"Lily and Tag's sparkling second-chance romance is the stuff Taylor Swift songs are made of, their boarding school world as cozy and close-knit as Stars Hollow. I loved the epic senior prank schemes, clandestine kisses, and every other twist and turn in this delightful story!"

—Kaitlyn Hill, author of *Love from Scratch*

"Walther builds romantic tension and develops some genuine nail-biting moments as the pranksters creep around campus, breaking into off-limits buildings, ascending a ropes course, and even hijacking a golf cart, all the while avoiding campus security."

—*Youth Services Book Review*

"Walther...fills this edge-of-summer rom-com with mischief and mayhem, delivering swift action and a swoony second-chance romance perfect for soon-to-be-grads suffering from senioritis."

—*Publishers Weekly*

"A complete delight! This is a swoony second-chance love story intertwined with a comedy of errors, performed by a lovable, vivid ensemble."

—Samantha Markum, author of *This May End Badly*

"Full of fun and charm... This sweet second-chance romance kept me smiling throughout!"

—Becky Dean, author of *Love & Other Great Expectations*

"Brimming with high-stakes hijinks and swoony romantic tension, *What Happens After Midnight* is a laugh-out-loud, perfect page-turner you won't be able to put down. Great fun!"

—Robin Reul, author of *Where the Road Leads Us* and *My Kind of Crazy*

Praise for *A First Time for Everything*

"Walther's strong young women characters truly shine in this quietly entertaining, character-driven tale... A lighthearted romance in which love comes to those who speak their minds and stick to their truths."

—*Kirkus Reviews*

"Walther's sweet, heartfelt, and warm novel blends a compelling family story with an undercurrent of romance... A cozy embrace of a novel that perfectly captures the feeling of facing life-changing experiences head-on."

—*Booklist*

Praise for *Maybe Meant to Be* (formerly titled *If We Were Us*)

"Gripping… Entertainingly depicts mature views on life, friendship, and romance."

—*Kirkus Reviews*

"An excellent choice for most YA collections, this will be welcomed by fans of Becky Albertalli's *Simon vs. the Homo Sapiens Agenda* and Molly Backes's *The Princesses of Iowa*."

—*School Library Journal*

Praise for *The Summer of Broken Rules*

"[It's] a rose-tinted romance that readers will want to toss into a beach tote for some relaxing, enjoyable fun."

—*The Bulletin of the Center for Children's Books*

"The mix of budding romance, competitive hijinks, a close-knit circle, as well as dealing with loss make for a satisfying read."

—*Kirkus Reviews*

"An engaging read… Recommended for larger collections with dedicated romance readers."

—*School Library Journal*

"Ideally suited for those who enjoy contemporary romance... A perfect summer or beach read!"

—Andrea Reid, *The Nerd Daily*

"Seamlessly weaves in the importance of family, and by the end, I felt like I had joined the Fox family and their traditions... A quick and easy read recommended for anyone who is looking for a lighthearted book sprinkled with elements of reality."

—Sachi Sharma, *Manhattan Book Review*

Praise for *What Happens After Midnight*

"An instant hit...carefully plotted [with] delightfully witty banter... The combination of engaging characters and plot successfully entertains while simultaneously asking big questions about legacy, memory, and the high school experience. Growing up is hard, but this book about transitioning from teen to adult makes for a fun book recommendation for a relatable life experience."

—*School Library Connection*

"An engaging story of personal growth and a second-chance romance."

—*Kirkus Reviews*

"Swiftie fans of *The Summer I Turned Pretty* would love everything K. L. Walther writes. Her books are full of heart, charm... Regardless of which book you choose, you will be met with a story you can't put down."

—*Buzzfeed*

Also by K. L. Walther

The Summer of Broken Rules
What Happens After Midnight
Maybe Meant to Be
While We're Young
A First Time for Everything
We're a Bad Idea, Right?

The Summer of Second Chances

The Summer of Second Chances

K. L. WALTHER

Internal design by Laura Boren/Sourcebooks

Published by Sourcebooks Fire, an imprint of Sourcebooks
1935 Brookdale Rd, Naperville, IL 60563–2773
(630) 961-3900
sourcebooks.com

Cataloging-in-Publication Data is on file with the Library of Congress.

Printed and bound in Canada.
MBP 10 9 8 7 6 5 4 3 2 1

For my grandparents.

Especially my grandmothers.

Especially Jo Ann.

ONE

I always held my breath when I signed in at the nurses' station, as if the visitor log was a test that I hadn't studied for. *Date?* it quizzed me. *Time?*

3:27 p.m., I wrote, later than usual today. The tropical storm had held off long enough for me to clock out of the bookstore and sprint to my car, but halfway to Elkins Village the thunder had rumbled its final warning before the sky opened up to shower Pennsylvania with its sorrows.

Sadly, I could relate to Mother Nature.

"It was a restless night," Tara told me after I scribbled my name on the visitor line. Not all the Elkins nurses knew me, but the team in Finlay House did. They offered me upbeat but heartfelt smiles four times a week. "But after sleeping in, it's been an uneventful day."

"Oh, good." I forced myself to exhale as she handed me a familiar green guest badge. Knowing the drill, I pressed the sticker to my chest and then saluted Tara before turning on my heel and heading down the hall. The carpeted floor somehow silenced my squelching rain boots.

I smiled when I reached the atrium, trying to appreciate its hominess. Colorful photographs of Bucks County flora and fauna hung on the taupe walls, and the overhead lighting was now warm thanks to a petition banning fluorescent bulbs. A skylight usually bathed the atrium in a cheery glow, but today raindrops thumped against the glass. Most of Finlay's residents gathered here during the day; I called it the "rally point." A couple women sat at the round table working on a jigsaw puzzle while hundred-year-old Bob Coleman relaxed near a window wearing big headphones. I knew the Elkins librarian hooked him up with audiobooks, since Bob's eyesight had abandoned him.

Other people had been herded around the huge TV, but *House Hunters International* held not one iota of their attention. Instead, they dozed in their wheelchairs. My chest tightened at the sight of Sally Jones—who slept silently under a blanket in her fleece-lined recliner chair on wheels. "Why is that lady in a stroller?" Maisie had asked the first time here, and before my dad could answer, Bryce had pointed to snoring Frank Richards and said, "Why are his eyelids see-through?"

They had both sounded so scared.

They didn't visit very often.

I said hello to several village elders as I crossed the floor, but my pulse quickened when I reached the other side—when I reached the third door on the left. Room F-18. An artificial but elegant boxwood wreath hung on the half-closed door. Once upon a time, the wreath would change with the seasons, but now one season slipped into the next without notice. Greenery worked no matter the time of year.

The door's nameplate read: ANNETTE LUPO.

But who am I? I thought, shifting from one foot to the other. *Who will I be today?*

Sometimes I was Olivia, loving granddaughter.

Other times I was not.

I took a breath and gently knocked on the door.

"Come in!" a slightly startled but kindhearted voice called.

I walked into the room to find my grandmother relaxing in her cushy white armchair by the window. My dad had nicknamed it her throne.

"Hello there!" Her face lit up in recognition. "What a surprise!"

I threw up my arms in a ta-da sort of way, having accepted that every single one of my visits—scheduled or spontaneous—would forever be a surprise. Time was no longer on my grandmother's list of priorities. "Hi, Annie," I said, upbeat. My grandmother had always been *Annie* to me, never Grandma or Grammy. "Delighted?"

"As ever." She beamed, and I hurried over for a hug before she tested her limits and tried to stand. Her left cheekbone was still bruised from her fall last month. "It's so good to see you, darling," she said as I held her close. For the overwhelming majority of my life, her signature scent had been Jo Malone perfume and L'Occitane soap, but I was getting used to the Dove the Elkins staff now bought her—or, I was trying to. "How long has it been? Weeks?"

"Mmm," I said noncommittally.

It had only been two days.

Forty-eight hours.

But Annie had thought I was a new aide on Monday.

The days she didn't recognize me felt like slaps in the face, but I'd learned that no matter how many times I insisted I was her granddaughter, her battlefield brain wasn't going to believe me. I'd never forget the first visit she hadn't known me, the first visit I'd had to *introduce* myself. She thought I was her neighbor's adult daughter. "It's a pleasure to meet you!" she'd said with her effervescent smile, so familiar it made my bones ache. "I have a granddaughter named Olivia. She turned ten a couple months ago..."

Now, I gently kissed Annie's cheek and played along with my supposed absence. It was easier. "I'm sorry, it has been a little while."

"I understand." My grandmother nodded. "School must be keeping you so..." She trailed off, wincing. I knew she was searching every nook and cranny of her vocabulary for "busy." After my grandfather unexpectedly passed away several years ago, my grandmother started losing and mixing up words. It had been one of the first signs that something wasn't right, that her mind was doing more than grieving. "On your toes!" she finally sputtered.

School must be keeping you on your toes.

"Mmm," I again neither confirmed nor denied. Annie hadn't been well enough to attend my high school graduation last spring. Not only was she becoming less steady on her feet, but her doctor had adjusted her medicine, and the side effects had hit her hard. Paranoia, in particular. She wouldn't stop accusing the Elkins chef of kidnapping her cat.

Annie hadn't had a cat in years.

Maybe she thought I was in college now, but after a series of arguments with my dad and Erica, I'd deferred Northwestern. Was I spending my gap year at a cooking school in Paris? Or hiking the Appalachian Trail? Or teaching English in Thailand? Or blowing glass in Brooklyn?

No, but I worked almost full time at Haddonfield's bookstore. That was something.

I know we are losing her, I remembered saying. *But I can't just suddenly* lose *her.*

My heart warmed when Annie invited me to curl up in her armchair, big enough for the two of us. "Those look pretty," I said once I'd gotten cozy, gesturing to the vase of pink flowers on her windowsill. Tulips were her forever favorite.

"Yes, aren't they gorgeous?" she said in the dreamy voice she'd developed. "I found them at the market yesterday."

No, you didn't, I couldn't help but think. *I brought them on Monday.*

But that doesn't matter! I quickly scolded myself. *Who cares how she got them? The point is they make her happy.*

We admired the tulips together, and then I stretched for one of the many Shutterfly memory books arranged near the vase. They all had a theme, ranging from Annie's childhood on the Chesapeake Bay, to my parents' wedding, to my dad's second wedding, to my Halloween costumes over the years. The newest book was titled *Beach Days with Maisie and Bryce*. (Erica had taken literally a thousand photos of the twins on vacation last summer.)

Today's selection was *She's Too Young to be Seventy!* Twelve years ago Pops had thrown Annie a surprise party with thirty of their closest friends. She'd thought the plan was a fancy family dinner, so she had looked stunned—blue eyes wide and hand covering her mouth—but also *stunning*, in a sophisticated black dress with gold jewelry and hair in her signature blond pixie cut.

I glanced at her now, feeling a twinge at the sight of her flat gray hair. I still couldn't get used to it. For as long as I could remember, up until Elkins had transferred her from assisted living to Finlay House six months ago, her hair had been blond and coiffed to perfection.

With each passing visit, she looked less like my grandmother.

I hadn't realized I'd been biting my pinkie nail until Annie lightly swatted my hand. "Olivia, stop," she said. "You need to break that habit."

Flushing, I folded my arms across my chest. I only ever chewed my pinkie nail, and it was only when I was lost in thought or a little anxious, but she was right. Plus, I'd just treated myself to my monthly manicure, keeping Annie's and my tradition alive. I didn't want to ruin it.

"Chris's nails were nothing more than nubs," she continued. "I couldn't stand it."

Chris. I hadn't heard her say his name in a while. Whenever we were together, Annie never referred to my dad as "Chris," or even Christopher. It was always "your father." Or, if she thought I was an Elkins aide or nurse or long-lost family friend, "my son."

"I didn't know he bit his nails," I said.

"Oh, yes, he most certainly did." Annie let out a deep sigh. "Sometimes I wonder where he is..."

It was silent for a beat, save for the pouring rain outside. I understood why she was disappointed. My pilot dad didn't visit Elkins as often as I did; American Airlines kept his schedule pretty tight.

"He had an exasperating flight to O'Hare today," I offered, smiling to myself. Every single time he flew to Chicago, my dad found its airport a hot mess. "One of his college roommates lives right on Lake Michigan, so they're getting drinks tonight."

"That's nice..." Annie said, but in her faraway voice again. She caught my gaze, and I tried not to let my heart sink at her distant smile, at her glazed-over eyes. Two tells that her thoughts had drifted to a mysterious elsewhere...

Before suddenly returning to the room.

"Look at my tulips!" she said delightedly, pointing to her vase. "Aren't they just lovely?"

"Yes." I swallowed the rising lump in my throat. "They're beautiful."

But dementia was not.

TWO

My exit from Elkins was five o'clock sharp, right when an aide came to escort Annie to dinner. I walked to the dining hall with them, holding my grandmother's hand, but then I gracefully fled. It was a strategic decision; Annie never liked when I left, especially when she knew I was her granddaughter. "Why don't you stay and eat with me?" she'd ask. "The food is probably better than whatever that woman is making..."

I smiled weakly, too tired to defend Erica's cooking skills. And honestly, what was the point? "I can't tonight," I said. "But I'll be back soon."

"When?"

It was a good question, one that almost brought tears to my eyes. Technically, I'd be back on Friday—only the day after tomorrow—but would Annie hug me then? Tell me how happy she was to see me? Or would she politely greet me, as if I were a new face at Elkins? I tried not to allow myself to dread the possibility of her being in a bad mood.

"I love you, Annie," was all I said as I gave her a goodbye hug, one that would hopefully last until she saw me again. "I love you very much."

"I love you too." She raised a slightly shaking hand to my cheek. Ridges of blue veins ran across her pale skin. "My dearest Olivia."

And with that, an aide distracted her so I could slip away, steeling myself to not look back. Thankfully, the storm had calmed; it lightly drizzled as I crossed the parking lot toward my car. Elkins Village—"the Ritz-Carlton of retirement communities," per my dad—was safe, so I never locked the Jeep. But after I hopped up into the driver's seat, I couldn't help but feel like something was strange. It seemed like the car was higher off the ground than usual, and why was my seat farther away from the steering wheel?

It was only when I noticed the backpack and lacrosse stick riding shotgun that I realized I was sitting in someone else's car. *Oh my god*, I thought, stomach dropping. *What the fuck, Olivia?*

My mind was always a little scrambled after leaving Annie, but seriously?

I slid out of the Jeep, hoping to flee the scene as fast as possible. *Funny story*, I didn't want to explain to its owner. *I* also *drive an Anvil blue Jeep Wrangler, and just like you, I don't lock it while I'm here…*

It luckily took less than a minute to find my actual Jeep, two rows over with its New Jersey license plate. I'd grown up in Pennsylvania—just up the road, actually—but Erica had convinced my dad to move to Haddonfield after Pops died and once Annie was transferred to assisted living. I'd been a sophomore and went with the flow, knowing that my time had passed. Life in the Lupo family was about prioritizing the twins. The house my dad and Erica ended up buying? It had five bedrooms, the smallest of which was gifted to me. "You don't mind, do you?" Erica had asked, pseudo-earnestly. "I just think it makes sense that Maisie and Bryce have bigger rooms, since they'll be living here longer..."

By the time I pulled into our driveway, the cloudy sky had darkened and the front lights flickered on to show Bryce waiting for me. His light brown hair was extra curly from the humidity. "Hey, Olivia!" he called whilst launching himself into a big puddle. Erica would be thrilled. "Guess what?"

"Your kickball team *finally* beat Maisie's at recess?"

My ten-year-old brother pointedly ignored my guess. "We got your favorite mac and cheese for dinner."

"The Hot 'n' Honey Pork?" I asked, stomach rumbling with hope. A gourmet mac and cheese restaurant had recently opened in town.

"No, the pepperoni pizza mac."

"Bryce, that's *your* favorite." I said, then wrinkled my nose. *Not to mention* disgusting*!*

He giggled. "Well, my mom said we all had to agree..."

"...so you *lied*," I finished for him as we walked into the house together. The kitchen smelled like pepperoni and cheese and

Swede bounded over to us, nearly knocking over Erica's tall Nikon tripod. "Hello, hello, my dude!" I cooed, crouching to give the golden retriever a hug. "Bryce, do you know if Swede's been fed?"

My brother shook his head, and our dog corroborated by barking.

"Swede…" a voice warned, and I glanced over my shoulder to see Erica walking into the kitchen. She wore black leggings and a white T-shirt that read JERSEY GIRLS DON'T PUMP GAS, but her caramel-colored beach waves and flawless makeup made her look camera ready.

"Did you shoot some content today?" I casually asked, gesturing to the tripod.

She nodded. "Tuckernuck sent a couple dresses, and I made a charcuterie board."

"Cool." Erica was a lifestyle influencer on Instagram; her almost 250,000 followers watched her do stuff like model preppy clothes, whip up hors d'oeuvres, mix cocktails, review books, and go on weekend getaways. Maisie and Bryce also made regular cameos, usually in coordinating outfits. "Where's the charcuterie board?"

"I brought it over to Hilary's house. She's hosting book club tonight."

My stomach sighed in disappointment, but if my stepmother heard it, she didn't let on. Instead, she opened the fridge and started taking out salad supplies—a sign that she also planned to pass on eating Bryce's favorite mac and cheese.

I waited for her to ask about my visit with Annie.

She didn't. In fact, she didn't say anything at all; instead, she admired the invitation posted on the fridge for the thousandth time. It had arrived last month. WELCOME TO CAMP CARMICHAEL! the letterpress heading read, and below that were all the details for Erica's family reunion on Martha's Vineyard this summer. Her parents were celebrating their sixty-fifth wedding anniversary, and we'd been invited up for a three-week-long celebration.

To say I didn't want to go was an understatement. Erica's family was not my family, and three weeks was almost a month.

That was a *long* time to leave Annie.

The oven timer jolted Erica back to the moment. "Bryce, will you go get Maisie?" she asked as I rolled my eyes. Still no inquiry about Annie. It was amazing how wrapped up my stepmother could be in her own life.

"I can't," my brother answered. "I'm making sure Swede doesn't eat too fast. Olivia said the vet said his stomach could twist, remember?"

(Swede had a tendency to wolf down his Purina Pro Plan.)

"I'll call her," I offered, then took approximately three steps across the tile floor before dramatically shouting, "MAISIE! DINNER!"

Out of the corner of my eye, I caught Erica flinch.

"COMING!" my sister called back, along with, "WILL YOU DO MY NAILS TONIGHT?"

Bryce groaned. "You guys are so *loud*."

Five minutes later, we took our unofficially assigned seats at the kitchen table. Swede followed suit and stretched out beneath us, resting his blocky head on my feet. The twins raved about their mac and cheese, and I thanked their mom for tossing a salad big enough for two. "You're welcome," she said, and after letting Maisie fill me in on first grade gossip—Violet P. thought her fish sticks tasted weird at lunch and then later threw up all over their science experiment—Erica spoke up again. "Olivia, how are Quincy and Gwen doing?"

"Good," I said. Quincy and Gwen were my best friends, but unlike me, a gap year hadn't been in their plans. With freshman year now in the books, they both had internships in New York for the summer. I'd helped them move into their apartment over Memorial Day Weekend last week. "They're taking the train to Ocean City for the Fourth. Gwen's parents rented a house."

"Oh, right." Erica took a sip of water. "I knew that. Chris ran into Gwen's mom at Acme."

I inwardly sighed. It was always *Chris*, not *your dad*. It sounded like I wasn't his daughter; instead, I was just some adult who lived with them. An au pair, perhaps.

Maisie hiccupped, a much-too-fast eater like Swede. "So where did we land on the whole painting-my-nails thing?"

I mustered up a smile. "What color?"

After letting Maisie dig through my stash and painting her tiny fingernails an Essie shade of hot pink called "blushin' & crushin'," I took a shower and then found Swede curled up in my room. He always started the night in his plush dog bed, but like clockwork, when it got to be around midnight, he'd invite himself into my bed and snuggle up next to me. He was, to use the technical term, a "Velcro dog."

"Don't look," I joked before I untied my bathrobe and changed into my new pajamas. A pale pink sleep set covered in flamingos and palm fronds.

I'd gotten my love for pj's from my grandmother. She always wore a fun pair when I slept over at my grandparents' town house as a little kid. My favorite was the silky blue-white-and-gold checkerboard pair. Very luxurious, very Annie.

There was a framed photo of her on the bookcase near Swede's bed; she was eighteen at her high school formal, wearing a Grace Kelly–esque white dress. It was a total glamour shot, and after a quick glance at my own prom photo, I admit it *was* a little eerie how much I resembled Annie. While my eyes were hazel and hers deep blue, we had the same wavy blond hair, our lips were shaped the same (a "Cupid's bow," my grandfather had loved to say), and our eyebrows had the same intrigued arch.

Despite my room being tiny, I had two walk-in cedar closets—one was for my wardrobe while the other now stored some of Annie's stuff. Most of her belongings were in a storage unit near Elkins, since she'd downsized to a single room. We didn't have space in our house for all her furniture, but Erica suggested we keep everything for now; some pieces were family heirlooms and others could furnish an apartment someday. "Whose apartment?" I'd deadpanned, because how often did she fantasize about me moving out? Was it secretly marked on her calendar? I knew she was being pragmatic, but it just rubbed me the wrong way.

I switched on the light in the second closet, then sat crisscross-applesauce on the needlepointed rug that used to sit in front of Annie's town house fireplace. She'd stitched it herself, white with intricate springtime flowers and a green border. "Needlepointing is cheaper than therapy!" she often said, though I never understood what she needed therapy for. She'd lived a wondrous life.

Lives, I corrected myself. *She's still living life.*

It just wasn't so wondrous anymore.

I usually hid in the closet after my Elkins visits, looking through Annie's old record collection—she loved opera, especially *La traviata*—or admiring her jewelry and precious little trinkets. Once I'd put on one of her favorite winter coats and found a grocery list in a pocket. *Dark chocolate* had been the first item, written in her elegant penmanship. My eyes had stung; Annie couldn't write anymore. Thanks to her dementia, she could barely spell her name.

Maybe it was a little embarrassing, but the closet comforted me. It felt like *Annie* was comforting me, the grandmother who had helped raise me and who I so fiercely loved and wasn't ready to lose. I only saw glimmers of that woman at Elkins, and they were becoming few and far between.

She's still here, I half-lied to myself. *She's still around.*

THREE

Friday was my day off, so I took Swede on a long run around Haddonfield before looping home to regroup for my Elkins visit. Per her calendar, Erica had lunch with friends, but I didn't realize her plans were to *host* her fellow elementary school moms, rather than rendezvous at the Bistro in town. Three extra cars were parked in our driveway, and I heard my stepmother's voice almost as soon as I reached for the kitchen door's knob. Someone hadn't closed it all the way, leaving it ajar. "Yes, I don't really know what to do with her," Erica was saying. "She seems to have lost all her drive and sense of direction." Pause. "It's awful, but I'm sort of dreading everyone seeing her next month."

My pulse skipped a step. Was she talking about *me*?

Swede whined to go inside. I scratched behind his ears, as if to say, *Shh, one second.*

"But she's wonderful at the bookstore," one of her friends said—Hilary, who loved any and all novels set in London. "She might not be *challenging* herself, but at least she's working hard and keeping busy."

"What does Chris think?" a second friend asked.

Erica ignored her, seemingly lost in thought. "I mean, my sister *still* can't believe we let her defer Northwestern..."

I gritted my teeth as Swede pawed at the door. This time I took his cue, and while my dog dashed over to his water bowl, I zeroed in on Erica and her friends. They looked like an aspirational stay-at-home foursome, sitting at our kitchen table together with a huge spread of food accessorized by Simon Pearce water goblets and blue-and-white MacKenzie-Childs plates. (Erica had gotten the entire Royal Check dinnerware set in exchange for an Instagram promo Reel.) "Really, Erica?" I asked. "You still don't get it? You still don't get me?"

The ladies who lunched were silent.

I didn't give a crap what they thought.

"*The* most important person in my life has dementia," I emphasized. "My grandmother is quite literally *losing her mind.*" My heart pounded. "College is extremely important to me, but unlike Annie, it can wait." The corners of my eyes prickled. I'd only weathered losing my mom at seven and my dad starting a new family a couple years later because I had Annie. I couldn't imagine life without her. "Graduating a year after my friends sounds much more appealing than coming home for Christmas break and having my grandmother have no fucking clue who I am."

Had deferring Northwestern been a no-brainer? Yes, but that didn't mean it had been *easy*. One reason I hadn't ever visited

Gwen or Quincy at college was because I worried it'd bum me out—make me jealous, even. I wanted what they had, a life away from home.

But I thought gradually saying goodbye to Annie as I knew her would be marginally better than the sudden shock that her memory had been wiped. "Please let me spend next year with her," I'd begged my dad last spring. "What if I leave and she remembers no one and nothing when I come back?"

Now, Erica took a deep breath. "Olivia—"

I couldn't even look at her; instead, I turned to her friend. "Hilary, I set aside a new romance for you," I said. "It's waiting behind the register."

And with that, I turned around, grabbed a Tupperware off the counter, snatched my keys off the hook, and left the house.

~

I drove to Elkins with white knuckles, and thanks to my sweat-soaked clothes and air-conditioning, I'd caught a chill by the time I parked. *Keep calm*, I told myself as I waited to be buzzed into Finlay House. Their inner double doors were always locked, to prevent Annie and other residents with memory issues from wandering off. I tried not to compare it to a psychiatric ward, but sometimes it was hard. "Hey, Tara," I said when I reached the nurses' station. I summoned a smile and presented her with my Tupperware. "Chocolate chip cookies!"

I baked for the Finlay team as much as I could. They did so much.

"You're too sweet, Olivia," Tara said, accepting the cookies but not returning my forced smile. Instead, she gave me a solemn look. "We had a sundown yesterday."

My squared shoulders slumped. "Oh."

"Yes." Tara nodded sympathetically. "We gave her something, but..."

I listened while the nurse told me how agitated Annie had been all afternoon, pacing the halls and then demanding to shower at 2:00 a.m. I'd learned that "sundowning" was common for those with Alzheimer's and dementia; manifestations ranged from increased confusion to anxiety to wandering to insomnia to hallucinations.

"How is she now?" I asked Tara.

"Comfortable," she answered, then hesitated a beat. "But you should prepare yourself to just be a friend today. She fought Kai every step of the way to breakfast."

"Okay," I said quietly. Kai was Annie's all-time favorite aide. She was only awful to him when she wasn't herself.

Suddenly, my bones felt weary.

It also wasn't a good sign that another nurse took over the desk so Tara could walk me to Annie's room. Her door had been propped open today, as if the staff agreed she needed extra monitoring. "Hello, Annette," Tara said gently. "You have a visitor."

My heart twisted when I saw Annie in bed, snuggled under

the fluffy violet throw blanket I'd given her for Christmas. (She loved anything and everything cozy.) Her bed back in her Elkins apartment and then assisted living had been queen-sized, but now she was tucked in to a twin. Barely big enough for me to sit at its foot.

And it didn't matter, anyway. I knew from the blank expression on her face that she didn't recognize me. "Hello," I said warmly, before she could aim a dagger at my heart by asking who I was. "I'm Olivia Lupo."

Even my full name did not ring a bell. I was truly a stranger to her; she wouldn't even recognize my laugh.

I willed myself to ignore the pang in my chest.

"Annette, Olivia is here to spend some time with you," Tara helped, guiding me toward Annie's armchair. "Doesn't that sound nice?"

Annie finally blinked. "Company is always nice," she said as she made direct eye contact with me. There was light there, thankfully. "You know my family *never* comes to visit me."

A hard lump rose in my throat. *Yes, they do!* I wanted to cry. *Dad visits; I visit; we visit all the time; I'm visiting* right now!

But that was exactly what I *wasn't* supposed to do. There was no winning when you tried to convince someone with dementia that they were wrong. It frustrated them. Erica limited her visits because she admitted she couldn't wrap her head around it. "Your Cartier watch is gone, remember?" she'd said back when Annie lived in assisted living, before her official diagnosis. "You may have accidentally thrown it out."

"No, I didn't," Annie disagreed. "I put it back in my jewelry box, as always." Her eyes narrowed. "Why would I ever throw it out? It's *Cartier*."

They'd gone back and forth until Annie outright accused Erica of stealing the twenty-thousand-dollar watch. Which, my issues with Erica aside, was really sad. Because it was Annie who'd encouraged my dad to start dating after my mom had died, and it was Annie who reassured my dad that, despite Erica being *a lot* younger than him, they made a great couple. Annie had loved my mom, but she also adored Erica.

"What brings you to prison?" Annie asked once Tara had left us alone.

"Tax evasion," I replied smoothly. Elkins was always "prison" on Annie's bad days. "What about you?"

She laughed, and I glanced around her room, so sparsely decorated compared to her previous homes. There was one oil painting above her bed—of a woman standing in a meadow, her face obscured by a straw hat and yellow skirt blowing in the breeze—but the rest of her impressive art collection was split between my house and her storage unit. Some family photos sat on her windowsill, and there was a world map hung over her nondescript wood dresser. Blue pins were scattered across it. My dad had the map framed as a shadowbox for Annie's birthday.

"Do you like to travel?" I asked.

"Oh, yes." Annie visibly brightened. "Very much so." She pointed to the map. "Each one of those pins is a trip I took."

I smiled to myself. Travel was always a safe, reliable topic with Annie. She might not be able to remember me, but her decades of globe-trotting? Always.

They were carved so deeply into her brain that dementia had nothing on them. Not once had she ever been at a loss for words when I asked about her adventures. One of my favorites was the six-week cruise she took to Australia before the *Queen Elizabeth 2* ocean liner had retired. When I was little, I remembered Pops telling me he had to mark *forty-two* days off the calendar before she returned home. As a kid, that sounded like an eternity. "Why didn't you go with her?" I'd asked him, to which he replied, "Someone had to feed the cat!"

I'd been ten when I found out about my grandfather's anxiety; even on medication, he could not fathom going anywhere beyond state lines. But he and Annie had meticulously planned all her amazing adventures together before she went on them with her best friend.

"What was your favorite trip?" I asked now, knowing the real answer was Milan. There was no better place to shop than the Via Montenapoleone.

"Oh, there are so many," she said excitedly. "Not to mention, my dear friend Kathy and I have been recently talking about going back to Milan next year..."

I nodded along, even though Kathy had died of pancreatic cancer three years ago. Her funeral had been one of Annie's final public outings.

"...but Martha's Vineyard has a special place in my heart."

Huh? I thought, her words sounding like a sudden record scratch. Martha's Vineyard? When had Annie gone to Martha's Vineyard?

If she'd been herself, I would've thought she was kidding. Because ever since getting the invitation in the mail, I'd told her how much I didn't want to go to Camp Carmichael.

But right now, Annie wasn't herself.

I squinted at her map, even though I was far from close enough to spot a pin off the coast of Massachusetts. Over the years, I'd heard all the stories behind her pins.

"How old were you?" I asked, half-confused, half-intrigued. "When you went?"

"Oh, I must've been—"

My phone chiming in my tote bag cut her off. *Shit*, I worried as I started digging around for it. For whatever reason, ringtones irritated Annie.

Her brows furrowed. "What is that dreadful sound?"

"Just my phone," I told her, and pulled out my iPhone to see Erica was calling me. I sent her to voicemail before switching my phone to vibrate. "I'm sorry."

She pursed her lips.

"Martha's Vineyard?" I prompted.

"Yes, I visited several summers."

"With your parents?" I tried. Maybe it had been a family vacation spot. Besides hearing about *Mother* and *Daddy* as people, Annie hadn't told me much about her childhood.

Annie shook her head. "No, I first went with Kathy, and then…"

I felt my phone start vibrating on my lap.

Erica, the screen read.

Ignore!

"With Chris," Annie answered, smiling fondly into the distance.

An all-capitals text had popped up on my phone.

EMERGENCY, Erica had written. CALL ME!

My heart rate spiked, mind going immediately to my dad. He was flying home today from his three-day stretch. *Did something…?*

I didn't let myself finish the thought. "Do you mind if I step out for a moment?" I asked Annie, gesturing out to the hall. "I need to make a quick call…"

Erica answered on the second ring. "You need to pick up Maisie from her Girl Scout meeting and take her to ballet," she said. "I'm on the way to the hospital with Bryce."

"*What*?" I gasped. "What happened?"

"He fell off the jungle gym at recess and decided not to tell anyone about hurting himself." She groaned. "He was clutching his arm when he got off the bus. I think it's broken."

I winced. *Yikes.*

"Maisie's ballet bag is in the laundry room," Erica continued. "Girl Scouts is at Violet P.'s house today."

"Doesn't Violet P. dance too?" I asked. "I saw her listed in the winter recital's program."

Violet Poindexter, *what* a name.

"Olivia, where have you been? She switched from ballet to tap this spring!"

"I'm sorry," I said as I heard Bryce moan in the background. Poor guy. "I'll get Maisie, don't worry."

"Great," Erica said, then promptly hung up.

I sighed. The one good thing about Annie thinking I was some random person was that she wasn't as disappointed when I left. *It was lovely talking to you, Annette*, I rehearsed in my head. *But I promised I would pick up my sister from—*

"Olivia, darling!" Annie exclaimed, a sparkling smile spreading across her face when I returned to her room. "Was that your father on the phone? Did he find my luggage?"

I couldn't speak. There was no air in my lungs. Not only did Annie suddenly remember who I was, but she was moving around her room...tossing clothes on her bed.

Tears pooled at the corners of my eyes. "No, it was Erica," I said softly, scared of what was coming. "Annie, what are you doing?"

"Packing to go home," she replied. "I don't know why I ever left."

I bit the inside of my cheek; this scene had played out before, but it'd been my dad who handled it, not me. *Take Maisie and Bryce to the car, Liv,* he'd whispered to me as Annie furiously folded sweaters. *I'll be there soon.*

"Let me go talk to Tara," I said. "She'll know where your suitcases are."

"No!" Annie's paranoia kicked in. "They've trapped me here; we have to sneak out."

"Right." My stomach swirled. "Then *I* will go find your suitcases."

"Hurry, dearest," my grandmother said. "We don't have much time..."

"I know," I whispered, and wiped away an escaped tear before speed-walking out of her room.

But instead of taking the elevator down to Finlay House's basement, where each resident had a storage cage, where I *knew* my dad had put a few of Annie's suitcases, I found the nearest aide. White noise filled my ears as I explained the situation—another sundown. Kai nodded, put a gentle hand on my arm, and his eye contact told me he'd take care of Annie. I just barely heard him say I could go, that everything would be okay.

And with that, I took off up the hallway, racing for the locked double doors. *Let me out,* I thought, quickly pressing the button. *Let me out, let me out...*

I felt like the world's worst granddaughter until I picked Maisie up at Violet P.'s house, where I felt like the world's worst sister. "I *knew* Bryce broke his arm!" she said, climbing into the Jeep in her patch-covered blue Girl Scout vest. "It was such a bad fall, Olivia." She buckled herself in and glanced around the car. "Where's my ballet stuff?"

Fuck, I grimaced. I'd forgotten to stop at home to grab it.

"That's okay," Maisie said a beat later. "No offense, but it looks like you've had a bad day." She smiled. "How about we go get ice cream?"

My sister knew ice cream almost always cheered me up.

"Sure," I said, but still started to cry.

FOUR

My dad found me in my room that night; he'd gotten home later than expected. His flight back from Charlotte had not only been delayed, but then the plane sat on the Philly tarmac for a while. Maisie and Bryce, ready for bed in coordinating pajamas (more swag sent to Erica), were waiting up for him. Bryce couldn't wait to show off his new neon green cast, courtesy of his fractured wrist. "Daddy!" I'd heard them shout around nine, and I smiled to myself. No matter how exhausted my dad was, he would give the twins all his energy before Erica hustled them upstairs for bed.

"Hey there," he said later, rapping his knuckles on the already open bedroom door. I turned to see him showered and wearing sweats with a TOP GUN T-shirt. The United States Navy Strike Fighter Tactics Instructor program, not the movie. Christopher Lupo had been a fighter pilot for years before transitioning to commercial aircraft. He owned the aviators to prove it.

"Welcome home!" I wanted to hop up and give him a hug, but for some reason stayed put on the floor. "How many cold brews are powering you?"

"Upward of three." He smiled and leaned against the doorframe, salt-and-pepper hair shining in the light. My dad wasn't old, but I knew he was considered an "older dad" among the elementary school parents. He'd turned fifty last month.

But there had been no one more willing or happy to get down on the ground with the twins when they were younger. He was always rolling around with them on the family room floor. I couldn't really remember him doing that with me; my mom had been the one who tickled me until I was nearly breathless, with a widespread smile and shining eyes. In hindsight, I knew it was because the fighter pilot lifestyle consumed him. Things being different with Maisie and Bryce made me happy, but I still sometimes felt a small sting.

"What are you appraising today?" he asked, noting that I was looking through Annie's jewelry. I didn't want to call her collection *mine* yet, because if it were mine, that meant...

I held up Annie's favorite ring: a gold band with two beautiful sapphires flanking a diamond. She'd worn it almost every day, as often as her engagement ring. My dad had brought back the sapphires from a postgrad trip to Thailand, but I actually didn't know where Annie had gotten the diamond. Maybe it'd been her mother's.

"We should talk," my dad said before I could ask. He gave me a long look. "I heard about today."

"Mmm," I mumbled, suspecting I was about to be admonished for basically ripping off Erica's head at lunch.

"It sounds like you were pretty tough on Erica, Liv," he continued. "You know she cares deeply about you; she's just trying to wrap her head around your perspective." He sighed. "Jumping down her throat, right in front of her friends, definitely wasn't the smoothest move."

I nodded. I didn't have anything to add.

My dad waited for me to respond.

"I'll apologize," I assured him, then took a deep breath. "But do I really have to come to Martha's Vineyard in July? I barely know these people, and Erica obviously doesn't want me there." I straightened my shoulders. "I don't mind staying home. You wouldn't have to stop the mail or pay someone to water the plants—"

"Well, that's very generous," he cut me off. "But *I* mind, and Erica would too." He half-smiled. "This is a family reunion, and our family isn't complete without *you*."

Then why haven't I ever made the cut for Erica's family shots on Instagram? I thought, but kept my snark to myself. My dad didn't deserve it.

All I did was nod.

He nodded back before shifting subjects. "Elkins also called me," he said. "They left a message about this afternoon."

Something thickened in my throat. "I'm sorry," I told him. "I know I shouldn't have left her, but I didn't know what to do. She didn't know me, then suddenly she *knew* me, and sounded so desperate..." My voice quieted. "I feel so guilty for abandoning her, but I had to get Maisie."

"No." My dad shook his head as I rose from the floor. "No, you did the right thing—*please* don't beat yourself up over leaving." He opened his arms, and I walked into them for a hug. "Everyone there knows how devoted you are to her and are amazed by your composure and stamina. They've told me you visit more often and for much longer than the average family member." He hugged me tighter. "You are such a wonderful granddaughter, and I am so proud of and impressed by you."

"I'm doing my best," I replied, my eyes welling up a bit.

"I know." He pulled back to kiss my forehead. "But I can see the emotional toll it is taking on you, and I wonder if you should ease up on yourself. Elkins isn't right around the corner, and I'm now worried about you driving down and back home when you're exhausted."

My stomach lurched. "What?"

My dad's face was somber. "You are a real trooper, Liv," he said. "You've gone through and done some things no kid should ever have to do." He hesitated, and I knew we were both thinking about taking Annie's jewelry from her when she began misplacing things, confiscating her car when it was no longer safe for her to drive, and the other ways I'd deceived her. It had been necessary—for her own good—but that didn't mean I didn't feel like shit for it. "I am so impressed," he repeated. "But we can tell you're burned out and restless... Maisie told me how upset you were earlier, and snapping at Erica like that isn't you. Plus, every time I come home these days you're up here in your room. Things need to change." He cleared his throat. "I plan to lighten my schedule for the summer so I can spend more time with Mom." He paused. "I know three weeks with Erica's family might not be your dream vacation—to be honest, I don't think it's *Erica*'s dream vacation—but I think it'll be good for all of us, good for *you*." He gave me a long look. "You need to take some time off from the bookstore and get out of Haddonfield for a while."

Blood coursed through my ears. He actually wanted me to leave? *Leave* Annie? That was already the plan, of course, but when he phrased it as something I *needed* to do rather than something I *had* to do...

Even if I was a little tired, how would leaving Annie be good for me?

"I'm going to raid the fridge for leftovers," my dad said after a few seconds of silence, no doubt to lighten the mood. He gestured downstairs. "You want anything?"

"No, thanks," I whispered, but when he was three steps from my bedroom door, a thought popped into my head. "When did you and Annie go to Martha's Vineyard?"

My dad stopped. "Hmm?" He turned around, brow furrowed. "She said she went to Martha's Vineyard?"

"Yeah," I said. "She mentioned it today. She said it has a special place in her heart, and that you two went there together."

An odd expression crossed my dad's face, one so confused that I wondered if Annie was mixing up Martha's Vineyard with someplace else. Or maybe it was a vacation she'd wanted to take but the puzzle pieces had never fallen into place.

"She also said she first went there with Kathy...?" I tried.

The fog seemingly lifted, my dad now nodding. "That sounds familiar," he said. "The only place those two didn't go was the moon." He lovingly rolled his eyes. "Erica introduced me to the Vineyard, though. I think Mom's mistaking it for Block Island, off the coast of Rhode Island. I was the twins' age, maybe? It was one of the last vacations Dad came on with us, before his anxiety really ramped up..." He trailed off. "Anyway, I remember not especially loving it. That New England water was *freezing*." He pretended to shiver. "If I were you, I'd pack a wetsuit for the reunion."

I laughed. Every summer, we drove ten hours south to spend the last week of July in the Outer Banks. The ocean felt like bathtub water there.

But Martha's Vineyard... I still thought, and wished Pops or Kathy Ryan was still alive to corroborate. Did Annie have any pictures?

Sadly, I doubted it. Because as much as my grandmother loved seeing the world, she didn't love documenting it. Most of the photos we had of her adventures were taken by Kathy.

"You sure you aren't hungry?" my dad asked again. "Erica told me there's something called a 'blueberry ricotta pudding cake' in the garage fridge."

I snorted. "Are you serious? Her friends didn't eat it?"

"I know, absolutely unbelievable." My dad shook his head, then smirked. "But how lucky are we?"

"Very," I admitted, smirking back. "Very lucky."

After my dad and I'd eaten two slices of Erica's cake (each), we fell into such food comas that we mutually agreed it was bedtime. Swede was softly snoring at the foot of my bed, but I was wide awake. My mind kept bouncing between my dad suggesting I take a step back from visiting Annie…and Martha's Vineyard. *Why am I obsessing over it?* I chewed on my pinkie nail. *Because it feels like there's a secret there?*

For as close as we were, there was a lot I didn't know about Annie's life. What was her favorite game as a little girl? Why did she drop out of college to go to secretarial school? Where did she and Pops go on their first date? I knew I could've (and, in hindsight, *should've*) asked her those questions.

Meanwhile, we'd talked about her travels *extensively*, and she had *never* mentioned Martha's Vineyard. New England? Yes. She loved Ogunquit, Maine, and charming Essex Harbor in Connecticut, and now that I thought about it, she *had* mentioned a cottage on Block Island once. Its toilet had overflowed.

Yuck, I thought, and a few minutes later, I threw back my

covers and tiptoed over to my closet. Who knew? Maybe she did have some record of this trip.

And hopefully it was here, not in her furniture-filled storage unit in Pennsylvania.

Quickly and quietly, I went through everything for clues. Annie's jewelry, records, the manila folders filled with receipts that she *never* threw out (her antique armoire even had a letter of authenticity), as well as a Rubbermaid bin labeled *decorative glassware*. I skipped that, since I'd helped my dad pack all her vases, small sculptures, and other fragile ornaments. We'd wrapped everything in newspaper.

Interestingly enough, after I found my grandparents' wedding album and got distracted by looking through it for the millionth time, I *did* find a box filled with old-fashioned slides, but my heart sank when I realized I couldn't tell what they were without a projector. "Dammit," I muttered.

Swede woke up and joined the treasure hunt after I'd lifted Annie's heavy typewriter off the closet's top shelf. The golden retriever stared at its blacked-out keyboard, then gave me a quizzical look.

I yawned. "Maybe it forced her to memorize the keys?"

He wagged his tail.

It wasn't until I was sifting through a battered box of miscellaneous items—old birthday cards, monogrammed stationery, yellowed postcards from friends—that my heart beat with hope.

There was an elegant Hermès box at the bottom, but her other signature orange boxes had been neatly organized in another container. Why was this one on its own?

Because there wasn't a silk scarf in it.

"Oh my god," I breathed upon seeing its contents—a collection of Polaroids and small watercolor paintings. "Swede, *look.*"

Ever the Velcro dog, Swede was half on my lap.

As silly as it sounded, I felt like I'd just unearthed Leonardo DiCaprio's long-lost sketch of Kate Winslet in *Titanic.*

I picked up a photo, recognizing my grandmother right away. Wearing a white tennis dress, she smiled for the camera and held a glass of white wine. Pinot grigio, I knew. She always ordered it at restaurants or had a bottle chilling in her fridge at home.

She's barefoot, I also noted. *She's standing* barefoot *in the grass.*

That was not Annie.

My eyebrows knitted further together at the Polaroid's setting. In the background was a clear sky and trees that looked perpetually windblown, along with a sandy road, but in the foreground was a tractor. A classic green John Deere tractor, one that looked like an antique—even back then. Annie posed in front of it.

What the...? I flipped the photo over to see Annie's handwriting. It gave me a millimeter of clarity. *Summer camp*, she'd written. *Year 3*.

She hadn't dated the picture, but she didn't look much older than her high school formal photo, so my guess was sometime back in the 1960s.

Huh, I thought. *Summer camp?*

Where?

I glanced away from the Polaroid, enough for one of the watercolors to catch my eye. It had been painted on a small piece of thick paper, and while it had aged, its subject was still vibrant. Whitewashed cliffs embraced by vegetation and streaked with shades of gray, burnt orange, and red that rolled into the blue ocean. A pink-tinged sky suggested a beautiful sunset, and I could make out a coastline in the hazy distance—another coastline.

Something sparked in my chest, powerful enough that I leaped to my feet and hurried to my desk. A photo of Swede and the twins dancing in the rain greeted me when I opened my laptop, and I couldn't open a Chrome browser fast enough. Cliffs, I typed into Google. Martha's Vineyard.

Enter.

Aquinnah Cliffs was the headlining search result.

And its accompanying photo?

It was identical to the painting I still held in my hand.

FIVE

My suddenly chiming phone made my heart lurch. It was a gorgeous afternoon in mid-June, so Inkwood Books had hit a lull—most people in town either soaking up the sun at the pool or down the shore—which meant I was allowed to read at the register. I'd happily lost myself in another fantastical world, but I blinked to see that Gwen Carlisle, Queen of My Heart wanted to FaceTime. Answering went against all proper bookseller etiquette, but the store truly was a snooze and I'd been missing my friends lately.

"Thanks a lot," I said once Gwen and her signature smile-smirk appeared onscreen. "You just yanked me away from the man of my dreams."

"Listen, if that High Lord is really the love of your life, he'll wait a hot minute for you to return," my friend said. She was on the subway, a banner ad for the latest iPhone above her head.

I laughed. "How's life with the bunheads?"

A lifelong ballet fan, Gwen was interning in the American Ballet Theatre's donor relations department this summer. It wasn't shaping up to be as glamorous a role as she'd thought.

"Mmm, fine." She shrugged. "More spreadsheets than I thought imaginable. What's up with you?"

"Not much," I said. "Just counting down the days to Erica's family reunion next month."

"Ah, I see we're still thrilled about that," Gwen noted drily, and when I didn't respond, she laughed. "But come on, it'll be cool to explore a new place, right?"

I conceded with a slight nod, because she wasn't wrong. The night I'd discovered Annie's stash of Polaroids and paintings, something had come over me. I became, as Lindsay Lohan so delicately phrased it in *Mean Girls*, "a woman possessed." I'd fallen down an internet rabbit hole, learning everything I could about Martha's Vineyard. Reading its Wikipedia page (fun fact: there wasn't a single vineyard on the island), scrolling through Google Images, and even skimming a Reddit thread on Martha's Vineyard restaurant recommendations. Apparently, the Atlantic was overrated.

"Annie has been there," I told Gwen. "She didn't say anything after I first told her about the reunion, but then she randomly brought up Martha's Vineyard when I was..." I hesitated. "A friend."

Gwen was quiet. Her grandfather had died of Alzheimer's, so she knew what I was going through and was supportive, but at the same time, she wasn't. She always waited for me to bring up Annie, and she never wanted to hear anything beyond an adjective. *Today's visit with Annie was good/fine/difficult.* Details were too much for her.

Which hurt, but I understood.

"I never knew she went there," I eventually said. "She never told me, and there's no pin on her globe-trotter map."

"Have you asked her more about it?" Gwen asked.

"Yes, but..."

I trailed off when the bell above the entrance cheerfully dinged. It was Erica's friend Hilary. "I'm *finally* here to pick up that book!" she said as I quickly paused FaceTime and put down my phone. "I'm embarrassed that it's been *weeks*, but things have been all go, go, go with the kids." Her eyebrows knit together when I handed her my recommendation, a romance set in Buenos Aires. "This doesn't take place in London."

"Hilary, it's time for you to read about a new city," I said lightly.

She skimmed the book's cover copy, then sighed and handed it back to me to scan. "Okay, I'll give it a shot!"

Gwen and I resumed our conversation once the bell rang again, Hilary back out on the mean streets of Haddonfield. "Olivia, don't take this the wrong way," Gwen said, "but I think it's really good you're going away soon."

I affectionately rolled my eyes but also felt the hair start to rise on the back of my neck. Why did Gwen sound like my dad?

"I meant that it'll be *healthy* for you to leave for a while. What you've been doing this year is so selfless, and I can't express how much I admire you for it, but..."

My stomach dropped, the rest of her sentence turning to white noise.

But I imagined it translated to something like:

Olivia, you need to get a life.

Later, I couldn't help but storm straight into Annie's room with tears pooling in my eyes. My grandmother was relaxing on her bed with what vaguely sounded like a sappy Hallmark movie on TV and I didn't even hesitate before collapsing next to her. "Oh, my," she said. "What—"

My sudden sobs cut her off. I didn't know if she recognized me, and I selfishly didn't care; I cried. Annie was the *last* person I should've been melting down in front of, but besides my dad, she was also the only person I'd ever let see me so low—the only person who made me feel better. When a group of girls had nicknamed me "Stilts" in middle school, I'd come home crying after it had caught on with the rest of the seventh grade. Annie grabbed her keys to her Mercedes and took me on a long drive to a small town up the Delaware River, where we wandered the streets and window-shopped and then couldn't stop laughing over a five-course dinner at a dreamy historic inn. She'd turned it into the best day.

Now, I let it all spill out. How I didn't regret taking a gap year, but also how restless, frustrated, and unhappy I was. I was jealous of my friends, who'd started new lives at college. I felt like Erica branded everything as "the Lupo Family" when the dynamic in our house was "the Lupo Family & Olivia." Gwen was right; I needed to *get a life*. I wanted to leave Haddonfield, and hated myself for it. I hated myself for feeling this inexplicable pull to Martha's Vineyard—now secretly *wanting* to go when Erica seemingly *didn't* want me to go. And I especially hated that I was leaving Annie for almost a month. "I love you," I told her at the end. "I love you so much, Annie, but…"

"You need time away from me," she said simply.

Not sadly, but *simply*—matter-of-fact.

Heart wrenching and half-horrified, I didn't know how to respond.

"Start packing, Olivia," she whispered. "If not for yourself, dearest, then for me." She took my hand and squeezed it. "Martha's Vineyard is a magical place. Go fall under its spell."

SIX

As much as I loved my dad, I hated his taste in music. Here we were, three hours into our six-hour Sunday drive to Woods Hole, blasting Tool's greatest hits. Rock-metal fusion wasn't my carpool karaoke cup of tea, but he was in the zone and it was my fault for not charging my AirPods.

No one else had an issue with it. From the way back of our Ford Expedition, I leaned forward in my seat to see my siblings totally focused on their iPads. Maisie was watching *Encanto* while Bryce played some LEGO game. "Crap," he'd mutter every now and again, but my dad had only reprimanded him once. *Language, pal…*

In the front, Erica had set up a mobile office. Over the past several days, she'd been working overtime to have enough stored content to cover her imminent three-week hiatus. "I hope you don't plan on bringing your lights, camera, etcetera…" I'd overheard a call with her mom last week. Erica had her on speakerphone. "This month is all about being *present*, Erica."

My stepmother was the youngest of the three Carmichael

kids and most definitely a "surprise." Her sister Beth was *eighteen* years older than her and next came her brother Jay. His age was hazy. She also had several adult nieces and nephews who she didn't see much, but as far as I knew, she never missed a birthday card.

At the thought of a big group, my stomach squirmed a little; Maisie, Bryce, and I were Annie's only grandchildren, and I rarely saw my two cousins on my mom's side of the family. They lived abroad in Hong Kong.

Would the Carmichaels want to get to know me? I'd only met them a handful of times and it'd been small-talk city.

To distract myself, I unzipped my backpack and pulled out a folder containing Annie's Polaroids and paintings. I shuffled through the stack for the shot of her standing in front of the John Deere tractor. It was my favorite; she looked so happy, so carefree, so *beautiful.*

Why did she go? I asked myself for the hundredth time. *Who was with her?*

It had crossed my mind to bring the pictures to Elkins and ask, but part of me worried Annie would spiral and accuse me of stealing her stuff. I didn't want to risk returning her memories, only for her to later rip them up and throw them out, as if they were nothing more than a promotion for a new credit card.

Plus, her words kept swirling through my mind. *Martha's Vineyard is a magical place... Go fall under its spell... If not for yourself, dearest, then for me.*

Now, in a startling twist of fate, I *could not wait* to reach Martha's Vineyard. I was excited, because I had a mission. I was going to let Annie's Polaroids lead me around the island and take pictures of myself at all the sights she'd visited. Then I was going to make a memory book with our photos side by side. Even if she didn't recognize her younger self, I knew she would love it.

But maybe she will recognize everything, I couldn't help but hope as I admired an intricate watercolor of a white lighthouse. I wondered if Annie had painted it herself. Her father had been an amateur artist, but the most artistic I'd ever seen my grandmother was helping Maisie work through a paint-by-numbers kit or assisting Bryce with a Lupo family–themed cartoon strip for school. Her caricatures of us *had* been pretty accurate…

After finishing my packing late last night, Google had helped me discover the inspirations for the rest of Annie's hidden artwork. Then I'd made a list.

Aquinnah Cliffs (Aquinnah)
Old Whaling Church (Edgartown)
Flying Horses Carousel (Oak Bluffs)
Grange Hall (West Tisbury)
Dike Bridge (Chappaquiddick)
Ocean Park Gazebo (Oak Bluffs)
Menemsha fishing village (Chilmark)
White lighthouse (Edgartown? East Chop?)

While I couldn't tell exactly *which* lighthouse the watercolor was—Edgartown's and East Chop's were practically identical—only one location was still a true mystery.

Tractor Polaroid (???)

Hmm, I mused and straightened up in my seat, determined. I was going to piece this story together one way or another.

Lo and behold, my dad turned down Pearl Jam (still not *my* jam, but at least he'd tired of Tool) when we finally made it to Woods Hole, home of the Steamship Authority! "Holy crap," I said to no one in particular, unbuckling my seat belt so I could move up front, near the center console. I wanted a better view; this place was bustling like a busy airport. "Are they going to give us a map?"

There were people everywhere, a blend of preppy Lilly Pulitzer and Vineyard Vines meets granola T-shirts and Birkenstocks, and cars upon cars were parked in numbered lanes facing the harbor. It looked like they were waiting in line to willingly drive into the ocean. Jeep Wranglers, Suburbans, Range Rovers, Subarus, and even an eighteen-wheeler Stop & Shop truck. How was *that* going to fit on the ferry?

My dad carefully circumnavigated the swarming lot before

parking in lane three. An Amazon truck was in front of us. "Okay," Erica said once my dad had cut the ignition. She unbuckled her seat belt. "Time to stretch our legs!"

Today's blue sky and puff-pastry white clouds were straight out of Andy's room in *Toy Story*, and I couldn't remember the last time I'd smelled such briny sea air. My stepmother led the way across the parking lot, toward a cedar-shingled restaurant called the Leeside Pub. It looked like they had a revolving door of customers, probably all hoping to grab a bite before their ferry. "Do they have clam chowder?" Bryce asked.

"Yes," Erica answered. "But their fish-and-chips are better, B. Remember the last time we were here?"

Bryce nodded, but Maisie looked at me confused. "When was that again?"

"Three years ago." I tickled her. "You were seven!"

Erica had taken the twins to Martha's Vineyard while my dad and I'd gone on an Alaskan cruise together. Annie had booked it a year earlier, as a girls' trip for the two of us, but when the cruise had finally come around…

"Liv, wait a second," my dad said before I could follow Erica and the twins into the restaurant. I let the door swing shut behind them.

"What's up?" I asked after we'd moved off to the side.

"I wanted to thank you," he said.

"For all the driving I did?"

(I'd volunteered; he'd said no.)

My dad chuckled. "No," he said, "for turning a corner and being so upbeat about this trip." He put a hand on my shoulder and squeezed. "I really appreciate it, and so does Erica."

"Well, of course." I smiled. "Annie told me the Vineyard's magical, and she would know, so…" I shrugged.

"Mmm." He nodded. "I still can't remember for the life of me when she would've come here." He considered, but before I could mention the Polaroids, he wrapped me in a hug. He smelled like Irish Spring soap and cold brew coffee. "I know you're going to miss her."

So much, I thought, but I reminded myself it'd be okay. My plan was to call her every couple of days. She didn't often pick up the phone anymore, but I'd spoken to the Finlay House nurses to schedule a standing call.

"I love you, Liv," my dad whispered.

"I love you too," I whispered back. "You're the best dad ever."

"I'm your *only* dad."

"Well, even if I had two dads, or three à la *Mamma Mia*…" I broke away to give him a dazzling grin. "You'd still be the *best*."

He smiled back, then nodded at the restaurant. "Fish-and-chips?"

"Fuck fish-and-chips," I said. "We're in New England; I'm getting New England clam chowder!"

We barely made it back to the car before it was our turn to drive onto the ferry. There was no sunshine to be found in its dimmed belly. "I am taking a nap," Erica announced once my dad put the car in park. "There's nothing better than a forty-five-minute Steamship Authority snooze…"

I was tempted to follow her lead, but when I noticed all the people disappearing into the nearby stairwell, I knew the upper deck really must be the best way to experience the ride. Grabbing Swede's leash, I looked at my siblings and said, "Let's go!"

The harbor breeze hit us as soon as we reached the top of the stairs, blowing my hair into my face and mouth; I felt like an idiot as I tried to smooth it back into place. Rows of metal seats were bolted to the deck, and I let Swede take the reins; he led the twins and me to the very front of the of the boat so he could introduce himself to a small Jack Russell Terrier. "Is your dog friendly?" I asked the owners, a middle-aged couple.

"Very!" the woman replied, and thus we let the dogs start enthusiastically smelling each other. "Although Loki doesn't like having his butt sniffed."

"I'll make sure Swede stays away," Bryce said as I scanned the horizon. The blue-green water glimmered in the sunshine, buoys bobbed along, and I squinted at the houses scattered along the coast.

"Have you been to the Vineyard before?" Loki's owners asked.

"Bryce and I have," Maisie answered. "It's Olivia's first time."

The couple smiled before lovingly looking at each other, as if remembering *their* first visit. "Where are you—" the man started to ask, but the ferry horn sounding cut him off.

It blared so loudly that my sister grabbed my hand and I nearly jolted out of my skin.

And then off to sea we went, with hammering hearts.

SEVEN

By the time Martha's Vineyard was in sight, Erica had joined us on the top deck with a coffee from the snack bar. She must've been desperate; Erica was kind of a coffee snob, and I couldn't imagine this brew was the best. "We're docking in Oak Bluffs," she told me while snapping some photos of Maisie and Bryce with her Nikon. They were laughing, T-shirts blowing and billowing in the ocean breeze. "It's one of the Vineyard's larger towns." She considered. "It's fun for a day, but otherwise too touristy."

All I did was nod, mostly focused on the horizon.

But I thought about Oak Bluffs' historic gazebo and carousel.

As we got closer to the island, all passengers were instructed to return to their cars, and walk-ons reported to the gangway. Bryce made a game of darting past and weaving between the parked cars, packed together like sardines. He'd literally just gotten his cast off. "Careful, pal!" my dad warned as he nearly cut a corner too close. "You might hurt someone…"

Or hit something, I thought, horrifically imagining a bike rack snagging my brother's sleeve, or an open car door stopping him in his tracks. There *had* to have been an accident like that before, right?

But Bryce made it back to the Expedition safely, and after coaxing Swede back into the car (the ferry was much more interesting!), we all buckled up—ready to disembark. The ferry unloaded efficiently, and I felt a thrill race through my veins when my dad drove onto the wide-plank dock.

I looked over the side of the pier to see people on the beach. A couple was napping together on a large blanket; three tween girls were taking selfies on the rocks; a young mother and her toddler stood at the water's edge, squealing and racing away whenever a ripple washed ashore. I smiled to myself, remembering my mom and me playing the same game when I was little. *Run, Livvy!* Her warm hand tugged mine. *Or do you* want *to turn into a mermaid?*

We cruised along the blue water, and when I glanced the other way, my heart jumped a little. Out the right side window, peering around Swede's blocky head, I saw a sprawling green park with a pair of fountains, network of pathways, and lush flowerbeds. Its white Victorian gazebo caught my eye; one of Annie's Polaroids come to life.

"How far away is Nana and Granddad's house?" Maisie asked, prompting me to blink.

"Twenty minutes," Erica said without missing a beat. She shifted in her seat. "Allison texted that Jay's flight was delayed, but everyone else is there."

Great, I thought, wondering if our arrival would make me feel like the new kid walking into a crowded high school cafeteria.

The other day, I'd asked Erica for a Carmichael family highlight reel; I didn't think about them very often (shocking, I know), and while I might not be able to put names to faces right away, I didn't want to have minimal background on top of that. My stepmother had been in the middle of updating her latest Pinterest board, but she seemed almost happy to take a break and give me the 411 on her family.

Her parents were Lawrence and Margaret. Their love story was an idyllic one: high school sweethearts turned patriarch and matriarch of a big family. Having met them only a few times, I should initially refer to them as "Mr. and Mrs. Carmichael," but only as a formality; they'd invite me to call them "Topper and Peggy."

What kind of nickname is Topper? was the follow-up question I did not ask.

Beth was Erica's older sister. She was a Boston neurosurgeon and married to Paul, who was German. They lived in the city during the week and coastal Connecticut on the weekends. Ashley was their only daughter.

And she has two kids, I remembered, but their names were fuzzy.

Jay, Erica's brother, worked in investment banking and was married to Allison. They also lived in Connecticut and had three children, but only Nick and Charlie—twins, funnily enough—would be "on-island" for the festivities. Erica mentioned their daughter lived in London—

Bryce's voice interrupted my train of thought.

"Look!" he exclaimed while we drove over a bridge. "That guy just did a backflip!"

Tons of teenagers in bikinis and swim trunks were catapulting themselves off the bridge and into the water. NO JUMPING OFF THE BRIDGE, a tall sign announced, but it must've been an inside joke.

"This is Jaws Bridge." Erica explained its tie to the 1970-something movie. "Jumping off the bridge is a rite of passage on the island."

"Have you done it, Dad?" Maisie asked.

My dad laughed. "Yes, but certainly not a backflip." He glanced at me in the rearview mirror. "You should jump, Liv."

"Maybe." I smiled, though my stomach tightened. The whole scene looked daunting. At our swim club, I'd only climb up to the high dive if someone dared me.

For the rest of the drive, I gazed out my window. I'd always associated the word *island* with *tropical*, but this place was different. There were trees everywhere, and none of them were palm trees. Instead, it was a blend of leafy green and pine, and every now and again, we'd pass a split-rail fence and a wide-open *beyond*—grassy fields, some with horses, others farmland. Cyclists rode along the paved bike path that ran parallel to the road, and cedar-shingled houses started popping up. Private driveways did too. A vintage orange car with white racing stripes sat at the end of one, a stone obelisk marking the driveway's entrance.

It wasn't long after we passed the airport that my dad flipped his left blinker and turned onto what a sign denoted as OYSTA WATCHA ROAD.

Which was unpaved. The smooth main road shifted into a tree-lined sandy-dirt drive. One so bumpy that I inadvertently started bouncing in my seat. The twins giggled, and Erica turned in her seat to smile at them. "It's like we're off-roading!" Bryce cackled.

Every now and again I spotted a mailbox, but there were no houses in sight. The road was so long that I lost all sense of space and time, the trees engulfing us. "And here we are," my dad finally said when we reached a navy-blue mailbox. CARMICHAEL was printed below the address in white lettering, and I was relieved to see a pebbled driveway. No more bumps.

And even though I'd seen pictures of the Carmichael family's summer home, it still left me speechless. New England cottage meets Gilded Age mansion, it was a long cedar-shingled house with white trim, black shutters, and three brick chimneys. A low stoop with a black front door and pair of lantern-esque sconces anchored the entrance while two beautiful sprawling wings flanked the historic house. The product of an intense renovation spurred by a growing family, I guessed.

My dad parked with the other cars, near the detached garage. It matched the house; cedar-shingles with rounded black doors.

"Hello!" someone shouted as my family deployed from the Expedition, our feet crunching over the driveway's pebbles. "At long last!"

Erica's mom was walking over, a huge smile on her face. She was petite and adorable in a wide-brimmed straw hat with a blue grosgrain bow. It didn't take a map to trace back Erica's preppy sense of style. "Nana!" Maisie and Bryce chorused and ran to her for a hug.

"Christopher, it's wonderful to see you," she said after the twins had released her and took off toward the house. I was almost envious; they hadn't been here in years, yet they already felt right at home.

"Wonderful to see you too, Peggy," my dad replied as he bent to give his mother-in-law a hug. "Thank you again for having us."

"It's our pleasure." She squeezed his arm after they broke apart, then turned to focus on me—and Swede, who was straining against his leash. "Olivia, it's been a while."

She sounded a little judgmental, and I didn't know what to say. *Yes? I know? I'm sorry, but also not really, because you're not my grandmother?*

"Your home is stunning, Mrs. Carmichael," is what I settled on.

As predicted, she told me to call her Peggy.

"Come into the house," she said after giving Swede some belly rubs. He was in heaven. "Don't worry about unpacking the car. I'll have the boys do it."

Erica stage-gasped. "They're here? In the house? Sitting still?"

Peggy laughed and kissed her youngest daughter's cheek. "No, no." She shook her head. "They're out sailing."

Of course they are, I thought, even though I wasn't entirely sure who Erica's mom was talking about. Erica's father and brother? Erica's nephews? A pair of bellhops? This place was beautiful beyond words, but it also seemed a little more than just sequestered—remote, on the edge of the world. I suddenly felt *very* far away from home.

Stop being so dramatic, I heard Annie's voice in my head. *This isn't* White Lotus*!*

I couldn't help but smile a bit as I let Swede lead me across the driveway. *White Lotus* had been too difficult a concept for Annie to grasp, but when I'd shown her a couple episodes a few years ago, she remarked how gorgeous the resort was.

She would've thought this house was gorgeous too.

Thirty minutes later, I was unpacking. Most of the Carmichaels were at the beach while others ran errands, so the house had been quiet until "the boys" got back from their sail. It turned out they weren't technically boys. "Family!" Nick Carmichael exclaimed once he and Charlie joined us on the back porch, which overlooked the water. Maisie and Bryce were racing across the rolling lawn with Swede and two other dogs, but my dad, Erica, and I'd been admiring the view of the gleaming blue-green Oyster Pond. Grinning, Nick stretched out his arms as if expecting a group hug, accidentally whacking his twin in the chest.

Charlie played it up with a cough. "Spatial awareness much appreciated, Knickknack."

Erica laughed and hugged them both. Nick and Charlie weren't identical twins, but they were both tall and unbelievably good-looking with red hair and matching Ray-Bans. I was pretty sure they were in their mid-twenties. "They're Jay's sons, and unequivocally my mother's favorite grandchildren," Erica had said with a sigh. "But I don't blame her; they're lovely. Charlie is in medical school at Harvard, and you know Nick is..."

A professional athlete, one of the rising stars in the NHL—and, as of last month, a Stanley Cup champion. With the exception of professional tennis and the Olympics, I was only a casual sports fan, but I was no less impressed. Nick had been drafted his sophomore year at Yale and now played for the New York Rangers.

"Olivia!" Nick didn't hesitate before wrapping me in a hug. "It's great to see you, step-cousin."

"For the record, *I* coined that term." Charlie winked at me after his twin and I broke apart, then stuck out his hand for me to shake. "And through trial and error, I know you're not a hugger."

"Oh, crap." Nick's smile dropped. "I'm sorry, I didn't mean—"

"No, no!" I felt myself flush. Charlie had hugged me hello a couple years ago at his aunt's New Year's Eve party, and I hadn't been expecting it, so I'd flinched and the vibe had been really awkward. "You give amazing hugs," I reassured Nick.

"Yes, doesn't he?" Peggy joined us on the deck, and offered everyone a glass of lemonade from the wicker tray she held. "Would you mind unpacking their car?" she asked her grandsons. "I want them to relax and enjoy this beautiful late afternoon."

In response, Charlie dutifully saluted his grandmother; Nick snorted and wrangled his twin into a headlock as they headed off for the garage.

Okay, maybe they *were* boys.

But boys who took their chores seriously! They had the Expedition unloaded in ten minutes, and I told myself it wasn't embarrassing how much stuff I'd brought—it was obvious which suitcase(s) were mine. For my high school graduation last year, Erica and my dad had given me an entire luggage set. It was white with camel-colored leather and my monogrammed initials: OBL, for Olivia Brooke Lupo.

Brooke was my mom.

"I know how much you loved Annie James's luggage in *The Parent Trap* when you were young!" Erica had said. "Isn't it perfect?"

Yeah, I thought. *Perfect to send me on my way…*

Although I couldn't deny that the luggage was stunning. My grandmother had agreed when I'd shown her photos. "Perfect for an adventure!" Annie smiled. "Bon voyage, my darling…"

Peggy showed me to my room, on the first floor of the east wing. SUMMER CAMP, a hand-painted sign on the door read, which made my spine straighten. Summer Camp, as in *Annie's* summer camp? Had the tractor photo been taken *here*?

I flushed a little, feeling silly for imagining a tractor in the garage outside. The building wasn't *that* big.

To my surprise, the door opened not to a bedroom, but a small square-shaped landing with wood-paneled walls. "Topper and I renovated after our first two grandchildren were born," Peggy explained. "Instead of singular bedrooms, we wanted to create nooks to allow each family some privacy." She shook her head. "And it's a good thing we did; Beth and Ashley *loved* to bicker..."

I laughed politely. Erica and my dad were getting the twins settled in the opposite side of the house, so it looked like I'd be escaping Maisie's snoring and Bryce talking in his sleep.

But there hadn't been a room closer to them?

"Who's staying in here?" I asked, hoping it wouldn't be weird.

"Connor," Peggy answered. "I'm sure Erica mentioned him."

Connor? I tried to connect the dots. *Had* Erica told me about him? Was he one of Ashley's kids? Or someone else's son? I didn't ask for any clarification, lest Peggy be offended I'd forgotten one of her grandchildren.

There were three doors off the hallway; Peggy gestured to the one on the right, then left me to it. The bedroom was cozy, with white shiplap walls and a green-and-cream striped rug overtop the knotty wood floor. A bunkbed had been built into the wall, against the slanted ceiling, and I was happy to see a copper wall sconce for late-night reading. Across the room, a vintage boat-in-a-bottle sat on an antique teak dresser, and I had no idea how I was going to fit everything into the narrow-looking closet.

The room was neat, but it also looked lived-in; a windbreaker hung from one of the multiple hooks on the wall, along with a baseball cap. Had someone forgotten them?

Before unzipping my suitcase, I closed my door to call Annie. She hadn't known me when I visited yesterday, not understanding that the tears in my teary goodbye were because I was going to miss her so much. Unfortunately, my call to Elkins almost immediately dropped; I checked my service to see that I only had one bar.

Crap. My palms started to sweat. Erica had mentioned something about spotty service on the drive here. But the Wi-Fi was reliable…

Multiple networks appeared when I investigated. XfinityWIFI, Sage's iPhone, DIRECT-9B-HP OfficeJet 4650, Let's Get Routy, and what was most likely the general router: Camp Carmichael.

Of course it was locked; I suspected the password was posted for us on the kitchen's fridge or something. I'd figure that out—

A text from my dad suddenly popped up onscreen: Wi-Fi PW is top+peg4ever, FYI.

An ode to the big anniversary, I surmised.

Thank you! I replied, then successfully connected to the

internet and enabled my Wi-Fi calling. Annie didn't answer her room's landline, but Tara picked up on the third ring when I called Finlay's front desk. She told me that Annie was in the atrium, sitting at the puzzling table with a few housemates. "I'll go get her if you like," she said, "but it's been a nice stretch—"

"Oh, no, I understand," I cut her off. "I'll call back later."

The more Annie's dementia worsened, the less social she'd become. If she was willingly hanging out at Finlay's rally point? That was a big deal, and I didn't want to interrupt.

We hung up after Tara made a note about a post-breakfast call tomorrow, and I rubbed my stinging eyes before any tears could spill.

Then I bristled at a knock on my door.

"Hello?" I said over the lump in my throat. It sounded like a question.

"Hi," the person on the other side said. A guy. "Olivia?"

"Yes." I nodded even though he couldn't see. "Connor?"

"I hope I'm not bothering you," he said. "But Teddy and Finn and I just got back from the beach, and I wanted to introduce myself."

Right, those were their names! *Beth's daughter Ashley has two sons*, I remembered Erica telling me. *Teddy and Finn are around the twins' age...*

"You can come in," I told Connor, realizing he was waiting for an invitation. I tried to make a joke. "I'm decent!"

Connor chuckled, his laugh cool and full-bodied and a little bit boyish. "Took you long enough," he quipped before twisting the doorknob.

Based on the Carmichael family genes, I was not surprised by the handsome guy standing in the doorway. But for some reason my pulse quickened, sort of caught off guard. Six-two or six-three, Connor was tall and thin with some shade of strawberry blond hair and startlingly pale blue eyes. Something sparked in them when we made eye contact, and I caught a muscle in his sharp jaw twitch. "Olivia?" he said again, a lock of hair falling over his forehead when he cocked his head. He was quick to smooth it back.

"It's nice to meet you," I said, smiling brightly and sticking out a hand at the same time Connor opened his arms to seemingly go in for a hug. Interesting—everyone here seemed to be a hugger. And despite what Charlie thought, I wasn't *not* a hugger, but…

Connor recovered easily, one arm reaching to casually scratch the back of his neck while the other swooped in to take my hand. I could feel the calluses on his palm as we shook. "It's nice to meet you too," he said, adding after a beat, "I'm Connor McCallister."

Wait, what? I thought.

Because while *Connor McCallister* rolled off the tongue, it certainly didn't sound like *Connor Carmichael.*

"Okay, who do you belong to?" I asked, confusion overwhelming my manners. "Does Erica have *another* sister? Because I know Beth's married name is Krause."

One side of Connor's mouth tipped up in a smile. "You think I'm a Carmichael?"

I raised an eyebrow. "Aren't you?"

"Not even a little bit." He shook his head. "But you're not the first to think so." He grinned and ran a hand through his fair hair, which was lighter but still similar-ish to Nick and Charlie's. "The twenty-fifth, maybe."

"At least I'm not the only one."

Connor good-naturedly rolled his eyes. "I'm hanging out with Teddy and Finn this summer," he explained. "Beth's grandsons. Her daughter Ashley is a family friend." He paused. "And, as Teddy will most definitely tell you later, also my tenth-grade math teacher."

I smirked. "You're a manny."

"Yes." He straightened his already confident shoulders and smiled. "Thank you—I'm a *manny*. My brother Liam won't shut up about me being a *babysitter*. Do I seem like someone who reads bedtime stories?"

"I don't know." I fought a smile to pull off a shrug. "I don't know you yet."

Though something about him was starting to seem *a little* familiar. His eyes maybe?

"Fair enough," he said. "You game for an icebreaker?"

"Sure."

"Do you like being on top?"

Heat burst on the back of my neck. *Excuse me?*

"I've been sleeping on the bottom." He gestured to the bunk-bed. "But if ladders aren't your thing—"

"Okay, *wait*," I interrupted, mind now whirring. "I thought this was *my* room."

"It is." Connor nodded emphatically before his eyes darted over to the windbreaker that hung under our porthole window.

Fuck, I thought, realizing that if I opened all six dresser drawers, chances were only three would be empty. And half the small closet would be full.

"What about the two other doors in the hall?" I asked. "Doesn't one of them lead to another bedroom?"

Connor shook his head. "No, it's the bathroom and then we have a little porch off the side of the house."

I swallowed, not knowing what to say. Sharing a bathroom was one thing, but breathing the same air in a bunk room with a stranger was different. Why hadn't I been given a heads up?

Did Erica know about this? Did *my dad*? I guess the Carmichaels were less conventional than I thought (not that they'd ever paid much mental rent), and while my dad had been far from oblivious about senior beach week last spring, I highly doubted that—

"I don't find it weird if you don't find it weird," Connor murmured.

Are you an axe murderer? I wanted to ask at the same time he said, "I promise I'm not an axe murderer."

We both laughed before Connor motioned to the bunkbed again. "Take your pick," he said. "Really."

"Oh, um..." I wanted the top bunk, but knew I should steal the bottom from him, especially if he wasn't a dog person. "The top's great."

"Cool. I'll let you start unpacking..." He trailed off to assess my spending-the-summer-in-Europe-sized suitcase.

"It was a graduation present," I said. "Erica picked it out."

"*The Parent Trap*, right?" he guessed, fondness in his voice.

"You've seen it?"

"Of course." Connor nodded. "It's one of my brother's favorite movies. My mom bought him a yellow duffel bag when he was nervous for his first sleepover, to give him some Hallie Parker chutzpah."

"That's really thoughtful," I said, doubting my Annie James luggage set went that deep. If it wasn't a message to move out, maybe it was a suggestion to study abroad? Who knew.

A sudden *ping* made me blink. "Speak of the devil," Connor said after digging his phone out of his pocket. He flashed his screen long enough for me to see a FaceTime request from Liam. "I'm sorry you're stuck in here with me," he said before leaving, blue eyes holding mine. I definitely recognized them, but from where? "I know you probably wish you were with your family."

I almost nodded. Because while I enjoyed my privacy, this nook felt really far away from the rest of the house. Peggy and I hadn't passed any other bedrooms on the way here.

Plus, I was sharing a room with someone I didn't even know. Someone who probably wanted some personal space too, since he wasn't part of the Carmichael family either.

"It's okay," I told Connor. "Maisie snores."

"Well, you're in luck," he replied. "I got my tonsils and adenoids out in elementary school, so I don't snore, and as far as I know, I also don't sleep-talk or sleepwalk."

"I'll be the final judge of that," I half-joked. "See you later?"

"Absolutely." He grinned. "I'll see you later, Olivia Lupo."

Huh, I thought once he was gone. *Did I tell him my last name?*

Maybe he'd asked someone.

EIGHT

I wasn't much of a cook, but the Carmichael kitchen made me want to captain a multicourse meal. It had white cabinets with butcher-block countertops and a retro but modern-looking lapis blue stove with gold accents. "Nana's pièce de résistance!" Charlie joked when he caught me marveling.

Across the room was an oblong farmhouse table, and beyond that were floor-to-ceiling glass windows that were actually *doors*; when I came downstairs, I saw that someone had folded them so that there were no walls between the kitchen and back deck.

The sun was starting to slip on the horizon, bathing the sky in a pink-orange glow while voices, laughter, and the smell of citronella candles drifted inside; a combination that signaled cocktail hour was in full swing. I spotted Erica sipping a peach-colored drink and nodding along to whatever her father was saying. Nearby, my dad was helping himself to an elaborate cheese plate.

Are you aware I'm sharing a room with a boy? I'd texted him once I'd made the executive decision to keep my Tampax in my suitcase instead of the bathroom's medicine cabinet.

I am now, he replied.

???, I typed when he didn't add anything.

Totally up to you, Liv, he wrote back a few minutes later. You know I trust you. And Peggy said Connor is a very upstanding and trustworthy young man.

He's preoccupied, I surmised. *Something else is on his mind*...

Nevertheless, I waited for him to offer me a trundle bed in Maisie and Bryce's room, but it turned out they were in a bunk room with cousins Teddy and Finn. The Lupo "nook" only had one bedroom.

After consulting with Erica, the best my dad could do was offer an air mattress in an upstairs reading room. As tempting as that was, I told him I'd do a trial run with Connor.

Because after asking myself what I was so worried about, I concluded that I wasn't worried about *Connor*; I was worried about being an afterthought—a.k.a. being cut out of this vacation. Especially since I was sharing a room with the only other person who wasn't part of Erica's family.

Now, there was plenty of action in the kitchen. Maisie and Bryce were playing with Swede and the other dogs while Charlie decanted a bottle of wine at the island and a pretty blond woman danced her heart out to the song playing over the speakers. "This band is terrible," I heard Charlie say.

"They are not," the blond protested, shaking her hips. "They take me back to Bexley!"

He snorted. "Exactly."

By way of a response, she threw up her arms and belted out the song's chorus. I swallowed my laugh. From casually stalking Nick's Instagram earlier, I knew this was his fiancée, Sage. And based on the amount of childhood throwback photos he'd posted, I surmised their story was a friends-to-lovers one.

Charlie noticed me skulking. "Hey, Olivia," he said, then tipped his head at Sage. "Have you met this character yet?"

"Olivia, hi!" Sage's smile lit up her face, and I weirdly felt like we were friends five minutes later. "So I kinda found you on Instagram yesterday," she said as Charlie glanced at his watch. "And I *need* to know where you get your clothes."

I tried not to blush. *In no way* was I trying to mirror Erica, but every Friday I posted a recap of my outfits for the week. Mirror selfies I took in my room. Maybe I'd done it to annoy her a little, but it'd had the opposite effect, especially after I hit five thousand followers—she'd started wordlessly leaving castoffs on my bed. "I'm always on Poshmark," I told Sage. "I also have some things from Erica, plus a lot of vintage pieces from my grandmother." I gestured to my top, a light pink eyelet blouse with billowy sleeves. "This is from the seventies."

"Amazing!" she said. "Your whole look is very Parisian chic meets Palm Beach."

"That's what I'm going for." I nodded excitedly. Tonight, I'd paired Annie's shirt with a sleek bun and barely there dewy makeup. "It's harder than—"

"Please tell me you lit the grill," someone said, and I turned to see Nick and another guy walk into the kitchen. They looked like the odd couple; redheaded Nick was built while his friend was thin with dark hair and tortoiseshell glasses. They both carried reusable bags with EDGARTOWN MEAT AND FISH printed on the side.

"Yes, Chef." Charlie nodded, all business. "The grill has indeed been lit. Uncle Paul's monitoring it by toasting marshmallows over the coals."

The chef rolled his eyes but kissed Charlie's cheek once he rounded the island. "Olivia, this is Luke," Charlie said. "Executive chef, Nick's BFF, and my husband."

"Obviously listed in order of importance," Luke quipped, then readjusted his glasses. "I hope you like swordfish and steak tips, Olivia. We were supposed to have tuna, but there was an incident earlier..."

Sage grimaced. "One of the dogs went counter surfing."

Prematurely mortified, my eyes widened. "Swede?"

Charlie shook his head. "Greta." He pointed to the black Lab whose belly Nick was rubbing. "My parents' dog." He chuckled. "She always listens, but never follows the rules!"

"Swordfish and steak tips sound delicious," I told Luke, who was unwrapping the fresh fish. My stomach rumbled, both hungry and excited. "Is there anything I can do to help?"

Dinner was ready right after the sun went down; with so many people, we served ourselves buffet-style in the kitchen before finding a place to sit out on the deck. I wanted to stick with Luke, Sage, and the Carmichael twins—at twenty-six, they were the closest to my age, not to mention *really cool*—but Erica's sister waved me over to the round table where her mother probably hosted multimillion-dollar-view bridge games. "Miss Lupo!" Beth called. "We haven't gotten to chat yet…"

I forced myself to smile. Erica's older sister was nice, but I understood why my stepmother kept her at a distance. Beth was intense. She'd pressed me on where I'd wanted to go to college when I was only a sophomore in high school and told me to find an SAT tutor stat.

"It's so nice you were able to make the trip up here," she said once we started eating, everything making my mouth water. "Erica mentioned it's been a busy summer."

For who? I wondered, savoring my steak. Luke had grilled it to perfection, medium rare, and the marinade was delicious, both sweet and savory. *For my family? Or* me*?*

"Oh, of course!" I told her sister, keeping my uncertainty to myself. "I wouldn't have missed it. I'm so flattered to be included."

Beth took a sip of water. "And your grandmother's doing okay? All things considered?"

Her eyebrows pinched together in concern, but her forehead didn't move. Erica had a Botox appointment now and again, but were her sister's monthly?

"She's fine," I said, and was relieved when Erica's brother Jay—newly arrived from Atlanta—sat down with a plate and wasted no time before sharing each and every detail of his roller-coaster trek here. It was more or less a smear campaign against Delta Airlines. "I'm going to take this up with your father, Olivia," he concluded as I swallowed my last spoonful of corn salad. "It was an absolute *nightmare*."

"It sounds like it," I said. "But my dad flies for American, so I'm not sure how much he'll apologize on Delta's behalf..."

"Wait." Jay cocked his head. "When did he switch to American?"

"A while ago," I said. "From United."

"He's never flown for Delta?"

I internally sighed. Erica's family liked my dad, but I felt like they made no effort to get to *know* my dad. I might've been young at their wedding, but I'd never forget how Erica's brother sarcastically referred to my dad as "Maverick" in his rehearsal dinner speech, and how irritated my grandparents had been when Jay had warned Erica about marrying a pilot. The ego! The drinking! The flirty flight attendants! "How original," Annie had deadpanned during the applause while Pops had rolled his eyes.

"Nope!" I told Jay with a bright smile. "He's never flown for Delta."

Everyone gathered around the deck's gas firepit for dessert later. I wasn't really a pie person, but the mixed berry pie made me think that whatever I'd eaten in the past could not have possibly been pie. *This* was pie: raspberries, blueberries, and blackberries all so light, sweet, and bursting with flavor wrapped in a warm, flaky crust. I also followed Nick's lead and plopped a scoop of vanilla ice cream on top…

"Alright, *who* made this?" I asked nobody in particular.

"Morning Glory Farm," Sage answered with a knowing look. "Best pie you've ever had, right?"

I nodded emphatically, my interest also piqued. Morning Glory *Farm*? Had Annie been there? Might the tractor photo even have been *taken* there?

My thought bubble popped when Sage held up her phone to show me Morning Glory's Instagram. It was a flash of colorful flowers, fruits, veggies, and baked goods.

Its bio also read: Local Family-Owned Farm Since 1975.

Okay, never mind.

"I worked there one summer," Sage said wistfully.

"Only one?"

"I wanted to spend more time outdoors." She settled back against the striped couch cushions. "I loved the farming part, but most of my shifts ended up being behind the register." She smiled. "I spent the next summer as a bike tour guide and also interned at the hospital a few days a week."

"You're a nurse, right?" I asked, even though the words I'd

snagged on were *tour guide*. Would she be interested in checking out Annie's Polaroids? Maybe hitting a few landmarks with me? Retracing Annie's steps sounded more fun if I had a copilot, and Sage seemed like someone who was up for anything. Plus, how was I going to get around? I had neither my bike nor my car here. Maybe I could borrow someone's?

She nodded and told me she worked in the NICU, but she was taking some time off before starting her new job at another New York hospital. "Otherwise I *never* would've been able to take off three weeks for this trip!"

We laughed, but before I could circle back to her tour guide days, someone whistled. "Attention, Camp Carmichael!" Nick called. "I'd like to say a few words..."

"Updating us on Lord Stanley's status, I hope!" Jay called back. "Are you having the Cup brought here?"

Out of the corner of my eye, I saw Connor's spine straighten with excitement. He'd been comfortably on the periphery all night, seemingly at ease with the fact that this wasn't his family. "He's a huge Rangers fan," Charlie had told me earlier. "You should've *seen* his face when Nick got here yesterday..."

Nick chuckled. "Sorry, Dad. I don't get the Cup until August. It's with our captain in Toronto now." He looked at his grandparents; Peggy was stealing pie from Topper's plate. It reminded me of whenever Erica passed on dessert but then always helped herself to my dad's hot fudge sundae. "I just wanted to thank Nana and Granddad for not only being an epic couple, but also for hosting us the next few weeks." He smiled, a dimple appearing in his left cheek. "Even with some of us missing, I think everyone will agree when I say that it's been way too long since we've been all together!"

The deck erupted in whoops, whistles, and cheers. I started biting my pinkie nail, but stopped when my dad caught my eye and winked.

"And as much as we love and adore one another," Nick continued. "It might also be fun—maybe even *healthy*—to add some friendly competition—"

"Oh my god, Nick," Beth groaned. "We are *not* playing Assassin."

Nick arched an eyebrow. "What's wrong with Assassin, Aunt Beth?"

"Nothing," Charlie piped up from nearby. He was squashed in an Adirondack chair with Luke and clearly biting back a laugh. "Except for the fact that you need to accept that you're not meant to be one." He gestured across the moonlit Oyster Pond. "They're never going to ask you to guest star; it's *their* game."

"That's exactly why *we* should play!" Nick countered.

"What and who are they talking about?" I asked Sage as the Carmichaels collectively shook their heads. "What's Assassin?"

"One of Nick's biggest dreams." Sage sighed. "Although I fear it will forever go unrealized."

Jay whistled when his sons started bickering. "Rein it in, knuckleheads!"

"Sweetie, it's really just not our cup of tea," Peggy told Nick, then squeezed his arm affectionately before turning to everyone else and smiling. "But I *promise* this trip will be full of fun family..."

Not part of your family, I couldn't help but think.

"...game nights, ones we all know and love!"

"Like Life?" Bryce asked, so excitedly that I caught my dad and Erica exchange a bemused look. None of us could understand why my brother was so obsessed with Life.

"Try glow-in-the-dark volleyball, Bryce," Jay said. "Or was it dodgeball?"

"Oof." Luke shook his head. "I preferred the pie fight."

"A pie fight?" Maisie gasped. "Actual pies in the face?"

"Coconut cream." Peggy beamed at the same time Erica said, "Mom, would it be okay if—"

"Absolutely not," Beth cut her off. "You can't vlog our vacation!"

Erica's smile slipped. Her family had capital-T Thoughts about her influencer career. Beth, for example, believed it was an invasion of privacy.

"Showing off your summer wardrobe while sipping one of Dad's golden hour cocktails is one thing," she continued, "but we don't need videos of us playing charades going viral..."

"Must be one hell of a game of charades," Charlie whispered to Luke, and they snickered as I rose from my spot on the couch.

"I'm running to the bathroom," I told Sage, but instead ran

into Connor in the kitchen. He was refilling his glass of water. "Correct me if I'm wrong," I said, "but is there maybe *a little* too much personality under this roof?"

"Oh, come on," he said, eyes shining. I still felt like I knew them from somewhere, but maybe not. "Quirky families are the best."

Yes, I thought, slowly and suddenly unsurprised. No one offered to spend a summer with someone else's family if they weren't going to embrace it. *Aren't they?*

~

My dad might've trusted me, but he low-key interviewed Connor after things had broken up, and I couldn't help but subtly eavesdrop as Sage told me about this week's Fourth of July party. Because Connor McCallister talked nonstop. No matter the conversation topic—family, sports, music, movies—he had something to say. I didn't catch where he was from, but he had a fourteen-year-old brother, rooted for New York teams, unabashedly loved Coldplay, and thought the Marvel universe was getting out of control. "I graduated a few weeks ago," he said when Erica asked about school. "I'm playing lacrosse at Notre Dame next year."

There it is, I thought. Connor looked like an athlete, but I hadn't been able to pinpoint his sport.

"He's a good kid," my dad said before hugging me good night, as if I'd introduced Connor as my prom date rather than a reluctant bunkmate. "I like him a lot."

"He's also not your type," Erica whispered, which annoyed me…even though she was right. I always went for…well, anyone but the nice-guy athlete.

Getting ready for bed later was awkward. There was no other way to say it. After fluffing up Swede's dog bed, I went to the bathroom to change into my pajamas. A pink-and-white sleep set that my dad called my "Eloise pj's." I braided my hair before brushing my teeth. It turned out Connor and I had identical electric toothbrushes.

"Is everything okay in there?" Connor asked once I'd moved on to moisturizing.

"Yeah!" I replied, busy rubbing in lavender lotion. "Why?"

He didn't respond, and the silence made me realize that it was getting late and he hadn't had a chance at the bathroom yet.

Oops.

At home, I shared a bathroom with the twins, but we rarely used it at the same time.

I tried not to blush when I stepped back into the bunk room. Swede was settled in his bed, and Connor was texting on the bottom bunk…wearing only a pair of striped boxers.

"All yours!" I chirped, to overcompensate for the swirl of heat on the back of my neck. No plaid pajama pants? Not even a T-shirt?

"Thanks." Connor looked up from his phone and smiled at me. "I'm sorry. I didn't mean to rush you."

"It's okay." I shook my head before giving Swede some

snuggles. Then I climbed the bunk's built-in ladder up to my bunk. The mattress could've been softer, but the cool covers felt luxurious against my skin. Smiling to myself, I switched off my light and settled into my pillows.

Suddenly exhausted.

I heard Connor pee and the toilet flush, the sink basin splashing with water as he washed his hands, and when he got into bed, his sleepy sigh was louder than mine. I also heard—and *felt*—Swede tense up in the corner.

No, I thought. *Please, no. No, no, no—*

"Oh, hello," Connor said from the bottom bunk. He sounded amused, but I doubted he actually was. "Buddy, I'm flattered..."

"We can switch bunks." I gritted my teeth and pushed back my coverlet. Below, Swede was trying to claim space next to Connor. "I'm sorry. I should've taken the bottom. I knew he was going to do this. Every night he starts in his own bed but winds up with me like clockwork."

Connor laughed. It was muffled, probably by Swede's fur. "Don't worry about it," he said. "I'm all good down here."

I winced. He was so *nice*.

"Okay, you may be comfortable now, but when you wake up at three a.m.—"

"He'll be a living furnace taking up most of the bed," Connor finished for me. "Trust me, I know, and it's fine. My best friend has two huge dogs, and I've shared the couch with them a thousand times over the years."

"What are their names?" my inner dog person asked.

"Arthur and Francine."

"Oh, cute," I said, then bit my pinkie nail. "If it doesn't work out, you get the top tomorrow."

"Deal," he agreed, and from there, all three of us shifted until we were comfortable. My spine straightened at Connor's sharp inhale. Swede had kicked him in the stomach.

But he didn't say anything until all was quiet. "Olivia?"

"Yeah?" I just barely asked, my eyelids drifting shut.

I heard him swallow hard. "You don't remember me, do you?"

NINE

On Monday, I found myself sleeping so deeply that I barely felt my wrist buzz at 6:00 a.m. I'd worn my Apple Watch to bed, not wanting my phone alarm to wake Connor. He hadn't seemed to be a night owl, but did that mean he was a morning person?

To be determined, I thought as I pushed back my covers and carefully descended the bunkbed's ladder. The wood was cool against my bare feet, maybe even a little slippery. In fact, the whole room felt cool—and damp—from our cracked window. Not in a gross way, just different.

Swede almost always knew the drill, so I was surprised to find him still asleep in the bottom bunk with Connor. They were spooning. My dog was the little spoon but had taken up most of the bed while Connor was all but pressed up against the wall, sleeping on his side with an arm draped over Swede.

"Swede," I whispered, and the golden retriever blinked open his brown eyes. He clambered off the bunk after I softly snapped my fingers. Connor's arm flopped lifelessly on the mattress.

Either he was seriously exhausted or a heavy sleeper.

Maybe both.

Out on the cute little porch I scooped two hefty cups of Purina into Swede's bowl while he relieved himself nearby. I'd left the leash on the hook. Swede was adventurous but had never been a bolter.

Connor was still passed out when I slipped back into our room, so I didn't bother going into the bathroom to change; I quickly stripped and pulled on a lilac-colored running set before twisting my hair into a bun and double-knotting my sneakers.

There was nothing better than starting the day with a run.

I couldn't help but glance at Connor again while sipping from my water bottle; he hadn't shifted sleeping positions since Swede had abandoned him. My empty stomach stirred a little, unable to hear him breathe or see the rise and fall of his chest.

Was he even alive?

What I did next was certifiably creepy; holding my own breath, I crouched next to the bottom bunk and let my hand hover over Connor's nose. Half a heartbeat later, I felt his warm exhale against my palm.

It's all good, folks, I thought. *Sign of life detected!*

Swede hadn't wandered far when I came back outside; he had his nose to the ground about ten yards away, under an ancient oak tree. "You coming, dude?" I called, careful not to wake anyone.

The sky was overcast, so no sun peeked through the trees as Swede and I jogged across the lawn together, eventually finding a sand-and-grass pathway that led toward keep Oyster Pond. I was used to my feet pounding the pavement back home, so it took a minute to adjust to the uneven trail.

The path ran along the pond; over the tall grass, I saw a few early-morning kayakers on the water—it looked like someone was even doing yoga on their paddleboard. Across Oyster Pond, the ocean must've been rough; I could hear the waves crashing against the shore. It made me want to pick up my pace, but I didn't want to wear myself out so early.

I rarely listened to music as I ran; instead, I ran with my thoughts. They ranged from the plot twist of whatever book I was reading to whether or not I should stop texting so-and-so to mentally adding sea salt caramel Talenti to Erica's detailed grocery list to Annie—of course, Annie. Always Annie. I hoped I'd get to talk to her today.

Right now, though, I thought of the guy barely breathing in my room. "You don't remember me, do you?" Connor had said last night, and I hadn't responded at first. Because what was he talking about? I'd found out he was from Pennsylvania, my hometown oddly enough, but he'd gone to public school while I was private until moving to Haddonfield. Unless we'd met at Newtown Swim Club one summer, I had no idea how we'd know each other.

"I'm sorry—" I started at the same time he said, "Camp Skytop? Eight years ago?"

I bristled in bed. Camp Skytop was the sleepaway camp my

dad and Erica had sent me to when I was eleven. "Olivia, you're going to *love* it!" I remembered Erica gushing while showing me the camp's website. It was in the Pocono Mountains, and they wanted to send me there for four weeks that summer. "I went when I was your age and made so many friends..."

"We were there the same monthlong session," Connor continued as it suddenly and finally hit me. "We crossed paths a lot..."

"Did you do horseback riding?" I asked. It was the one activity that I'd really loved, so much that I'd begged my dad for a horse upon getting home. Our compromise had been riding lessons for a couple years.

"Oh, no." Connor chuckled. "I'm allergic to horses."

"Sailing?" I tried, since I'd had some pretty memorable (and mortifying) capsizes. Maybe that was how I'd made an impression.

"I was more of a canoer," he said. "It was mostly the—uh, landline that brought us together."

The landline.

My stomach twisted. If a camper ever wanted to call home, they had to use one of the camp landlines during certain hours, and calls were limited to five minutes. I'd never forget that... because I went to the mess hall *a lot* to call my dad or grandparents. Annie always asked to hear every detail of my day then told me about her latest round of golf and ladies' lunches.

Now that I really thought about it, there *was* a group of six or so kids that showed up for phone time like clockwork. The supervising counselor called us "the Homebodies."

That was it—*that* was where I knew Connor's blue eyes from. The line for the landline.

"You were one of the Homebodies," he unknowingly confirmed. "Literally always first to call your family."

I shifted on my mattress, sensing some sarcasm in his voice. It wasn't a crime that I went to the mess hall early to ensure I was first in line for the phone; I knew my priorities. "I'm sorry," I said. "Maybe I don't remember you because you never challenged me for the gold medal."

Connor snorted, seemingly amused even though my words had come out sharper than I'd intended. "Yes, I definitely didn't," he agreed as my heart hammered. "Since I volunteered to go *last*."

"What?" I asked, even though this was all sounding familiar.

"I always went last," he repeated. "With no one after me, Ava let me stay on the phone longer. I usually got two or three extra minutes."

He sounded proud of himself.

"Good for you," I deadpanned, then squeezed my eyes shut to imagine the mess hall. His eyes were something—I *had* to remember the rest of him.

"I was ten but looked seven," he added after a couple seconds of silence. "Short and skinny—"

"With a buzz cut and freckles!" I finished for him, way too pleased with myself. It was all coming back to me. "You also wouldn't take off your Red Sox jersey…" My brows knitted together. "Didn't you tell my dad you root for New York teams?"

"I do." I could *hear* his blush in the bunk below me. "But back then, I was strictly a fan of the front-runner."

I laughed. "Why do you remember me? Because I look pretty much the same?"

Whenever Annie and I used to look at my old school photos, she pointed out that I looked seventeen in fifth grade. Taller than almost all the boys and more developed than every other girl. Puberty had hugged me earlier than expected.

"No," Connor answered. "I recognized you because you're beautiful."

Something stirred in my chest, but I rolled my eyes.

Connor was smooth, and he knew it.

So much for remembering him as an innocent little pipsqueak, I thought.

Connor yawned. "Good night, fellow Homebody."

"I grew out of that," I told him. "It just took a series of slumber parties."

"Same here," he said as I closed my eyes. "Lacrosse camps."

"Mmm." I snuggled further under my blankets. "It's good you play lacrosse."

"Why?" Connor asked, but I felt my face literally melting into my pillow before I could answer.

The house was buzzing when Swede and I got back from our run, sweaty and panting. "Swede!" Bryce and Maisie cheered from the crowded kitchen table, but the golden didn't acknowledge them or the other dogs wagging their tails; instead, he all but dunked his head in the communal canine water bowl.

"You want some French toast, Olivia?" Nick called from the stove.

I smiled but shook my head. "Maybe later!"

Without looking up from his phone, Luke offered me a banana from the island's fruit basket. He must've been a fellow runner; we didn't eat much right after runs.

"Thanks," I said, but when his response was an exasperated sigh followed by some furious texting, Charlie stepped in.

"He technically took two weeks off, but a case of his is suddenly heating up."

My eyebrows knitted together. "A case?"

"Agent Morrissey is with the FBI," Charlie said, smiling proudly. "White-collar crime."

Holy crap, I thought, impressed. *Does everyone here have a cool job?*

"Yes, I packed the sunscreen," someone said, and Charlie and I turned to see Connor pulling two lunch boxes out of the fridge. He handed the red one to a wickedly sunburned little boy in glasses and the blue one to a slightly older boy wearing a backward baseball cap. Teddy and Finn.

"The spray kind?" the bespectacled kid asked.

"Ted, are you serious?" Connor gave him a look. "Am I new here?"

"He's a natural with them," Charlie murmured as Teddy and his brother giggled. "Their parents aren't here, so everyone was a little worried..." He trailed off. "But it's been three weeks and Nana said it's been easy. He takes them to sailing and tennis camp a few days a week, spends hours with them on the beach, and even supervises bedtime."

"Jeez," I said. "Where are their parents?"

"Handling something," Charlie answered vaguely while Teddy and Finn said goodbye to their grandparents and great-grandparents. Beth barely looked up from her laptop, but Topper put down his coffee for fist bumps. I glanced over at Connor; it was hard to believe I'd needed to check his breathing earlier, that he'd seemed like someone capable of sleeping through his alarm. Now he looked more awake than anyone in the room, humming some song while casually swinging his keys around a finger.

He quickly caught me looking at him, winking when we made eye contact. My stomach swirled, but I forced myself to peel my banana and take a bite. "How'd you sleep last night?" Connor called.

"Fine." I shrugged, even though I hadn't woken up once—a rarity for me. "How about you?"

"Swede and I had the sweetest dreams," he replied, then checked his watch and whistled. "Troops, time to head out!"

I watched him shuttle Finn and Teddy outside, and for some

reason, I pushed away from the island and followed them. The early-morning clouds had cleared, the sun now shining brightly and a breeze rippling.

"Remind me how often you're going to reapply?" Connor was asking Teddy as they headed down the front walk.

"Every time we switch sessions," he replied.

"You're a genius, my man," Connor patted his shoulder, then turned to his brother. "Finn, the hat."

He groaned. "But..."

"Girls don't like backward hats," Connor said. "Mary-Grace Van Cleve is never—"

"He likes Claire Dupré now," Teddy chimed in.

"I do not!" Finn's voice jumped, but I caught him peek at Connor's front facing baseball cap before he flipped his around to match.

Someone was clearly an icon.

"Hey!" I called right before they hit the driveway, all three guys turning to face me. "I..." Totally didn't have anything to say. "Uh, have a question."

"What is it?" Teddy asked. "We have a schedule."

"And we're actually running ahead of time for once," Connor said. He smiled at me. "What's up?"

I thought quickly. "We don't have a shower."

"Because you're staying at Summer Camp," Teddy said, as if that explained everything.

Summer Camp. Our nook's name again made me think of my

favorite Polaroid of Annie—barefoot and smiling with a glass of wine as she posed beside that mysterious green tractor.

"No, our bathroom doesn't have a shower," Connor confirmed. "But the outdoor shower's right off the porch." He sighed happily. "If heaven were a place on earth…"

I made a face. "An outdoor shower?"

"Wait, have you never taken an outdoor shower?" he asked and laughed when I wrinkled my nose. Finn and Teddy did too. "You're missing out!"

Was I? Because I didn't really see the appeal of a shower that didn't involve steaming up a mirror. Maybe my dad and Erica would let me use their shower.

By way of goodbye, Connor nodded toward the garage; I did a double take when I saw the boys climbing into *my* car, a blue-gray Jeep Wrangler. Except no, it wasn't my car, because I hadn't taken its top off or driven up here or have a Pennsylvania license plate.

I also definitely did not have a Hilton Head sticker on my back bumper.

But a shiver still ran up my spine, not only recognizing that sticker, but also realizing something. I'd seen Connor's car before—I'd seen it only weeks ago, in a parking lot on a drizzling, dreary night.

And I'd mistaken it for mine.

Last night he'd said he was from *Newtown*. Elkins Village was in Newtown—it'd definitely been his Jeep I'd accidentally climbed into that night. Beyond embarrassing, but it also made me wonder what relative of his lived there.

Did he visit often?

Now wasn't the time to ask, and I found I didn't want to ask. Because while I could talk about Annie, I knew I would tear up if I also mentioned Elkins.

"Have fun at camp," I told Finn and Teddy.

"You're welcome to tag along," Connor said. "We can walk around Edgartown after dropping them off."

"Oh, that's really nice," I said, truly tempted. Because one of Annie's Polaroids showed her in front of the island's Old Whaling Church, and, thanks to my research, I knew the Old Whaling Church was in Edgartown. This was the perfect opportunity to start following in her footsteps.

Although I hesitated, as if I weren't ready to explore Annie's past yet.

"But I should take a shower and then actually eat breakfast before we leave for the beach."

"Will you still be there at three?" Teddy, eavesdropping, called from the Jeep.

"I can teach you how to crab!" Finn added.

Connor chuckled. "Dude, what about Claire Dupré?" He shook his head, then turned to salute me. "Duty calls…"

"I see you met Connor," Sage appeared at my side once Connor's Jeep had disappeared down the driveway. "He's something, right?"

"Yeah." I nodded. "He's definitely…happy."

That was the only word for him.

"Oh, yes," she agreed. "I've only known him a couple days, but I think he's living his best life." She smiled. "It's hard not to on the Vineyard."

I smiled back, hoping it was true.

The Carmichaels had a small stretch of Oyster Pond Beach, but Nick—who seemed to be the unofficial cruise director—hustled everyone and their beach gear down the dock and into a bobbing Boston Whaler. This group was all cousins; someone would circle back for my dad, Erica, and other, older adults. "Where are we going?" Bryce asked once Nick fired up the boat's engine.

"Over there." Charlie pointed across the pond, toward the horizon. I could see the bright blue ocean, but there was a beach in the foreground, dotted with a rainbow of beach chairs and umbrellas. "Since we don't have ocean access, our friends let us use their beach."

"You mean they *own* it?" I asked, incredulous. The closer the Whaler puttered, the bigger the beach looked. "The whole thing?"

Charlie nodded. "The whole *mile*, yes."

Wow, I thought. *And I thought the Carmichaels' spread was something…*

Sage dropped the anchor several yards from shore; the sun-bathed water came up to my knees, but it was refreshing as I waded to land, the sand soft beneath my feet.

Although my heart lurched when I felt something scuttle over my toes.

"Hey, are there crabs..." I started to ask, but trailed off upon noticing a pack of children wielding tall nets in the pond's shallows. What had Finn told me earlier?

"I can teach you how to crab!"

As if on cue, a curly-haired boy skillfully scooped a blue crab out of the water, its orange-tipped claws tangled in the netting. "Everyone, look!" a girl in a pink suit shouted. "Look what Oliver caught!"

Bryce and Maisie couldn't join the scene fast enough; once Charlie had scouted out the perfect place to make camp, my siblings dumped their stuff and fled back to the pond. I watched in wonder; Bryce immediately started helping Oliver untangle his crab while another kid offered Maisie her net.

Oh, to be ten, I lamented, but I unlocked my phone to snap some photos. Annie would love them.

Soon I went from photographer to lifeguard. "I'll keep an eye on them," Luke offered as I shifted from one foot to the other. His pinging phone was nowhere to be seen; he now looked like he was in total vacation mode, wearing a frayed baseball cap with his sunglasses. He popped the tab of a lemon La Croix once he'd collapsed into his beach chair. "You relax, alright?"

I nodded, then unfolded my own beach chair and spread out my striped towel behind it, for a little shade. I liked to bake in the sun for a while before taking a dip, so after stretching out on my towel, I flipped open my book.

But someone called my name mid-sentence. "Olivia!"

I glanced over my shoulder to see Nick waving me toward him.

"Guys, this is my elusive step-cousin, Olivia…" he joked when I joined him and Sage. They stood near a huge circle of beach chairs. Music played from a nearby speaker and some people held playing cards while others sipped iced coffee.

"Hi." I summoned a smile and wave. "It's nice to meet you."

"You too!" One woman smiled back. Her sun-streaked hair was up in a Tinkerbell top-knot and she wore funky sunglasses. Tortoiseshell with flecks of pink, white, and yellow. "I'm Meredith."

"Our fearless leader." The blond guy next to her affectionately squeezed her knee, then looked at me. "I'm Stephen, her groom."

"But we call him Wit," said the tanned brunette on his other side. "Even though his is questionable…"

Wit laughed. "I love you too, Luli!"

Luli smirked before introducing her husband, and then a guy in a T-shirt reading JUST FLOSS cleared his throat. "Olivia, have you met Connor McCallister yet?"

I raised an eyebrow. "You know him too?"

The court of beach chairs collectively cracked up, and the man nodded. "I've met him once or twice—"

"Austin!" A sophisticated blond kicked some sand at him. Austin caught her foot and she squealed when he squeezed it. His wedding band glinted in the sunlight.

"Get a cabana," Wit said, even though there were none in sight.

"Name a year, Olivia," Austin ignored him. "Name a year and I'll be able to tell you what Connor was for Halloween. I've known him forever; he's best friends with my younger sister."

"Small world!" I said, because wow, was it ever. A *really* small one. First a near-rom-com moment at Connor's and my grandparents' retirement community, and now this?

The blond raised her sunglasses to give me a look. "Be gentle with him, okay?"

"Katie..." Meredith sighed as a ripple went up my spine. *Be gentle?*

What was that supposed to mean?

"I'm serious!" Katie exclaimed. "He has—"

"A big heart," Austin finished for her. "Connor has a really big heart."

Hmm, I thought, but before I could turn that over in my head, the entire vibe shifted—from fun and lighthearted to serious and all business.

"Mer, he's here!" Luli whisper-yelled. "He's unloading the surfboards from the Scout."

"Here we go..." Sage said at the same time Meredith dropped to the sand and reached for a Super Soaker stowed under her chair. Nick clapped his hands and rubbed them together, excited for whatever was about to play out, but Sage made eye contact with me. "You feel like floundering?"

"What's floundering?" I asked as she elbowed her distracted fiancé.

"Oh, man." Nick turned to us, his blue eyes twinkling. "You have much to learn, cousin."

Not your cousin, I thought, even though I smiled and raced after him and Sage into the water.

~

By the time we left the beach, I had less than fifty pages left in my book. Nick, Sage, and I had "floundered" in the ocean for a while (*floundering* [v]: floating on your stomach in the shallows and letting waves wash over you, which more often than not results in spinning out of control and laughing your ass off), and after that, I collapsed on my towel to read. Bryce handed out lunches a couple hours later, full of pride. He'd volunteered to help Peggy pack them this morning.

"Ooh, what's this?" I started to unwrap the tinfoil as my stomach growled. "Turkey and cheese?"

"Peanut butter and fluff," he reported.

My appetite squirmed.

"I told Nana you wouldn't like it," he whispered. "But she said it was tradition..."

"Don't worry about it." I smiled at him. "It looks delicious!"

And then I forced down a sandwich that vividly took me back to puking all over myself at Jenna Randall's house in third grade. Her mom had made them as an after-school snack; the thick marshmallow spread had turned to cement in my stomach.

But this was Camp Carmichael! I was going to embrace it!

Fortunately, dinner was much better: a huge pasta salad with cherry tomatoes, zucchini, mozzarella, and basil. "What about you, Erica?" Jay asked my stepmother while we ate. "You up for a match tomorrow?"

"Jay, I don't think Erica plays much tennis anymore," Beth said, then turned to her sister. "You're into pickleball now, right?"

Next to me, my dad stifled a snort. Erica *did* play in Haddonfield's pickleball league—while modeling cute outfits and swinging monogrammed paddles that various brands sent her—but her inner tennis player loathed it. *What kind of sport doesn't make you sweat?*

"I thought you'd never ask," she told her brother, pointedly ignoring Beth. "Name the time and place..."

I offered to do the dishes later, but I didn't know what to do with myself once I'd finally started the dishwasher at nine thirty. Nick, Sage, Charlie, and Luke had said goodbye before they'd headed out to hang with friends, and who could blame them for not inviting me? They were twenty-six; I was nineteen. Even though I felt exhausted beyond my years, they probably saw me as a kid. Meanwhile, Maisie and Bryce had hunkered down in their bunk room, and my dad had texted me that he and Erica had gone out for ice cream.

I'll bring you back some salted caramel! he promised. One of my favorite flavors.

Most of Erica's family was watching TV together, but after I made myself a cup of tea and stole the remainder of last night's pie, I retreated to my room. My footsteps were quick and quiet, but I almost stopped short when I noticed a framed needle-pointed canvas. It was a lakeside landscape—all blues, greens, creams, and grays—featuring a majestic heron.

Peggy's work, I surmised, but it made me think of Annie. There was nothing more comforting than watching her stitch and sip chamomile tea while we watched a movie together.

I missed her, even though we had spoken today. I'd called after getting back from the beach, and miraculously, Annie herself had picked up her landline. "Annie, hi!" I'd exclaimed from the Carmichaels' dock, hoping the service wasn't too spotty. "It's Olivia!"

"Who?" she replied. "Please speak up; my doctor says I don't need a hearing aid, but I disagree. I can't hear anyone when they whisper..."

Meanwhile, her voice came through in broken pieces, so I hung up and called back from my bunk bed. Annie didn't answer, but Tara did at the nurses' desk.

"Olivia, darling." I could hear my grandmother smile once Tara gave her the phone, which made *me* smile. "How are you?"

I told her all about the beach today, from Nick driving the Boston Whaler across the pond to Maisie and Bryce crabbing to floundering in the ocean to the decades-old cowboy hat Topper always wore on the beach. I also described how the bright sun made Oyster Pond glimmer like glass. It was unlike anything I'd seen before.

"What a beautiful painting," Annie remarked.

"Don't worry, I took *a ton* of photos," I replied, knowing she meant *picture*, not painting. I swallowed. "How was your day?"

"Oh, it was wonderful," she said dreamily. "Ellen and I…"

My heart sunk at *Ellen*. Ellen had been one of Annie's good friends, her longtime golf partner. And while Ellen was still alive and well, she and Annie no longer played golf together. They didn't even see each other anymore.

Because Ellen didn't visit.

"…played eighteen holes this morning, then had lunch on the patio and spent the afternoon at the pool."

"That sounds like the perfect summer day," I told her. "Did the handsome lifeguard ask about me?"

There was always a handsome lifeguard at the country club.

"He's too old for you, dearest," she said. "Eighteen."

I bit my nail, not wanting to know how old she currently thought I was. "I'm sorry, but I have to go now," I said a beat later. "Erica's calling me for dinner."

Erica was still at the beach.

Annie sighed. "Oh, that woman…"

I ignored the dig. "I'll call you again soon, Annie. I love you."

"I love you too," she said. "Bring back a painting, okay?"

"Yes, of course!" I promised. "I will bring back plenty of pictures."

A moment of silence, and then, "Wonderful, another photo book."

Her delivery was dry, probably outright rude to anyone else, but I laughed. I laughed even after my grandmother had abruptly hung up on me.

It had just been so long since Annie last made a joke.

And little did she know that I was going to make her the photo book of all photo books.

~

When I slipped back into Summer Camp, I thought I was alone…for half a second. "You're *kidding* me!" I heard Connor say from behind the bunk room's closed door. "Mads, he really said that?"

Well, I thought. *This complicates things.*

My plan had been to change into my pajamas and climb into bed with Annie's Vineyard memorabilia and my phone. Consulting my list again would help me come up with an actual itinerary…or should I be more spontaneous and just pick a place?

I hesitated knocking until Connor laughed, a confirmation that his conversation wasn't that serious. "Welcome!" he called, and I was surprised when I opened the door to find him not in his bunk, but casually hanging with Swede on his dog bed.

It would've made for a funny photo.

"Keep talking," I whispered. "I just need to grab a couple things..."

"No, it's okay." He tapped his mute button. "Mads can summon her one shred of patience." He smiled at me. "I see you have pie."

"Indeed, I do." I set the mostly empty box down on the dresser so I could quickly find some cozy clothes. Then I unzipped my backpack and pulled out my folder of Annie's stuff. The back of my neck prickled, feeling Connor's eyes on me. He'd brought Finn and Teddy to the beach late this afternoon, but I only saw them from afar; their intense Frisbee game, played in Oyster Pond's shallows, had been serious business. "Tell Mads I say hi," I added before retrieving my pie and making my exit.

In the bathroom, I changed into sweats and one of Annie's worn cashmere sweaters, then went out to the porch. It was secluded and snug, with cushy furniture and an amazing view of the stars. I charted out what I was pretty sure was Orion's Belt.

Fantastic, I thought upon flipping on the outdoor light to assess the pie leftovers. There was more or less a slice and a half left, but I'd forgotten to grab a fork.

Rookie mistake, Olivia!

What I did next wasn't ladylike, let alone civilized, but I didn't care. No one was around, and I really wanted to finish my day with this magical dessert. So I carefully picked up the remaining slice, preparing to bite into it like a piece of pizza…

"That's certainly one way to eat it," a voice said out of nowhere, and not only did I drop the pie in surprise, but it crumbled in the box.

Heart shattered, I closed my eyes.

"You seem a little edgy," Connor noted. "Are you usually edgy?"

"No," I said, eyes still closed. "I've actually been praised for my calm and collected demeanor, especially in high-stress situations."

"Hmm," he hummed. "I'm sensing some invisible quotation marks."

My muscles tensed. "No, I'm paraphrasing," I said, since my dad, teachers, bookstore boss, *and* the Elkins staff had all paid me some version of that compliment. "The direct quotes are much more—" I dropped off when I blinked to see Connor standing front and center on the porch, wearing nothing but a blue towel wrapped around his waist.

He held up his hands, as if I'd suddenly trained a gun at him. "I'm taking a shower!"

Oh, I thought. *Right.*

The outdoor shower was off to the left, attached to the side of the house. Post-beach I'd shampooed and conditioned in Erica and my dad's bathroom.

I glanced down at my pie, and Connor took that as a signal that it was safe to move. "You know I won't judge you," he said once inside the wood stall, towel now probably hung on a hook. I heard him turn the faucet, officially committed to a cold shower. "If you eat that pie with your hands, there will be zero judgment on my end."

Already licking raspberry off my fingertips, I rolled my eyes. "Well, in *that* case…" I almost choked on a bite of crust when I saw steam rising from the shower. The water was *hot*?

Not only did that make *a lot* of sense, but it also made me feel like a total idiot.

Of course it's hot, Olivia! the snarky voice in my head said. *The not-at-all-recent invention of pipes makes it entirely possible…*

Cheeks warming, I debated whether or not to sneak inside the house; it was a little awkward sitting here while Connor lathered himself with body wash three yards away, but my phone chiming distracted me.

Finally hit the front of the line, my dad had texted. They're out of salted caramel. "Lotsa Dough" sound like a solid plan B?

Thank you, I typed back. But I devoured any and all remnants of mixed berry pie, so that'll tide me over!

My dad: Topper called dibs on those.

Me: Oh shit.

Connor: "I'll be back out in a sec!"

"What?" I looked up to see Connor back on the porch, once again shirtless and running a hand through his still dripping hair. It looked darker when wet, more red than blond.

"I'll be right back," he rephrased. "We can hang out."

Hang out? I thought. *You have* energy *to hang out?*

I mean, he and Finn had broken out their lacrosse sticks to play catch after dinner. *How* was he not exhausted?

"Okay," I said, wishing my muscles would unwind. "Sure." I rolled back my shoulders. "Let's hang out."

TEN

As advertised, Connor returned to the porch, in sweats and barefoot with Swede in tow. He'd thrown a wool blanket over his shoulder and held up a pack of Oreos. "Want one?"

"I'm good," I said as he joined me on the couch. Our shoulders brushed, and I caught a hint of his shampoo. I couldn't pinpoint the exact scent—watermelon?—but it smelled *delicious*. "This is all getting a little too *Parent Trap* for me."

I mean, us isolated together in "summer camp," his reddish hair, and now the Oreos...

What was next? A jar of Jif?

"What do you mean?" Connor smirked. "I'm allergic to tree nuts, which are commonly mixed up with peanuts, we're not related, and most importantly, Sean and Miranda McCallister are happily married."

I made a ballpark guess. "Twenty years?"

"Twenty-two."

"I was close."

"You were," he agreed then bit into a cookie.

Crunch.

Crunch, crunch, crunch.

Crunch!

Dude is a loud chewer, I thought while making Swede sit for the Milk-Bone I'd stashed in my pocket. He deserved a sweet treat too.

"So," Connor said, "how've the last eight years treated you?"

I raised an eyebrow. "The last eight years?"

"Yeah." He shrugged. "I'm down for the scenic route or the supercut."

But what if I'm not? I wondered, feeling a pang in my chest.

I'd never considered myself an especially private person, but something about Connor made me want to put on my winter coat and zip it all the way up. It wasn't that he made me *uncomfortable*, it was something else. Something I couldn't pinpoint.

"Where do you go to college?" Connor coaxed.

"Northwestern," I told him. "But I haven't started yet. I took kind of a gap year..." I trailed off, the night breeze suddenly sweeping through the porch. Connor wordlessly offered me some blanket when I tried rubbing goose bumps off my arms. "Thank you," I said, but felt the pinpricks multiply once his trapped heat hit me. Too abrupt a temperature change, maybe.

"No worries." Connor took a breath. Luckily, my phone chimed before he could exhale and prompt me to pick up on my life story.

I assumed the notification was a text from my dad, letting

me know that he and Erica were back at the house. Or even Erica, asking me to peek in on Maisie and Bryce to make sure they were asleep.

I didn't know when my phone had slipped in between the couch cushions, but it took a few beats to dig it out of the crevice. QUINCY, my screen read.

"Who's Quincy?" Connor casually asked. I must've read her name aloud. "Boyfriend?"

"One of my best friends," I said as I scanned Quincy's message: Hey, girl! Just checking in... "And last year's Haddonfield High School homecoming *queen*."

(It was times like this when Quincy rolled her eyes at her parents' choice to give her a most-of-the-time boy's name.)

Connor and I looked at each other once I'd locked my phone, and from the way his eyes held mine, I knew what he was going to say before his lips formed the first word.

"Do you have a boyfriend?"

My heart rate heightened, suddenly aware of the hazy tension in the air. What was it Nick and Sage's friends had said on the beach? That Connor had a really big heart?

Likely translation: Connor was a huge flirt.

Well, I thought, letting both his blanket and body heat wrap around me. *Why not, pipsqueak? Let's see what you've got.*

"Do you have a girlfriend?" I countered.

"No." The corners of his eyes crinkled. "Not right now."

Not right now.

Why add that? Why not leave it at *no*?

To gauge how curious I am, I realized as soon as I said, "But there *was* someone?"

Okay, he was good.

He nodded. "There's pretty much always been someone."

"Ah." Catching his drift, I casually reached for an Oreo. "Well, you *are* a lacrosse player…"

"Wow, I'm not offended at all." He rolled his eyes, but I caught their twinkle. "I don't play the field. Mads calls me a 'serial monogamist.'"

I tilted my head. Interesting. "So, what? You've had two or three girlfriends?"

Connor counted to five on his fingers, then raised another to make six. "Only three have been serious, though."

I snorted. "What was the deal with your last relationship?"

"Leah and I dated for six months but called it after prom. I was coming up here for the summer and our colleges are nowhere near each other." He shrugged. "I don't think either of us was that into it." He raised an eyebrow. "What about you?"

"What *about* me?" I asked.

"How long was your last relationship?"

Okay, wait, I thought. *This is getting very personal, very fast.*

What happened to us just hanging out?

I didn't respond at first. Back in high school, I'd hang out with guys for a few weeks or couple months before we stopped texting each other so we could devote time to texting other people. Things with my prom date had been *a little* different, since Trevor and I ended up hanging out through the summer...

But everything grew complicated when he left for college. Once I began dodging his FaceTime calls and dreading his visits, my friends suggested that the relationship had run its course. When Trevor didn't fight to stay together, I was relieved.

"A little over three months," I told Connor. "But I don't know if I'd categorize it as a *committed relationship*."

Connor looked incredulous. "He cheated?"

I shook my head. "It's more like we didn't want to commit to the relationship itself."

"Hmm." A pause. "Does that bother you?"

"No," I said truthfully, but I knew I sounded irritated. And I didn't really know why. I also didn't know why I was suddenly telling Connor all this. "I mean, some of us aren't serial monogamists."

"Oh, so *you* play the field?"

I shifted in my seat. Man, was he quick. "I prefer hanging out."

Connor was quiet, as if weighing whether he wanted to poke that. "What are you doing tomorrow?" he eventually asked.

"Not sure," I said. "Maybe the beach again? I think Erica's playing tennis, and then she and my dad are taking the twins kayaking."

"Not your scene?"

"It's not *not* my scene. It's just..."

No matter where I go with my family, I feel like a spare tire.

Under the blanket, Connor's knee nudged mine. "Come with me when I drop off Teddy and Finn," he said. "Wear a swimsuit."

"Why? What are we doing?"

He smiled, and leaned close to whisper in my ear. "Something fun."

I rolled my eyes to ignore the two words rippling up my spine.

When I got back from my run the next morning, Nick was at the stove again. "Here you go, Bryce!" he said as I snagged a spot at the island. "Your nine-cheese omelet. Sorry it looks more like scrambled eggs…"

"You still get an A for effort," Sage remarked, in between bites of something that resembled a deconstructed take on a veggie omelet. She blew him a kiss.

Nick lightly slapped it on his cheek with a dimpled grin. "I worked at Dock Street during the summers in college," he told me. "I mastered everything but flipping an omelet."

"Then how'd you get this gig?" I joked.

"I know, right?" He chuckled and cracked an egg in a bowl. "Our omelet guy sadly skipped town at sunrise."

"Luke?" I guessed. Life as an FBI agent must not have been as glamorous as it was on TV.

Sage nodded. "But he'll be back before the Foxes' Fourth party tomorrow night."

"The Foxes?"

"Our friends across the pond," Nick said. "You met Meredith on the beach."

"Oh, yeah—she was hiding that huge Super Soaker. Are the Foxes the family that plays that game? Assassin?"

"Yes." Nick sighed, then asked for my breakfast order while Sage laughed. I noticed Nick gaze adoringly at her before cracking an egg. When was the wedding?

"We're going fishing off Cow Bay later," Sage said once I'd eaten half of my dilapidated but delicious caprese omelet. "Do you want to come?"

"Oh, thank you," I said, "but—"

"The actual fishing is optional," Nick added. "My mom's coming with firm plans to nap on the bow."

I laughed. "That's tempting, but I already have plans."

Nick and Sage looked at me, intrigued.

"I don't know the particulars," I said after pointing to Connor, who was currently lecturing a strawberry-averse Teddy on the long-term effects of scurvy. "But he's advertised it as something fun."

~

From what I gathered, Connor's topless Jeep usually had a DJ, but instead of blasting whatever it was nine- and seven-year-old boys were into, Finn and Teddy asked me a bunch of questions. "I don't have a favorite fudge flavor," I said, gripping the passenger seat's safety strap while Connor drove. He was a steady driver, but Oyster Watcha Road was no less bumpy than it'd been the other day. *Off-roading*, indeed. "I've only had fudge twice. The first time it was as hard as a rock, and it totally crumbled the second time."

"Then it wasn't good fudge," Teddy declared from the backseat then said to Connor, "Don't take her to Murdick's without us!"

Murdick's? I felt the urge to take out my phone.

Out of the corner of my eye, I saw Connor shake his head. "I wouldn't dare, Ted. It's obvious she needs your guidance."

"Hey!" I said, mostly to make Teddy laugh.

"Do you have a boyfriend?" Finn asked once we were cruising along the beautifully paved West Tisbury Road, toward town.

"What about Claire Dupré?" I lightly deflected.

"She says she wants to focus on sailing and surfing this summer," Teddy answered when his brother only blushed. "I did some recon."

"Yeah," Finn stewed, "but I didn't *want* you to—"

"Welcome to Edgartown, Olivia!" Connor exclaimed. "Isn't she something?"

Two blinks later, I was immersed. Despite it being early, Edgartown's Main Street was a *scene*. There were cars tightly parked on the road and plenty of people wandering up and down brick sidewalks sipping iced coffees and walking dogs. Teenagers moved in packs across the green-painted crosswalks while college kids jaywalked without a care in the world, too busy laughing at each other's jokes. Traffic was at a standstill, a sea of red brake lights. I suspected Connor knew a shortcut to the yacht club but was battling Main Street for my benefit.

I did a double take at the Old Whaling Church's soaring white pillars. *Take your picture for Annie!* my mind screamed. Farther down the street, a blue mermaid swam on the sign for a boutique called Nell. Scoops Ice Cream was on the corner. "We don't go there," Finn informed me after I asked if he was a waffle cone guy. "We only go to Mad Martha's."

I nodded. "Noted."

The Edgartown Yacht Club was a historic cedar-shingled clubhouse on the harbor, a red-white-and-blue triangular flag waving in the salty breeze and all types of boats moored in the water. Everything from tiny dinghies to sweet sailboats to a gigantic wood-paneled yacht. I couldn't unlock my phone fast enough to take a photo, knowing Bryce would be agog. Meanwhile, the modest parking lot had more or less turned into an elementary school drop-off line. When Connor pulled up to the front of the clubhouse, Teddy and Finn quickly unbuckled their seat belts and climbed out of the Jeep. "Murdick's afterward?" Connor asked by way of goodbye and got a pair of grins in reply.

It was adorable.

Connor shifted the car back into drive once a camp counselor had visibly checked in the brothers. I liked that their "manny" had waited. "Okay," I started when he pulled into a recently deserted spot to recalibrate. "*Now* will you tell—"

"Connor, hey!" someone called. "How's it going?"

I turned to see a familiar-looking blond guy walking toward us, double-fisting coffees and a pastry bag. "Aw, Wit," Connor said. "You shouldn't have." He held out his hand for a to-go cup. "Vanilla latte, I hope?"

"With two percent." Meredith's husband smiled then started to pass the coffee to Connor before suddenly swerving. "Which is also my bride's milk of choice!"

Connor shook his head. "Where is Meredith?"

Wit nodded toward the yacht club. "Wink asked her to do him a favor, so she walked in with Claire—"

"Claire?" My gasp was embarrassing. "Claire *Dupré*?"

Why was I so invested in this?

"Yes..." Wit looked both confused and amused. "When did you meet my goddaughter?"

"She hasn't," Connor answered as I blushed. "But she's heard the glowing reviews."

"Ah," Wit said. "Finn." He took a sip of his coffee, keeping Claire's feelings—or lack thereof—close to the vest. "What are you up to today?"

"Connor is taking me to an undisclosed location," I said, then shrugged. "He's kicking himself for forgetting the blindfold."

Wit raised an intrigued eyebrow, and Connor waved him over to whisper in his ear. "Of course," Wit said. "Because starting simple, with a lighthouse, is overrated."

"Totally," Connor agreed. "We should start with a cannonball."

"Or a dive," Wit cryptically quipped. "Maybe even a flip."

"*Where* are we going?" I asked, curiosity now coursing through my veins. A lighthouse—maybe Annie's lighthouse—sounded perfectly good to me.

Connor popped open his center console and pulled out a classic red bandanna. "You'll see not long after you put this on."

~

With my sight gone, I focused on my other senses. The briny air whipping through my hair, the sun on my shoulders, and the Coldplay song pulsing through the Jeep's speakers. Connor sang along, completely off-key, and every now and again, he flipped his blinker or stopped at a red light. "Oh, perfect!" he said at one point. "A spot!"

I reached to pull off my blindfold. "We're here?"

"Not yet," he told me. "You do *not* need to see me parallel park..."

Three excruciatingly long minutes later, Connor cut the ignition and tugged off the bandanna. "I don't know what your parking strategy is," I said. "Because it didn't feel like there was one, so you should try imagining your steering wheel as a pizza..."

Connor nodded, and nodded, and pleasantly nodded until I'd finished explaining how Erica—of all people—had taught me to parallel park. Then he smiled and said: "Look around, Olivia."

I blinked to see that Connor had parked the Jeep in a long

line of cars on the side of the road. Wetlands were on one side while the other looked out to sea, boats bobbing on the calm water. The vignette was beautiful, but what was so special about this place? Or cool enough that Connor ranked it as a sightseeing cannonball?

Equipped with beach towels, Connor and I ducked around the cars and started walking along the road's shoulder, and up ahead…

My stomach plummeted, because *up ahead* was what Erica had called the "Jaws Bridge." We'd driven over it two days ago, on our way to the house. People had been practically pushing and shoving to launch themselves into the air, and today was no different. The bridge crawled with jumpers, at least twelve people balancing on the railing's top rung. I saw two tween girls take the plunge holding hands, but even that cuteness didn't buoy me.

"Hey." Connor was suddenly in my face, wide-eyed and caring. I took a step backward; he was too close. "Are you—"

"Are we going to jump?" I asked, as if it were a question.

He nodded enthusiastically. "It's tradition!"

"Have you done it before?"

Another nod. "My second day, with Teddy and Finn."

"What?"

The brothers were so young!

"Oh, no—absolutely not," Connor quickly reframed. "It was their idea to drive out here, but they *watched* me jump from the beach."

Okay, I let out a deep breath. *Phew.*

"It's incredible," he added.

"Even if you don't do heights?" I mumbled.

"You're scared of heights?"

"Yes." I folded my arms across my chest. "Thank you for asking."

Connor turned toward the bridge, to consider. We were only several yards away now; something in me squirmed as I watched a man execute a perfect flip. His fellow jumpers cheered once he hit the water, a wide channel. Was there a current?

"Listen, I don't love heights either," Connor admitted. "I got stuck at the top of a roller coaster when I was ten, and it was *terribly* life-changing." He motioned to the madness. "But this is a *good* kind of life-changing. You'll see."

I cocked my head. "Are you trying to twist my arm?"

Connor shook his head. "I'm not an arm-twister."

"Oh, well..." I didn't know what to say. "I appreciate it."

"Of course," he said, then ran a hand through his hair. "I think you should at least walk across the bridge, though, to experience the energy."

"And to watch you do a cannonball?"

"Olivia, you have far too much faith in me." He laughed. "I only pulled off a pencil dive last time..."

Before braving the bridge, Connor and I made a detour to the beach—to the ancient boulders lining the channel, where most of the spectators sat. "Excuse me, sir," Connor said to an older man wearing a pair of aviators, an artist whose collapsible chair was precariously perched on a rock. He seemed to be working on something in his sketchbook. "Would you mind keeping an eye on these for us?"

Without glancing away from his drawing, he gave us a thumbs-up. We left our towels at the edge of his boulder and then retraced our steps to higher ground. A blast of adrenaline knocked me back, catching me so off my guard that I almost didn't clock a moped speed by. "Watch out, Elle Woods!" someone shouted at me and my pink bikini.

"How original," I muttered as Connor put a hand on my waist to guide me farther along the bridge. Sunlight swirled on my skin.

We snapped up the first break in the crowd, and Connor didn't hesitate before scaling the railing's five rungs. He stretched his arms above his head once he'd gotten his balance on top, and the girl next to us openly checked him out, fascinated by his flexed shoulder muscles.

"Nice view!" He obliviously scanned the bright horizon. "I think I see Nick's boat."

"Really?" I asked. There were a couple boats bobbing in the distance. "*Island Girl*?"

"Olivia, I'm not *that* farsighted. She's blue and white, right?"

"Per his Instagram," I said, and wanting to get a better look, I carefully climbed the wet but sturdy wooden fence. I didn't realize what I was doing until Connor offered a hand to help me. He smirked once we stood side by side.

"So you'll brave the higher altitudes for Nick?"

Heat rushed to my cheeks.

"It's okay," he said. "I would too."

I rolled my eyes, ignoring the tremors rolling up the backs of my legs. Connor shifted so that his arm brushed mine before he sidestepped closer, as if worried I'd slip. "Is his boat even out there?"

Connor pointed, and sure enough, I made out two people fishing off a white boat with two blue stripes.

Bare feet gripping the rail, I was suddenly very aware of being so high in the air. Blood pounded in my ears, and I told myself not to look down—to keep looking at *Island Girl*. "Are you ready?" I asked after a beat, stealing a glance at Connor.

"Yes." He gently elbowed me. "It sounds like you are too."

I shrugged, but a strange lump formed in my throat. "When am I going to get the chance to do this again?"

"Any time over the next twenty days," he quipped. "But I get what you're saying."

I snorted. "Thanks for ruining the moment, smartass."

"That wasn't *the moment*," he countered. "The moment is imminent; the moment is *airborne*."

Jump! I thought, unexpectedly so excited I couldn't breathe.

But Connor's outstretched arm blocked me from leaping. "The current is strong," he warned. "Be ready to swim, okay?"

I nodded, the butterflies in my stomach stirring. I might not like the diving board, but I'd always been a solid swimmer. Everything would be okay.

"Three?" Connor asked.

"Two," I answered.

"*One!*" He grinned, and at the very last second, when only the tips of my toes touched the bridge, I reached for his hand.

ELEVEN

I knew I was in trouble as soon as I broke the surface, completely miscalculating the meaning of *strong current*. I'd expected something intense, something that wouldn't stop jostling me. But no matter how hard I kicked underwater, I felt powerless. There was nothing violent about the channel; instead, the water was calm. It was even *smooth*, the flow like a conveyor belt...but one I couldn't escape. "Connor!" I called as I fought being carried out to sea. Our entwined hands had been ripped apart upon hitting the water. "Connor, where are you?"

"Let it carry you!" he called back. I thrashed around until I could see him bobbing behind me, seemingly in control. "Let it carry you a little farther, then start swimming toward the seawall!"

This wasn't Connor's first rodeo, so my pounding pulse and I believed him. I took a deep breath, then stopped kicking and surrendered to the current; it scooped me up and swept me away in a diagonal direction. Only when I was in line with the boulders did I channel my inner Katie Ledecky, breaking into my best freestyle.

Unfortunately, exhaustion soon struck. My arms and legs shrieked, and while I was aware of Connor cheering me on, I could barely hear him over the blood pulsing in my ears.

Just keep swimming, I chanted to myself. *Just keep swimming...*

But when the seawall didn't seem to be getting any closer, I started to lose steam. Being swept into the bay wouldn't be the end of the world, right? *Island Girl* was out there! Nick and Sage would see me!

It wasn't until someone onshore waved at me that I snapped out of the fantasy and back into motion. A tall man in a blue baseball cap was walking down the wall, to the last rock. "Right here!" I distantly heard him call, arms over his head. "Focus on me!"

Okay. I inhaled, then exhaled. *Okay, okay, okay.*

"Olivia, you've got this!" Connor shouted right before I sucked in another breath, closed my eyes, and ducked underwater.

And slowly but surely, I made progress, coming up every several seconds for air and to make sure my coach was still in my crosshairs. Closer, closer—I was getting *closer*. The man nodded encouragingly as I swam and stretched out his hand the moment I could grab it. "Breathe," he said once I was safely ashore, bent over and my body burning despite being sopping wet. "Just..." He trailed off when I managed to stand and we looked at each other. He was much older than I'd thought, maybe even close to Annie's age with white hair under his sun-bleached hat and deep creases around his wide green eyes.

"Thank you." I continued gulping for air. "Thank you so much. That was"—I mustered a shallow laugh—"a disaster."

"It was my pleasure," he replied. "I've dealt with many *disasters* over the decades." He paused, tilted his head intently. "Was that your first—"

"Olivia!" Connor blurted, and I unsteadily spun to see him emerge from the water, hair plastered to his forehead. "I'm sorry! That was so much rougher than last time..."

"Don't apologize," I said, feeling something untangle in my chest. "It ended in a meet-cute."

Connor smiled, but the older gentleman didn't pick up on the joke (he must not have been a rom-com fan). "That current was *wild*," Connor told him. "Thank you for helping her."

"You're welcome," he said, then added, "I like that."

Connor furrowed his brows. "Like what?"

"'Thank you for helping her,'" he quoted. "Not 'thank you for *saving* her.' You recognize the distinction."

Color rushed to Connor's cheeks. "Of course." His Adam's apple bobbed and goose bumps bloomed on my skin. "Olivia doesn't need saving."

"Oh, yes, I can tell." The man smiled and pointed to the bridge, right as a teenage boy in blue board shorts executed an off-kilter flip. He whistled. "Let's hope my grandson doesn't either."

After wrapping ourselves in our towels and unsuccessfully sneaking a peek at our guardian artist's sketchbook, we trekked back to Connor's Jeep and silently sat in the car for a few minutes. "Your body is so red," I finally remarked. "Are you getting a rash?"

"Maybe..." Connor mused. "Or it's just the aftermath of my belly flop."

I winced. "You belly flopped?"

"I was aiming for feetfirst," he said, chuckling. "Clean and simple, but I got distracted."

"By what?" I asked.

"Your smile."

"Oh my god." I shifted in my seat. "Why do you *do that*?"

"Do what?"

"Just..." I glanced away, willing my heart rate to slow. "Just say stuff like that."

"I'm afraid I'm not following."

I looked back to see Connor with his head cocked. "You are so easy with your compliments," I clarified. "I mean, first you call me beautiful, and now—"

"That's because I *like* you, Olivia." The corners of his blue eyes crinkled. "I've always liked you."

I've always liked you.

When I tried to take a breath, I discovered my lungs had turned to stone. If someone asked me when I'd met Connor, I would've said yesterday, but if someone asked Connor when he'd met me, I had a suspicion he'd dial back almost a decade.

And I suddenly wondered if *Connor has a really big heart* went deeper than his penchant for flirting; I worried it better translated to *Connor catches feelings fast*.

I didn't catch feelings *period*.

And I didn't want to start now.

Be gentle with Connor also echoed through my mind.

"I'm sorry," Connor said when I was quiet. "Do compliments make you cringe?"

"No..." I mechanically shook my head. "They're just really up-front." No guy I'd hung out with had handed compliments to me like flowers. *You look nice* or *you smell so good* was as blush-inducing as it got.

Connor smirked. "Up-front has yet to fail me."

His Jeep suddenly felt way too small.

"How many times have you seen *The Holiday*?" I almost asked, especially because "meet-cute" had struck a chord earlier. "*The Holiday* should be required viewing for all men," Erica had once written in an Ask Me Anything Instagram story. "My husband and I watch it every Christmas, and he agrees that no line is more enlightening than Kate Winslet's 'I'm looking for corny!'"

An unfamiliar ringtone popped whatever bubble we were in; I unlatched the glove compartment and pulled out Connor's phone. Liam, its screen read.

"Hey," he said to his brother. I watched him cradle the phone with his chin while he dug his AirPods out of the Jeep's cupholder. "What's up?"

"Okay, guess—" I heard Liam say breathlessly. "Guess what—" It sounded like he was laughing. "*Guess what* Miranda did this morning!"

"You call your mom by her first name?" I asked later, as we inched back into Edgartown. Connor had spent the drive on the phone, animated as ever. I didn't mind, contemplating whether or not I should put some space between us.

"Oh, yeah." He nodded. "She's 'Mom' to her face, but Liam and I pretty much always refer to her as 'Miranda' with each other." One side of his mouth tipped up in a smile. "She thinks it's hilarious."

"Huh," I said. "I can't imagine Erica ever being cool with the twins doing that."

And I couldn't say one way or the other how my own mother would've felt. I'd lost her so fast, and she'd been gone so long. Sometimes I felt like I could barely remember her, but I would never forget hugging her goodbye when I was seven; she'd dropped me off at Annie and Pops's town house to spend the night with them while she celebrated her best friend's birthday in New York. She never came to pick me up. An aneurysm, I'd learned.

A lump formed in my throat.

Connor coughed. "We're really close."

"Aww," I cooed, needing to joke my way out of this mood. "Are you a mama's boy?"

"Yes." He adjusted his hands on the steering wheel. "I absolutely am, and she loves it."

"Oh, I'm sure..." I rolled my eyes, stomach rumbling before I could tease him more.

"Hungry?" he asked lightly.

I nodded. "*Starving*."

He nodded back. "I know a place."

~

While Teddy and Finn had gone into the yacht club together, they emerged separately. Teddy came storming out to show Connor his wounded elbow. "They didn't even clean it!" he exclaimed after giving us the full scoop on the scrape (tripping out of his sailboat). "I just got this Band-Aid, which isn't the right size..."

"Okay." Connor nodded easily, which I noticed slowed Teddy's shallow breathing. "My first aid kit has antiseptic wipes."

"And a variety of Band-Aids?"

"And a variety of Band-Aids."

Teddy smiled, and when his older brother joined us, he said, "Finn sailed *really* well today."

"Really?" Connor asked. "How well?"

Finn shrugged but couldn't hide a little smirk. "Claire Dupré told me she's now reexamining her wants and needs."

Where is Claire Dupré getting this mature language? I wondered.

Connor grinned and offered Finn a fist bump. "This definitely calls for fudge!"

The brothers cheered, and after stopping by the Jeep to clean and rebandage Teddy's scrape, we walked through town toward Murdick's Fudge. Earlier Connor and I'd gotten lunch at Behind the Bookstore, a cute open-air café tucked behind Edgartown Books. "Pace yourself," he'd said when I'd made my intentions to devour my Italian toast clear. "Fudge should be highest on your list of priorities..."

A bell chimed overhead when Finn pulled open Murdick's screen door, and an aroma of sweetness immediately wrapped around me. Pure chocolate, vanilla, and nuttiness all at once. I found myself transfixed by the marble tables in the front window; my mouth watered as I watched a fudge-maker pour batter into a mold on the thick stone slab. "Olivia!" Teddy called, and I turned to see cases full of different flavors of fudge. He frantically waved me over. "What do you want?"

Everything, I thought.

"You're the expert," I told him, wishing Maisie and Bryce were here. "What do you recommend?"

Connor held our place in line while the boys and I assessed our options. "Good afternoon, ma'am," Teddy said when it was our turn to order. He rose up on his tiptoes in an effort to make eye contact with the bemused cashier. "We are going to take six slices..."

I looked around the shop while he listed our flavors—double chocolate, sea salt caramel, vanilla, rocky road, chocolate peanut butter, and something called *penuche*—and the gift box display caught my eye. The biggest one not only had the Murdick's Fudge whale logo but also had featured an illustration on the lid: a warm red-orange sunset behind a lighthouse. This rendering's window placement looked familiar. "Is this a real lighthouse?" I asked Finn, pointing to the box. "Or *inspired* by a real lighthouse?"

"Of course it's real," he said. "It's the Edgartown Harbor Light."

My heartrate skipped. *Yes!* The lighthouse in Annie's painting was either the Edgartown Harbor Light or the East Chop Lighthouse. And right now we were *in* Edgartown, which meant we could probably walk to the Edgartown Harbor Light. Right?

"And we'll also have a slice of maple walnut," Teddy concluded, ever the professional. "But in a separate box, please."

That's sweet, I thought. *He's looking out for Connor.*

His tree nut allergy was only the beginning. "Oh, there's an entire list," Connor had told me at lunch. "Tree nuts, cats, ice when it directly touches my skin—"

"No way!" I'd laughed. "*Ice*? Who's allergic to ice?"

"Dust mites, soy, and shellfish."

"Yikes," I said. "Don't New England and shellfish go hand in hand?"

"Yes, but I can be around it with zero issues," he said. "You could be devouring a lobster roll right now and I'd be fine..."

Connor paid for our fudge haul with an American Express card; my guess was it belonged to Teddy and Finn's parents.

"This is for the entire family," Connor said firmly, holding up our Murdick's bag before his expression curled into a mischievous smile. "But where are we sneaking the first few bites?"

"Olivia wants to see the lighthouse," Finn replied as I felt a swirl of excitement. "It's right up the street."

Connor nodded. "Lead the way."

With Finn on point, we pushed out the door and continued up North Water Street, passing Vineyard Vines, a couple restaurants, and a collection of art galleries before the street shifted from commercial to residential. It was lined with white picket fences, monstrous blue hydrangea bushes, and cedar-shingled and white clapboard homes. I blinked a couple times; it really felt like I had been transported to a Hollywood soundstage, one outfitted for "quintessential coastal New England town."

Annie must've loved it here, I thought with a pang. Edgartown looked like all her guilty pleasure Hallmark Channel holiday movies. Only instead of Christmas lights and a dusting of snow, the homes were decorated with American flags and buntings for the Fourth of July.

"What's that?" I asked when we passed a lane entirely backed up with cars.

"The Chappy Ferry," Teddy told me.

"It's a two-car ferry that goes to and from Chappy," Connor explained. "Chappaquiddick is a small island about five hundred feet across the harbor. The only way to access it is by ferry, boat, or kayak."

"Claire told me her dad once swam over," Finn added as I

thought of my list. Dike Bridge was somewhere on that little island.

"How do you know all of this?" I asked. Forget about a few weeks; Connor spoke like he'd spent years here.

"I've been exploring while these two esteemed gentlemen sail." He gestured at the boys. "They send me to all the hot spots."

"Very cool." I nodded, realizing that if I asked Connor to follow Annie's trail with me, he would. The idea might've even stirred some excitement in my stomach, as long as I could keep whatever he thought was between us at bay.

"There it is!" Teddy shouted when we reached the top of the street. He ran ahead and pointed to the right, but the massive Victorian hotel on the left caught my eye first. THE HARBOR VIEW, its sign read, but before I could marvel at the hotel's beautiful wraparound porch, I felt hands lightly land on my shoulders.

"Don't fight me when I try to spin you around," Connor said, the warmth of his skin soaking through my coverup's thin fabric. "Okay?"

"Okay." I closed my eyes, and one, two, three hard heartbeats later, he guided me 180 degrees. "What do you think?" Finn called, which was my cue to blink. "Does it live up to the hype?"

Yes, I thought. *Yes, it does.*

This was it. This was Annie's lighthouse.

It was stunning and stood steadfast on the coastline, white with a dark wrought-iron railing that circled around the glass lantern room. I suspected the lighthouse had been restored over the years, but Annie's half-finished watercolor had still captured its essence.

"Do you want to see it up close?" Connor asked, nodding his chin at the wooden causeway. It led to a grassy slice of land with a network of sandy trails running across it. Beyond the lighthouse was the beach, dotted with families and colorful beach towels. "Or maybe even go inside? We can triumph over our acrophobia again."

"Okay," I said, my voice breathy. "Sure."

"To the lighthouse!" he shouted to Teddy and Finn, and as we crossed the causeway together, I watched him subtly snap some photos of them.

"For their parents?" I guessed.

"Oh, yeah," he said. "Their family uses a Vineyard shot for their holiday card every year, and since Ashley isn't here…"

A beat passed.

"Is everything okay?" I asked, trying not to pry. "Did something happen?"

"Everything's fine." Connor stayed tight-lipped. "There's just some stuff going on with her husband's side of the family. They're helping with that."

"Got it." I looked toward the horizon. The lighthouse shone in the sun, and I suddenly felt *determined* to see its view. Annie had been here; I wanted to see everything she'd seen.

"You seem especially fired up about this," Connor noted once we'd paid our five-dollar entrance fee and were spinning up the spiral staircase. "Any particular reason why?"

"My grandmother came here," I said with sweat trailing down my spine, the humidity almost fooling me that I was out of shape. "I don't know exactly when or why, but she visited the island."

"You haven't asked her?" Connor responded at the same time Teddy loudly sighed and said, "Do you think the fudge has melted?"

"It'll be fine, Ted," Connor said. "We're almost at the top."

The top.

My knees weakened, but I pushed onward and upward, and when we stepped out onto the balcony and I saw Edgartown's idyllic harbor and the Cape Cod coast in the distance, I was too awestruck to worry about how high off the ground I was. This was even more breathtaking than the bridge.

Out of the corner of my eye, I caught Connor snapping a picture.

Stay cool, I told myself, and for the next couple minutes, all was lovely and quiet.

"Fudge?" Teddy eventually suggested.

"Fudge," Finn concurred.

Connor dutifully broke out the provided plastic knife. "So," he ventured upon slicing me a piece of double chocolate fudge. "Did your grandmother go anywhere else?"

"Yes," I told him, breaking into a smile. I couldn't help it, not when it came to Annie. "Would you like to see?"

TWELVE

I took a photo of the lighthouse—to pair with the watercolor—and on our way out of Edgartown, Connor pulled over near the Greek Revival masterpiece that was the Old Whaling Church. Originally built for Methodist whaling captains way back when, it now hosted various events. A few celebrities had even gotten married there. I didn't have Annie's Polaroid with me, but I knew it showed her posing near one of the columns with a straw bag and a small bouquet of daisies. A sign that her love for freshly cut flowers had bloomed ages ago.

I'd kept Annie's diagnosis to myself, but I did show Connor the list and tell him about my plan to make her a new Shutterfly book, this one full of both her Vineyard memorabilia and photos of me in the same places two generations later. He'd grinned, a smile that I hated to admit rivaled today's sunshine. "Oh, she's going to love that!"

I nodded, knowing she would…

Especially if she recognized and remembered her summer here.

Connor offered to take a picture of me, and I put my hand on my waist and smiled when he'd framed me in my iPhone's crosshairs. "Relax!" he called to me. "You don't need to be so stiff."

"I wasn't aware I *was* stiff," I said, but I rolled my shoulders back. He wordlessly took a couple shots, both horizontal and vertical, then stepped closer and even crouched down a little.

"What are you doing?" I asked.

"Covering every angle," he answered as a light breeze rippled through the warm air. "Liam taught me this one!"

I started giggling.

Smiling, Connor captured it.

"Thank you," I said after he handed back my phone. "Hopefully there are one or two good ones."

"Olivia, come on." Connor lifted his sunglasses, to give me a look that made my stomach drop. His eyes—his eyes were so hypnotically blue that I felt the urge to dive into them. "You know you're gorgeous," he said, then turned toward Teddy and Finn. "Right?"

"Right!" the boys echoed, both cracking up when I shrugged and casually flipped my hair to play off the moment. Hopefully no one caught the embarrassment warming my cheeks.

You know you're gorgeous.

How was I supposed to respond to that?

Even if I knew, I couldn't. I was tongue-tied.

Connor played Finn's favorite playlist on the drive home,

and once back, they raced inside to change for the beach. "Their turnaround time is usually ten minutes," Connor informed me. "Late-afternoon snack selection is a serious business."

I nodded knowingly. "The kitchen's closed!" Erica told Bryce multiple times a week, usually after dinner.

"I'd love to see your grandmother's photos," Connor added, making my heart spark, and together we retreated to Summer Camp. I spread out the Polaroids and watercolors on top of our dresser and watched Connor's eyes slide across them. "Wow..." He picked up the Aquinnah Cliffs painting. "Did she do this?"

"I don't know," I said. "I mean, I would *think* so—my great-grandfather was apparently a pretty good artist—but I've never seen her paint. She does draw a little, though."

Drew, I silently corrected. Annie *drew* a little, since she could no longer hold a pencil.

"You haven't asked her...?" Connor trailed off, his attention stolen by a Polaroid. The tractor photo, of course. Something in my chest twinged when he flipped it over to read Annie's elegant handwriting. "Where's 'summer camp?'"

"I don't have the slightest idea," I told him. "But something tells me it's not *our* summer camp."

He laughed and studied the photo again and then looked all too quickly back at me, this time with a glint in his eye. "You look just like her."

"I know," I told him. "You aren't the first person to call me gorgeous."

At that, Connor arched an eyebrow, but he didn't seem to have any words.

I thought, *Who's tongue-tied now, pipsqueak?*

~

It seemed like games were the theme of Wednesday, since Maisie and Bryce spearheaded a volleyball match with all the younger kids on the beach while Erica and my dad challenged Jay and Allison to a surprisingly less-than-competitive game of cornhole. (They sipped beers and High Noons as they tossed beanbags.) I read my book, ate a peanut-butter-and-fluff sandwich, and then collected shells with Sage and Meredith. "I wonder what Teddy and Finn are up to this afternoon," Sage mused once we were back on her beach blanket, sorting through our haul. Meredith had run off at the sight of her aunt with a water gun. "They're usually asking to bury Nick alive by now..."

I felt myself flush, never slow on subtext. Peggy thankfully appeared before Connor's name could officially come up. Her brown eyes were bright under her wide-brimmed hat. "I hope you girls don't have any plans tonight," she said, and after Sage and I shook our heads, she instructed us to be in the upstairs den after dinner.

"Secretive as always," Sage whispered to me, reading my mind. She winked. "We never know the game ahead of time..."

The upstairs den, I discovered post–shish kebabs, was up a

narrow staircase that opened up into a panoramic room. *Wow*, I thought, even though I'd seen the rounded third story from the outside. *How many surprises does this house hold?*

Large glass windows showed off tonight's waterfront slow sunset, gold light reflecting off Oyster Pond, and wood-paneled walls made the den feel especially cozy. A chunky plaid sectional looked like it could fit a dozen people, and while it was July, I didn't mind the fire burning in the grate. The temperature had dropped with the sun. "Everyone over here, please!" Peggy waved us over to the couch then clucked at her son when he sniffed around the mysterious boxes on the coffee table. "Jay, you know better…"

"Granddad, what's up with the hat?" Maisie asked, since Topper wasn't donning his beach Stetson. Instead, he wore a blue-white-and-silver embroidered fez, similar to the one Daniel Craig wore while soaking in the bathtub in *Glass Onion*.

"It's an old favorite," he told my sister. "I bought it years ago in San Francisco. Cable Car Clothiers."

"I think it's fantastic." Erica snuck up behind him so she could playfully flick the hat's silver tassel. "Do they make a child version?"

Bryce would look adorable… I silently agreed.

Topper chuckled as his tassel twirled. "Perhaps you can check their Instagram."

"Perhaps I will," Erica lightly replied before Jay spoke. "Why are you wearing it tonight, Dad?"

Most of us looked at Peggy. Try as the Carmichaels might, no one had figured out tonight's specifics. Sage hadn't been exaggerating; Carmichael family game nights involved much intrigue and drama.

"Mom," Beth said. "Tell us."

"What a thoughtful way of saying *hurry up*," I just barely heard Erica mumble, the dry inflection sounding unlike her. I knew her sister got under her skin, but she wasn't normally this sarcastic.

Had something happened earlier?

Smiling, Peggy pulled a blue Bugs Bunny–style sleeping cap from one of the boxes. "If everyone could please draw a marble..." She offered the cap first to impatient Beth. "Tonight's game will involve plenty of teamwork. As your judge, I will explain more once teams are chosen."

Beth pulled a blue marble, her husband yellow, and Sage red. Nick cheered when he drew yellow too. The more people pulled marbles, the more everyone seemed almost *giddy* with excitement. I caught Connor's eye; he shrugged and smiled amusedly, as if to say, *This might be bonkers, but I'm here for it!*

It felt somewhat strange to be participating. A game of Monopoly would've been one thing, but this—an unknown game—was another. Did my dad also feel like an outsider?

It didn't look like it. He and Charlie executed a perfect high five, both members of Team Blue. I wished I could talk to Annie; I wished she could give me advice. She had been able to light up any social situation, whether that was being the consummate hostess, making others feel welcome, or charming people at a party where she knew few.

If you want to be a part of things, I distantly heard her say. *Then* be *a part of things!*

Embrace this.

Teddy waved around his green marble as soon as he pulled it out of the hat, and then it was my turn. I also picked green. "Yes, I've got Olivia!" Teddy cheered, which made me smile. "Who's jealous?"

"No one!" Maisie and Bryce called, as if it were a rehearsed joke. My sister giggled when I rolled my eyes.

I felt a rush of love for her.

Teddy and I ended up with Allison and an extra person on our team…Erica. My enthusiasm deflated a bit, but at least she was fired up from whatever had gone down with Beth.

"Wonderful!" Peggy clapped her hands when Bugs Bunny's nightcap was finally empty. "Now it's time to go over the game…"

"Oh my god," Beth gasped when her parents brought out what looked like an old-fashioned men's nightshirt. "I know what this is!"

"What, Gram?" Finn asked, everyone now officially on the edge of their seat.

Too overwhelmed, Beth shook her head. "We did this as little kids," she said, then looked at Jay. "Remember?"

I noticed she wasn't tugging Erica down Memory Lane.

Jay jokingly stroked his chin. "Vaguely..."

"It was before I was born," Erica told him. "But maybe *balloons* will ring a bell?"

As if on cue, Peggy held up a package of colorful balloons.

What the hell? I thought as Jay's eyes widened in an epiphany and Topper held up a nightshirt that looked straight out of Ebenezer Scrooge's wardrobe. Had they gotten them at that kooky vintage store Sage had mentioned? That old fishing shack? I liked thrifting with Gwen and Quincy but preferred the organized chaos of Poshmark.

"Where did you get these?" Beth asked her parents. "They're too clean to be the ones we used when we were kids."

"Hopefully not from the Mermaid's Trove," Charlie said. "That place looks like it should be condemned..." He side-eyed Sage.

"Stop!" She playfully slapped his arm. "They have some hidden gems!"

But do they? I almost asked.

Peggy laughed. "Of course not, sillies," she said. "They're from Amazon."

Now that I knew the nightshirts wouldn't be moldy or visibly stained with sweat, my interest returned. The room's volume soon escalated, and it didn't help that Teddy and Bryce stole two of the nightshirts and started running around with them on their heads.

Finn and Maisie looked unimpressed while Connor was

failing miserably at swallowing his laughter. Warmth flooded my chest as I had a flash of what he looked like at ten years old.

A buzz cut and freckles, I remembered.

Nick whistled, the sharp sound a shock to my eardrum. Even Swede's head snapped up from resting on my knee. "Everyone settle down!" he called. "Let Nana explain the rules!"

"Yes, I'd love a refresher course." Beth eyed her brother. "Some of us need to understand that you can't sabotage another team's balloons..."

Jay chuckled. "Bethany, I will not apologize for being a competitive child."

The room heeded Nick's words, and Peggy explained that the game would involve one player from each team wearing an enormous nightshirt over their clothes. Each team also would be given a bag of balloons and an air pump.

"Using your team's pump and good old-fashioned lung power, you have ten minutes to blow up as many balloons as you can and stuff them into your team's nightshirt," Topper instructed. "The team with the most balloons in their nightshirt takes the cake."

"You all have five minutes to strategize!" Peggy concluded, and just like that, she took a stopwatch out of her pocket and pressed start. Every team laughed and made a mad dash to different corners of the room.

"I want to wear the nightshirt!" Teddy exclaimed, waving it over his head.

Erica and Allison exchanged a look before my stepmother

jumped into mom mode. "Teddy, we need your superfast arms to help stuff the balloons into the nightshirt." She turned to me. "Olivia, how about you wear the shirt while Allison and I blow up the balloons?"

"Dibs on the pump," Allison said. "My lungs don't compare to yours, Erica."

Erica smiled. She'd lifeguarded in high school and still swam regularly. "What do you think, Teddy?" I asked, trying to channel my inner Connor. He was so natural with kids. "You want to stuff me like a turkey?"

Grinning, he surrendered the nightshirt, and I pulled it on over my clothes. Meanwhile, Sage wore her team's nightshirt with Connor and Bryce doing breathing exercises to ready their lungs. *Of course*, I thought at the sound of Connor offering pointers on how to most effectively expand lung capacities. He'd mentioned his mom taught yoga on the weekends.

Our five-minute strategy session felt more like thirty seconds, but somehow, everyone seemed pseudo-organized by the time Peggy called time. "Ready..." she teased as Topper raised a plastic whistle to his lips. My heart started to pound. "Set..."

Go!

Swede barked and Beth's little Posey yipped when the whistle blew, the room exploding with excitement and frantic energy. I identified as the latter. My nightshirt's hem stopped mid-calf, so I worried the balloons would fall out the bottom. "We've got to stuff the balloons in really tightly," Erica said, reading my mind. "It'll expand the shirt Santa Claus–style and prevent the balloons from slipping out and getting away."

She and Allison took turns using the hand pump and blowing up the balloons while Teddy stuffed them under my nightshirt. I caught the two moms motioning to each other, agreeing that they too would shove balloons in, but subtly so they didn't hurt Teddy's feelings. It reminded me of when I was a little girl; we'd been on vacation and I'd told my mom I could eat an entire banana split sundae myself. She told me to go for it and congratulated me after I all but licked the bowl clean. It was years later that I found out she'd been sneaking bites while my dad distracted me. Brooke Lupo hadn't even liked bananas.

Heart twinging, I glanced over at the other teams and couldn't help but raise an eyebrow at their strategies. How had Maisie ended up in the nightshirt? It was so big on her; she looked like a ghostly bride with her long train. All she was missing was a veil. My dad, Charlie, and Beth—my sister's teammates—were going for optimal balloon production, having formed a full-on assembly line.

I smiled, shook my head, and refocused on my own team. Beads of sweat had formed on Allison's forehead, and Erica's hair was falling out of her ponytail. My stomach had also grown *enormous*, blocking my view of Teddy.

Are we winning? I wondered, pulse racing at the possibility.

Because okay, this was fun.

"Five more minutes to fill your nightshirts!" Peggy said, then held up something that looked a lot like a sewing needle.

"What is she going to do with that?" I asked at the same time Jay shouted, "Mom, you're *evil*!"

Beth knowingly laughed, but neither she nor her brother enlightened us. "Ouch!" I squeaked when someone poked me hard in my stomach. "Watch where you put your hands, Theodore…"

"I'm sorry!" Teddy shouted. "And it's Edward!"

Apologizing, I bent my knees to stop several balloons from escaping my nightshirt.

"Good idea, Olivia…" Erica was almost breathless from the pump.

"Erica, let's switch after five more," Allison said. Slowly I was starting to resemble Father Christmas getting ready for bed.

My sister wasn't far behind; she had started to blow up à la Violet Beauregarde from *Charlie and the Chocolate Factory*. Beth urged them on like a field general while stuffing in balloons with both hands. "I—can't—breathe!" Maisie squealed.

Pop!

Pop, pop, pop!

I stiffened at the balloons bursting against my skin. "Teddy—" I started, but then felt someone's arm snake up my back.

"It's not me!" he cried.

"Don't worry," Erica said. "I'm squeezing in more balloons."

At the cost of others! I thought, again feeling the sharp snap of plastic.

"Watch your fingernails," I gritted out. "They're popping balloons faster than you're adding them."

Erica didn't respond; instead, one of her nails scratched my back.

"One minute left!" Topper warned as I winced.

"Go, go, go!" Beth yelled from across the room, eliciting an eye roll but also a couple giggles. What *was* this? What was this level of sheer craziness? And why was I enjoying it so much? Despite Erica's perfectly manicured fingers, laughter bubbled up in my lungs.

The whistle blew. "Drop your balloons!" Peggy shouted. "I want to see all hands in the air! *Top Chef* hands now!"

"Nice reference, Nana," Charlie weakly said, one of the many raggedly breathing, coughing, and exhausted balloon-blowers. Almost everyone fell to the floor, as if just barely surviving Erica's favorite kickboxing class. (Per her vlog, it seemed like a nightmare.)

"Now comes the fun part." Peggy beamed with steely eyes.

"Mom, don't scare the children!" Erica choked out.

She waved a dismissive hand, already approaching my corner. "Team Green, I will start with you." She raised her sewing needle. "One pop equals one balloon." She smiled at me mischievously. "Olivia, this will be quick and painless…as long as you stay still."

My stomach's churning was so choppy that I almost asked to go to the bathroom.

To, you know, vomit.

But Peggy was too quick. With expert precision, she stabbed her needle through my thin nightshirt. Maisie laughed when I flinched at the first pop.

Erica surreptitiously filmed the scene. I glanced over my shoulder at Beth, hoping she wouldn't notice her sister. *We need evidence*, I thought. *Otherwise, Quincy and Gwen will never believe me when I tell them…*

"Sixteen balloons for Team Green!" Peggy proclaimed.

Teddy hit me with high fives.

Team Yellow was up next. Nick was still standing, but he massaged his biceps while Finn had gone green. Beth's husband still looked thin in his bloated nightshirt. Their tally was ten balloons.

"Thirteen balloons!" Peggy told the red team, and I laughed when Sage and Connor hoisted Bryce in the air. They were in second place.

Last but not least, we turned to Team Blue. Maisie looked stone-cold serious as Peggy went to work. All smiling smugly, Charlie, Beth, and my dad counted each pop aloud. "*Boooo*!" people chorused once even Maisie relaxed enough to join in: "Fourteen, fifteen, sixteen, seventeen, *eighteen*!"

"And we have our winners!" Peggy grinned. "Team Blue has won an all-expenses-paid trip to Backdoor Donuts at midnight tonight!" She turned to Nick while I did a double take at the mention of *midnight*. What bakery was open that late? "You don't mind driving, do you, sweetie?"

"Not at all, Nana," Nick said, mumbling, "As long as I get an apple fritter."

Topper had filmed tonight's shenanigans and broadcasted it once us losers had cooled off later. It turned out Erica accidentally popping balloons and scratching my back hadn't been *that* bad, but my expression had been caught on camera. "You look like you want to *murder* her," Bryce oh so sensitively commented, garnering more than a few laughs.

But it kind of made me feel like a bitch...and a little bad for Erica. If I'd known I'd given her a death glare, I would've apologized in the moment.

Tail between my legs, I went looking for her later, finding her in one of the house's small studies with her laptop. "Scrolling through summers past?" I guessed, spotting the Shutterfly icon on her MacBook screen.

Erica visibly jumped at the sound of my voice. "Oh, it's you," she said, exhaling. "I thought you were my mother." She muttered. "Or Beth."

I gave her a look. "I sound like them?"

"Not at all." She shook her head. "I'm a little paranoid because

I'm working..." She trailed off, but I got the gist. Erica set her own hours and answered to no one, so why was she working when she could be spending time with her family? She cleared her throat and gestured at her computer. "I want to tweak the Hill House campaign before I post tomorrow."

"Oh, nice," I said. Hill House had sent Erica and Maisie matching nap dresses, and they'd done a "Like Mother, Like Daughter" themed photo shoot in one of Haddonfield's gardens. Afterward, Maisie had begged me to take her to Starbucks... where she'd accidentally spilled her Frappuccino all over her dress. Erica had been less than pleased, but she *had* admitted it'd been *a little* funny. "I love those photos."

"They turned out beautifully." Erica raised an eyebrow slightly. "Do you need something?"

"No, I'm fine." I took a deep internal sigh. "I just wanted to apologize for being a bit of a bitch earlier."

"Don't worry about it," she said. "It happened in the heat of the moment; we were really into it..." She trailed off to look at her manicure. Before leaving for the Vineyard, Maisie had talked her into Essie's "clambake" red for the Fourth of July. "And my nails *might* be a little too long."

She half-smiled before returning to her laptop, which I knew was my cue to leave; at home, she always needed a silent office. "What's with the scrapbook?" I asked though, pointing to her right. A light green album sat on the desk, seemingly untouched.

"Oh, Beth thought it would be nice for us to give our parents an anniversary gift. We're each responsible for several pages before the grandchildren fill in the rest." She shrugged. "I have to get some work done first, though. Which has been hard with everyone watching me."

I shifted from one foot to the other. It was so strange that Erica felt like she had to hide her work from her family, strange that the Carmichaels were so judgmental about her job. Annie had loved hearing about Erica's projects and even brainstormed ideas with her. Nothing rivaled their seasonal tablescapes, a blend of Pottery Barn or Williams Sonoma pieces with fine china from Annie's personal collection. "This is your best yet, honey," I remembered Annie remarking several Februarys ago. For Erica's Galentine's Day dinner, place cards were cute retro Valentines and each wineglass had a pink or red ribbon tied around its stem. Blush-colored candles also added to the rosy mood. "Truly, I marvel at your taste."

A lump in my throat, I swallowed and said good night before going to find my dad and the twins. Nick and Sage were leading a stargazing session on the deck. "Sweet dreams, Olivia!" they chorused when I said I was turning in for the night. It wasn't that I didn't want to hang out with people, but I was feeling drained from the day. It had been surprisingly fun, but *long*.

Connor's voice hit me the second I closed myself in our nook. "I'll see Austin and Katie tomorrow," I could hear him from inside our room, talking or FaceTiming with someone. "Meredith's family is hosting a party for the Fourth. I'm bringing Finn and Teddy for dinner and the fireworks."

"*Hosting* a party?" a bemused voice answered as I sighed, just wanting to read. My book was on my bunk. "Or *throwing* a party? Because I've always gotten the impression that Meredith's family *knows* how to party..."

"I'll be sure to update you," Connor chuckled, and when he asked how someone named Marco was, I headed for the bathroom.

This is ridiculous, I thought once I'd gathered up my shampoo, conditioner, body wash, loofah, and face wash. Plus, my towel. *You're going to go parading though the house with all this? Announce to everyone that you're taking a shower?*

Why was Erica and my dad's bathroom so far?

Which made me debate whether or not to even take a shower, but then I remembered Connor's and my *outdoor* shower; it was only a leap away on the porch.

One deep breath later, I pushed out onto the porch. Its warm light was on, and I could faintly hear Oyster Pond lapping up against the shore. The breeze blew through my clothes as I took a couple steps down to the shower and slipped inside to find a flagstone floor. I squinted in the porch light's dim glow to see that the shower was big. A few hooks on the wall signified a changing area, and farther along the wall was the showerhead. Pipes ran down the side of the cedar-shingled house. One of them was red, and I clocked the *H* faucet.

Connor's shower stuff lined the ledge—classic Old Spice body wash, but not some generic guy shampoo. ORIBE, the fancy black bottle read. He *also* had a loofah.

Interesting.

I made room for my things then refocused on the shower. "Here we go…" I muttered before turning the hot tap and quickly dodging the water's spray.

Still clothed, I hung my towel on a hook and undressed. Goose bumps shivered on my skin, able to feel the hot water's steam. It encouraged me to sneak toward the shower, and after one more burst of breeze, I surrendered.

It took me approximately five seconds to understand why Connor considered an outdoor shower close to heaven. The water was indeed hot and absolutely *gushed* from the shower-head. I hadn't requested a back massage, but I was getting one anyway.

Oh my god, I thought, fighting the urge to moan. *I love this…*

As the cherry on top, this shower had a window. I gazed out at Oyster Pond while rubbing lavender shampoo though my hair. The bright moon made the dark water shine, and I could see all the stars sprinkled across the sky.

It was a beautiful night.

I didn't usually take long showers, but my skin was a deep pink when I pulled on my pajamas an extravagant thirty minutes later. Connor had disappeared somewhere.

As relaxing as the porch was, I couldn't resist climbing my ladder and getting cozy in bed, switching on my reading lamp and snuggling into my pillows. My friends had sent a couple texts, so before diving into my book, I replied with a photo of me outside the Old Whaling Church. Goddess divine! Quincy wrote while Gwen hearted the picture. Who took this???

"Is that the one you bought yesterday?" Connor caught me off guard a while later, during a spicy scene. "From Edgartown Books?"

"Yes." I reluctantly placed my bookmark in between pages 199 and 200, then looked up to see him leaning against the doorframe in a dark green sweatshirt. Swede was at his side. "Where have you been?"

He raised a suggestive eyebrow. "Where have I *been*?"

I felt a couple pinpricks at the back of my neck. *Been* had come out with a dramatic emphasis, maybe even an unintentionally sexy undertone. "No, that's not what I meant," I backtracked. "What have you been up to?"

"Bedtime," he replied, scratching Swede behind the ears. "Did you know your brother does a spot-on Irish accent?"

"Uh," I said. "He does a few funny impressions..."

Connor shook his head. "Bedtime is a production," he said. "I mean, Finn is pretty easy. He and Teddy are superheroes about staying off the screens during the day, so I give him a half hour on the iPad before bed. He's really into nature documentaries." He paused. "But Teddy is old fashioned; he picked out a ton of books at the library last week, and we're now making our way through them."

I sighed. "Let me guess, you have a talent for voices."

"I do." Connor beamed. "And tonight I was entertaining

enough that Finn and your siblings joined us." He rubbed Swede's belly. "The story was also pretty compelling."

"Oh, that's sweet," I said genuinely, imagining all four kids and Connor, plus Swede, crammed together on Teddy's bunk. "How did my brother wind up speaking in an Irish accent?"

"We took turns reading. I cast them in different roles; Bryce played the Irishman. They wanted me to read longer, so I told them it was to protect my vocal cords." He slyly dropped his voice. "It also gets them to practice their reading. They don't even realize it."

I raised an eyebrow, impressed. Bryce followed the Lupos' twenty-minutes-a-day reading ritual, but Maisie *hated* to read. "That's really clever," I said at the same time I wondered, *Why haven't I ever thought of that?*

Probably because I was too wrapped up in my own reading material.

"Thank you," he said, then motioned to the porch. "I'm going to grab a quick shower."

"Oh." I felt myself flush. Fingers crossed I hadn't used all the hot water.

Connor cocked his head, as if waiting for me to say more.

"I took an outdoor shower earlier," I admitted, and before he could tease me, added, "I want my dad to build one on our back deck. Even if our water lines need to be reconfigured..."

He laughed, the corners of his eyes crinkling.

It made me smile. "I also didn't expect you to use such high-end shampoo."

"Really?" Connor smirked. "You thought I was a Head and Shoulders guy?"

"Or Dove," I said. "What's Oribe?"

"The shampoo my salon uses."

A snicker snuck out.

"What?"

"Nothing," I said. "Nothing, except... You go to a *salon* to get your hair cut?"

"Yes, I do," Connor said confidently, but I caught some redness creep across his cheeks. "I like the experience better than Great Clips or the barbershop."

I started laughing.

"The *salon* treats me like the greatest person to ever exist," he continued. "Jill cares about my life and tells me about hers, and they have snacks and a fridge full of delicious drinks. Plus, a killer playlist. They *love* me there."

"I bet they do," I said and rolled my eyes.

Even though I secretly thought it was cute and could picture it without even blinking. Connor was probably the mayor of his salon.

"Where do *you* go get your hair cut?" Connor asked cheekily. "Somewhere that serves champagne?"

"How did you guess?" I deadpanned, then shook my head. "My grandmother cut my hair when I was little. We played beauty salon in her bathroom."

"This is Annie, right?"

I nodded. "I'm not that close to my other grandmother."

Patricia—Grandma—was nice, and I enjoyed spending Easter with her and the rest of my mom's side of the family, but she lived across the country in San Francisco.

She also wasn't Annie.

"She sounds really special," Connor said, then took a breath as if trying to muster the courage to say something else, but instead, he simply added, "One of a kind."

"Yes," I agreed, wondering what words he'd swallowed. "There's no one like Annie. I wouldn't be who I am without her." I considered. "I'd probably have a couple tattoos."

Annie hated tattoos.

"Oh, yeah?" Connor arched an eyebrow. "Where?"

"That's for me to know and for you to speculate."

Then I winked.

Connor laughed, but it sounded a bit uneasy, and he took a clumsy step backward into the hall. "Shower." He motioned around vaguely. "I'm going to take a shower, then I'll be back."

"Okay," I said casually, settling back in with my book. "Looking forward to it."

Excellent work, I berated myself after Connor practically ran for the porch. *Truly, an outstanding performance!*

Over the past day, I thought I'd done an okay job of keeping things light with Connor—keeping things *friendly* instead of *flirty*—but here I was, flirting with him again. Why did he have to make it so easy?

Why did he have to make it so fun?

~

For the third night in a row, Swede leaped into bed with Connor while I had the top bunk to myself. "He *will* forgive you for pushing him off," I told Connor, who'd just made an *oof* noise. "I promise."

"I'm sorry, but I don't totally believe you," he replied. "Arthur—Mads's dog—is always furious whenever I kick him from the couch."

"Mads?" I prompted, even though I knew.

"Madeline," he answered. "My best friend."

"Mmm."

Connor snorted. "She has an *mmm* too."

"What does hers mean?"

"Oh, a variety of things." Pause. "But she's very protective of me."

"Of course she is," I said.

"What does that mean?" Connor asked, a slight edge in his voice.

Note to self, I thought. *Do not make fun of Mads.*

"I don't know," I admitted, but I wondered if there had ever been something more between them. Billy Crystal's iconic line echoed in my head: *Men and women can't be friends.*

Connor cleared his throat. "Mads and I did try to date once," he told me. "I can hear you wondering."

In response, I deployed my *mmm*.

"We don't like each other that way."

"Mmm."

"She's obsessed with her boyfriend."

"Mmm."

He was indignant. "Olivia!"

I broke down laughing, so hard that tears stung my eyes. "I'm sorry," I said after he groaned, getting myself together. "I believe you; I'm just teasing."

Connor was quiet, and then, "Mmm."

"Touché," I quipped before asking more about Mads. She and Connor had been friends since childhood; she played field hockey, loved her never-ending Spotify playlists, and was both the kindest and most judgmental person Connor knew.

"I love her," he said. "Just not like that."

"I believe you," I said back, for real this time. Mads sounded like the best of all best friends; someone who Connor was wholeheartedly open with and who was open with him.

We said good night, but my heart twisted when I shifted onto my side and heard Connor's slow breathing beneath me. Was he already asleep?

"I've been in your car before," I heard myself say softly.

Connor heard me too. "What?"

"I've been in your car before," I repeated, a little louder.

"Well, yeah..." he said. "We went to Edgartown."

"No, I'm not talking about that," I said, then closed my eyes and asked, "Who do you visit at Elkins Village?"

Crickets. The bottom bunk was very quiet for a few moments. "My grandfather," Connor eventually said. "He moved into independent living this spring. We have dinner with him every other Saturday, and I also bring him his favorite sushi on Wednesdays."

A lump formed in my throat. "That's really nice," I whispered, wishing Annie still lived in the independent wing.

"Thanks," he replied. "He's happy there. He's dating a woman a few doors down from him. Fliss something."

"Fliss Williams," I surmised, swallowing hard. "Don't you just love her name?" I remembered Annie saying about the woman she'd met in chair aerobics. "Fliss is short for *Felicity*..."

"Yes, that's it." Connor's nod was in his voice. "Fliss Williams."

I waited for him to ask me how I knew that, but he didn't; instead, he circled back to how I'd ended up in his car. "It was an accident," I said. "We drive the same Jeep—"

"Seriously?"

"—and I always leave mine unlocked at Elkins."

"Well, of course," Connor said. "There's no place safer than Elkins Village."

"Until I climbed in your car," I quipped. "I didn't bother checking the license plate. It was raining and I was..." I trailed off, thinking of how I'd fled Finlay House after Annie begged me to help her escape into the night. Every inch of my body felt coated in guilt.

Swede, the only one sleeping, let out a loud snore. "How'd you realize it wasn't your Jeep?" Connor asked.

"I'm very attuned to details," I answered. "The driver's seat was set too far back, and your Jeep is higher than mine. I didn't have a lacrosse stick riding shotgun either."

"Wow." He laughed. "If only I'd seen you…"

That would've been some meet-cute! I thought, but the sudden heat in my chest burned the joke before I could make it.

Connor let silence hang in the air then shifted on his mattress. My pulse started pounding. *Who do* you *know at Elkins?* I imagined him asking, realizing he already knew when he asked what photo of Annie's I wanted to follow next.

I mentally scanned my list. Edgartown lighthouse? *Check.* Old Whaling Church? *Check.* "How does the Flying Horses sound for tomorrow?" I suggested.

"Like an adventure, because I haven't been yet. Finn keeps saying it's for little kids." He took a beat, then a breath. "Do you want to summon your inner child and go?"

"Only if you summon yours."

"Already done," he said brightly. "Everyone says I'm a child at heart."

THIRTEEN

We agreed to visit the Flying Horses, the world's oldest carousel, on Friday. Today was the Fourth of July, so Nick advised us not to go near the center of Oak Bluffs. It would be swarmed with people.

Tomorrow it was.

Instead, I spent the day on the beach and spoke to Annie before getting ready for the Foxes' party. She told me she was watching reruns of her favorite HGTV show, *Love It or List It*, and insisted that she and Pops had lived down the street from the house being showcased. It was in Durham, North Carolina.

My grandparents had only lived in New York and Pennsylvania, never North Carolina, but I listened as Annie told me about the elaborate treehouse the owners had built for their children.

It was identical to the treehouse Pops had built for my dad.

I liked hearing her paint the picture, even if it was out of context. It was still pretty.

Per Erica, her parents used to host Oyster Pond's

Independence Day festivities, but after Topper had lost a bet with Meredith's grandfather a handful of years ago, the Foxes had pocketed hosting rights. Assuming the dress code was patriotic, I zipped up a white linen shift dress. "You're missing a couple colors," Connor commented after I posted my mirror selfie to my Instagram. People had loved my beach look the other day.

I pointed to my lips, which were red.

"Okay, *a* color," he corrected, running a comb through his hair. "Where's the blue?"

"Where's the white?" I countered, assessing his outfit. Nantucket red shorts, a pair of Allbirds, and a navy blue polo that showed off his biceps.

That was hard to ignore.

"Right here." He pulled sunglasses out of his pocket. Not his usual Oakleys, but a pair of white Ray-Bans. "What do you think?"

I offered my honest opinion by wrinkling my nose.

"Really?" He proceeded to put them on. "Why not?"

"They're just..." I couldn't find the right word. "*A lot.*"

Connor chuckled. "I stole them from Liam."

"And I'm sure they look great on Liam," I said carefully. From the way Connor talked about his brother, and the recon I did of Liam McCallister's Instagram, it was clear he had style. "Maybe you should mail them home."

"Maybe." He shrugged. "Maybe not."

I rolled my eyes. "Are you driving or taking the boat?"

"Driving," Connor said, looking ridiculous. "You?"

"Boat," I told him. "I can't risk being associated with you and those glasses."

And with that, I put on my own sunglasses and rushed out of the room, holding in my laugh until I was out in the hall and Connor couldn't hear it.

The Carmichaels' Boston Whaler was so packed that Maisie sat on my lap, and I was slightly worried we were testing the weight limit. "What's the Foxes' house like?" I asked Luke and Charlie once a seventh person climbed in, hoping to distract myself.

"Which house?" Luke answered as he draped his arm around Charlie's neck. He'd returned from Boston late last night, his confidential case under control.

My eyebrows knitted together. "There's more than one house?"

"There's eight," Maisie spoke up. "Oliver Epstein-Fox told me on the beach." She paused. "He also asked me out today."

"*Eight*?"

"The property is called Paqua Farm," Luke added. "*The Farm* for short."

"The Farm," Maisie repeated. "Are there horses and cows and stuff?"

"It's not a working farm," Luke said. "Although Wit told me

they had sheep back in the day, and there still are a couple barns standing."

"Two." Charlie nodded, lowering his voice. "Legend has it that Meredith's grandfather and his brother burned the third one down in their twenties. Fireworks show gone wrong." He winked. "Their parents were so angry that they gave the Fourth of July to our family."

"Ooh and now they've got it back," Maisie said, intrigued.

"Smells like redemption!" I teased.

Charlie groaned. "Granddad *never* should've made that bet…"

We clung to each other once Nick powered up the speedboat, but instead of gunning it, he took things slow and steady across the pond. I felt Maisie's muscles relax.

"Did you agree to go out with Oliver?" I whispered in her ear.

"No," she whispered back. "But I told him I was flattered."

I let out a low whistle. *Way to shoot your shot, kid.*

"Are you going out with Connor?" Maisie asked.

"Excuse me?" I bristled.

"Teddy says he's in love with you."

Yikes.

"I wouldn't say *in love*," I mumbled.

"But you do think he likes you, right?"

I kept my lips zipped.

My sister elbowed me.

"Connor is just a friend, Maze," I said, heat flaming on the back of my neck—worried that Luke and Charlie could hear us. "He's not my type."

"Right..." Maisie rolled her eyes. "You like dorks."

With Erica policing the twins' language, *dork*, in Maisie-speak, translated to *douche*.

She wasn't right, but she also wasn't wrong. "Oh, he's a douche," was almost always my official reason for breaking off things with a guy, even if it wasn't totally true. I couldn't explain why, but I knew it needed to end when knots tangled themselves in the pit of my stomach.

"Hey," Charlie said, oblivious to our code. "No one is more lovable than a dork!"

"Were you a dork?" Maisie asked, not at all embarrassed.

Her cousin gave her a look. "Of course not."

"That would be my department," Luke said smoothly. "Though I prefer the term *nerd*."

Maisie giggled. "What's the dif—"

"Land ho!" Captain Nick called, and after disembarking our water taxi, our crew climbed a creaky driftwood staircase that deposited us at the party's edge.

"Wow," Maisie breathed. "This is awesome."

"You can say that again..." My heart skipping, I didn't know where to look first; everything was a sight to behold. There was a sprawling cedar-shingled ranch house overlooking Oyster Pond and the ocean and horizon beyond it. An upbeat band jammed on the house's low deck, and I marveled at the huge American flag spread across the roof. Maisie tugged me across the lawn, dotted with partygoers. Some were playing cornhole, others badminton, and there were picnic tables and circles of Adirondack chairs. I spotted Peggy, who'd driven over earlier, by the serpentine buffet. She had baked the Barefoot Contessa's classic American-flag cake for the party. Nearby, Erica had set up her tripod. *Only if you have everyone sign a release form*, I imagined Beth sniping.

"Mom!" Maisie waved.

After Bryce appeared out of nowhere and just as quickly ran off with Maisie, I got a drink at the bar—there was a specialty mocktail with glitter in it—and took a huge lap, wrestling over what to do. My dad stood with a group of other dad-looking men in the gravel driveway, admiring an orange car with white racing stripes on its hood. "It's a 1973 International Scout Harvester," a handsome Black guy said, an adorable toddler sitting on his shoulders. "I found it…"

I eventually located the twins with Teddy, Finn, and a bunch of other kids. Someone had built a massive obstacle course. "Go, Claire!" Maisie cheered as a girl with a long auburn ponytail army-crawled under some netting.

Claire? I wondered. *Claire Dupré?*

One glance at Finn gave me my answer. He was waiting at the finish line with flushed cheeks…or maybe he was out of breath from his obstacle course run.

I smiled when they high-fived, before the rest of the Farm caught my eye. It was a seemingly boundless meadow, with tall green grass, yellow flowers, and a web of sandy trails running through it. There were tall trees that looked permanently whipped by the wind and another blue pond in the distance.

"It's something, isn't it?" someone said, and I turned to see an older gentleman standing behind me. He smiled and sipped a glass of wine, and the rings around his eyes—

Holy crap! I realized. It was the man who'd all but rescued me at the Jaws Bridge.

"It's beautiful!" I said quickly, a little embarrassed. "*Breathtaking.*"

"I quite agree." He stood beside me, and together we gazed at the Farm. "Even after decades and decades, the view never gets old."

Even after decades and decades…

My ears perked up. "You've been here before?"

"Many times." He nodded, then pointed to the far pond. "My will stipulates that my ashes be spread on that shoreline. I have my coffee and read the *Gazette* there almost every morning."

Too much information, I thought, but I didn't really mind.

"Are you Meredith's grandfather?" I asked.

He chuckled. "Oh, no. My brother Andrew has that highly esteemed honor." He gestured across the lawn, where an old man sat behind an easel, seemingly painting something.

Wait. I recognized his aviators. *Is that the Jaws Bridge artist?*

"Was Andrew at the bridge the other day too?" I asked. "Sketching on the boulders?"

"Yes, he finds the jumpers a dynamic subject." His brother nodded, then he offered me a hand to shake. "Christian Fox."

"Olivia," I said. "Lupo."

"What brings you to the Vineyard, Olivia Lupo?" Christian asked.

"A family reunion," I answered. "Topper and Peggy's wedding anniversary."

Christian tilted his head. "You're a Carmichael?"

Carmichael-adjacent, I supposed, but left it at a cheerful, "Mmm."

I wasn't in the mood to explain the connection, that I was technically an interloper.

"Did you *really* burn down a barn?" I asked a couple seconds later, sounding like Maisie.

Something flashed in Christian's eyes. "How do you know that?"

"Hey, Grumps!" someone shouted before I could respond, loud enough that Christian and I turned to see a teenage boy with his hands cupped around his mouth. I wondered if he was aware of the curly-haired girl sneaking up behind him. "Meredith's—*no*! I *hate* you, Hannah!"

Christian sucked in an audible breath as the girl doused the boy with a bucket of water, dumping it right over his head. "That's Ty, my youngest grandson," he told me once Ty took off after Hannah. "He sadly was just assassinated."

"Never would've guessed," I said drily.

Remembering Meredith on the beach, I concluded that game unhinged people.

The corners of Christian's mouth twitched. He looked both bemused and intrigued, and like he wanted to ask me something. I waited, but no questions came. "Meredith makes excellent potato salad," he finally said. "Shall we go try some?"

Eternally friendly, the chef herself waved me over to her picnic table once I'd grabbed a seltzer and made myself a plate. She wore a red-and-white-striped tank suit with jean cutoffs, and her friend Katie sat next to her in a corresponding blue suit with white stars. "Olivia, how are you?"

"Hungry." I raised my loaded plate. "An older gentleman told me the potato salad was *to die for*."

Meredith smiled knowingly, and others at the table laughed before settling into easy conversation. "Connor, hey!" Wit called later, and I followed his gaze to the make-your-own ice cream sandwich station. Connor was helping Teddy scoop ice cream onto a palm-sized chocolate chip cookie. His obnoxious sunglasses still reigned supreme.

He gave us a goofy salute.

"That kid," Wit said, "is a literal golden retriever."

Austin chuckled. "His parents raised him well."

Right, I thought. *Austin is Mads's brother.*

"No, I'm serious," Wit said. "Have you ever met someone that *happy*?"

"Oh, I don't know," Katie said lightly. "How about *you*?"

"Funny." Wit smirked. "But you know that even I have my moments."

Meredith coughed. "*Moods.*"

Austin shrugged after the table laughed. "He's always been a glass-half-full guy. My sister says he even takes heartbreak well."

"Maybe he hasn't ever truly had his heart broken," I piped up without really thinking about it. Connor caught feelings easily, but he was proving to be an enigma. Had he actually *fallen* in love with his ex-girlfriends? Or were there so many because he just *loved* love?

Or the idea of love.

Why can't I be like that? I thought. *Why don't I want that?*

My friends always supported me when I told them I wasn't hanging out with Rob or CJ or Luca or Trevor anymore, but the way Erica sometimes looked at me once I casually mentioned it to her and my dad…

There was that knot again.

"It's a fair point, Austin," Katie said. "Even after that one girl—"

"Okay, *Entertainment Tonight*." Meredith winked. "Leave him alone."

Her friends chuckled before Nick asked about some renovation happening on the Farm, but someone stole my attention.

Connor, in the corner of my eye, alone and solemnly gazing out over Oyster Pond.

My heart stirred in my chest; I wasn't used to his face without a smile.

What is he thinking about? I wondered, and wondered again later, while my dad and I made our own ice cream sandwiches. The sun was slipping in the sky, which meant we couldn't be too far off from the fireworks.

"This is a mistake," I told him as he scooped Mad Martha's peppermint ice cream onto a peanut butter cookie. "Of epic proportions."

"We'll see..." he mused, then nodded at my dessert. A hefty scoop of sea salt caramel between two snickerdoodles. "You're playing it safe."

"Safe can still mean *delicious*."

"Touché." He smiled. "My mother would go for the white chocolate macadamia nut." He gestured to the far platter of cookies.

"Oh, definitely," I said through a bite of bliss. "With raspberry sorbet."

Annie had never met a sorbet she didn't like.

"Have you spoken to her?" my dad asked, a little tentatively. "Recently?"

I nodded. "She was watching HGTV this afternoon."

"*Love It or List It*?"

"Of course."

"How'd she seem?" he asked.

"Fine," I said. "She sounded sharp as a tack while telling me about your idyllic fictional childhood in North Carolina."

One side of his mouth tipped up in a smile. My dad always appreciated an extra dose of humor when it came to Annie's dementia. It was how he coped.

"What about you?" I realized he and I hadn't been alone in a while. There were so many people in the Carmichael house, doing so many different things.

"I spoke to her a couple days ago," he said. "Not for very long, though." He took a big bite of his eccentric ice cream sandwich, chewed, and swallowed...all with a pained expression on his face. Peppermint and peanut butter together were indeed disgusting. "She was tired and under the impression I was her gardener. We spoke briefly about her tulip border." He cleared his throat. "And her doctor and I touched base this morning."

"About what?" My eyebrows knitted together. "Her medicine?"

Erica appeared before he could explain. "I am taking Maisie and Bryce back to the house," she matter-of-factly announced. "It's getting late."

"But the fireworks haven't been set off yet," I said. "They shouldn't miss the show..."

Both my siblings were so excited.

"No, they won't." My stepmother shook her head. "Jay sets them off with the Fox brothers on Oyster Pond. We'll see them from the back deck."

I tried again. "But—"

"They stayed up extremely late last night," Erica told me. "I want them back on a normal sleeping schedule."

My dad didn't argue, which meant the twins really must've been on the precipice of overtired. Maisie would be grouchy, and woozy Bryce would fall asleep on his feet. "I'll take them home," he offered. "You stay and enjoy the rest of the night."

By way of a response, Erica smiled and slung her arms around my dad's neck. "Do you mind wrangling Teddy and Finn too?" she asked after they kissed. "My mother told me Connor is supposed to take them back soon, but I think it'd be nice to give him the night off."

Connor would never take Teddy and Finn home before the fireworks, I thought.

"I couldn't agree more," my dad said. "He's a hard worker and deserves to have some fun." He turned to me. "I'll see you back at the ranch, Liv?"

"Definitely." I tried not to show my disappointment; fireworks had been my dad's and my *thing*, ever since I was a little girl. Before he married Erica, we'd always take the train into New York and watch the Fourth of July fireworks together on the USS *Intrepid*. There was no better place to see all the razzle and dazzle than its flight deck. Granted, for the last several years we had gone to Haddonfield's fireworks show, but it was still special. I summoned a smile and welcomed his hug. "I'll see you later, Dad."

Erica walked off with him to help wrangle the kids, and I too set off after grabbing a napkin for my now-dripping dessert. "Hey, Olivia!" someone called, and I turned to see Nick on the dance floor off the deck. "You want to dance?"

The band was currently on break, so someone's summer playlist blared. I recognized James Taylor. "Where's Sage?" I called back.

"With her favorite dance partner!" He gestured across the floor, where Luke twirled the future Mrs. Nicholas Carmichael. Despite their uncontrollable smiles and laughter, it looked like they had a solid sense of rhythm.

"I'm a *terrible* dancer," Nick added. "But my lifts are epic!"

"Do you know the one from *Dirty Dancing*?" I joked.

He gave me a look that said, *Is that even a question?*

Laughing, I started toward him.

~

After Nick spun me, dipped me, and even flipped me, I grabbed a water bottle from one of the many drink coolers and gratefully sipped while a white-haired woman with colorful jewelry got on the mic to announce a ten-minute warning for fireworks. The sun had indeed said its goodbye. "Assume your positions!" she teased.

People migrated all different directions, most of them popping a squat on the lawn and others disappearing down to the beach. I pictured the twins and Finn and Teddy back across the pond, all settled on the Carmichaels' back deck together. Knowing my dad, he'd probably turned on the gas firepit and brought out s'mores supplies. He might've agreed with Erica about a better bedtime, but that didn't mean the kids couldn't go out with a bang.

It's vacation! I imagined him saying. *The Fourth of July!*

I felt a lump rise in my throat, suddenly wishing I were there too. Why hadn't I gone with my dad and the twins? Watching the fireworks with them would've been just as, if not more, special than watching the show here. It would be closer to tradition.

Wanting to be alone now, I searched for a secluded spot. The lawn was a patchwork quilt of people and blankets, and all the blue Adirondack chairs were taken. Clusters of children sat on top of picnic tables while the older crowd held court on the low-slung deck. I was on the verge of giving up my hope for solitude when Christian Fox caught my eye, standing with Meredith's grandfather and her grandmother, presumably. "Looking for the best seat in the house?" Christian asked at the same time I heard a stage-whisper: "Andrew, doesn't she sort of look like..."

Grace Kelly, I'd heard it before. "You caught me," I told Christian. "Any suggestions?"

He nodded once. "The side of the house."

The side of the house? What kind of view is that?

But I felt I had no choice but to heed his words when he smiled and emphatically pointed to the right. "Thank you!" I walked past the ultimate lineup of grills—gas, charcoal, and a Big Green Egg—before stepping off the deck and rounding the corner of the house. Only to see…

Bursting white hydrangea bushes.

Of course he was joking, I thought, some embarrassment creeping up my neck. *What magical view of the sky was waiting around the bend?*

It wasn't until I squinted for dramatic effect that I noticed the hidden rope ladder running down the cedar-shingles. The rope certainly wasn't pure white anymore, but the ladder still looked sturdy enough to climb.

I told myself to go for it.

The house was only one story, so its roof didn't spur my fear of heights. I carefully sat down and stretched out my legs, the breeze swirling around me. *I owe Christian Fox a thank-you note*, I thought to myself, as I gazed starry-eyed at the smooth inky water and night sky. *This* is *the best—*

"Want some company?"

I leaned forward to see Connor standing below me on the deck.

"How did you find me?" I asked.

"I heard you climb up there," he answered. "The ladder is right next to the bathroom window."

"Oh." I wished I hadn't squeaked whenever the ladder swayed. "Cool."

"Very," Connor agreed, then he attempted to calm his disheveled hair, running a slow hand through it. "Do you want some company?"

"Two-minute warning!" came over a megaphone. "Two minutes until the show!"

"Sure," I told Connor, surprising myself. Hadn't I wanted to be alone? "You have a minute and fifty-six seconds."

He grinned, but before I could smile back, I all but squawked. Rather than ascending the ladder, Connor simply leapt upward, his fingers curling around the edge of the roof.

I expected for him to cleanly rip off the gutters, but instead I watched with wide eyes as he elegantly hoisted himself up onto the roof.

"Okay, no." I shook my head, refusing to be impressed. "You did not just do that. You *did not* just do a perfect pull-up."

"The stitch in my side says otherwise," Connor said, and he took a deep breath once he relaxed next to me. The air around us warmed. "How's your night been?"

"Both calories and cardio," I said. "Nick's name was on my dance card."

"Was it everything you ever dreamed it'd be?"

I sighed. "Everything and *then* some."

Connor snorted. "You *do* know he has a fiancée?"

"With his great-grandmother's stunning emerald-cut diamond." I nodded. "I also heard through the grapevine that he's seven years older than me and my sort-of cousin."

Silence, and then: "I'm totally rooting for you two."

Laughter bubbled up inside me, and I found I couldn't stop it from overflowing. Connor's lips twitched in amusement, but a shot sounded before he could comment.

Yes! I thought as red sparks lit up the sky. *Here we go!*

The first firework sequence was a blend of peonies and chrysanthemums, their patterns both spherical and flowerlike upon crackling. If you blinked, you'd miss the peony, but I loved the chrysanthemum's finale. Its big, bright burst was followed by smaller pops of gold.

I shifted in my seat with excitement, goose bumps blooming on my arm when I accidentally brushed against Connor. "You love fireworks," he said softly.

"Yes." I nodded. "But I'm not a pyromaniac."

"Mmm," he hummed. "I don't know about that..."

I offered him something that resembled a glare.

"You saying you're not a pyromaniac when I said *nothing* about you being a pyromaniac suggests you *are* a pyromaniac," he explained.

I flushed. "It was *one* New Year's Eve."

When I was thirteen, my grandfather and I had driven to a hole-in-the-wall fireworks store to wow our family at midnight. I hadn't been able to stop smiling...until one of my cherry bombs went rogue and nearly nailed Pops in the leg.

Connor laughed, but then we refocused on the sky, a series of green comets now center-stage. *Crossette*, I pinpointed almost immediately. It was one of my favorites; a comet that broke into multiple comets, resulting in unique cross shape.

"I love these," I heard Connor remark several minutes later, as we entered another phase. His voice was barely a whisper above the crackle and the party's applause. "It sort of looks like a spider in the sky."

"Or lace," I said, nodding as the gold glitter shimmered. "The technical term is *brocade*."

Connor coughed. "Pyromaniac."

In response, I flicked him on the arm.

"*Hey*!"

"Really?" I raised an eyebrow. "That hurt?"

"Yes, courtesy of…" He took my hand, and I felt my heart softly skip when he lifted it up and squeezed my fingers. "Your claws."

Excuse me, I thought. *Claws?*

"Okay, *rude*." I shook him off to admire my manicure. My nails were far from talons. I did wince a little at the sight of my right pinkie nail, wondering if I'd been chewing on it in my sleep…because it had been whittled down. Annie was right; the look was not cute.

As the brocade fireworks disappeared into strobes, I folded my arms across my chest. Out of sight, out of mind.

Connor seemed comfortable falling into another silence, but for some reason, I didn't. "How was your night?" I asked him. "The boys behave themselves?"

"It was fine," he answered. "Teddy's sugar rush presented some challenges, and Finn suddenly wants to learn to surf for Claire…" He shrugged. "It's just been a little tough today. I would give anything to be home right now."

"Oh," I said, caught a bit off guard by his honesty, but also quickly connecting the dots back to an earlier vignette; Connor looking out over horizon, notably not feeling tonight.

"My family has been hosting our Fourth of July cookout for as long as I can remember," he continued. "It's not as big as this…" He gestured around Paqua Farm. "But it's still a *big* production. Decorations, goofy pool floats, games, everything. My dad literally spends all year planning the menu. He engineered a whole guacamole and margarita bar for tonight."

One corner of my mouth tugged up in a smile, and even though the fireworks were still in full swing, Connor unlocked his phone to show me photos his mom had sent him. Red, white, and blue paper lanterns; pitchers of pink, yellow, and orange margaritas; people in sailor hats; hot dogs and hamburgers; and even human-sized cardboard boats in the pool. A girl with braids was rowing as if her life depended on it, despite her boat already sinking. MAD MADS, was written in bubble letters on the side. "I've missed this cookout once or twice," Connor told me. "But it never felt like a big deal… There was always next summer." He paused. "But now, *will* there be next summer? Tonight kind of feels like the last one." He nodded at *Mad Mads*'s determined captain. "Mads and I are going to college; who knows what we'll be doing a year from now?" He sighed. "And Liam…"

"And Liam?" I prompted when he trailed off.

"Nothing." He shook his head. "Just that I know Liam's really going to miss me when I leave for Notre Dame, so sometimes I feel shitty about taking off this summer."

A lump formed in my throat, wishing I didn't feel almost exactly the same way. My dad, and my phone calls with Annie so far, had reassured me that everything would be okay while we were away, but I had no idea how to prepare myself for the end of the summer. *How* was I going to say goodbye to Annie? After a year of spending most of my days with her?

I hadn't thought of that when I'd begged to take a gap year—the idea that I'd be able to see her so often, but once twelve months ran their course, both of us would have to adjust to far less regular visits. *Will she even notice?* I wondered. *When I'm gone for months instead of days?*

Her mental calendar was nonexistent, and I hated that that sounded promising. If I left in August and didn't see her until Thanksgiving, it might seem the same as me visiting Wednesday after stopping by on Monday.

The thought made my heart hurt.

"I know how you feel," I told Connor, but I couldn't find the words to elaborate. The more time I spent with Connor, the more I wanted to tell him everything about Annie…but the moment never seemed right. Now, for instance. I didn't want to end the night in tears.

In fact, I really wanted to *avoid* tears on this vacation. I wanted to believe I'd left them all at home.

Connor didn't ask any questions; instead, he subtly turned his palm face up on his thigh. *Hand's here if you need it*, the gesture said.

Swallowing hard, I forced myself to return to the fireworks. Silver flying fish squirmed and swam through the air—my dad's favorite—but once the last one burned out, I snuck another peek at Connor's upturned palm.

I'm here if you need me, it reiterated.

Blood suddenly pulsed through my ears, and all I could hear was distant cheering while Paqua's pyrotechnicians geared up for the finale (no show was complete without a medley). *Look back at the fireworks*, my conscience coaxed me, but instead I found myself glancing at Connor.

Something in my chest seized when we made eye contact, starlight reflecting off his blue irises. Holding my gaze, he tilted his head in either amusement or intrigue. I couldn't tell.

Although I was surer than sure of what was next after he reached out and tucked a lock of my frizzy hair behind my ear (thank you, humidity).

What are you doing? I asked myself as Connor slowly leaned in. *What are you doing, what are you doing, what are you doing?*

I couldn't kiss Connor McCallister; I *wouldn't* kiss Connor McCallister.

Because someone, not me, would get hurt.

However, my mind didn't stop my eyelids from fluttering shut, and I felt a thrill spiral through my veins when I heard him take a deep breath.

But when my heart lurched, it wasn't because Connor McCallister was kissing me; it was from a startling shot around us. My eyes snapped open just in time to see every color of the rainbow light up the world. They shined, shimmered, and glimmered. "Incredible," I breathed.

"Yes," Connor murmured, but I felt his still eyes on me, not the sky. "Incredible."

FOURTEEN

"I don't want to go to the Flying Horses," Maisie said mid-munch of Cinnamon Toast Crunch. "My mom said she might take Bryce and me to the candy store later."

I glanced over my shoulder, the kitchen thankfully not as crowded as usual. Topper and Peggy were sipping coffee and absorbed in a crossword puzzle, and across the room, Connor was busy helping Teddy man the waffle maker. Erica and my dad had gone on a walk. The others were sleeping in after a late night.

"You have all day to swing by the candy store," I told her instead of pointing out that Erica's *might* was code for *maybe*, not an iron-clad *definitely*. "Please, Maze?"

My sister slurped some more cereal.

"Annie went there once," I tried. "Don't you want to go somewhere she's been?"

Maisie's brow furrowed, a sign that she was now truly considering. Because before Annie's decline, she used to find our grandmother's adventures fascinating—*fantastical*, even. "No, no,

I don't believe you!" she said when Annie once told her about a long-ago tour of Russia. "You went to a circus and actually *pet* the tigers?"

"Of course I did, darling," Annie told her with a smile and mischievous glimmer in her eye. Circus? Yes. A face-to-face with the felines? Hmm. "Their fur was like butter on warm toast…"

Butter on warm toast.

It was such an *Annie* expression, one that now made the corners of my eyes sting.

"Okay." Maisie nodded as I blinked twice. "Bryce and I will come—"

"Yes!"

"—*if* you promise to drive us to the candy store afterward."

I gave her a look. "What about your mom?"

Maisie shrugged. "I'm not sure she'll really take us," she said. "Aunt Beth keeps telling her she needs to work on the scrapbook."

Ah, the scrapbook, I thought. *Topper and Peggy's anniversary album.*

The other night, Erica hadn't seemed too enthused about it. Maybe she was just tired and behind editing footage, but maybe something else was stopping her from crafting the crap out of those blank pages.

I wondered which one it was.

If Connor was caught off guard when he saw my siblings, he had a master poker face. "Excellent!" he called when we all rallied outside. "A full bus for today's field trip!"

Bryce grinned, but Maisie extended a small fist to Connor, her pinkie finger raised. "The Candy Bazaar?" she prompted.

He arched a brow. "The Candy Bazaar?"

"*Yes*," my sister clarified. "Do you promise you'll take us to the Candy Bazaar after the Flying Horses?"

Connor smiled, and then before my eyes, locked in a pinkie promise.

"I call shotgun!" Bryce chirped as we loaded into the Jeep, and I wished more than anything that my brother *could* legally ride in the front seat. But alas, he wasn't thirteen.

I admit, part of why I wanted my siblings to come with Connor and me was because I didn't love the idea of being alone with him. Things had ended awkwardly between us last night, and Teddy and Finn weren't here to buffer; they were spending the day with their grandparents. Apparently, Beth and her husband had a surprise for the boys. Connor claimed he knew nothing.

The fireworks finale might've ruined the ambiance for rooftop romance, but Connor hadn't been deterred. "Tell me I'm not off base, Olivia," he'd said, blue eyes bright in the flashing light. "Tell me you feel something too."

"I..." I started, but my tongue thickened before totally lolling in my mouth. It stopped me from mindlessly spouting off that while I liked spending time with him, I knew anything more wouldn't go well between us. No, my loss of words was forcing me to *think*.

But being so close to him made that nearly impossible; we hadn't kissed, and I knew we weren't *going* to kiss—the mood had dampened—yet my heart still hammered hard, and I could feel each and every single hair on the back of my neck standing tall. The air around us felt charged with electricity.

Fantastic, I thought. *Fan-fucking-tastic.*

"Olivia?" Connor prompted.

I closed my eyes to focus on stringing some words together. "You're not off base," I barely heard myself say over the blood in my ears. I couldn't outright lie to him; he didn't deserve that. "But..."

But?

But what?

What was I trying to say?

I aborted, switched to a half-baked tactic. "You're so nice, Connor."

"And let me guess..." He released a deep sigh. "That's the deal-breaker? You don't go for nice guys?"

Again, I weighed what to say. Most of the guys I'd hung out with *were* nice—well, nice *enough*. And that was all they needed to be for me. I preferred to keep an arm's length between us. No guy had ever seemed to have a problem with it.

But Connor will, I knew, my stomach stirring. *Forget about an arm's length.*

Because everything I'd learned about Connor McCallister in the last few days signaled that he would want to be *close*. Not only physically, but emotionally—*especially* emotionally. I mean, he'd been more than happy to open up about his relationship history during our first true conversation. He also genuinely wanted to know about my life, and when I clammed up, he wasn't deterred. Instead, he waited. It was like he wanted to someday smile and take my hand and spin me into this shimmering world, one where there was no secrets between us.

That, I thought, imagining *La La Land*'s planetarium scene, *is what being more than friends with Connor would be like.*

Meanwhile, I didn't have the courage to show him my favorite hiding spot. It was too good; I was rarely found during hide-and-seek. If Erica had given up searching, I didn't blame her.

Now, I shook my head, trying to shake away the scene, but Connor kept looking at me. I had to say something, had to say *anything*. "Listen, Connor—"

"Olivia!" someone unknowingly swooped in to save me. "Connor!"

We both leaned forward to see Charlie below us, standing on the deck and giving Luke a goofy piggyback ride.

"Sweet spot." Charlie sounded bemused. "I don't mean to interrupt—"

Flushing, I resisted the urge to cover my face with my hands.

"—but if you guys want a lift home, Nick's firing up the boat."

"That'd be great!" Connor said before I opened my mouth. He promptly rose from the roof and descended the same way he'd ascended: a calculated leap.

"Smooth," Luke noted once Connor's feet hit the ground.

"Not smooth enough," I swore I heard him say, and I tried to swallow a lump in my throat as I carefully climbed down the rope ladder.

There's no point anyway, I told myself later, after stealthily climbing up to my bunk. I'd helped my dad, Nick, and Allison cut into and polish off a peach pie to give Connor space to get ready for bed. He'd taken the liberty of turning off all the lights. *There's no point whatsoever. Even if he could be casual, we're only—*

His voice in the darkness jolted my pulse. "We're still on for tomorrow?"

"Yes," I whispered after a beat of surprise, thinking of Annie and her Martha's Vineyard memory book. She was far more important than whatever was or wasn't happening with Connor. "I wouldn't miss it."

~

It was an overcast day, so most people were forgoing the beach in favor of town. Oak Bluffs was buzzing. "Look over there!" Bryce shouted and I turned in my seat to see him point toward the water, to a beige-shingled restaurant. Big blue letters spelled out NANCY's on the side, and underneath hung a great white shark sculpture. "It's Nancy's!"

I gave him a blank look. "So?"

"Teddy says they have *the best* hot dogs."

"Hmm," I said. "Teddy sounds bound for a bigshot job at the island's chamber of commerce."

"What's that?" my siblings asked as Connor chuckled.

I felt a smile twitch at the corner of my mouth. "A chamber of commerce is..." I began, but quickly lost the twins; they were all but craning their necks out of the Jeep. There was too much to see. Big Dipper Ice Cream, a bike rental shop, and more restaurants. Just the masthead for Martha's Vineyard Chowder Company made my stomach rumble, remembering the amazing clam chowder I'd eaten before our ferry out here. Connor skillfully navigated around the other cars and black dog and menemsha blues T-shirt-wearing pedestrians, but he shrugged back his shoulders while inching up Lake Avenue. "There it is!" Maisie exclaimed. "Up ahead!"

And I had to beg you to come, I thought to myself.

The historic carousel was housed in a barn-esque building, red with white trim. FLYING HORSES was written just below the roofline in antique lettering. My heart turned with excitement, ready to see the merry-go-round in Annie's picture come to life.

Connor's voice made me blink. "How about I drop you guys off and then find someplace to park?" He scanned the street, which was tightly lined with cars. "Options here aren't too promising."

"A Mini Cooper literally just left," Maisie pointed out. "You can definitely fit." Pause. "Well, maybe."

"And a Subaru is pulling out right now," Bryce added.

Connor was quiet, and I knew what that meant. The parallel parking scene was too intimidating. "I'm happy to teach you Erica's pizza steering wheel trick," I told him, then I checked that the coast was clear before unlocking my door. Maisie followed suit.

But Bryce adorably offered to stay with Connor. "He might need me to spot him," he justified. "And if we walk by Nancy's, we can stop for hot dogs..."

"America's oldest carousel," Maisie read the sign aloud as we climbed the front steps. She turned to me. "How old is it again?"

"Almost a century and a half," I said, recalling what I'd read on the Vineyard Preservation Trust's website. "It was built in the 1870s, and originally was a ride on Coney Island. I think it was moved here ten years later, give or take."

Maisie looked intrigued, oblivious to the modern-day arcade lobby we were passing through. Out of the corner of my eye, I spotted a pair of pinball machines. "Why?"

"I'm pretty sure there were plans to dismantle it so they could sell it off in pieces, and the Vineyard Preservation Trust didn't want that to happen." I nodded at the doors to the carousel's ring. "Do you want to go in? Or wait for Bryce and Connor?"

"Go in," Maisie said. "Otherwise, we'll be waiting forever."

She rolled her eyes. "You *know* Bryce is going to talk Connor into hot dogs." She swiped my phone from my back pocket. How she knew my passcode, I had no clue. "I'm going to text him to get us some!"

"Don't read my messages!" I blurted before I could stop myself.

"Why?" My sister grinned evilly at me. "Do you have a secret?"

"In your dreams." I rolled my eyes, because I technically didn't. I'd just sent an idiotic text to my friends this morning: This vacation might have a plot twist.

Quincy: What?

Gwen: WHO?

Why? I'd asked myself, internally groaning. *Why did you tease that?*

Hadn't I already decided Connor would want to get too close for comfort?

Because you wanted to hook them, reel them in, and get their advice, I thought now, snatching my phone the second after Maisie texted Connor.

I hadn't had the time or guts to respond to my friends.

Maybe I already knew what they would say.

"Shall we?" I gestured toward the doors.

Maisie squealed with delight once we pushed into the center ring. The Flying Horses were in full swing, the platform carousel spinning to upbeat, old-time carnival music. I grinned, thrilled to see the green painted platform and hand-carved wooden horses in real life. "Their tails are *real* horsehair!"

"Who told you that?" I asked.

"Teddy."

"Shame on me for even asking," I said as we weaved our way through spectators and paid our carousel fee before joining the patient line waiting behind a white picket fence. Tourists had definitely gotten the memo to visit. My guess was we'd have to wait a couple rides before mounting our noble steeds.

Connor responded to Maisie's text a few minutes later, confirming that he and Bryce were indeed making a pit stop at Nancy's, and did we need any condiments with our hot dogs?

I pretended to gag when Maisie said relish and mayonnaise.

Fries too? Connor asked.

Depends, I answered. Does Teddy think they're up to snuff?

"Did Annie ever get the brass ring?" Maisie asked while we watched children and adults alike stretch to grab a ring when they passed the overarching dispenser. I'd read that there were many iron rings, but only *one* brass. Whoever seized it won a free repeat ride.

I shook my head. "She never said."

"Oh." Maisie's brow furrowed a little. "Maybe she didn't win then. I feel like that's something she'd tell us."

I felt a twinge in my chest. Annie and Maisie bonded over their shared love of competition. Our grandmother had rarely missed Maisie's softball games, tirelessly cheered for the twins during elementary school field days, and taught Maisie to play gin rummy when we had Sunday dinner with her. I lost track of how many games they'd play, but they almost always ran after the kitchen timer chimed. "Would someone *win* already?" Erica would tease. "The food's getting cold!"

It almost broke my heart that Maisie probably wanted to tell Annie about the other day's nightshirt caper, but the chances of Annie understanding were slim.

"I think she would've told us too," I said slowly, then squeezed my sister's shoulder. "She might've won, Maze. Let's believe she did." I paused. "The reason she didn't tell me was because I never spoke to her about the Flying Horses."

Maisie's eyes widened. "What?"

"I tried talking to her about Martha's Vineyard," I said, "but she didn't share much beyond telling me she went. She wasn't..."

My sister's gaze fell to the floor when I trailed off, which made me remember that she was ten—a precocious ten, like I once was, but *only* ten. Finlay House frightened the twins, with its village elders, and Maisie had gotten so frustrated with Annie before our grandmother had been moved there, unable to fully understand what was happening. I knew she was also disappointed in herself, which killed me. "Thank you for staying," she'd whispered to me last year, right after our dad agreed to my gap year. "Annie needs you."

Now, I swallowed the lump in my throat when Maisie took my hand. "How do you know she came here, then?" she asked quietly. "To the Flying Horses?"

"I have this," I answered, reaching into my purse and pulling out Annie's Polaroid from a zipped inner pocket. I handed it to my sister. "I found it in one of her boxes in my closet."

"Wow," Maisie marveled. "She looks so *young*."

"Yeah," I agreed, also admiring the photo. Someone had taken it from a distance; Annie wore a floppy straw hat and a light pink sundress, and she was waving at the camera as she rode a horse with a white mane and tail. She was smiling so widely that I wanted to smile back. "She's the most beautiful woman in the world."

"*Second*-most beautiful," Maisie pointedly corrected, then said, "I wonder who that man is."

"What man?" I asked.

Maisie pointed at the picture, not at Annie in the foreground, but to the background. It was a little hazy, and captured plenty of other carousel riders, but I suddenly realized there was someone else meant to be in the photo's focus. *A man*, as my sister had said. His hand held onto the pole that anchored Annie's horse, but higher up than her clasped hands, so I hadn't noticed at first. He was tall and wearing a white polo shirt, although I couldn't see his face because he had turned away from the camera's crosshairs, as if someone behind him had called his name.

"Do you think it's Pops?" Maisie asked.

"No." I shook my head, mind whirring. Our grandfather's travel anxiety hadn't set in until he was older, but I knew this wasn't him. "Pops had really dark hair."

Mystery Man's looked light brown, and upon squinting, it curled at the edges.

It kind of reminded me of my dad's hair.

"Hmm." Maisie was stumped. "I guess we'll never know."

I gave her a look. "Your investigative journalist skills need some work."

"Why? I don't want to be an investigative journalist anymore."

"Okay, what do you want to be?"

Maisie shrugged before the carousel slowed and a woman with red hair cheered. She waved around something small. "The brass ring!" My sister locked eyes with me. "I *want* it, Olivia."

"Then let's get it," I told her. It looked like we were going to make the cut for the next ride. "I believe in you!"

~

Naturally, Maisie *did* triumph and grab the brass ring, so I took a video of her victory lap for my dad and Erica. "Maisie's riding without me?" Bryce was incredulous when he and Connor (and a to-go bag from Nancy's) found me at the picket fence.

"You snooze, you lose," I joked.

His disbelief turned indignant. "We weren't snoozing! We had to park all the way up near the Steamship Authority, and then walk to Nancy's—"

"How about we get in line?" Connor suggested. "I'm sure Maisie will be game for another ride."

"Especially if she wins the brass ring again," I said, pocketing my phone. "I nearly pulled a muscle trying to grab those rings."

Connor cocked his head, bemused. "You didn't stretch first?"

Not wanting to flash my middle finger in front of Bryce, I stuck out my tongue.

By way of a response, the corners of his eyes crinkled and he held up our food after Bryce took off to stake out our spot in line. "Teddy advised two hot dogs per person, so I got you the requisite two and Maisie three."

"Very observant," I commented. My sister could lowkey put away *a lot* of food. "And..." I gave him a smile, one that surprisingly caught me off guard and warmed my face. Usually one reserved for Annie. "Thank you."

"My pleasure." He smiled back, then reached into the bag, surreptitiously pulled out a french fry, and offered it to me. There was probably a no food or beverage sign around here somewhere. "These are also Teddy-endorsed."

Our fingertips touched when I accepted his fry, and I felt blood rush to my cheeks after I fumbled the handoff and the fry fell to our feet.

If this plot twist is A GUY, Olivia, Gwen had texted when I didn't respond, then YES, you should go for it! For once in your life!

"Party foul..." Connor teased as my lungs secretly sped up, but his eyes found mine when I didn't laugh, let alone react.

"Are you okay?" he asked. "You seem a little..."

"Do not say edgy," I said, remembering our first time hanging out on our porch. "I am not on edge."

Just painfully attracted to you, I realized. *And I need to get out of here.*

I was suddenly claustrophobic from all the people, the cutesy cloying music, the carousel, and Connor's elbow brushing mine. *I need to leave, I need to breathe, I need to—*

My chiming phone cut through the feeling that I was in a bizarre funhouse; I pulled it out of my pocket and was confused to see a call from La Maison d'Annie. Was it Tara? Or one of the other nurses? Annie rarely called me from her room's landline anymore. I mostly called her.

"I'll be right back," I told Connor, already half-heading for the exit. The last thing I wanted was to send Annie to voicemail. "My grandmother's calling me. Will you keep an eye on the twins?"

"Of course." Connor nodded. "Tell her I say hello."

"She doesn't know who you are," I tried to joke, but the words cut deep—deeper than Connor knew.

"It doesn't matter," he said as my eyes started to sting. "I still say hello."

"I will," I said, and only when I turned away did I realize we hadn't taken my picture for Annie.

FIFTEEN

I worried something was really wrong. My heart hammered as I swerved through the carousel chaos and darted across the arcade-filled lobby. "Hello!" I burst out the front door on the final ring. "Tara?"

"Tara?" a familiar voice replied—a warm voice, a kind voice, my favorite voice. "Whyever do you think I'm *Tara*?"

I felt myself melt into a smile. "Hi, Annie."

"Dearest," she said. "How are you?"

"How are *you*?" I asked, hoping to gauge where her head was. She sounded like *herself*, but I still wanted to manage my expectations.

"I'm wonderful," she answered. "The weather's beautiful today, so Fliss Williams and I took a long walk on the trails…"

Okay, not bad, I thought. Not *true*—Annie wasn't allowed to freely wander Elkins Village anymore, or even walk with only a friend—but not bad. Fliss occasionally visited my grandmother in Finlay for a cup or two of tea.

"And then we had tea in my room."

I released a relieved breath. *There we go.*

"She just *loves* the photo books Erica makes for me," she said. "Today I showed her *A Night to Remember*."

A Night to Remember was a collection of my high school dance shots. Pictures of me before homecoming, the winter SnowBall, junior prom, senior prom, etc. Erica and I had fun, actually, picking out the photos together.

"Well, you can expect another one soon," I told her, speed-walking along the sidewalk. There had to be a bench somewhere. "I've been taking a lot of pictures..."

And so had Erica. "Don't worry," I'd overheard my stepmother tell her sister the other day, when Beth had given her a look for snapping shots of the cousins playing an intense game of croquet and another of the delicious summer lasagna Peggy had made for dinner. *Influencer-ing, are we?* Beth's expression read. "They're for Annette, not social media."

"Yeah, relax, Beth," Jay had chimed in. "It's not like people are going to stalk us for Mom's lasagna recipe!"

Not stalk, I thought, feathers a little ruffled on her behalf. *But if Erica shares a photo, followers* will *ask.*

I wondered if her siblings had even seen her Instagram.

"I can't wait," Annie said now, as I settled on a bench near the Steamship Authority. With today's cloudy sky, the ocean looked more green than blue. "How are the Outer Banks?"

Just go with it, I told myself, biting the tip of my fingernail. *Just go with the flow. Surf the Outer Banks wavelength.*

But for some reason, I couldn't.

"We're on Martha's Vineyard, Annie," I gently said. "Not the Outer Banks."

The line was quiet.

I counted my heartbeats. *One…two…three…*

"Yes, forgive me," my grandmother said slowly, a line she hadn't used in ages. "I remember you mentioning that."

Do you? I wondered, because my meltdown in her room seemed like a little *more* than a mention. I suspected Annie had no recollection of that visit, and she was *aware* of that, but didn't want to hurt my feelings by admitting it.

It didn't matter.

"We went to the Flying Horses today," I told her brightly. "Maisie grabbed the brass ring on her first ride."

"Oh my!" My grandmother laughed, delighted. "Of course she did. Our Maisie never backs down from a challenge."

"No, she does not…" I hesitated. She *knew* what I was talking about; she *remembered* the Flying Horses and its brass ring. What should I ask her next? I needed to make the most of this.

"What's on your mind, Olivia?" Annie picked up after a moment. "I can hear those cogs turning."

Warmth filled my chest. *I can hear those cogs turning*. Annie said that to me a lot growing up, whenever I was clearly wrestling with something but couldn't bring myself to talk about it.

Did something happen here, Annie? I asked. *Why didn't you ever* really *tell us about Martha's Vineyard?*

The opportunity was right there, but something got the better of my curiosity. "I might've met someone," I said, the words sounding too serious but also the most accurate. "Connor."

"Mmm," Annie distantly hummed.

I grimaced. By saying so little, she made me feel heartless. I historically never talked about the guys I hung out with, beyond sharing their first names and a fast fact. *Rob plays the drums… CJ lives three streets over… Luca works as a busboy… Trevor loves Ultimate Frisbee…*

Their best quality always went unsaid: *They only want to have fun.*

"What is this boy's name?" Annie asked, as if I hadn't just told her.

"Connor." A flurry of butterflies swirled in my stomach, to the point of near-nausea. I felt like I was about to jump off the Jaws Bridge for the first time. "Nothing's going to happen, though," I quickly added. "I just…" My voice wavered. "I just like him."

"Does he like you?" Annie prompted.

I couldn't help but let out a laugh. "Yes." I nodded, even though she couldn't see. "He has been very…" I searched for the word. "*Up front* about that."

"Ah," Annie said lightly. "Then why is nothing going to happen?"

A lump formed in my throat.

"You return each other's feelings," she stated. "I don't see the problem."

"Because there isn't one." I said, swallowing hard. "It's more *pointless*. We're only here for two more weeks, which is no time at all, and he's working here for the summer—"

My grandmother cut me off. "Where is Connor from? New England?"

"Pennsylvania."

"That sounds vaguely familiar."

I blushed. "But it's not like we're going to the same college."

"Oh, who cares?" Annie asked, in a tone that straightened my spine. Not unkind, but one that would pair perfectly with an eye roll. Her loss of a filter was another symptom of dementia. "What does it matter?"

I opened my mouth before gathering words.

"You don't have to marry him, dearest," Annie told me. "A couple weeks of fun never hurt anyone, and the Vineyard..." She sighed. "It's a fantastic place for fun."

"How do you know?" I blurted, for fear that she would forget in the next three seconds.

"Because *I* had plenty of fun there," she replied. "Before I met your grandfather, I was in your shoes. I *met* someone."

My pulse was pounding. Annie had *never* spoken of any romance other than the one she'd had with Pops. Some high school admirers, of course, but those didn't really count. "Annie, who was—" I started at the same time someone on Annie's end said, "Annette, lunch is being served."

"No, thank you," I heard her tell Kai. "I'm speaking with my granddaughter."

About groundbreaking matters! I thought, but kept quiet when Kai suggested Annie call me back later.

"Kai, that would be rude," my grandmother said, as a knot twisted in my heart. I knew I had to hang up; Annie had lost her fondness for eating in the dining room, but everyone agreed it was important for her to keep up socializing.

I refused to be her excuse.

"Go have fun at lunch, Annie!" I chirped, but while closing my eyes. I'd been so close, yet so far. "I should go, anyway. I promised I'd take Maisie and Bryce to the candy store."

"Well, alright," she replied. "But don't think about what I said, Olivia. Just *do*. Otherwise, you'll only keep talking yourself out of it." She took a breath. "Because, dearest, I can hear how much you want this in your voice."

Every muscle tensed when I rejoined my siblings and Connor at the carousel. (Maisie had snagged the brass ring twice more; Bryce had gotten in trouble for climbing up on his horse in order to reach the ring dispenser.) My hot dog from Nancy's was now cold, but I ate it anyway, needing to fixate on something other than Connor's glinting blue eyes.

It was so delicious that I wondered how it had tasted when hot.

"Smile!" the twins chorused from the sidelines while Connor snapped a shot of my second and final spin around the carousel.

Like Annie, I'd chosen a white horse. All I was missing was her fabulous straw hat and a mystery man.

I met someone, she'd said.

Who? I wondered on our way back to Edgartown. The Candy Bazaar was on the water near the yacht club. Maisie and Bryce raced into the cute cedar-shingled cottage; the screen door slammed shut behind them.

"Ladies first," Connor said upon grabbing the door for me, but a family of five poured out first.

"Thank you!" called the mom with a toddler on her hip. Her little boy was multitasking, licking an old-fashioned Fudgsicle while also trying to pull off his mother's sunglasses.

"My pleasure!" Connor smiled, then he held the door for two Twizzler-wielding teenagers before finally gesturing me inside.

"The consummate gentleman," I commented, but I felt my lungs contract, imagining his hand landing on my lower back to guide me through the doorway.

"You okay?" he asked when he didn't touch me.

Because why would he?

I'd made things clear on the roof last night.

"Just a little thirsty," I lied.

"I can help with that," Connor said, a mischievous smile curling.

My cheeks flamed, catching the double entendre too late. Why hadn't I said *dehydrated*?

He pointed toward the far side of the store, to a tall drinks fridge. "Over there."

I flashed him the middle finger.

He hit me with a smirk that straightened my spine.

Again, I was an idiot.

"Olivia, look at these!" Maisie called before I could flee the store. "Cigarettes!"

"What?" I blinked to see my sister waving around what looked like a Marlboro pack. "They're candy, right?"

Grinning, Maisie nodded and added them to her already impressive haul. Wicker baskets lined the shelves, containing candy from your everyday M&M's and Nerds Gummy Clusters to flying saucer wafers, sour strawberry belts, and blocks of chocolate.

"Oh, man!" Connor exclaimed as Maisie offered me a candy necklace to match hers. "I was *obsessed* with these when I was a kid."

"What is it?" Bryce asked, a pack of Razzles in hand.

"Building Blox," Connor answered as he showed off a hefty bag full of what looked like colorful Legos. "I'd always build something before eating them." He grimaced. "They can be a little hard on the teeth, though."

Eyes alight, my brother basically mugged Connor and dropped the Blox into his basket, which, like Maisie's, was about to overflow.

Dad and Erica are going to love *this*, I thought once my brother and Connor started talking about potential construction projects.

My siblings' sugar rush might be fun, but I didn't want to be anywhere near the later crash.

I saw Connor grab an empty basket, presumably to pick out a few things for Finn and Teddy, and I followed suit. My dad loved any and all types of gummies (save for those of the recreational drug variety); I grabbed him a bag of blue sharks. Erica wasn't normally a big fan of candy, but I couldn't resist the Fun Dip. It'd been her top craving while pregnant with the twins.

Why are you being so nice to her? the voice in the back of my head asked. *You're rarely this nice to her.*

Because she needs to loosen up, I answered, trying to shake the thought away. *No one should be this tightly wound on vacation!*

I felt a twinge in my chest, realizing the statement wasn't solely applicable to Erica.

"Hey, Olivia!" I heard my name and turned to see Connor standing by the case of gourmet chocolates. "Are you a chocolate lover?"

"Try a chocolate *snob*!" Maisie answered for me, as Annie's words drifted through my mind: *A couple weeks of fun never hurt anyone...*

"It's true," I said with a shrug. "A Hershey's bar doesn't do it for me."

"Or Dove," Bryce chimed in. "Or Godiva."

"Got it," Connor said, bemused. "No drug store chocolate for the queen."

My siblings giggled. "Olivia isn't the queen," Bryce said. "That's Annie!"

I couldn't help but laugh a little too. My dad sometimes referred to Annie as "the queen," usually when she beckoned him over to fix something ASAP.

Connor raised an eyebrow.

"Lupo family lore," I explained and joined him by the chocolates. "Do they have chocolate-covered orange peel?" I sidestepped closer to him to better peer into the case.

But I closed my eyes when I felt heat radiating off his skin. He smelled like sunscreen, laundry detergent, and whatever delicious watermelon-hinted scent his shampoo was.

I felt like melting.

"Sophisticated," he remarked, and the accidental bump of his hip against mine forced my eyes back open but sent my pulse off to the races. "Top shelf, left side."

"Are you going to get anything?" I asked after selecting a bag of orange peel and a few of Annie's favorite Turtles.

"Caramellos," he said. "Caramel and marshmallow nougat covered in chocolate."

I laughed when he sighed dreamily, but once we finally made it to the register, I had to focus. "You each need to put five things back," I told the twins and their bursting baskets. "I don't have enough cash for everything."

"But you have your debit card," Bryce countered.

Ignoring him, I suggested they leave behind the more generic goodies.

We still spent sixty bucks.

This island was getting more expensive by the day.

"No way," Finn said when we returned home later, the twins immediately showing off their treasure. "You went to the candy store without us?"

In response, Connor (gently) pelted him with some packs of Pop Rocks. "Dude, you know I'm always thinking of you."

"You're the best, Connor!" Teddy exclaimed after a bag of tangled blue raspberry laces hit him in the shoulder.

Connor smiled. "Where'd your grandparents take you today?"

The afternoon had flown by; Luke was already marinating chicken in the kitchen while Nick performed his best juggling routine (big beefsteak tomatoes instead of colorful balls), and I spotted Charlie and Jay out on the deck, husking corn. "Grandpa took us hiking in Aquinnah," Finn said, sparking something in my chest.

Aquinnah.

I *had* to see those cliffs, to see if they were as incredible as their rendering in Annie's watercolor painting.

Had she gone to see them with her summer love?

God, that sounded so *Grease*.

"And then we got lemonades," Teddy added. "Gram had a lot of phone calls, so she stayed here."

"But she still has a *surprise* for us," Finn said as I fought the urge to roll my eyes. Couldn't Beth be an attentive grandmother for once? I had yet to see her spend any quality time with the boys. "Something is happening later."

"Huh." Connor nodded slowly, seemingly in the dark. "That's exciting—"

"Liv!" I pivoted to see my dad and Erica coming in front the deck, faces pink from the sun with the twins in tow.

"Hey, Dad," I said once Maisie and Bryce took off with Teddy and Finn. "What's up?"

He gave me a look. "That's *a lot* of candy."

Oh, okay, I thought, a little taken aback. I'd been expecting Erica to come at me.

"Yeah, I know," I said, "but believe me when I say I *did* force them to narrow it down..." I blindly reached into my tote bag and grappled for his sweet treat. "Will this make things better?"

My dad chuckled at the gummy sharks. "Funnily enough, there were a few sightings today on Shark Watch," he told me as he popped a piece of candy in his mouth and chewed. "Mmm, that's the stuff..."

I smiled and quickly presented Erica with her Fun Dip, bracing myself for her to admonish me for the massive amounts of candy. But instead, she laughed. "I haven't had this in *years*!" she said, excitedly ripping open the package.

"Really, Erica?" her brother called. "Don't upset Mom by spoiling your dinner!"

"Take a hike, Jay," Erica said. "It's not my fault your daughter isn't here to bring you Fun Dip."

And with that, she spun on her heel and waltzed back outside.

Daughter? I thought, sort of stunned. *Since when am I Erica's daughter?*

For as long as I could remember, I'd been *Chris's* daughter.

My dad squeezed my shoulder before I could decide how I felt about that. "We love you, Liv," he said, then planted a kiss on the top of my head and whispered, "But you're on call if Maisie or Bryce boots."

~

Finn and Teddy's surprise revealed itself after dinner, when I offered to help Charlie clear the table. "*Mom*!" Finn shouted, and everyone turned to see a woman walking into the kitchen. Her brown hair was trying to escape her messy bun, but her face lit up when her sons practically fell out of their chairs so they could race over to her. The Carmichaels cheered, which encouraged Nick to pump his fist and start a chant.

"Ashley! Ashley! Ashley!"

"Are you our surprise?" Teddy asked once they'd hugged.

Ashley nodded. "A good one, I hope."

By way of an answer, her younger son squeezed her again. A lump rose in my throat, unable to imagine being seven and not seeing my dad for an entire month. Because I knew what it felt like to be seven and not see my mom…for much, much longer than a month.

"An *epic* surprise," Finn clarified, then he dropped his voice a little. "Is Dad coming?"

"Not yet, sweetheart." Ashley gently smiled and touched his cheek. "He misses you so much, but he still needs to help..."

With what? I wondered if Connor would fill me in, now that Ashley was here.

Beth clapped her hands. "Let's make Ash a plate, okay?"

Crickets.

"*Are* there leftovers?" Jay ventured tentatively. "Because I had thirds—'"

Erica pushed back her chair. Her brother was really on her nerves today. "How does soup and oyster crackers sound, Ashley?"

"*Amazing*," her eldest niece said, smiling gratefully. "Thanks, Aunt Erica."

"I can't believe I didn't know!" Connor said once Ashley was settled at the table. Only a few people remained; the others had funneled out onto the deck for the Carmichael ritual known as "sunset drinks." Next to me, Charlie loaded the dishwasher at lightning speed so he didn't miss it. "Why didn't you tell me?"

"Maybe I wanted to surprise you too," she teased, then she stretched to tousle Connor's hair. I bit the inside of my cheek, yearning to do the same.

Well, I more wanted to *run my hands* through it—again and again, over and over, perhaps even endlessly.

"We also need to talk," Ashley said while I considered whether or not some fresh air would do me good. "Right now."

Even from dish-rinsing duty at the island, my ears perked up.

Connor nodded. "You have my attention."

"Good." Ashley paused to accept a glass of white from her dad. "Then you'll hear me—loud and clear—when I say that you are to take the next week off."

My heart leaped. *What?*

Connor's wide eyes signaled the same, but he quickly shook his head. "I *really* appreciate it, Ashley, but no. A week is too—"

"It's *not* too much," she cut him off. "You have spent day in and day out with my children for the last month."

"You're paying me to," Connor reminded her.

"That doesn't mean you don't need or deserve a break."

Her manny didn't say anything; for once, he looked a little tired. Wiped out, even.

"I'm only here for a week, Connor." Ashley took a sip of her wine. "I promise to return them to you."

"Well..." Connor started, sighed. "I haven't picked up my stick in days."

"Perfect," she said, as Erica set down her bowl of soup. "Play some lacrosse." She laughed. "And afterward, *please* have some fun!"

Have some fun.

"I'll try, boss," Connor chuckled, and I swear I felt all of space and time freeze when he caught my eye and winked.

Instead of downing a drink for liquid courage, I sat on the deck and dug into my chocolate spoils. Connor, upon accepting his PTO, was nowhere to be seen. "You're *really* not going to share?" Nick prodded for the umpteenth time, as I chewed a nutty Turtle. It had been ages since I'd had one; they were far more delectable than I remembered.

"Are you serious?" I swallowed. "I offered you an orange peel."

"Yeah, but..." My step-cousin sheepishly rubbed the back of his neck. "I don't like mixing chocolate and fruit."

I laughed. "Candied orange *hardly* qualifies as fruit."

Nick considered my waxy white bag, but before he could step out of his comfort zone, someone put their hand on his shoulder. We looked up to see Sage with a bright smile on her face. "You ready?" she asked.

"Now?" Nick answered, seemingly surprised. "What about your headache?"

"Oh, I'm sure it'll stick around." Sage shrugged. "But we can't miss these stars, Nicholas."

Her fiancé broke into a grin that rivaled tonight's dazzling celestial display before leaping up from his Adirondack chair to loop his arm around Sage's waist. "Marry me, Morgan," I heard him whisper.

She laughed. "I'd be careful," she teased. "If you keep asking me, I might change my mind..."

Something tightened in my chest once they stepped off the deck and set off across the lawn hand in hand, toward the beach, to do whatever it was they were going to do.

If I had to wager a guess, I'd say skinny-dipping.

I squinted to see Nick scoop Sage up in the darkness, then I blinked hard and rose from my seat. "Good night," I said, softly and to no one in particular.

Blood pumped through my ears as I all but ran through the house, the last of my chocolate coating my thickening throat. I vaguely registered Swede, Greta, and Posey tailing me, sensing excitement, but when I reached Summer Camp, I opened and closed the door before they could slip inside too.

All was still in the bunk room; all was silent.

He's out on the porch, I surmised, and sure enough, I found Connor standing in the lamplight; he was trying to stay as close to the house as possible—or, in other words, as close to the *Wi-Fi router* as possible.

Because God forbid his call dropped.

"Can we rewind?" I blurted, too keyed up to hold back. "Back to last night?"

Connor raised an eyebrow, but the voice I heard wasn't his. "Rewind?" I heard a girl squawk, and when no one responded, she pressed on. "*Back to last night*?"

"Sweet dreams, Madeline," Connor said smoothly, but I was *mortified*. "Please don't forget to give Arthur and Francine my best..."

"Wait!" Mads tried to put up a fight, but Connor mercifully ended the call and tossed his phone on the couch.

Then looked at me.

My heart flared.

"I'm sorry," he said. "I missed what you said."

Liar, I thought, able to tell from the slight tilt of his head. But I indulged him, with a deep sigh. "I said, 'Can we rewind to last night?'"

A nod. "To which part?"

My voice came out as a croak. "You know."

"I'm not sure I do."

"Connor."

"What?" He held up his hands, as if I'd caught him in my flashlight beam. "I need some clarification." He took a step toward me. "Are we backtracking to when you made fun of my sunglasses?" A second step. "To someone almost nailing me with a water gun?" Third step. "Which was when you were dancing with—"

"After the sun set!" I cut in. "Specifically, after the sunset, on the roof, and during the fireworks, but before the finale."

Connor stopped in front of me, one of the porch's wood planks creaking under his feet. I could feel the shift, very aware that his fingertips were dangling only inches from mine. Sweat beaded on the back of my neck.

"It's been tormenting me all day," I added. "I keep thinking about it."

"Join the club," he said lightly, then cleared his throat. "I really like you, Olivia, but I'm not sure what you want. I don't want to be pushed away every other day."

"You won't." I quickly shook my head. "I promise."

Because I'm not going to let you get that close.

Connor and I were just going to have fun together. I wouldn't feel that knot.

Pulse skipping, I dared to take his hand, slipping my fingers between his and squeezing tight. My stomach somersaulted when Connor squeezed back.

"Okay," he agreed, and when he grinned, I started mentally counting the seconds until he leaned in and kissed me.

Instead, he took a step backward.

My heart sank, and my face must've said it all.

What?

"I'm sorry," Connor said, clearly trying not to laugh. "But I can't kiss you now."

My brows knitted together. "Does my breath smell?"

"Yes, like chocolate."

"My Turtles."

"Right." He nodded. "Your Turtles."

It hit me a beat later. "Oh, no..." I groaned, suddenly wishing Turtles had peanuts instead of pecans. Because Connor didn't need an EpiPen for *peanuts*; he was allergic to *tree nuts*.

Literal distance, I reluctantly supposed, made the heart grow fonder.

SIXTEEN

It took me ages to fall asleep that night; I didn't know how Connor's breathing could be so steady beneath me. Didn't he feel the current of electricity in the room?

After the kiss that didn't happen, I ended up reading on the porch while Connor grabbed his lacrosse stick and played catch by himself. He'd set up a pitch back in the side yard, and he cradled the ball so intensely that I wondered if he too had nervous energy he needed to channel. In a way, the movement was mesmerizing. I kept waiting for him to miss the ball.

He never did.

Eventually, I surrendered to sleep, but I lurched awake what felt like only moments later. A phone chimed, but it wasn't mine. I groaned. "No…"

"Sorry!" Connor whisper-yelled. "I hoped you wouldn't hear it."

I didn't ask why he'd set an alarm for the wee hours of the morning; I simply rolled over, snuggled into the other side of my pillow, and promptly fell back asleep.

But not for long.

My heart reeled when I felt a hand on my arm. "Olivia," Connor murmured. "Wake up."

"You're kidding me," I replied, though it sounded garbled. But was he? Kidding? Joking? What was with the alarm? Was Connor secretly a nocturnal creature?

After all, he *was* impossible to wake in the morning…

"This is not a joke," he told me. "This is a drill."

"I don't hear the fire alarm," I deadpanned, begrudgingly pushing back my covers. Sleep had set me free. "Explain."

"Okay, not really a drill," he amended. "More like the perfect time to practice." He gestured out our window, to the shining night sky. "Let's go flex our stargazing skills."

"When did Nick mention he was going to grade us?"

Connor laughed as I started down the bunkbed ladder; my body pulsed when I felt his hands hovering only centimeters over my waist, ready to right me if I slipped. Heat swirled through my thin pajamas. The sensation made me shiver.

"Just let me grab a sweater," I said once my bare feet hit the floor. Our room was a little chilly, and I could hear the night breeze outside. "Where did I—"

"Here." Connor handed me one of his sweatshirts. It smelled like his sweet shampoo and sunscreen, and I smiled to myself as I tugged it over my head.

Shoes were skipped.

"Wow," I breathed when we stepped off the porch, the stars looking like spilled sugar against the inky sky. I'd seen them earlier tonight, of course, but I hadn't really *noticed* them until now. They glittered so brightly that I didn't have to squint to see the Big Dipper. It practically waved hello to me.

Out of the corner of my eye, I also couldn't help but mentally trace Connor's perfect jawline, so stunningly outlined by moonlight.

"I should've grabbed a blanket," he said once we'd walked halfway to the beach. The grass was cool and damp under our feet, but I didn't mind. It reminded me of Annie's Polaroid collection, especially the photo of her standing barefoot by the tractor.

Would I ever figure out where it had been taken?

"It's okay," I told Connor, reaching for his hand to thread our fingers together. His palm was calloused and warm, and my heart twisted when he pressed it hard against mine. "I won't deduct that many points."

"Oh, interesting." He kept ahold of my hand, but teasingly bumped my hip. "Are you calling this a *date*?"

"No." I hoped he couldn't see me blush. "Not when it's obviously a private astronomy lesson."

"Taught by whom?" Connor asked, his voice suggesting a smile tugging at his mouth.

I comically furrowed my brow. "You didn't coordinate with Nick?"

We both glanced back at the house; all the windows were dark, save for the dimmed kitchen lights.

"I took an astronomy class this spring," Connor said once we went back to staring at the sky. "It was a disaster."

"Really?" I asked. "Astronomy was known as one of the easiest electives at my school."

"Did you take it?"

I shook my head. "I couldn't get off the wait list."

"I hope you weren't too heartbroken."

"I'm almost finished piecing it back together."

Connor snorted and then wriggled out of my grip so he could wrap an arm around my shoulders. My stomach somersaulted as I shifted my weight from one foot to the other, aching to lean into him. He was a safe haven from the briny breeze—and, in the moment, from everything else.

"I can feel your heartbeat," I murmured after slipping my arms around him. "Hear it too."

He laughed. "What's it saying?"

I giggled. "It's telling me that—" I dropped off, suddenly distracted by a bright flash on the horizon, a swift glimmer of light. "Look, a shooting star!"

"Make a wish!" Connor's voice cracked. "Quick!"

I closed my eyes and mouthed something to myself.

"What was it?" he asked three heartbeats later.

Eyes still shut, I smirked. "Nice try."

"Come on, tell me."

"No," I said. "Because if I tell you…" I trailed off, caught by Connor's blue eyes within a single blink. His gaze was steady, but strong—I felt its pull deep in my chest. "If I tell you…" I swallowed hard. "It won't come true."

"Ah." He nodded then moved away only to move close again. I felt one hand go to my hip, and flushed when starlight swirled in his eyes. "I believe I've heard that before," he said as something in my chest sparked, hoping to catch fire. I felt his hand leave my side, only for goose bumps to bloom when he gently cupped my face. His thumbprint burned against my cheekbone. "Is it okay to wager a guess?"

"I suppose." I breathed with tight lungs, my dry eyes *screaming* at me to blink. There was no way Connor could be right or wrong, because right now I was so spellbound that I couldn't really remember my wish. Like the shooting star, it was already gone.

His lips slowly curved into a smile, but at the first crinkle of his eye, I tipped my mouth up to his.

Every nerve in my body reacted when he kissed me back, so hypnotically that light flickered behind my eyes. The breeze swept up around us, but we were impervious. If anything, the air between us *crackled*. Small shock waves ran through me, and I tried not to groan when he pushed up the hem of my sweatshirt, to rest his hands on my waist.

"You weren't supposed to tell me," he breathed when I moved to tangle my fingers in his thick hair. "I was supposed to guess."

"I couldn't wait any longer," I whispered, right before I realized that I *should've* waited longer. "Holy shit!" I pushed him away, maybe a little too suddenly. "Connor!"

He made an *oof* sound, like I'd knocked the wind out of him. "What?"

"We kissed," I pseudo-squeaked as he righted himself. "I kissed you, and I..." Chocolate, caramel, and all things tree nuts came to mind. "Your EpiPen." I took Connor's hand and tugged. "Where is your EpiPen?"

"Back in our room," Connor said with zero sense of urgency. He didn't even move; instead, he attempted to twirl me back into his arms. "But I don't need it, Olivia." He looked a bit sheepish. "It's okay to kiss someone tree nut–free after several hours."

"Oh." I said, exhaling in relief. "It's been several hours?"

"It was several hours when my alarm went off."

It was quiet for moment, all calm except for a wave crashing in the distance. "You didn't wake me up for the stars," I ventured as I spotted a second shooting star. "Did you?"

He sighed. "It was a happy coincidence."

"Mmm, I see." I looped my arms around his neck, heart swelling in my chest. "You couldn't wait until tomorrow."

You couldn't wait until tomorrow either, part of me expected him to say. *You couldn't wait until tomorrow* first.

Instead, he nodded—slowly, then very quickly. "Yes." He broke into an unashamed grin. "I couldn't wait until tomorrow."

"Because you've been waiting to kiss me?" I asked, hoping to milk it just a little bit.

He laughed and pressed his lips to my temple. "Yes," he repeated as a ripple went through me, his voice a whisper in my ear. "I've been waiting to kiss you."

I did not know what to do when the sun rose; I was vaguely aware of my Apple Watch buzzing on my wrist, but I only slipped deeper into dreamland. It was almost nine when I woke up for real, tucked into the top bunk. "Do you tuck Teddy in like this every night?" I remembered teasing Connor while he so chivalrously arranged my covers for me.

"Not quite," he'd replied. "He's much more particular."

Then he'd given me quite the good-night kiss, leaving both of us breathless for more.

Every moment of last night felt like a dream.

But I didn't know what we were supposed to do next. Walk into the kitchen for breakfast and announce that we were going to hang out more together?

I could hear Maisie's voice in my head. *You already* do *hang out a lot together.*

God, what was my dad going to think?

Connor was supposed to be strictly a nice young man.

A good kid.

I descended my ladder deep in thought and let out something akin to a *meow* at the bottom, caught off guard by Connor's awake presence in the room. "Hey," he said, fully dressed and texting on his bunk. "You sleep well?"

"You're awake," I observed.

"Yes."

"But you're *never* awake."

"False," he countered as I pictured him passed out, barely breathing in the bottom bunk. "I am never awake *first*." He smirked. "Today must be a fluke."

"Try a once-in-a-lifetime event," I quipped, then I turned to hunt for some clothes more acceptable than my silky pajamas. My heart flipped when Connor stood and spun me around for a kiss.

"Come to breakfast with me," he murmured afterward, breath warm on my lips. "I was thinking Waterside Market, in Vineyard Haven. You haven't been to VH yet, right?"

"You want to go out for breakfast?" I asked, but of course he did; the Carmichaels weren't his family, and he was on vacation.

He nodded. "Breakfast is almost always a high-stress time for me. I want to enjoy it for once." He paused. "I also want to give Ashley some space with her boys."

That made sense too.

"Okay," I said, pulse picking up—thrilled at the thought of being alone with Connor. "Yes, I'd love—"

"Olivia!" I heard someone emphatically knock on Summer Camp's door, and my sister's muffled voice. "Olivia, are you alive?"

"What is it, Maisie?" I called back.

"You need to hurry up! We're getting ready for the game, and Nana's also going to announce tonight's theme..."

Oh, right, I remembered. Last night at dinner, Peggy had casually mentioned another family activity today. And we were also going out to some type of themed dinner tonight, another Carmichael tradition.

I'll be right there! I tried to muster, then looked at Connor. He gave me a thumbs-up in understanding, but that didn't make me feel better.

"I actually have plans," I told Maisie, reaching for Connor's hand. He started shaking his head, but I squeezed his fingers. "Connor and I are grabbing breakfast in town."

"Well, you didn't need to drag *me* into it..." he whispered.

"There's nothing for you to be dragged into," I whispered back. Because attendance wasn't required, was it?

"Oh, okay," Maisie said, still out in the hall. "I'll let everyone know."

I grimaced, not loving the sound of that.

"Will you be at dinner, though?"

"Yes, of course," I said. "I wouldn't miss it."

"Promise?"

"*Promise*," I told her, and five seconds later, she retreated down the hall. Ten minutes after that, Connor and I left the house by way of our porch. Swede bounded up to us as we crossed the driveway, and when Connor opened the Jeep's passenger door for me, I had to stop my golden retriever from leaping into the car.

Nice try, buddy, I thought as I gave him three big pets goodbye.

Connor offered me his aux cord, and after DJing for a handful of songs, we cruised into Vineyard Haven. Like preppy Edgartown, there were countless cedar-shingled houses, but from the storefronts and people strolling the sidewalks, I could tell Vineyard Haven had its own vibe.

Eclectic, I thought. *Homey.*

Waterside Market was on Main Street, with a black-and-white awning and porch covered with wicker tables and chairs. There was not one empty seat, and the aroma of fresh coffee, blueberry pancakes, and bacon made my stomach rumble.

Thankfully, the line wasn't that long. There was more seating inside, a massive beverage case, and tables that showcased homemade chocolate chip cookies, baskets of fruit, and a selection of wine. Plus, shelves lined with jellies, jams, and hot sauce. Two fancy chalkboards flanked the front registers, one advertising breakfast and the other Waterside's signature sandwiches.

"You first," I told Connor when we hit the front of the line.

Smiling, he shook his head. "No, you first."

"I can't decide what to order." I bit my lip in consideration. "I'm torn between the Tex-Mex and flapjacks."

"Ah, the never-ending debate between sweet and savory," he said before shifting his gaze to the cashier. "We're going to share the Tex-Mex and flapjacks..." He glanced at me. "Chocolate chip?"

I nodded, my chest filling with warmth. I liked that he didn't think twice about sharing.

"And we'll have two cold brews, along with a Tractor Farmer's punch because that sounds *incredible*." He cleared his throat, then said in a serious, almost solemn tone: "I'm also allergic to tree nuts and shellfish."

"What was that voice?" I asked as our cashier input our order. "You sound like a doctor delivering bad news."

"Very funny." Connor rolled his eyes. "I always sound that way when I tell someone about my allergies. When I was little, I wanted people to pay attention and know I wasn't messing around." He shrugged. "It stuck."

"Have you ever had a serious allergic reaction?"

"No, which leads me to believe my doctor-delivering-bad-news voice is extremely effective."

I laughed, and after Connor insisted on paying, we took our iced coffees and managed to find an empty table on the porch. *Miss Lupo!* I thought I heard someone shout behind me, but nobody waved when I glanced over my shoulder.

"So..." Connor ventured a while later, in between bites of breakfast. I'd never eaten such light and fluffy pancakes, and the Tex-Mex *sauce*... "May I ask you something?"

I took a sip of his punch. It was sweet, but not too sweet. Refreshing. "Sure."

He opened his mouth, then closed it, then opened it again. "What made you change your mind about me?"

"Oh," I said, feeling my stomach stir. Chocolate chips and pico de gallo weren't a match made in heaven. "Well, I—"

"Don't get me wrong," Connor quickly added. "I'm happy—*really* happy—that you did change it, but..." The tips of his ears reddened. "You seemed pretty set on the Fourth and when you brought Maisie and Bryce as a buffer yesterday."

I grimaced. "You noticed that?"

He raised an eyebrow. "You're surprised?"

"No." I sighed. "No, of course not. It was pretty obvious..." I wanted to bite my nails, but instead I started to stir my straw around in my iced coffee. Was he actually going to make me admit it? "I like you, Connor, but I haven't liked anyone—or really, *let* myself like anyone—in a long time."

Maybe even ever.

"I don't totally have a handle on why," I thought aloud, then mused. "Sometimes it just feels like I've been too busy for a boyfriend." I bit my lip, wondering if that was true. It didn't seem like it. Because what was I so *busy* with? I'd taken the year off to work part-time and visit my grandmother; I didn't have a full college course load like my friends. I stopped fiddling with my straw to look at Connor. His eyebrows had furrowed, but more with interest than confusion. "Anyway." I smile-shrugged. "When Annie called me yesterday, she encouraged me to stop fighting it with you and have some fun. She said she once met someone on the island and had the time of her life."

"Your grandfather?"

"No." I shook my head. "She didn't give me any details, but no."

Though now that I was talking about it, I *was* starting to really wonder about the story there. Did her love interest live here? Or was he just here for the summer, like her?

"Annie lives at Elkins," Connor said gently. "Doesn't she?"

"Yes," I admitted, knowing it was finally time to open up to him about her. "But she doesn't live in independent living like your grandfather. She did when she and Pops first moved there, but after he passed away..." Something in my stomach started twisting itself into a knot. "It pretty much went all downhill from there."

"How so?"

I took a breath, then I told him about Annie's dementia. Her memory issues before the official diagnosis, moving from her apartment to Elkins' assisted living unit, her tendency to wander off, sustaining some scary falls, moving again to Finlay House, and her terrible sundown episodes. "She's also forgetting who I am," I said. "No matter how often I visit. Sometimes I'm Olivia, but more and more often, I'm someone else."

"I'm so sorry, Olivia," Connor said. "I can't imagine how hard that must be." He hesitated. "It sounds like you two are really close."

"Annie has always, always been there for me," I responded. "She really stepped up and helped my dad raise me after my mom died." I didn't wait for a response, not wanting to veer into that right now. "She knows me better than anyone else." I took a deep breath. "And I thought I knew everything about her too, but her secret connection to this island is throwing me off a little."

Connor raised an eyebrow. "She's never talked about Martha's Vineyard?"

I shook my head. "Not the way she's talked about her other travels."

"Hmm." He rubbed the back of his neck. "Ashley's been

dealing with something similar," he said after several seconds. "That's where she's been this summer. Her husband's grandfather has Alzheimer's, and Mike's been managing his care for years. I don't know why his parents never stepped up, but it's all Mike." He paused. "It apparently took a lot to get his grandfather into a memory care facility, and he's declining quickly. Mike's grandmother isn't handling it well either. Ashley doesn't think she should live alone anymore, but she refuses to move in with them."

"That's..." I took a breath, not having the words. Well, I did—terrible, awful, unbearable, and cruel. Dementia and Alzheimer's disease were both cruel to the person suffering and devastating to their loving families.

"I thought that was you two!" Someone thankfully stopped my thoughts from spiraling, and I turned in my seat to see Christian Fox and another familiar-looking old man. Andrew, his older brother. I remembered him mostly sitting next to an easel at the Foxes' Fourth party.

Swiftly and suddenly, I felt the tug of a thread in the back of my head.

What *had* he been painting?

And how long—

"Good morning, Mr. Fox," Connor said, rising from his chair and extending his hand. "You here for breakfast?"

"We just finished up." Christian chuckled as they shook hands. "Please call me Christian. Our father was Mr. Fox, even to us occasionally." He glanced at Andrew, who'd seemingly missed the inside joke, focused on something else.

"Meredith has told me about you," he said to me, his blue eyes bright but a little intimidating, "Forgive me for being remiss, but which one of Topper and Peggy's children do you belong to?"

In other words: *How are you related to the Carmichaels?*

"Erica is my stepmother," I said politely. "This is my first time on the Vineyard."

Oh, how wonderful! I expected him to say, but instead, I caught him imperceptibly elbow Christian, who nudged him back. The motion turned them from old men into young brothers.

What is going on? I wondered.

"We should head out," Christian said. "We're due to meet our daughters for a match."

"Tennis?" Connor asked.

"That's a generous way to phrase it," Andrew said with a wink. "It was lovely meeting you, Olivia. Feel free to come to the Farm anytime." He looked at Connor. "A little birdie told me we'll be seeing you tonight?"

Tonight?

Connor nodded. "I volunteered to bring s'mores supplies."

Andrew tipped an invisible hat. "Good man."

"You're hanging out with Meredith tonight?" I asked once the Fox brothers had taken off for the tennis courts.

"Yeah," Connor said. "I figured since you guys have your dinner..."

Right, I remembered. We had reservations at a restaurant called Alchemy and would arrive in full Carmichael costume. Maisie had texted me earlier from our dad's phone to say that the theme was "Historical Figures."

It was a little more dignified than the "barnyard" theme Nick had been teasing.

"But that's later." Connor waved his hand. "What matters is *now*."

"Now?" I casually raised an eyebrow, but I felt my pulse quicken.

"Do you have your list of Annie's hot spots?" he asked. "We can pick our next place."

Chilmark, I immediately thought of the blue-gray photo with tiny cottages and big nets and faded red buoys. *The Menemsha fishing village.*

I gave him a look. "You sure you want to do this with me?"

"Of course." Connor pulled off a goofy shrug. "I'm on a mandatory vacation. What else do I have to do?" I felt my heart spin when his lips spread into a slow smile. "And there's no one I'd rather spend my time off with than you."

He truly is fearless, I thought. *Fearlessly up-front.*

Feeling myself blush, I glanced around at Waterside's crowded porch before leaning across our table and raising my hand as if I were going to whisper a secret in his ear.

But instead, I used it to cover our faces so no one would see us kiss.

SEVENTEEN

Everyone wanted to ride to dinner in Theodore Roosevelt's blue Bronco. Nick was wearing a thrifted three-piece tweed suit with a red tie but had given his look a nineteenth-century spin by adding TR's famous glasses. They had two lenses, but they reminded me of a monocle because they didn't have arms that extended behind the ears. "The style is called *pince-nez*," Nick—who'd also gelled his hair and shaved his stubble so that he had the shadow of a mustache—told Maisie. She too had gone full Americana as Rosie the Riveter, wearing her favorite denim jumpsuit (ICON was tastefully bedazzled on the back) with her beloved black patent leather Doc Martens. Her hair was tied up in one of Peggy's red polka-dot cloth napkins.

"What's so special about Nick's car?" Luke-masquerading-as-Albert-Einstein asked. His white lab coat and wacky wig were hilarious, but his mustache kept falling off. "I have the better playlist!"

"Bryce and I will go with you, Luke," Lilly Pulitzer—I mean, *Erica*—said. Her brown hair was up in a bouffant, and her green-and-white shift dress was vintage. I thought her hoop earrings and bright pink lipstick were a nice touch.

Meanwhile, my brother had dressed up as Davy Crockett. I couldn't say his coonskin cap—I had no idea where he'd gotten it—was very cohesive with Erica's Palm Beach uniform.

My dad offered to drive everyone who couldn't fit in Nick's and Luke's cars; I rode squashed between Teddy and Finn in the backseat. They were both in togas, while I was trying to pull off Princess Diana's iconic running-errands outfit. Black spandex, white midcalf socks with sneakers, and Charlie's oversized HARVARD MEDICAL SCHOOL sweatshirt. He'd also let me borrow his black Ray-Bans, and I'd slipped on Annie's amazing sapphire-and-diamond ring. "You look incredible, Olivia," Sage/Amelia Earhart said, and I'd grinned.

Though I admittedly felt underdressed for dinner.

Once we rolled into Edgartown, our Expedition circled for a while. Cars not only lined Main Street but also all its offshoots. "*How* did he find something?" my dad said, incredulous, when we spotted Nick and everyone in his car strolling along town's brick sidewalks.

"Connections," Ashley said. "The Foxes have a reserved parking spot behind the Old Whaling Church. He charmed its location out of Andrew one night."

"Why am I not surprised?" My dad chuckled as my mind drifted to the Foxes, and Connor, who had driven over to Paqua Farm for dinner earlier. How much fun was he having?

We scooped up a spot by Espresso Love about ten minutes later. It was only yards from a cedar-shingled building with a white clapboard storefront and double-decker porch. Patriotic bunting hung from the second floor's white railing, and ALCHEMY was painted across the front windows in gold script. *Three… two…* I waited for everyone to be stunned when we walked through the front door. *One…*

The hostess didn't bat an eye. "Carmichael?" she confirmed, and after Ashley smiled and nodded, she gestured to the stairs. "The rest of your party's up on the side balcony."

I was keenly aware of the restaurant's other patrons either raising their eyebrows while sipping their cocktails or setting down utensils to applaud when we walked by—something told me they were somehow in on the joke—so I was relieved to discover our table was sequestered from the rest of the restaurant. It ran the length of the balcony, whose twinkly lights made everything cozier. "Perfect for people watching…" Beth joked when my dad commented on the view.

"Good evening, everyone!" Our waiter appeared seconds after I opened my menu. He looked dapper, as Annie would say, in a white button-down, navy-blue vest, and a cream-and-navy striped tie. "I'm Dylan, and I'll be taking care of you tonight." He paused. "Are we celebrating something special?"

Nobody answered at first, but then I heard none other than Erica clear her throat. "No, Dylan," she said. "Whyever would you think that?"

The table burst into laughter. "That was good, Erica," Jay said, wiping his eyes. Topper nodded in agreement. "Really, really good."

Erica smiled, and I noticed her sit up a little straighter in her seat.

I could almost hear Annie's voice in my ear: *She makes a wonderful Lilly, doesn't she?*

Yes, I thought, feeling a pang of something like pride. *She does.*

Alchemy didn't leave us wanting for dessert, but Teddy and Nick threatened to mutiny if we didn't swing by Mad Martha's before driving home. And me, admittedly. My stomach rumbled in agreement, suddenly craving two scoops in a waffle cone.

Would you like anything from MM's? I texted Connor as we weaved through people on the sidewalk. My heart skipped at the thought of seeing him later.

Gray dots popped up in our chat, but before Connor's response appeared, I felt a familiar hand on my shoulder. My dad. "You have a minute to talk?" he asked, which had always been his way of saying, *We need to talk.*

"Yes." I quickly locked my phone. "What's up?"

"Maisie told me you went out to breakfast with Connor today? That's why you weren't at the house this morning?"

I grimaced, already feeling guilty enough. When Connor

and I'd gotten back from Vineyard Haven, Bryce and Maisie had quite literally dragged me into the spacious garage, where twelve gingerbread houses were on exhibit. "Christmas in July," Maisie explained as I admired the twins' creation. Instead of a pitched roof, it had a flat one with gumdrop solar panels.

"You should've been there, Olivia," Bryce said. "Nick and Charlie squirted frosting at each other, and Aunt Beth kept licking the candy canes." He giggled. "Swede stole one of the gingerbread men…"

"I'm sorry," I told my dad weakly. We were standing outside a sophisticated boutique, having fallen behind our fellow historical figures. "I didn't realize it was mandatory. Connor and I—"

"Seem as thick as thieves lately," my dad noted, then tilted his head. "Anything I should know about there?"

I felt my cheeks warm. "He's helping me retrace Annie's steps." I quickly told him about discovering the sketches and photos. "I want to visit each place she did while she was here."

My dad's eyebrows furrowed a little, intrigued. I took that to mean he had never seen her mementos. "Okay, so she *did* come here with Kathy Ryan," he said. "Long ago."

"No, I don't think so." I shook my head. "It seems like she was here with a boyfriend."

His intrigue shifted to confusion. "A boyfriend?"

I shrugged. "Maisie spotted this guy in one of her Polaroids, and when I called Annie yesterday, she told me that a summer romance—"

My dad snapped his fingers. "I knew it," he said, smirking a little. "There *is* something going on with Connor."

I gave him a look. "That's your key takeaway? Connor and me? You aren't curious about Annie's past here?"

"Of course I am," he said. "She's my mother, but I'm your father. Having a handle on my daughter's dating life is a higher priority for me."

"I'm not *dating* Connor," I mumbled as I folded my arms over my chest, as if to calm the butterflies fluttering inside. "We're having fun."

With the exception of my prom date, I'd never introduced a guy to my dad. Only Erica had casually met them; she was polite, but I could tell she wasn't very impressed.

My dad laughed. "Well, I hate to break it to you, Liv, but I don't see much of a difference." He slipped his arm around my shoulders. "Either way, we need to find you some new sleeping accommodations."

I didn't object. Part of me knew that was coming.

"Tell me more about these watercolors," he said once we started up the sidewalk again. "Because I don't think I've ever seen your grandmother pick up a paintbrush."

"I know," I said, heart racing. "Which makes me think she isn't the artist."

Connor didn't get home until after I'd packed up all my stuff and attempted to surreptitiously drag it to the other side of the house, to a cozy reading room near the bunk room. It had a comfortable daybed, but Ashley—finished putting her boys to bed—peeked in and told me there was an air mattress and linens in the back of the closet.

"Thanks for the tip," I said, and I considered asking her about her father-in-law's memory battle, but I couldn't find the words. And maybe I wasn't supposed to know. Connor made it sound pretty private.

I hummed as I unzipped my suitcase, then I organized my other belongings. I had somehow collected so much stuff over the last week that I'd borrowed the yellow duffel bag I'd found under Summer Camp's bunkbed. *Connor stole it from his brother*, I surmised, remembering the two of us shooting the shit about *The Parent Trap*. "My mom bought Liam a yellow duffel bag when he was nervous for his first sleepover," he'd said, "to give him some Hallie Parker chutzpah..."

Connor's cup runneth over with chutzpah, I thought, biting back my smile. It was stupid how excited I was to see him. Be back soon, he'd texted fifteen minutes ago. Can't wait for my midnight snack!

After changing into my pajamas and a sweater, I grabbed his generous scoop of Menemsha Mint Oreo from the freezer and waited for him on Summer Camp's little porch. The air was cool and comfortably damp, but I felt beads of sweat on the back of my neck.

Especially when a pair of headlights appeared in the darkness.

My pulse leaped when his Jeep's door popped open, and it leaped again when it slammed shut. "Lady Spencer!" Connor softly called upon spotting me in the porch light's glow. "How was dinner?"

I opened my mouth but had no idea what I said. The world blurred and went to white noise; all I could focus on was Connor's breeze-blown hair, blue eyes, and grin. He played up the Princess Diana bit by kissing my hand before tugging me into a warm hug. A wave of campfire, citronella, and the sea air wrapped around me. It smelled like an incredible night.

I pulled out of the embrace to smile and loop my arms around his neck. "Dinner was delicious," I said. "And really fun."

"I'm so glad," Connor said, hands resting on my waist. Even through my sweater, my body hummed from his touch. "I had fun tonight too."

"Good," I murmured, and then we smiled at each other for half a heartbeat before I rose up on my tiptoes and kissed him. He tasted like s'mores and strawberry rhubarb pie, and I couldn't get enough of it. We kissed fast and furiously, but my breath didn't catch until his tongue slowly started running along my lower lip.

I broke away to breathe, only to fall a hundred stories into his gaze. He made me feel safe but also undeniably starry-eyed. It was almost unsettling, and I was suddenly grateful to my dad for insisting I sleep elsewhere. Just thinking about saying good night to Connor made me ache, but I was also relieved I had a space of my own to retreat to later.

"Do you want to go for a walk?" he asked.

Yes, I thought, but heard myself say, "Your ice cream's going to melt."

"That's okay," he said. "I like milkshakes."

"Nice try." I smirked. "Melted ice cream is *not* a milkshake."

"Have you been talking to Mads?" Connor jibed, but he caught my drift. He grabbed his to-go cup and popped off its plastic lid once he'd gotten cozy on the couch. I needed no invitation before snuggling into his side.

"My dad knows about us," I said after he offered me a bite of ice cream. "He knows we're..." I hesitated. "Having fun."

"Okay, cool," Connor said, seemingly unfazed. "Should I prepare myself for a talk?"

I giggled. "That's not really his style."

Because, as far as I knew, it wasn't.

"Got it." Connor nodded. "But just so you know, I am excellent at those talks."

"Oh, yeah? You have references?"

He laughed, and the sheer delight in it made me smile and my heart spin around in my chest. I wasn't sure I'd ever felt a glow like this before, or at least not in a very long time.

Don't let it worry you, I told myself. *You might be getting swept up, but you're not getting swept away.*

EIGHTEEN

The next morning, Connor and I left the house after breakfast. "Where are you two headed?" my dad asked, and in response, I showed him Annie's watercolor of the Aquinnah Cliffs. He carefully studied it, the expression on his face both mesmerized and puzzled. Captivated by the small painting's intricate details but probably confused why Annie never displayed it for all to see. It was gorgeous.

He handed the watercolor back to me and smiled.

Do you want to come? I almost asked, but I knew he and Erica had plans to take the twins on a boat ride around Edgartown Harbor with Ashley and the boys.

The sky was so blue and the sun burned so bright that not even Connor's roofless Jeep stopped us from sweating on the way to the western end of the island. "Looks like we aren't the only great minds," Connor commented while we searched for a parking spot. There seemed to be tourists everywhere. A family of five bobbed in bucket hats toward the cliffs' historic brick lighthouse. Gay Head Light, I'd learned on Wikipedia. Back in the nineteenth and twentieth centuries, Aquinnah had apparently been known as "Gay Head."

I could imagine all the jokes.

Connor maneuvered his Jeep in between a dusty Subaru Crosstrek and a black G-Wagon, the spacing between the cars so tight that I had to leap down through the trunk. "Nine-point-eight," Connor quipped after offering me his hand to ensure I stuck my landing. Smiling, I laced our fingers together, and we set off for the iconic overlook.

Nearby, there were a series of small, cedar-shingled souvenir and snack shops. It hadn't hit me how thirsty I was until I spotted a sign for freshly squeezed lemonade. Suddenly, I felt *parched*. "Should we get a roadie?" I pointed out the sign to Connor. The line wasn't that long.

Ten minutes later, we climbed the overlook's steps with refreshing drinks in hand. Sweat slipped down my back, but the lemonade packed a punch, its icy sweetness soon spinning through my veins. My body felt lighter, my head cooler. I started sucking it down so quickly that I didn't notice one of the overlook's warped steps. "Whoa there!" Connor's arm slid around my waist before I could totally trip. My heart skipped as he raised a comically inquisitive eyebrow. "Do I need to confiscate that drink?"

I laughed. "Maybe."

Fellow tourists greeted us up on the wide plank observation deck, their phones raised to snap pictures while a few children looked through mega binoculars. My pulse began to pound once Connor and I weaved our way toward the edge, and not solely because his hand rested on the small of my back, gently guiding me. The Aquinnah Cliffs were *breathtaking*, even more beautiful in person than in Annie's painting. The bluffs practically rolled into the glimmering ocean, burnt orange and red clay streaks shining bright against the blue sky backdrop and surrounding tall green grass and yellow flowers in full bloom. "Wow," I whispered.

"Wow," Connor concurred, then motioned for me to give him my phone. "Let's get this photo shoot started..."

"How do they look?" I asked afterward. He'd taken a burst, of course, even crouching down for a couple shots.

"Eh." He shrugged. "Maybe one or two good ones."

I rolled my eyes, knowing he was mocking me. "Hopefully there are one or two good ones," I'd said at the Whaling Church, his reply making me now blush instead of flush.

You know you're gorgeous, right?

Now, someone tapped his shoulder. A petite woman in a sun visor and sunglasses with a pair of binoculars around her neck. "Would you like me to take a picture of you two?"

"That would be great!" Connor smiled. "It saves us a selfie."

She gestured for him to hand over his phone. We moved to stand side by side by the cliff's edge, Connor wrapping his arm around my shoulders. His skin nearly scorched mine, but I didn't hesitate before leaning into him. "Say cheese!" our photographer shouted.

We indulged her, kind of. "Provolone!" I called at the same time Connor went, "Mozzarella!"

We jolted out of our pose, eyes locking as if to say, *What was that?*

"It's from when I was a kid," Connor said. "I wanted to make my mom laugh. After Liam was born, she was sad for a while." He half-smiled. "What about you?"

"Annie," I said. She'd later introduced me to fancy cheese plates.

And you should call her today, I told myself.

"Eh, not great, kids..." the paparazzo told us. "Look at the camera next time!"

Connor gave her an affirmative thumbs-up, and I reached up to take his hand, threading our fingers together. Out of the corner of my eye, I caught his lips twitch up before spreading into a smile.

We gave *say cheese* everything we had.

"Smoked Gouda!" I shouted as Connor went, "Wisconsin cheddar!"

And then we started laughing like we were the funniest people on the island.

~

There were a handful of cars in the driveway when we got back, but the house was empty, save for the dogs sprawled out on the cool kitchen floor. "They're all at the beach, right?" I asked Swede as I gave him some belly rubs.

His response was a huge yawn.

Sure enough, Connor and I checked the dock to find the Boston Whaler gone. "Crap," I said after squinting to see it anchored on the far side of Oyster Pond. "How are we going to get over there now?"

The obvious answer was to text Nick and ask if he could putter back and get us, but I didn't want to interrupt his Sunday soaking up the sun. Should we just set up camp on the small beach here?

"I've got it," Connor said. "Let's get our stuff!"

We raced back to the house and split up once inside, Connor retreating to Summer Camp and me hurrying upstairs to my new room. I changed into a bikini and threw on a crocheted cover-up before grabbing my beach tote. On my way back through the kitchen, I grabbed water bottles from the fridge and some fruit salad left over from breakfast. I also filled a Ziploc bag with Sage's homemade granola. It was addicting.

Connor beat me back to the dock, now in blue swim trunks and a white Notre Dame T-shirt. He hadn't rubbed all the sunscreen in on his face, seemingly too eager to tug a green canoe and pair of oars out of the small boathouse. "Oh my god," I said. "I haven't canoed since camp."

Just short of a decade ago.

"That makes two of us," he said as my stomach started swishing with excitement. "But I think I remember how..."

Instead of setting off from the dock, we positioned the canoe on the beach, in Oyster Pond's shallows. I loaded our beach bags and towels, then I climbed while Connor held the canoe steady. We'd decided I would sit in the front and he'd be in the back. One thing I remembered from Camp Skytop was that the rear rower did most of the steering. While my sense of direction was solid, Connor was definitely stronger than me.

"Ready?" I asked even though our canoe was still ashore; Connor would push it into the water before jumping in with me.

"Almost," he answered, then dug through his backpack and pulled out a small Bluetooth speaker. "We need the right playlist…"

I was impressed when George Ezra started crooning through the speaker.

Connor raised an eyebrow. "Acceptable?"

I grinned. "Acceptable."

After pushing in our canoe, Connor dashed through the water to swiftly swing himself up over the side. The canoe rocked only once, a graceful maneuver. We both started paddling. It took a few beats, but we found ourselves in sync. "And we're off!"

The water was placid—not even a hint of a breeze. There was only one speedboat boat out—towing a water-skier—plus a couple kayaks and paddleboards. The sun had also still not let up from this morning, so all too soon I was sticky with sweat. I glanced over my shoulder to see Connor lean over to dip his hand in the water before running it through his hair for some relief.

We paddled and paddled, eventually putting the Carmichaels' house in our rearview mirror, but I noticed our speed flagging when we were halfway across the pond. "Is it just me..." I said over our music. "Or are we slowing down?"

"Not just you." Connor stopped paddling, and I followed suit. "Rowing is becoming more intense too, which is weird. The pond is like glass." He paused. "Please don't take this the wrong way, but are you actually paddling?"

I spun around in my seat. "Did you really just ask me that? You think I'm—" I dropped off, a sudden shiver ran through me. It took a second to register that it had stemmed from my feet, because what felt like a lot like water was tickling my toes.

My pulse started pounding. Had our Poland Spring bottles leaked? We hadn't even opened them yet...

"Shit," I heard Connor breathe. "*Shit*—Olivia, I think the canoe's leaking. Look at the floor."

I dared myself to glance down, only to see rivulets of water running across the canoe's belly. The bottom of my tote bag was already soaked through. How much water could we take on before trouble really hit us?

I cursed myself when I realized we didn't have life vests. *How* had Connor and I forgotten life vests? Especially after I'd gotten mixed up in the Jaws Bridge channel!

"Let's start paddling back to the house," Connor said after I informed him that both of us were spectacular idiots. "It looks farther than it is. We can make it."

"What if we don't?" I asked.

"Then we'll call for help."

"Our phones don't get service," I reminded him. The only reason we could listen to Spotify was because Connor downloaded his playlists.

"I meant with our lungs." Connor poised his oar. "Ready?"

We may have rowed thirty yards, or maybe fifteen. The house still looked so far, and now that we were aware the canoe was taking on water, it was *really* taking on water. My oar kept slipping in my slick hands, blood thumping wildly in my ears. *Come on*, I thought, trying not to panic. *Come on, come on, come on—*

My pulse spiked, then it soared when I heard the putter of an engine. "Is everything okay?" I turned to see Charlie at the bow of the Carmichaels' Boston Whaler and Luke at the wheel. Dripping wet, Sage stood next to him, cradling her water skis. "When we spotted you guys earlier, it looked like you were heading for the beach."

"We were." Connor's voice was hoarse. "But our ride's about to crap out."

"We have a leak," I translated, and from there, no time was wasted. The water was now up to our ankles, making the canoe tougher to row, but Luke was able to maneuver the Whaler so we could easily hand Charlie our stuff before bailing.

"You're not wearing any life vests," he commented once our heart rates had returned to normal. "*Where* are your life vests?"

Our sheepish silence said everything.

Luke shook his head. "Connor, you're a childcare professional."

Connor, already bright red, went even redder.

Sage, wearing a life vest, fake-coughed. "And Olivia, you're an Eldest Daughter!"

Point taken, but I let a smile slip out, the plethora of TikToks, Reels, and memes coming to mind. Eldest Daughters could rule the world, competent in all areas of life.

"Well, let this be a lesson learned," Charlie said with an air of finality, then he flicked his eyes to his husband. They quickly warmed. "To the beach, Captain."

Luke saluted him. "Aye-aye, C."

Must we? I thought, embarrassment now seeping in. Someone had to tell Topper and Peggy that their old canoe was foundering in the middle of Oyster Pond.

I hoped they hadn't hung on to it for all these years for sentimental reasons.

"I'll explain everything to the Carmichaels," Connor whispered in my ear after Luke cranked up the Whaler. "It was my idea."

"And I thought it was a good one," I whispered back. "We'll explain together."

Then I took his hand and squeezed it as we sped toward the shore.

Charlie recruited his dad and Nick to rescue the canoe on their grandparents' behalf, and Nick was surprisingly pretty pissed about it. "Don't give it another thought," Topper told Connor and me once we came clean. "That leak has been there for years, and it's our fault for not patching it." He shook his head. "I've just never been able to tell where the damn thing is!"

"We're so glad you're both safe," Peggy said, fanning herself with this month's issue of *Vanity Fair*. "You *did* have life vests, right?"

I gritted my teeth, never wanting to hear the word *life vest* again, but my family had other ideas. Maisie and Bryce ran up to me after I'd showered and changed for dinner, grinning mischievously. "What's that?" I asked, noticing that Maisie had something hidden behind her back.

"Dad says you have to wear this!" Bryce was giddy when our sister revealed a lime green life vest. "Until you go to sleep tonight!"

Touché, Christopher, I thought but couldn't help but be a little amused. "This doesn't match my outfit at all," I stage-grumbled as I slipped on the bulky vest and zipped it up before adjusting its straps. The twins couldn't stop laughing.

"Connor has one too," Bryce said. "It's pink and has ruffles."

I snorted. "He's hilarious, our father!"

At least he wasn't reading Connor the riot act for putting my safety at risk.

But did I maybe want him to?

Before dinner hit the grill, we all said goodbye to Luke and Charlie, who were catching a late-afternoon boat back to the mainland. Agent Morrissey needed to work this week, but they would be back next weekend for Topper and Peggy's big anniversary dinner.

The house quieted not long after dessert. "I'll be back in a bit," Connor told me while I settled in with everyone for a movie. "I really owe Liam a FaceTime..."

Nick randomly suggested the original *Mulan* and was astounded that Maisie and Bryce had never seen it. I, on the other hand, still had the soundtrack memorized, so after the first twenty minutes, I slipped away to grab my iPad.

I wanted to look at the photos I'd taken for Annie's book, maybe even experiment with some Shutterfly book templates. "Oh," I said when I turned the reading room's doorknob to unexpectedly find Erica sitting on the daybed. Her eyes snapped up from the big book on her lap. "Hi..."

"Hi." Erica got straight to the point. "I'm hiding from my sister."

"Okay." I wanted to ask, *You couldn't hide in your own room?*

"I'm sorry," she added. "I know this is your space, but our room is obvious and she knows all my other spots." She tucked a pencil behind her ear. "She won't think to look here."

"Mmm," was all I said, then I nodded at her reading material. A light green album with a creamy white pages. "Is that the scrapbook?"

"Yes, I'm supposed to be hard at work on it."

I raised an eyebrow. "Supposed to be?"

Erica sighed. "Well, with squeezing in work and Beth hounding me to hurry up on this, it's been difficult to really dig in." She tapped her pencil. "I'm sketching out some ideas, though."

My stepmother was a meticulous planner; in all the years she'd been compiling scrapbooks, she'd never been one to glue down a photo without considering the rest of the page.

"What brings you here?" she asked.

"I sleep here," I deadpanned.

She rolled her eyes, but I could tell she was amused. "I thought you would be spending time with Connor."

"He's FaceTiming with his brother," I said. "We'll"—I hesitated, then used her words—"spend time together later."

There was a beat of silence. Was "spending time together" some type of euphemism? It came off so parental, but "hanging out together" didn't sound right either. Connor and I weren't going to talk about next-to-nothing before hooking up.

"I can leave if you would like," Erica offered before I could reflect too much. She closed the scrapbook. "Hide-and-seek aside, this is your personal space—"

"No, that's alright." I shook my head. "I just need my iPad to go through some photos I took today." I took a few steps over to where it sat charging on the little room's end table, figuring I'd trek across the house to Summer Camp's porch.

Then I changed my mind and asked Erica if she could scoot over a bit on the daybed. "Oh, sure." I caught the surprise in her voice. "Of course."

"Thanks," I said, and for the next half hour, we worked side by side in silence. She didn't peek at the humble beginnings of my Shutterfly project, and I didn't ask about the grand vision for her assigned scrapbook pages.

But still, it was nice.

NINETEEN

The next couple days passed in the blink of an eye. Sunday's scorching temperatures had burned off, and a light breeze blew through the air as Connor and I took an early-morning jog on Monday. I teased him for his incessant yawning, but I suspected it was all for show. He'd brought his lacrosse stick and only dropped the ball he cradled once.

Just because I'd jokingly elbowed him.

We visited three more places on Annie's list, this time with Maisie and Bryce in tow. "Thanks, Liv," my dad had said. "Erica and I could use some time together."

Yeah, I thought. *Some time away from her family…*

"You said you were sent this set for *free*?" I'd heard Peggy say when Erica set up an extremely aesthetic game of Mahjong on the deck yesterday. It was a lot of fun once you grasped the rules. "It looks very expensive."

"Did you volunteer to post it?" Topper asked. "In exchange for the game?"

"No, Dad," Erica answered. "After I hosted a Mahjong night

with my friends, the company reached out to me about a brand partnership."

"Oh," her mom said. "They really paid you?"

Ashley then intervened, as if sensing her aunt was going to lose it. That's when it sort of struck me: Erica had spent so much time with Annie and Pops, and I couldn't remember her getting frustrated once. Maybe over a couple little things, but that was it.

Was it because Annie understood her career? And Pops tried his best to? And they both cheered her on, no matter what?

I suddenly wondered if Erica missed my grandmother as much as I did, if she was just trying to stay strong for the twins.

And maybe for me.

Anyway, while she and my dad drove up island for a day alone, Connor ran Maisie and Bryce wild in Oak Bluffs' sprawling green Ocean Park. They dodged people spread out on picnic blankets, curved around fountains, and nearly trampled a few flowerbeds—all the while tossing a Frisbee back and forth. He really was good with kids.

Whining, Swede strained at his leash. "Sorry, dude," I said, gesturing to some magenta flowers. "I just don't think that hibiscus bush is safe if you're on the prowl…"

"Can we go back to Nancy's?" Bryce asked after I'd taken a picture of him and Maisie in front of the park's big Victorian gazebo, to match Annie's Polaroid. I wasn't Annie's only grandchild, after all. "Those hot dogs were *awesome*."

Connor caught my eye, his gaze glinting in the sunlight. "We can..." he started.

"But that means we can't get cheeseburgers," I finished.

"Cheeseburgers?" the twins burst out. They loved hot dogs, but burgers held a bigger place in their hearts.

"Yes." I nodded. "Nick told me about a place."

If there was one person who knew more about casual Martha's Vineyard cuisine than Teddy, it was Nick.

"To the Lookout!" Connor cheered.

"To the Lookout!" we echoed.

Swede even barked in agreement.

I hoped they allowed dogs.

Tuesday found us exploring the popular Martha's Vineyard Museum (not on Annie's list, but a Teddy recommendation) and then the Grange Hall in West Tisbury. Built in 1859, it was the original home of the island's agricultural society and its annual fair. I had never seen such a grand barn, and I felt like I'd stepped back in time. The whole drive I wondered if Annie's tractor photo had been taken there. The context didn't make a lot of sense—her sipping wine in her tennis whites—but maybe the hall had hosted a party of some sort? I'd read online that they could host weddings.

Annie's rendering of the Grange Hall was neither a painting

nor photo; instead, it was an intricate ink sketch. In both the drawing and real life, it looked more like a Victorian cottage than the quintessential red barn—cedar-shingled with an angled roof, wide front porch, and white fretwork details at the top of the porch columns and eaves. "This is incredible," Connor commented, and while I nodded, I couldn't really focus on the hall. Of course there was no John Deere tractor, but even the topography didn't seem to be the same. There were no sandy dirt trails, no car-worn grass, and no distinctly wind-whipped trees. *How am I going to find this place?* I wondered, feeling a twinge. By visiting every single farm on the island?

Why hadn't Annie included the location in her caption? "Summer Camp" told me absolutely nothing.

"You're very quiet," Connor observed on the way home. He had one hand on the steering wheel and the other on my knee. Every few heartbeats, I had to remind myself to breathe. I usually liked his easy affection, but right now it felt a little much. "Everything okay?"

"Uh-huh." I took his hand off my leg and lazily threaded our fingers together. "I just need to call Annie when we get back. It's been a while."

Connor squeezed my fingers. "You can use my humble abode," he said. "If you want some privacy."

I smiled at him. I had discovered the walls of my little reading room were thin; I heard every step taken in the hallway, along with every faucet turning in the bathroom across the way.

I did call Annie not long after we got home and was still thinking about the call the next day, during an afternoon playing "musical board games." Scrabble, Monopoly, Clue, chess, and Chutes and Ladders were set up in the living room, and after playing one game for ten minutes, Peggy instructed us to switch to someone else's seat at another game. I'd just abandoned Colonel Mustard to take up my dad's Scrabble letters. He had four E's.

As I contemplated my next word, I thought back to what she'd said. "What did you say your name was again?" she asked mid-conversation. I'd been telling her about lunch at the Lookout Tavern. Bryce had chugged a glass of milk after dumping Tabasco on his burger.

"Olivia," I said. "It's Olivia."

"Oh, how pretty," she said dreamily. "My gr—and—daugh—ter's name is O—wiv—ia."

Phone pressed against my ear, I closed my eyes. Hearing Annie trip over her words wasn't new, but she'd never fumbled my name before.

I told myself that my grandmother was just exhausted. Tara had mentioned Annie hadn't slept well the past few nights. Then she insisted on getting up at 6:00 a.m.

"Your turn, Olivia," someone said, and I blinked to make eye contact with Ashley. She smiled gently at me from across the table, and I noticed she had just spelled out "bisque" on the board. I glanced down at my letters, having nothing prepared.

"Where is that SAT vocabulary, Miss Lupo?" Beth teased, but when I managed to use two of my dad's stockpiled e's to form "exuberant," stealing the lead, she excused herself to refill her iced tea.

"My mother can certainly dish it out," Ashley commented when it was just us, "but she can't always take it." She laughed as she jotted down my triple-word-score points. I love *exuberant.* It's what my grandfather-in-law always called Teddy."

I shifted in my seat, "grandfather-in-law" ringing a bell loud and clear. The whole reason Connor was here this summer was because Ashley was helping her husband care for his Alzheimer's-ridden grandfather. Did she know about Annie? Had Erica told her? They seemed pretty close.

"Exuberant definitely sounds like Teddy," I tried to smile, then snuck in, "My grandmother has called Maisie *spirited* ever since the twins were born. Bryce is *lively.*" I shrugged. "I guess there's a distinction."

Ashley's nod was thoughtful. "And what about you? How does she describe her eldest granddaughter?"

"A snot," I said before I could stop myself, eyes welling up. "She called me a snot."

Yesterday, I'd hung up with less tact than usual. Bryce had started knocking on the door, asking me to play croquet with everyone, and as awful as it sounded, I found myself itching to end the call. And it must've been obvious. "You're such a little snot, Ophelia," Annie had said, disdain in her voice. "Wanting to say goodbye as soon as you have something better to do."

"Well," Ashley said after I told her. "Technically, she called Ophelia a snot, not you." She gave me a sympathetic look, one that signaled she was in the know about Annie. "You know that woman calling you a snot is not your grandmother, right? It's the disease?"

"Yeah." I tried to blink away my hot tears. "I do, of course I do, but…" A lump rose in my throat. "Sometimes telling myself that doesn't help."

"I know." Ashley reached across the table to squeeze my hand. "Believe me, I know." Her voice dipped to a whisper. "I would give almost anything to hear Ed call Teddy exuberant again." She smiled faintly. "And Finn noble."

We sat there in silence together, until Beth returned with a fresh pitcher of iced tea. "Alright, alright, alright," she said in a McConaughey drawl. It made me smile a bit. "You ladies better buckle up for a dramatic comeback…"

~

As much as I wished it would leave, my melancholy stayed with me the rest of the day, until Nick mentioned a bonfire after dinner. "We're leaving in five," he told me as *Encanto* was cued up for the twins. "Connor's grabbing sweatshirts!"

It was him, Sage, Connor, and me. We climbed into the Boston Whaler with blankets and some beers and started across Oyster Pond. I could see the fire burning bright in the distance, and once we made it to the beach, I heard the crackle itself. It made the hair on the back of my neck stand up. Connor slipping his arm around me didn't help.

A shiver swirled up my spine.

Beach blankets and chairs surrounded the fire; I recognized some members of the Fox family, but not others. Meredith sat in between her grandparents with a little dog asleep on her lap, and Christian Fox was intensely focused on a card game with his grandson.

I felt a twinge, thinking of Annie, Maisie, and their Sunday rummy games.

"Greetings!" someone called, and we turned to see Wit. Of all things, he wore a striped bathrobe and had a water pistol tucked into his waistband.

"No way!" Nick said. "I heard you were out."

Wit shook his head. "Upon further investigation, a window equates to a door, and the shot was only six feet from the window." He smirked. "I'm in it to win it."

Assassin, I thought, *is ridiculous.*

But maybe a little fun.

Wit accepted Nick's six-pack and put it in one of the three YETIs to chill while we dug out already cold drinks from another cooler. Sage pulled out two short and squat yellow cans. TIP TOP was printed in green across both cans. "You want one, Olivia? It's allegedly a margarita."

"Sure." I nodded, a little buzz sounding good tonight. I just wanted to relax and have fun. While Nick and Sage went to scout out a good spot for our blanket, Connor volunteered to assess the snacks situation.

"Olivia!" someone said before I could offer my opinion on brownies. "It's nice to see you!"

"Hi, Christian." I couldn't help but smile. There was something so *warm* about him. He didn't remind me of my grandfather, exactly, but... "It's nice to see you too." I gestured around the blazing bonfire. "This is amazing."

"It is," he agreed. "My brother knows how to rally the troops."

"What game are you playing over there?" I asked.

"Egyptian Rat Screw. Ty is cheating."

"Or maybe you're just a sore loser, Grumps!" his grandson called.

Christian chuckled. "Have you played?"

"Never." I shook my head. "My family is more into rummy."

"Rummy?" He looked impressed. "It's been years since I've played."

Then his brow furrowed, and I noticed him just barely tilt his head. His lips parted to say something else, but it was Connor who spoke instead. "Okay, Christian," he said, appearing at my side with goodies. "What do you put in these grasshopper brownies? Your daughter said you made them?"

Christian smiled. "You bake, Connor?"

"Absolutely not," Connor said. "But my mom does..."

"He distills his own mint leaves," Meredith said later, when she joined the five of us on our blanket, giving up her great-uncle's secret. She stole the last minty brownie from our paper plate. (Nick looked absolutely heartbroken.) "No one makes better brownies than Christian Fox."

"Except his brother, arguably," Wit countered. "Every batch of his brownies has been on point this summer."

"Yes." Meredith bemusedly rolled her eyes. "Betty Crocker has ensured that."

"He buys the box mix?" I guessed.

"Always," she said. "My grandfather has many talents, but I wouldn't say basic chemistry is one of them." She nodded at Andrew, who was passing a journal back and forth with his wife. She couldn't stop laughing as he dramatically scribbled something. It looked like they were playing some sort of game.

I felt a slight pang in my ribs, somehow reminded of my dad and Erica. Individually, they could be pretty serious people—*poised*, Annie used to call Erica—but together they brought out each other's goofy sides.

Sipping my drink, I tuned back into my beach blanket's conversation. Wit was talking about how much he dreaded the day they had to choose outlet locations in the house.

"House?" I asked, intrigued. "What house?"

"Our house," Meredith said. "After bopping around the past couple years, we're putting down roots in our favorite place." She gestured in some direction. Save for the fire, the beach was now all darkness. "It's being built near Paqua Pond." She winked. "We got a really good deal on the land."

"But we still haven't decided on its name," Wit told me. "Any and all ideas are welcome."

"What does the house look like?" I asked Meredith.

She opened her mouth, then closed it. Her eyes darted to Connor, who had been texting for a while, then made eye contact with me. "You know..." she said. "You should come and see it sometime. We'll show you not only the actual progress, but also the rendering."

"It's fantastic," Wit said. "Grumps designed it."

"He's a retired architect," Meredith explained.

Ah, I thought. *Christian must be a math-science guy, while Andrew...*

I glanced across the bonfire again, my heart rate heightening. Wait, what did Andrew do once upon a time? I blinked to see him on the Jaws Bridge boulders with his sketchbook, then on the Fourth with his easel...and suddenly felt like an idiot for not putting these possible pieces together sooner. *Because, what if—*

"Does that sound good, McCallister?" Meredith said.

Connor looked up from his phone, expression a little sullen. He'd mentioned Liam had asked a guy on his swim team out for pizza tonight... Maybe it hadn't gone well? "Sorry." His throat bobbed. "What'd I miss?"

"You and Olivia are coming over for dinner on Friday," Wit said. "Meredith is going to cook you an incredible meal, and in return, you'll consult on where the outlets should go in our new house."

"I'm down for that as long as there's dessert," Nick said. "What about your tres leches cake?"

"Nicholas, we're getting dinner at Atria with your parents that night," Sage reminded him as Meredith and Connor exchanged a sort of sly look. Maybe an inside joke about tres leches cake? I'd forgotten that they'd known each other for a while.

"Dinner sounds delicious!" I heard myself say, then I nudged Connor. "To celebrate your final days of vacation."

Starting Monday, he was back on the clock.

Connor laughed, and I couldn't help but grin at the sound. It was infectious, swirling into the sky with the bonfire's *snap, crackle, pop*. My heart swelled, and before I could stop myself, I leaned over and whispered in his ear. "Do you want to go for a walk?"

My insides squirmed when Connor looked at me with a raised brow.

"I mean, not *now*," I quickly amended, thinking about everyone watching Connor and me disappear into the darkness. My entire body blushed. "But maybe later?"

"Mmm." He hummed, then pressed a kiss to my temple. My eyelids fluttered shut, and the world suddenly didn't feel so heavy on my shoulders. "Maybe later sounds nice."

TWENTY

On Thursday morning, I ran alone, then I walked around the back of the house to Connor's outdoor shower. My dad might've banned me from sleeping in Summer Camp, but I could not give up that shower's ten minutes of bliss!

Speaking of my dad, I could see him and Erica through the shower's window, out on Oyster Pond together. I'd recognize my dad's neon blue and green-striped swim trunks anywhere. Their paddleboards weren't far from the shore, and Swede watched them from the beach. Erica was perfectly balanced on her board, but my dad wiggled all over the place. Even with the shower on full blast, I could faintly hear my stepmother's laugh. Something warmed in my chest, happy that, even with so many people here, my dad and Erica were finding some alone time.

I felt a little guilty for spending so much time with Connor, but my dad didn't seem to mind. "I'm just glad you're having so much fun," he said, then gave me a lopsided smile. "You look happy, Liv..."

Do I not usually seem happy? I'd worried. This year hadn't been easy, but I didn't want to think it always outwardly showed.

Today Connor and I had plans to visit Chappaquiddick, the island five hundred feet off Edgartown Harbor. Connor had explored it earlier this summer and described the ferry as "two baby barges going back and forth."

One of Annie's photos had been taken on the Dike Bridge.

We'd agreed to head out around 10:00 a.m., but Connor never showed up in the kitchen for breakfast, and he still hadn't made an appearance by 10:10. You ready? I texted him, but didn't receive a reply.

"OJ, Olivia?" Topper asked when I climbed onto an island barstool at 10:15.

"Please," I said, because it was freshly squeezed, smelling delightful. Plus, it didn't look like I was going anywhere. I could be pretty neurotic at times, but seriously, where was Connor? "Thanks, Topper."

He nodded like it was nothing, then he asked about my plans for the day. He and Peggy were having lunch with the Fox elders up island. "Christian will bring his sketchbook," he mentioned, chuckling. "He always does."

He means Andrew, I deciphered. Christian didn't strike me as an artist.

"Is Christian married?" I asked, curious nevertheless. "I met his grandson, but…"

"He was," Topper said as he started wiping down the

countertop. "For a very long time. Jane passed away several years ago."

"Oh," I said, latching onto the phrase, *For a very long time.*

That sounded like code for *high school sweethearts*.

"And what about Andrew? How long have he and Meredith's grandmother been together?"

"Also a very long time." Topper chuckled. "But back in the day, the entire island was in love with Andrew, and he was far too aware of it. It wasn't until he met Bea at a Boston Christmas party that he changed his ways."

"Oh, wow." I'd tried to shake away the thought of Andrew Fox potentially being Annie's summer romance. It could totally just be a coincidence that he was an artist and definitely too convenient that he was so close. There were probably countless octogenarian artists on the Vineyard, right?

I just had this *inkling*—

"Hey!" Connor appeared in the kitchen, in swim trunks and sunglasses. "We ready?"

I've been *ready*, I thought, but bit my tongue. Why was I so bothered by this? He was late, big deal. We weren't operating on a tight schedule. Everything was on "island time," as Peggy called it. It was all about going with the flow.

We sat in a comfortable silence as Connor drove into Edgartown, listening to his Spotify. "You like Taylor Swift?" I asked when a sign reading CHAPPY FERRY told Connor to turn left. "Cruel Summer" pulsed in the Jeep.

"Not particularly," he said. "This is a playlist coauthored by Liam and Mads."

"Mmm," I replied.

"Uh-oh..." Connor chuckled. "Am I in trouble?"

"Why do you say that?"

"I got the *mmm*."

Flushing, I looked out the windshield to focus on the road. Instead of several lanes, the Chappy Ferry appeared to only have one. Minutes and minutes and more minutes passed before we rolled into the harbor, which in no way compared to the massive Steamship Authority back on the mainland or even in Oak Bluffs. This road was so narrow.

Then I noticed the signs. Off to the right, streetlamps highlighted easy FAQs like operating hours and ticket rates.

I raised an eyebrow at Connor. "We have to pay? I thought you said the ride is five minutes?"

"*Less*," he told me, then he put the Jeep in park and unbuckled his seat belt to pay cash-only for our ticket. I followed his lead. There were probably a few more trips before we made the cut.

"Seriously?" I muttered when he selected the "car and driver" option. It was fifteen bucks for a round trip!

Connor gave me a wry look, lips turned up at the corners. "Have you always been this grouchy?"

The ferry could only transport three cars at a time, so it was another wait after we buckled up again. We found ourselves sandwiched between a forest-green Subaru and a silver Range Rover.

ALL PASSENGERS MUST BE SEATED WHILE UNDERWAY, a sign read, appropriate since a pack of people had boarded and were squeezing onto the foot passenger benches.

Three and a half minutes later we pulled off the ferry to see the beach parking lot off to the left; it looked full, but after two laps, a sandy Suburban started backing out of its spot. "Thank you!" Connor chirped, then he swiftly pulled in between the two faded lines. Dike Bridge was a bit of a drive, so we'd decided to lounge on the beach and have lunch first. Sage had mentioned it was her favorite one.

I quickly understood why, with its breathtaking view. Little Chappaquiddick had a front-row seat to the show that was Edgartown Harbor. Sailboats of all sizes glided by, speedboats filled with tourists chugged along, and even celebrity-worthy yachts were anchored in the blue water. I could finally see Edgartown's historic homes from the waterside. Flowers bloomed in sprawling green backyards, American flags waved in the breeze, and I couldn't fumble for my phone fast enough. I *had* to take a picture.

Families had set up camp in the sand, the water calm enough that plenty of children splashed around in the shallows. It looked like gentle waves only washed ashore when a boat sailed by, its wake rolling across the harbor. Connor and I walked along the beach until we reached a stretch of unoccupied sand. Farther down, I squinted to see a row of red-white-and-blue cabanas. Some type of beach club, I guessed.

After spreading out our beach towels, we traded a bottle of Sun Bum and lay back at the same time, letting it soak in. I let my eyes drift shut, but they flicked back open when Connor spoke. "I'm sorry I was late," he said. "You know, earlier. My dad called. He was on his way to work and wanted to catch up."

"Oh," I said, then for no particular reason, asked, "Didn't you talk to him the other day?"

"Yes."

I swallowed. "You're really close to your family."

Connor reached for my hand. I let my eyelids flutter again, let my heart float. "And you're not?"

I opened my mouth, but then I considered. My dad and I were close, being an older sister was one of my favorite things ever, and, oddly enough, Erica had been pretty okay the past couple weeks.

What made me hesitate about saying we were close was that I could imagine my family without me in it. I didn't like that. I couldn't shake this nagging feeling of displacement.

Connor let the subject trail off, and several beats later, we both hummed with happiness when the sun captured us in its crosshairs. The light felt decadent against my skin, and it slowed my heart rate…until Connor moved to wrap his arm around me. Everything in me leaped then melted once he tucked me into his side.

Shining in a sunbeam, I thought. *But warm because of Connor.*

We baked in the sun for an hour, then we decided to take a dip in the harbor. "Not too bad," Connor commented, letting the water lap up over his feet. His hair shined in the sunlight, almost rose gold. He winked at me. "Should we race?"

"On three?" I asked once we'd backed up five or so feet and taken our marks in the sand.

He reached to zap my waist. "One..."

I pretended to slap his hand away. "Two..."

"Three!" we shouted as we took off, but before my toes could touch the water, Connor scooped me up into his arms.

"Rude!" I protested, but I started giggling when he splashed into the shallow surf. He held me tight, laughing too, until the beach suddenly got the better of us. Neither of us were prepared for the harbor's steep drop-off. The water went from three feet deep to a sudden seven. All the air left my lungs once it enveloped us.

"Holy crap!" Connor sputtered once we'd broken the surface. One arm was still crooked around my side. "Did you see that coming?"

"Not at all." I laughed as I started to tread water. "I don't hate it, though."

The water was cool, refreshing with the sun still so bright overhead. Connor and I splashed each other a few times before floating on our backs. We talked about this and that, how summer was the best season and winter was the worst, before he casually brought up a not-so-casual topic: the future.

Not *our* future together, but still, our futures. "What's in the cards for you?"

"Northwestern," I said, slowly running my fingers through the water. "You know that already."

"Right," Connor said. "But I meant beyond college. What do you want to do? Where do you want to live?"

"Oh..." I trailed off. Those questions shouldn't have sent a shudder up my spine, but they did for some reason. "I haven't given it much thought yet. I'm just trying to focus on the next four years in Chicago." I paused. "Have you?"

"Well, I haven't *decided*," he said. "But I've thought about it a fair amount." His leg brushed against mine. "I'd like to be an accountant."

"An accountant," I echoed, trying not to snort. "Really?"

"Yes, really. Is there something wrong with that?"

"Of course not," I told him. "But you're just so good with kids. Isn't that a sign of a good teacher?"

"Eh, I would roll my eyes too much."

"Connor, when have you ever rolled your eyes in front of Teddy and Finn?"

"All the time, on the inside."

Now I really snorted, not believing him whatsoever; I moved so that I was treading water again. Connor did the same, his smile bemusedly amused.

"Math is my favorite subject," he continued. "I like numbers, and the world will *always* be in need of CPAs."

"Good point," I conceded. "Where are you going to live?"

"East Coast," he said automatically. "Maybe not in Pennsylvania, but still relatively near..."

"Your family," I guessed, then gave him a look. "Do you think it'll be hard at Notre Dame? Being so far away from them?"

"I'll get used to it." Connor shrugged, but there was nothing nonchalant about it.

Something twinged in my chest, suspecting that it was hard being away from his family *now*. I thought of how he'd waited in the mess hall line to call his family at Camp Skytop, and how often he talked about them and Mads in the here and now.

Might he still be a homebody?

And was there anything wrong with being a homebody?

He cleared his throat. "You really don't know what you want to be when you grow up?"

"No," I said, feeling heat at the back of my neck even while swimming. "I really don't."

And I also couldn't say how Connor responded, because my mind had started whirring. I'd wanted to be a jewelry designer once, but only because I loved Annie's collection. She'd let me try on everything.

I loved books, but I didn't necessarily want to be a writer or librarian.

And my dad and the Elkins nurses told me I had an excellent bedside manner, but I could never get into medical or nursing school. Biology was the bane of my existence.

"I took a look at Northwestern's psychology department," I remembered Erica saying after I'd gotten my acceptance letter. "The courses look fascinating!"

"Cool," I said, but I hadn't engaged with her. In fact, I'd been hurt. What did she mean by that? I'd heard from friends that psychology was the major for people who weren't particularly interested in or good at anything.

And her words from lunch with her friends last month were a whisper in my ear: *She seems to have lost all her drive and sense of direction...*

"But I could see myself living a lot of places," I told Connor, and by that, I meant I had no idea where I wanted to live. I tried to shift the subject. "Meredith said she and Wit were kind of nomads?"

"Yeah." Connor nodded. "They would book an Airbnb for a few months, then pack up and move somewhere completely different." He lightly splashed me. "Speaking of Meredith, you still game to go to the Farm for dinner on Friday?"

"Definitely," I said, then I suggested we swim back to shore for lunch. My stomach rumbled. Before getting in line for the Chappy Ferry, we'd stopped in Edgartown for BLTs, potato chips, and fizzy drinks. Muffins too.

"This is insane," Connor said after finishing half his sandwich. "So good, right?"

"The best," I agreed, even though I wasn't paying my BLT nearly enough attention. I'd only taken two bites.

I was too busy wrestling with the idea that dinner with Meredith and Wit, who were important to Connor, felt serious. Like more than a casual dinner date.

And if I hadn't been busy worrying, I not only would have raved about how delicious the BLTs were, but I also would've immediately picked up on the hives blooming on Connor's neck.

Neither of us noticed until he started touching his lips. Slowly, and sort of in awe, as if he'd only just discovered he had a mouth. "Connor..." I said after a beat. "Are you okay?"

By way of response, he smacked his lips once.

They were *puffy*.

"I need my EpiPen," he said, now itching the hives on his skin. He sounded calm enough, but there was a hitch in his voice. "God, this hasn't happened—"

He didn't finish his thought; instead, he sprung up from his towel and bolted up the beach. Heart spiking, I grabbed my tote bag and followed.

"But you didn't eat anything!" I called after him, not caring how silly I looked. "Last time I checked, a BLT doesn't have tree nuts or shellfish." I paused. "Or horse DNA."

Connor didn't answer, and I pumped my arms harder to keep up with him. I considered myself a runner, but this guy could *run*. We sprinted past children building sandcastles and a father-daughter game of Frisbee. I nearly plowed into a couple of bookworms reading in beach loungers.

My bare feet burned when I hit the parking lot's pavement. *Shit, shit, shit*, I thought, heat scorching my feet, but I plowed onward. Connor had beaten me to the Jeep, but his hands were fumbling with his key fob. (He'd tucked it under the wheel well when we'd arrived, trusting our fellow islanders.) "Give them to me," I blurted, and upon snatching the keys, pressed the unlock button as hard as I could and yanked open the driver's side door. "Where is it?"

Connor wheezed. "...Center...console."

I barely heard him over the blood pulsing in my ears, but thankfully I managed to unlatch the console. I didn't have to dig around long before locating the EpiPen, but I had no idea how to use it. "*Here*!" I screeched at the same time Connor grabbed it from me.

And then in one swift movement, he pulled off some type of safety cap and stabbed himself in the thigh. I heard a faint *click*, and after three hard heartbeats, Connor slumped against the car and closed his eyes. He was pale and dripping with sweat but seemingly okay.

I let out all the air in my lungs.

"We have to call 911," he said once our pulses calmed. "I need an ambulance."

"Why?" I asked, confused. No one in my family had any allergies. "Didn't the EpiPen do its job?"

"I think so." Connor blinked open his eyes, and god, they were so blue. Staring into them made me feel like the world was tilting over, even though my feet were firmly on flat ground. "But the ER is protocol, in case the EpiPen is only temporarily effective." He glanced over at the humming Chappy Ferry and sighed. "It's going to take the EMTs forever to get over here."

We made the executive decision to leave the Jeep and our stuff so we could quickly hop back over to Edgartown. I forked over our pedestrian passenger fee, and Connor used my phone to call 911 from the barge. The wind whipped through the air, but I heard him explain and give the dispatcher our location.

We're about five seconds from getting off the Chappy Ferry.

I took Connor's hand and squeezed it once he hung up the phone. "How do you feel?"

"Prematurely mortified," he said, lips no longer so puffy. "You are about to witness the most embarrassing moment of my life."

"Oh, come on!" I laughed a little. "That can't be true! Didn't you embarrass yourself in high school?"

My mind flashed to me sophomore year, tripping down the library steps in a pair of ridiculous high-heeled boots.

"No, I did not," Connor said lightly, then he dropped his voice. "But there might've been something in middle school." He paused. "Involving a water park's wave pool."

I battled back a laugh.

By the time we disembarked, a red Edgartown Fire Department ambulance was somehow maneuvering its way past the ferry line. Connor casually waved, as if the ambulance were his Uber.

He keeps his cool, I thought, impressed. I was internally freaking out again. Had the EpiPen done enough?

"Allergic reaction, right?" one of the paramedics asked after putting the ambulance in park. Her partner went around to the back and opened its double doors. "Shellfish?"

"Or tree nuts," Connor said. "I'm not sure. I was eating a BLT."

"Hmm." The paramedic motioned for him to follow her to the mobile examination room. "Sounds like a cross-contaminant situation…"

My phone chimed in my bag, and knowing Connor was now in safe hands, I scooped it out to see Finlay House onscreen. I felt my stomach drop as I stared. What happened? Why was Elkins calling me? If something was wrong, they always called my dad.

Had he not picked up?

I wanted to ignore the call, to focus on Connor, but everything in me screamed that I couldn't. What if something was actually wrong and they needed to contact us?

I glanced over at the ambulance—the open door blocked me from seeing anything, but I heard the paramedics laughing at whatever joke Connor had probably just cracked.

I tapped to accept the call. "Hello?"

"Olivia, hi!" Tara chirped. "You busy?"

The sunshine in the nurse's voice was artificial but still brought me some relief. "No," I said. "What's up?"

"Your grandmother would like to talk to you," she said. "Hold on a moment."

My heart leaped, delighted. Annie wanted to talk to *me*, Olivia.

One, two, three seconds passed, but when I finally heard a voice at the end of the line, it wasn't Annie's. "Just a minute!" Tara told me, and then, off to the side, "Annette, this is your granddaughter. You asked to speak to her, remember?"

"No, I asked to *see* her," I faintly heard Annie reply, her voice icy. "That's entirely different."

"Annie, hi!" I exclaimed before I considered that I might be blowing out Tara's eardrum. "I'm right here!"

Tara must've convinced her to take the phone, but my grandmother's response was less than enthusiastic—a heavy sigh. "You're not," she told me. "You are *not* here, Chris. You never are."

The corners of my eyes stung. Why was this disease being so hard on my dad? Maybe he couldn't show up all the time, but he still showed up as much as he could. I swallowed hard. "We'll be home soon, Annie." I pretended nothing was wrong. "And I have so many pictures—"

I dropped off when I felt a hand on my shoulder and turned to see Connor. A little color had returned to his face, and he gave me a smile before stealing my phone and pressing it against his ear. "Hello, Annette," he said gently. My pulse pounded. "How are you this afternoon?" Pause. "I'm Connor McCallister, Olivia's old camp friend."

Excuse me? I thought. *Old camp friend?*

It wasn't until Connor winked that I realized he was teasing me, trying to slip under my white-hot skin. It started to burn as he walked back toward the ambulance, making sweet small talk with my sick grandmother, knowing he'd also given me something to think about.

If I didn't want to call Connor my "old camp friend," what *did* I want to call him?

TWENTY-ONE

Even though Connor seemed stable, it was protocol for him to spend several hours under observation in the ER. "You should stay here," he said before the EMTs chauffeured to Martha's Vineyard Hospital. He nodded at the Chappy Ferry. "Head back over and check out Dike Bridge." He pressed his Jeep keys into my hand. "I'll let you know when I've been discharged."

I made him promise that I'd be his first call.

"And my ride." He kissed my cheek, and when we got home five hours later, a totally fine Connor disappeared to call his mom and update her on his medical incident while I sought out my dad. I showed him the picture of me striking a silly pose on Dike Bridge (thank you, self-timer), then I told him about my conversation with Annie. He calmly nodded, but I could see something flickering in his eyes. "She always just seems weirdly pissed at you, for no reason." My voice unexpectedly wavered. "Dad, I hate it."

He wrapped me in a hug. "She's not really upset with me, Liv."

"Yeah, I know," I whispered, tears welling up. "The disease is."

We kept telling ourselves that, and it *was* the truth, but it was still difficult to separate the evils of dementia from our happy memories of Annie. They wouldn't overshadow them, but they'd still be *there*, woven into our family fabric. I would always remember my grandmother calling me a *snot*, just like Erica knew she was *that woman* every now and again.

Does that crush her? I wondered.

"Thanks, Dad." I pulled away to give him a small smile. "I love you."

"I love you too." He squeezed my shoulder. "Keep up your spirits for the rest of the trip. Don't worry about Annie. She's in the best hands, and we'll be back soon enough." He gave me a long look. "Okay?"

"Okay," I agreed, but it was easier said than done. The next day, on Friday, I called Elkins before Connor and I left for dinner on the Farm.

"I'm sorry, Olivia," one of the nurses said. "It's been a challenging day. How about you call back tomorrow?"

I didn't like the word *challenging*. What did that mean? Was she irritated and restless? Or had there been a bad sundown episode?

Connor interrupted my spiral. "What are you thinking about?" he asked as we puttered across Oyster Pond, Ashley at the helm. She and her dad were taking the kids—all wearing fluorescent life vests—tubing after dropping us off on the Farm's dock.

I waved my hand, as if to say, *Nothing!*

"Connor, remember to remind Meredith about your

allergies,"Teddy said when the dock was in sight. "She might fry something in the same oil as—"

"I don't think Meredith has a fryer, sweetheart," Ashley bemusedly cut in, "but I'm sure Connor will let her know."

"Absolutely," he said before offering the kids fist bumps. "Kick butt out there, guys!"

Ashley maneuvered the Boston Whaler as close as possible to the dock. I thought Meredith would've been waiting for us, but instead it was a life vest–wearing Claire Dupré and her mom. "Just up the dunes." She smiled at Connor and me and gestured up the rickety stairs.

And while Maisie practically pushed us overboard, wanting to get her tube on, a flushed Finn offered Claire his hand to help her onto the boat.

Manners matter, dude, I imagined Connor telling him. *Girls like manners.*

We do, I would've concurred, even though before meeting Connor, I'd tried to convince myself that chivalry had gone extinct. Who cared that Rob had always texted me from his car instead of knocking on my front door?

Heat sparked on the back of my neck, embarrassed.

Connor and I hiked up the hill, but again, neither Meredith nor Wit waited for us. Instead, there were two mountain bikes leaning against an ancient split-rail fence with wildflowers spilling down the side. "What are you doing?" I asked when Connor confidently mounted the red one. "That is totally someone's bike."

"Trust me," he said, and I found myself completely and utterly powerless against his smile. It weakened the backs of my knees.

But I still managed to swing my leg over the side of the silver bike, and once we started pedaling, it was off to the races. The sun bathed the Farm's seagrasses in a golden light as we rode along a well-worn sandy road. I wanted to close my eyes and throw my hands up in the air, feeling so incredibly carefree. Music drifted from the one of houses we passed by and there looked to be a cutthroat cornhole game happening outside another. Something sizzled on a grill somewhere.

I was so swept up that I had to slam on my brakes; Connor had slowed to a stop in front of a tiny cedar-shingled cottage with a pitched roof and green shutters. THE ANNEX, a sign over the door read. Two matching Adirondack chairs sat on its tiny porch, and a picnic table lounged out front. It was set for dinner with a vase of fresh wildflowers as the finishing touch.

"Welcome to the Annex," Connor said once we'd hit our kickstands. "It's nice, right?"

"It's adorable." I nodded, then I stole another glance at the dressed up picnic table and noticed it was only set for *two*. "Meredith and Wit live here?"

"Yes, until their house is finished," Connor said. "It's really her parents' place." He winked. "But it's ours for the night!"

My breath caught.

Meredith and Wit were never meant to be here, I realized, heart starting to hammer. It had all been a charade so Connor could surprise me.

"How?" I asked, stunned. "When?"

"I had some help this afternoon," he said coyly. "Sage and I kayaked over here while you and Erica were playing"—he made air quotes—"hide-and-seek with Beth."

I couldn't help but smile a bit. Erica seemed to be more focused on her "East Coast Summer" Reel than her parents' scrapbook, but Annie's memory book was starting to take shape.

"Bombing around the island and retracing Annie's steps has been a lot of fun," Connor added when I didn't say anything. "But you deserve your own unforgettable summer snapshot, Olivia." His voice softened, turned tender. "And I wanted to make it happen for you."

Pinpricks at the corners of my eyes, I felt a sudden and hard lump in my throat. Knots of thoughts tied themselves together in my head, but I swallowed and spoke over them: "You really do know how to make a girl swoon, Connor McCallister."

"Practice makes perfect," he quipped, then he grinned, took my hand, and squeezed it. "What can I get you to drink?"

Our menu was simple and so very summer. Connor skillfully turned two sweet potatoes into a cookie sheet of cinnamon-sugar sweet potato fries while I offered to make the salad, adding in a generous amount of sweet corn, tomatoes, and mozzarella pearls.

We sipped glasses of strawberry lemonade while Connor grilled our marinated chicken. "Do you normally cook?" I asked after kissing the chef. "Or is tonight…?"

"*Tonight* is a special occasion," he said, tips of his ears pinkening. "Miranda might've texted me detailed instructions for the sweet potato fries."

Smiling, I kissed him again.

By the time we sat down at the picnic table, it was almost seven. We talked about everything from Teddy wandering off and getting lost on the ferry last month to Quincy and Gwen's internships to our nearly identical middle schools. I nearly choked on my giggles when Connor brought up the ballroom dance routine he and Mads had to perform in seventh grade gym. "Oh, we did that too!" I exclaimed. "I had to dance with my friend Jenna, because no boy wanted to be *Stilts'* partner."

Connor raised an eyebrow. "Stilts?"

My cheeks warmed. "I was really tall, remember?"

He shook his head. "Middle school boys never play the long game."

"Yourself included?"

"Oh, myself absolutely included."

I smiled.

For dessert, we devoured Meredith's promised tres leches cake (left behind in the fridge with a sweet note). "This place is in a league of its own," Connor remarked after polishing off his third slice. He nodded at the horizon. "The Carmichaels' house is spectacular, but every time I've been over here this summer..." He trailed off. "I mean, have you ever *seen* anything like this?"

I looked out at the Farm's great beyond, to soak it in all over again. A wide-open meadow rolled out before us, speckled with yellow flowers. Scattered scrub trees swayed in the evening breeze, and beyond a small placid pond were the beach's sandy dunes and the ocean. I squinted to see a boat on the deepening blue-purple horizon. It looked like we were in the middle of nowhere, but my swishing stomach suddenly told me we were in a special *somewhere.*

And I was starting to think it wasn't only special to the Fox family.

Being here made me wish I'd brought Annie's Polaroid. The wind-whipped trees and sandy roads looked eerily familiar.

Is this it? I wondered, pulse speeding up. *Has it been Paqua Farm the whole time?*

How had I not noticed?

"It's magical," I murmured at the same time Connor's phone started vibrating its way across the tabletop. Like the Carmichael family house, it appeared the Farm had temperamental, borderline terrible, service. Thankfully, the Annex's Wi-Fi info had been posted on the fridge.

"Impeccable timing, as always," Connor snorted upon seeing

Mads's FaceTime request. He reached for his phone to reject it. "Sorry not sorry, Madeline—"

"No!" I blurted. "Answer it."

Connor gave me a quizzical look.

I also wondered what the hell I was thinking, but I nodded like I'd never been surer about anything in my life. "I've heard so much about her."

"Alright, then," Connor said. "Don't say I didn't warn you..."

He accepted the call, and once our connection cooperated—it took a few seconds—a pretty girl with brown hair in two braids appeared onscreen. Connor angled his phone so that his camera caught both of us. "Okay, *listen* to this—" Mads started before her eyes bugged comically wide.

"Mads, this is Olivia," Connor said happily, unable to play it even a little cool. "Olivia Lupo."

I summoned a smile and waved. "Hi!"

In response, Mads made a show of pinching her arm. "Just checking," she said with a guilty but sly smile. Next to me, Connor went *red*. It must've been an inside joke. "What are you guys up to?" she asked.

I only realized why I'd wanted to FaceTime her when Connor got up from the table to show her the Farm's vast view. I'd grown curious about his life. His life back home, not his manny existence on this island. I wanted to meet the people who were so important to him. Who meant the world to him.

But that didn't mean I was dying for a one-on-one

conversation with his best friend. "I'll be right back," Connor said a few minutes later, offering me his phone. "Nature, uh, calls."

"Literally," Mads chimed in. "The Annex has an outhouse, right?"

I reluctantly took the phone, but I didn't say anything until Connor had disappeared into the woods. "It really is great to finally meet you," I said, half-hoping our connection would crumble and the call would disconnect. "I know he's missed you a lot."

"I've missed him a lot too," Mads said. "We've never been apart this long, and I know being away hasn't been a piece of cake for him." She paused. "It's also great to meet you. I've been super curious, to be honest."

I blinked. "You have?"

"Yeah, of course. Connor went from asking how everyone at home was to talking about you nonstop." Mads raised an eyebrow. "You're surprised?"

I shook my head. No, I guess I wasn't. Not really.

"I'm not usually the overprotective type." Her cheeks flushed a little. "But then again, Connor has always had the upper hand in relationships. I haven't needed to worry about him. Everyone jokes that he falls hard and fast, but he always, *always* looks before he leaps, which hasn't been too often." She laughed. "And I have you to thank for that."

"Me?" I snorted. "What did I do?"

"You're his dream girl, Olivia. The camp crush that got away. Whether he knew it or not, I think he was saving his heart for you."

A lump formed in my throat.

You're his dream girl, Olivia.

I think he was saving his heart for you.

"I know that's probably scary to hear," Mads said as I heard a chugging noise in the distance. Was it my hammering heart? The blood in my ears? Or something else? "But it's the truth, and I think you need to know that..." Her eyebrows knitted together. "Wait, shit, I'm sorry. You look terrified."

"Yes," I said, then winced. "I mean, no. I mean..." I sighed. "It's just a lot of pressure."

My stomach squirmed. I'd known Connor less than three weeks, and I definitely wasn't the person he'd been romanticizing in his head for all these years. I hadn't remembered him without prompting, but he'd really been pining over me?

You messed up, I started berating myself. *Everyone told you—*

The chugging intensified, and before Mads could say more, a sound between a *pop* and a *whistle* made me blink. "Olivia!" I heard Connor call as I just hung up on Mads and looked over my shoulder to see not only him and his knee-numbing grin emerging from the mouth of the woods, but also...

A tractor.

My breath caught.

The green antique John Deere tractor from Annie's Polaroid, here all along. "It's been on the Farm since the 1930s!" Wit called from the driver's seat, as if reading my mind. He guided the tractor onto the lawn, revealing Meredith and a few others on the flatbed trailer. THE OYSTERCATCHER had been painted across the back in yellow letters.

"Sunset tractor rides are a Fox family tradition," Meredith told us. "We go from house to house and pick up more passengers. It's the best way to see the Farm!"

"And I am a gold-star tour guide," Wit added, "if you need further convincing."

One of their friends sitting crisscross-applesauce on the trailer bed nodded. "His narration is quite good," another guy offered in a dry Australian accent. "He does all the voices."

"Oh man, voices?" Connor chuckled. "I'm in!"

"Me too!" My voice cracked. I was still in shock, but calmed down long enough to climb on board with everyone. Then my heart started its now familiar hammering again. Here I was, about to see the Farm the way Annie had once seen it. Time seemed to slow and the Farm began to take on this glow. Nostalgia right in front of me.

It looked like it was going to be a gorgeous sunset.

"We should've brought sweatshirts," Connor whispered once we were settled on the flatbed. The temperature was already dipping and the breeze whipping up. He hugged me close. "You warm enough?"

"Yes." I smiled at him, because it impossible to shiver with his arms around me.

Maybe I was definitely in too deep with him, but I knew I could swim for a while longer.

TWENTY-TWO

You would think a tractor ride was only fun for little kids, but whenever Wit pulled up outside a house, people couldn't wait to join us.

"And, as most of you know, this is the Big House," Wit explained, steering the tractor up the sandy rock road toward a Victorian farmhouse. "It's the oldest house on the Farm." He turned back and winked at us. "And it just got a much-needed renovation!"

The Big House looked like it had been entirely re-sided in cedar shingles, since they weren't weathered brown like the Annex. Instead, they were a light maple color. My guess was they darkened with time. *A job well done*, I thought to myself, admiring the fresh green shutters and porch that wrapped around the house like a hug.

"Evening!" Andrew Fox called from the porch. "Do you have room for two more?"

"*One* more, darling," his wife corrected him. She was relaxing on the porch's daybed but waved her book around, determined.

"Book club meets tomorrow, and I'm only halfway through." She blew a kiss to everyone. "Next time!"

Someone moved to help Andrew Fox onto the Oystercatcher, but he was capable of hoisting himself up without assistance. Seemingly a spring chicken.

Meanwhile, my heart threatened to pound its way out of my chest.

Did you date Annette Lupo? I was desperate to ask once he had settled near various generations of family and friends. *Or did you know Annette Lupo, once upon a time? Did she come here?*

But I swallowed the words, realizing he wouldn't. "Lupo" was Annie's married name, and before I could internally rephrase the question with her maiden name, Andrew cupped his hands around his mouth and called, "Onward, Wit!"

I can ask his brother, I thought, knowing Christian's house was the next stop. I knew him better, anyway. The Jaws Bridge disaster had been quite the icebreaker.

The sun was low on the horizon when the tractor reached the Pond House, the site of the Fourth of July party. It truly had an incredible view of Oyster Pond. The water glimmered in the waning light, and I spotted a couple peaceful evening kayakers.

Jay and Allison, I recognized the green and yellow kayaks. After discovering Nick and Sage's love for kayaking under the stars, I'd learned his parents preferred paddling at sunset.

I turned to the Pond House at the sound of pounding feet. Two children charged across the back deck, with blankets wisely thrown over their shoulders, and while other Foxes followed, none of them were Christian. Andrew stuck two fingers in his mouth to sharply whistle. "He's not here," a middle-aged woman told him. "He went straight to the barn after dinner."

Straight to the barn? I wondered.

The tractor resumed its journey.

"Am I not comfortable enough?" Connor asked when I shifted against his chest.

"Comfortable?" I felt my face melt into a smile. "Try *cozy*." I glanced around; we had left the houses in the dust, now rolling along a meadow trail. "Where do you think this leads?"

He kissed the top of my head, murmuring, "I have a hunch..."

Wit slowed the tractor several minutes later, after impressively winding to a grassy oasis overlooking a small, placid pond. The sun had officially started making its descent, the blue sky bursting into shades of orange and pink, but you couldn't miss the house several yards away. Or, the bones of a house. It was mostly framework, but you could tell a sweet Cape would someday stand here.

Wit and Meredith's house, I surmised. This was where they were putting down roots.

"Everyone, everyone!" Meredith stood on the flatbed after Wit made a bird call to get the group's attention. "We've brought you all here tonight to make an announcement!"

"You're having a baby?" Claire asked.

Her mother gasped. "*Claire!*"

Meredith smiled as people laughed, but I caught the tiniest wince behind it. "No, Miss Dupré," she said. "No bun in the oven."

"We can't afford a kid," Wit joked, slipping his hand into Meredith's and squeezing it. "We've sunk our savings into this house." He gestured to the cottage. "Which we've *finally* thought of a name for..."

Too many people spoke at once, suggesting that this had been a Farm topic of conversation all summer. "Wave Watcher!" someone shouted.

"The Beachcomber's Bungalow!"

"Plover House!"

"Wit's End!"

"We appreciate all your suggestions," Meredith said, "but ultimately settled on one of our own." She grinned. "Drumroll, please!"

Her grandfather pulled off the perfect drumroll.

"Introducing," Wit said, "in late September..."

"Clair de Lune Cottage!" he and Meredith chorused.

Moonlight, I translated from the French. *Moonlight Cottage.*

And while that meant nothing to me, I could tell it meant everything to them. Their family and friends were excited too.

"We should get them some fudge," I whispered to Connor. They'd been so nice to us.

"We should," he whispered back. "For them and for us."

A few lanterns were switched on after the sun had set, but the stars and moon were bright and guided the tractor back the way it'd come. "Thank you for riding along with us," Wit said at each drop-off point. "Tips are not necessary but much appreciated..."

Meredith hopped off the Oystercatcher at the Annex, and Connor moved to follow her—he'd whispered that he had one more surprise for me—but I found myself frozen in place. My pulse picked up, not ready to leave this moment—*the tractor*—yet.

What more do you want? the voice inside my head asked. *You found it, isn't that enough? You know Annie was here.*

Did I have confirmation?

Everything but. I hadn't had the guts to talk to Meredith's grandfather before he'd disembarked at the Big House. He'd winked at Connor and me once during the ride. "Having fun?" he asked us, and I only mustered a smile and nod. Maybe I was afraid he wouldn't remember Annie, or I was scared that he'd broken her heart.

"Where does the tractor live?" I asked Wit now, as if the John Deere were a living, breathing thing.

"The barn," he told me, scratching his ankle. Someone had forgotten bug spray. "It's not far, if you want to check it out."

I looked at Connor, who looked at me—and that was all it took. One look. I didn't need to open my mouth and explain. "Keep rolling, Witry," he said. "We've heard the lore behind Paqua's barns."

My lips tipped up in a smile. I'd told Connor about the Fourth of July legend: the Brothers Fox accidentally burning down one of the barns during their fireworks show. Their parents had been so pissed they gave the Fourth of July to the Carmichaels.

Wit chuckled. "Copy that, McCallister."

He shifted the tractor's gear stick, and we rolled forward again. I couldn't help but shiver when we disappeared under a canopy of branches that shielded the road from the sky. Branches snapped and critters scuttled. It was also *dark*.

"Scared?" Connor teased.

"No." I shook my head, even though I couldn't imagine being out here alone. "You?"

"Terrified."

I giggled into his shoulder.

"Here we are!" Wit announced a few beats later, as we pulled into another whorl of darkness. But this one had bright spots of light. Two cedar-shingled barns squared off in a wooded clearing, one much larger than the other. THE BARN, a carved sign read in the lamplight. Connor helped Wit roll open the wide doors, welcoming the tractor back home. I peeked inside to see a smaller red tractor, as well as a Kawasaki mule and a pair of dirt bikes. The enormous American flag from the Fourth of July party hung on the back wall.

Then I turned back to the John Deere.

"I know," Wit said. "She's a stunner."

"Absolutely." I nodded, then I took a deep breath and asked if Connor could take a picture of me next to the tractor. He'd already fished his phone from his pocket. "I know it sounds silly, but..."

This was the final photo I needed, the one I thought I would never get the chance to take.

Wit grinned. "Not at all. I take a picture of Claire with the tractor every summer." He offered a suggestion as Connor framed me in his crosshairs. "Maybe rest your arm on the back wheel?"

I did, since I had no glass of white wine to hold.

"Say cheese!" Connor smirked.

"Feta!" I smiled wide when he laughed.

"Good turnout tonight?" someone asked, and the three of us turned to see Christian Fox step into the Barn's lamplight. Baseball hat atop his head, he wore a pair of faded jeans and frayed crewneck sweatshirt. There were dark stains on it, some faded, others fresh. He was wiping his blackened hands with a rag, which smelled to the high heavens.

Motor oil? I wondered, the scent taking me back to a catastrophe in our garage. My dad used to love tinkering on his college Saab, determined to bring it back to life. (After the sludge had been cleaned up, Erica had gently encouraged him to give up on resuscitation.)

So Andrew's an artist, I thought. *And Christian is a motorhead.*

"A new record," Wit bragged. "I cleaned out every house."

Christian smiled and shook his head, bemused. "I'm sorry I missed it."

"What are you working on?" I asked despite not having much of an interest in cars. "Someone mentioned—"

"I'd stop right there, Olivia," Wit warned. "Grumps doesn't unveil his genius until it's *genius*."

"He speaks the truth, I'm afraid," Christian said, with a hint of bittersweetness. He hesitated. "But if you count to a hundred so I can hide the current bane of my existence, I'd be happy to show you some of my finished pieces."

Finished pieces? How many cars did he have?

"One..." I responded, keeping it light. "Two..."

With a chuckle, Christian turned and started back toward the second barn. It was a little smaller, so I hadn't given it much of a look earlier, but it was pretty and warm in the darkness. It was newly cedar-shingled with arched windows and copper trim. I wondered if he'd designed it himself. Meredith said he'd been an architect, right?

THE WORKSHOP, its sign read when I'd hit ninety-nine and reached for the doorknob. Connor said he'd join me after helping Wit put the John Deere to sleep, fascinated with it.

"Ready?" I asked before pushing open the door.

"All set," Christian answered. "Welcome..."

I immediately blinked upon crossing the threshold, expecting to walk into a large garage space; instead, I'd been transported to a whole other world. Wood-planked walls with old beams for rafters, the entire room had a golden glow that begged you to sit down and stay a while. Weathered brass pendant lights and salvaged lamps lit the room, and art was *everywhere*. Majestic framed oil paintings kept company with unframed watercolors, pencil sketches, and black-and-white photographs. I couldn't help but think how wonderful Erica would think this studio was; she always wanted her office to be homier but could never find the right Pinterest inspiration photo.

Andrew's studio, I realized with a twinge. The Workshop belonged to both brothers.

"All of this is incredible," I said, slowly walking around the space. My gaze hooked on an intricate charcoal sketch of a horseshoe crab, and then a monstrous painting, one that truly had to be as tall as me and must've taken ages to paint. The watercolor was set by the sea, a vignette of a woman sitting on a jetty and staring down into the water. Her feet were bare and her linen pants cuffed, but you couldn't see her face; it was like a picture that had been snapped from behind...

But from the way her blond hair fell, I knew. Andrew Fox was not only the artist of Annie's artwork but also her long-ago island love.

"I call that one *Girlhood*," Christian offered, a seemingly casual comment that turned my world entirely upside down.

"What?" I truly felt like I'd been clocked in the head. "*You* call it *Girlhood*?"

"Yes," Christian said. "It was the title from the first brushstroke."

From the first brushstroke.

Blood pulsed in my ears, keeping time with my frantically beating heart. "Andrew didn't paint this?" I waved my hand around. "Any of this?"

Christian opened his mouth then covered it with his hand, as if to hide a laugh. But the crinkling corners of his wrinkled green eyes gave him away. I squinted at the inky, pungent pigment still smeared across his knuckles.

Not motor oil, it dawned on me. *Oil paint.*

"No, most of this is my work," Christian confirmed, but he reached for a sketchbook resting on his drafting table. He handed it to me. "Here is a representation of Andrew's."

I flipped over the cover to see a watercolor on the first page, and while I was neither an artist nor qualified art critic, it was...

Half-finished and not good.

Was I looking at a sun*rise* or a sun*set*? And was that a whale or a dolphin? There were no dolphins on the Vineyard, right?

"But he's everywhere," I mumbled. "The bridge, the Fourth of July, the beach... He's always painting...or sketching..." I gave Christian a confused look. "He's so *dedicated*."

"Yes, because he's been unusually bored this summer." Christian shrugged. "I suggested he take up art."

"Oh," I said. "Well, he certainly plays the part."

Christian chuckled, then he let a beat of silence pass between us before he murmured, "You look so much like her."

Heat rushed to my cheeks. *Like who?* I could've asked, but I didn't see the point.

"You've known?" I said softly. "This whole time?"

Christian shook his head. "No, not at first. After meeting you and Connor at the bridge, I told myself I was greatly exaggerating the resemblance—maybe even *seeing* things. You were a Carmichael; you couldn't look *that much* like Annette Clark."

The way he said her name.

Annette Clark.

He coughed. "And then I found out you were adorable little Erica's stepdaughter..." He took off his baseball cap and ran a hand through his white hair. "Well, I'm not particularly proud of what I did next."

My silence begged the question: *What did you do you next?*

"I asked my grandson to find your Instagram." He blushed a bit. "I recognized a blouse you were wearing in one photo; I remember her sewing it. And you write the most beautiful birthday tributes."

I swallowed hard. Annie had never been the most technologically savvy—"I am not meant to live in the age of the smartphone!" she often lamented—but she *had* gotten the hang of Instagram before her diagnosis. And I'd loved posting throwback photos of her on her birthday, some that made her smile, some that made her laugh, and others that made her say, *What was I thinking with that haircut?*

"She has three grandchildren," I finally said. "I'm the oldest. She is the most wonderful person in the world."

Christian nodded. "I always thought she was astonishing."

Then what happened? I wondered, deep in my soul. *What were you to each other and what went wrong?*

And why does she still think about you?

Because, spotting his bitten-down fingernails, a theory was suddenly unspooling in my mind. "Chris's nails were nothing more than nubs," I vaguely remembered Annie saying, and I'd thought she meant my dad. In fact, *every time* Annie mentioned "Chris," I assumed she was talking about my dad.

Maybe she hadn't been. Maybe the Chris who was *never there* for her wasn't and had never been my dad. *Chris* might've been a nickname.

We had to start at the beginning, though.

"When did you meet Annie?" I asked, hands clasped so that *I* didn't start biting my pinkie nail. "*How* did you meet?"

"It was the summer before college," he said. "I introduced myself to her on the ferry." He smiled softly. "She and her friend were sharing a pair of binoculars."

Kathy Ryan, I didn't need to ask. Her forever travel buddy.

"Her hair kept blowing in the wind, and after every bluster, she tried smoothing it down. I mustered up the courage to go over and offer her a rubber band to tie it back."

I smiled a little. Annie always had a hairband handy in her purse in case I forgot one. "Did she accept it?"

Christian nodded, but before he could say anything else, the studio's door opened and Connor slipped inside.

"Wow..." His eyes widened, then darted around the room.

My heart ached; I loved his innate sense of childlike wonder. "Where do I start?"

"Here." I pointed to the big watercolor. "This is called *Girlhood.*"

"It's amazing," Connor marveled, moving closer to the painting. He studied it, then side-eyed me. "It actually reminds me of you."

"Thank you." I smiled, warmth building in my chest. "You know everyone says I look just like my grandmother."

TWENTY-THREE

Before Connor and I walked back to the Annex, Christian asked if I was free for lunch tomorrow. "It would mean so much to talk more," he told me. "I would love to hear how Annette is, and if you have any questions..."

I had so many. We hadn't really returned to the reality of Annie and Christian after Connor had done a double take at the artist's identity. Christian mostly spoke about his creative process, and I caught his drift. His history with Annie felt a little too intimate to share with anyone else.

"Yes," I told Christian. "I'm free tomorrow."

We agreed to meet in Edgartown, and I tried not to let thoughts of tomorrow preoccupy my brain for the rest of the night. Both excitement, nerves, and dread coursed through my veins. The former for obvious reasons, and the latter because I knew I had to tell Christian about Annie's dementia. I had to tell him that we were losing her.

I'd all but forgotten about Connor's final surprise until I asked how we were getting back across Oyster Pond. Would

Meredith take us back in the boat? Had Nick and Sage been given a pick up time? What time even was it?

Connor's raised suggestive eyebrow made my stomach flip-flop. "Who said anything about going home?" he said, then he turned to grab a Coleman lantern off the Annex's porch.

A flush crept up my neck; I hoped Meredith and Wit were brushing their teeth and not watching us from the kitchen window.

Okay, Olivia, I told myself. *They're mature adults, not middle schoolers.*

"Where are we going?" I asked Connor once we'd set off hand in hand. "The beach?"

"Mmm..." he mused. "Beach is a bit of a cliché, wouldn't you say?"

I laughed and grinned when he twirled me around while humming a familiar song. "I thought you didn't like Taylor Swift," I said.

"I am ambivalent," he replied. "But that doesn't mean she can't get stuck in my head."

He continued to hum, and I softly sang along. We might've been totally off-key, but we sounded perfect to me.

"This is one of Annie's favorites," I said after totally hitting—or entirely missing—the bridge. "She asked me to cue it up every time she picked me up from school. She also loved all Taylor's outfits in the music video."

"Set on safari in Africa, right?"

I raised an eyebrow.

His shrug was visible in the lamplight. "Liam."

"Of course." I smiled, then I heard myself say, "I'd like to meet him sometime."

"I think we can arrange that." Connor smiled back at me before we broke into another harmony.

But after a bend in the trail, my breath caught. A green tent waited patiently for us in the moonlit meadow. It was so simple, yet everything about it made me ache. I gave Connor a look.

"Your summer snapshots," he reminded me. "You need more than one."

I bit my lip. Part of me was tempted to ask if Connor watched *The Bachelor*, since this did kind of follow the famous one-on-one date formula, but most of me was too busy feeling like the luckiest girl in the world.

It was like a windowpane shattered in my head. Would any other guy plan *this* romantic an evening? If I'd let them?

Thinking so much about Annie tonight, I was starting to understand why I didn't.

"Connor, it's not like I'm leaving tomorrow..." I tried to joke before being hit by a sharp realization. "Oh my god, wait, my dad—"

"Don't worry, he knows you're here," Connor said quickly. "I spoke with him."

"You spoke with him?"

"Yeah, we had a talk yesterday."

A talk.

Connor coughed. "It went well," he assured me. "I said they were my specialty, remember?"

"Vividly, but I didn't totally believe you..."

He put a hand to his wounded heart.

"Until now."

Because any conversation must have gone well if I was allowed to be here overnight. I mean, Connor and I were camping together. Alone.

My dad wasn't a romance reader, but had he really never heard of the *tent trope*?

Blushing hard and fast, I moved to unzip the tent flap. Pillows and sleeping bags were inside, as well as a smaller cooler with water bottles and a retro plaid thermos. "Did you make this too?" I asked Connor. My mouth watered when I unscrewed the lid to smell hot chocolate.

He nodded. "Lee's recipe."

"Lee?"

"One of Mads's dads."

"Ah." Not wanting to think about Mads, or our tête-à-tête earlier, I suggested we sip while staring at the stars. Connor grabbed one of the tent's thick wool blankets and spread it out on the grass before we snuggled together. "Hold on," I said after a few minutes, wriggling away from him. "I need to get my phone. I want to take a video of this."

The sky was so hypnotic tonight.

"So you can show Annie?" Connor guessed, his voice laced with an unfamiliar something. It sounded like sarcasm, but it couldn't have been, right?

Just in case, I tossed my phone across the blanket once I'd captured the brilliant night sky on video. "This really is an incredible night," I murmured, a montage playing in my mind. Our delicious dinner, the tractor ride, discovering Annie's ties to Christian, and here and now with Connor.

"It is," he whispered back. "I've never been so grateful to Erica."

"Erica?" My eyelids fluttered when his hand slipped up the back of my sweatshirt, fingers dancing across my bare skin.

"Yeah," he breathed. "She told me you love to camp."

"Um…" I didn't know what to say, because back in ninth grade, Erica had jokingly bought me an all-weather air mattress and a legitimate hot-water bottle for my mandatory freshmen camping trip.

My family knew I didn't like to rough it.

Usually.

"Relax," Connor said when I tensed. "I know she was bullshitting me." He knocked his foot against mine. "I've met you, Olivia."

My laughter was loud in the gentle night. "But you're okay with that?" I asked as he resumed drawing circles on my skin. I melted into him again. "Her bullshitting you?"

"Definitely not, but there's a silver lining to almost getting got…"

Grinning, I rolled over to pin Connor to the blanket. His blue eyes were bright in the moonlight, something flashing in them before I leaned down and kissed him. "What's the silver lining?" I murmured, able to feel his heart beating against his chest.

It dared my pulse to match his.

In response, Connor tangled our legs together and used his strength to flip us over so that we were side to side. "Must I really spell it out?" he whispered, our foreheads now pressed together.

"Of course," I teased. "To ensure we're on the same page."

As if the heat building between us wasn't proof enough.

His hand found mine again, but instead of lacing our fingers, Connor stroked the inside of my wrist with his thumb. It sent ripple after ripple up my spine. "The silver lining," he began, voice low and a little strained, "is..."

I didn't let him finish; instead, I grabbed his face and kissed him so he would see more stars. Half a heartbeat later, he kissed me back, and then we were kissing each other like we were running out of starlight. Connor's tongue slipped inside my mouth, sweet but persistent, and it sent my pounding pulse straight up to the sky. My fingers tangled themselves in his hair, trying to pull him closer than close.

Distantly, I heard a dog bark.

Please, I thought. *Please stay far away from us.*

We shifted so that Connor was on top of me, the weight of his body a calm but also exhilarating feeling. Every inch of me was alive, my senses in overdrive. He tasted like hot chocolate, and I was consumed by the amazing but indiscernible scent of his shampoo, citronella candles, and the briny island air—and best of all, something that was just Connor McCallister. His five-o'clock shadow rubbed against my skin, but I didn't care. I couldn't get enough of him.

"Do—you—want—to—go—inside?" he asked when we finally pulled apart to breathe.

"Oh." I blinked, my mind moving a hundred miles a minute. "*Oh.*"

"We don't have to," Connor said quickly. "I know the timing is—well, we've only known each other two weeks." He started tripping over his words. "And I don't want to rush—I mean, pressure—you, and despite what some people believe, I *never* move this fast. I don't want you to think that, but we're here and we're alone and—"

"Connor." I covered his mouth with my hand. "Calm down."

He nodded, then he melted into a smile against my palm when I flicked my gaze toward the tent. He was right; we might've had a long history, but we'd only truly known each other two weeks. Less.

It was safe to say the upstanding young woman somewhere inside me was not impressed.

But I wanted this. Spellbinding magic had been sprinkled in my veins, and my expanding heart felt like a balloon about to pop. From my head to my toes to the depths of my core, I wanted to make the most of this moment with Connor.

I removed my hand from his mouth, and said, "Ask me again."

He was quick. "Do you want to go inside?"

I answered him with a light brush of my lips, then unzipped the tent myself.

Afterward, our limbs were entwined in a single sleeping bag. My body had liquefied at Connor's touch, and now my pulse felt faint, in tune with his slow and steady breathing. *What a wonderful way to fall asleep*, I dozed, my head against Connor's chest. I wanted nothing more than for his heartbeat to lull me to sleep.

If only that dog weren't *still* barking.

Someone was out looking for it now. "Loki!" we heard a man and woman shout every other minute. "Loki, *come*!"

Their calls and whistles seemingly went unanswered.

"So," Connor ventured once it was clear we weren't drifting off to dreamland anytime soon. He yawned. "What'd you and Mads talk about earlier?"

"Earlier?" I asked, because dinner now felt like three years ago.

"Yeah, while I visited the outhouse."

I willed myself not to clam up, Mads's words haunting me all over again.

Dream girl...

Got away...

Saving his heart for you...

"Oh, you know," I stalled. "Girl stuff."

"I'm surprised." Connor playfully zapped my waist. Goose bumps burst on my skin. "She didn't ask about your intentions?"

I knew he was only teasing, but my body reacted before I could tease him back.

"Whoa, whoa, whoa…" he said, incredulous. "She *did* ask?"

Shit, I thought. *Shit, shit, shit.*

I didn't want to get Mads in trouble, because even if her words worried me, I knew she meant well. And she technically hadn't asked after my intentions. The tractor's cinematic arrival had made sure of that.

Connor prodded me. "Olivia?"

"Mmm?"

"Jeez, don't *mmm* me…"

"No," I said, wincing at my voice. It sounded a little too firm. "No, there was no interrogation." I bit the inside of my cheek. "She's a really great friend, Connor."

"I know," he said as he shifted to prop himself up on an elbow. We made eye contact in the lantern's dim light. "Can you please loop me in here?"

My heart twisted. "Only if you promise not to get upset at Mads."

"I promise," he said, no hesitation. "Mads usually has a method to her madsness."

Mads-ness.

If the night were less charged, I would've laughed. "Okay, it's not a big deal," I said, stupidly making it sound like the opposite. "We were just talking about you, and Mads mentioned how much I mean to you, and that you've haven't felt this way about any other girls."

Connor didn't even blink. "I don't understand. What's the problem?"

I opened my mouth, but he fit puzzle pieces together too fast.

"Unless the issue is on your end," he said. "You mean a lot to me, but I don't mean as much to you."

I shook my head. "That's not what I'm saying. Not at all. It's just..."

"It's just?" he prompted when I trailed off. "It's just what?"

"It just wasn't supposed to be like this!" I blurted, sitting up and suddenly feeling very naked. Too naked. "We're supposed to be having fun together—we *are* having fun together—but what does that mean to you, Connor?"

He didn't speak for a second, so I took the silence to snatch my shirt off the floor and pull it over my head.

"It means exactly that," he finally said as the nighttime breeze rustled our tent. "We're having fun together... It's the truth, but to me, it's also an understatement." He ran a hand through his hair. "I think about us picking up where we left off when I get back home next month. I want to invite you over for dinner so you can meet my family. I imagine us taking turns visiting each other at school. You know Notre Dame is only a hundred miles from Northwestern, right?"

"That's so Troy Bolton," I mumbled, thinking of the corny but still swoony *High School Musical* line. "Thirty-two point seven miles away from you," Troy pointed out to Gabriella, when telling her about his college choice.

But I didn't hate hearing it.

Not at all.

Quite the opposite.

Yet...

There was this knot in my stomach, and I didn't know if I could untangle it.

"What do you think?" Connor asked. His eyes had grown glassy. "How does that sound to you?"

"I think that sounds really nice," I said truthfully, because I couldn't find the strength to agree or disagree. "Connor, you are the most—"

"*LOKI!*" came a call, and I nearly jumped out of my skin at the sharp whistle that followed. It sounded like the dog's owners were right outside our tent.

"Jesus Christ," I mumbled, heart thudding hard.

"You can say that again," Connor said, then sighed. "Should we walk back and sleep in the Annex? I don't think Meredith will mind if we crash in the sitting room."

Wanting out of this tent and away from my guilt, I agreed.

Loki barked our whole way back.

TWENTY-FOUR

I woke up early and a little achy on the floor. Worried about waking Wit and Meredith, Connor and I hadn't done much to make ourselves comfortable last night. We'd cobbled together a couple patchwork quilts and couch cushions for pillows.

It also appeared that we'd fallen asleep holding hands. It took a couple blinks to realize where I was and that I was holding our clasped hands to my heart.

Connor was still passed out, so I lightly kissed his knuckles before unlacing our fingers and rising from our nest on the floor. Something delicious-smelling wafted in from the kitchen, and I followed it to find Meredith slicing strawberries at the small granite countertop and Wit pouring coffee. "Morning, Olivia!" He smiled and held up a pink-and-blue cow printed mug. "Coffee? We suspect you didn't get much sleep last night."

"I am *so sorry*," Meredith said. "Loki is my family's dog, and he's unfortunately gone rogue in his old age." She shook her head as I faintly remembered Swede meeting a "Loki" on the ferry. A

Jack Russell Terrier. "And I feel awful you slept on the floor when the bunk room was empty…"

"Please don't worry about it," I told her as Wit handed me my coffee. "We were mentally prepared to camp already."

Meredith laughed. "Right, so now you deserve a five-star breakfast. The frittatas are in the oven, and based on the aroma, I think they have plenty of promise."

"I'll go wake Connor," I said, then I retreated to the cozy sitting room. Connor was unsurprisingly still dead to the world, although he'd shifted so that he was on his back with an arm thrown lazily over his head.

He looked both adorable and handsome, and the warmth blooming in my chest told me I needed to take a picture. I needed to capture Connor, in case…

Well, in case nothing. I refused to let my mind drift to last night.

But my phone wasn't hidden in our blankets or under the couch cushions. I couldn't even find it in the deep depths of my tote bag, which probably meant I'd accidentally left it behind in the tent last night. After Connor and I'd decided to bail, we'd hurried to grab only the essentials and left the rest until we returned to dismantle the tent. My phone must've been forgotten in the late-night shuffle.

Paqua Farm was very gray today. Above was an overcast sky, and in the distance churned a dull ocean. The trees, meadow, and flowers all appeared muted, and I shivered when the breeze snuck up on me. There was no one around, not even a distant bark from Loki. It felt gloomy, maybe even a little ominous.

Have the Foxes have ever considered renting to Hollywood? I wondered as I followed the trail toward our abandoned tent. *You could film a seriously melancholic period drama here…*

I doubted Meredith would find that flattering.

My phone lay face down a few feet outside the tent; I must've dropped it when we fled. I crouched to pick it up, and was surprised to find it still had some battery. And even more surprised to see some notifications since I had next to no signal. A couple emails, an Instagram DM from Quincy, several texts, and about forty minutes ago, I'd missed a call from my dad.

The last one spiked my pulse.

Why had my dad called me?

He'd also left a voicemail, but it wouldn't load. Everything alright? I texted him, and when the message took its sweet time to send, I tried to call him. Twice. The first attempt made a valiant effort to connect; the second immediately dropped.

Heart hammering, I ran back toward the Annex. Because something had to be wrong, right? My dad wouldn't call *and* leave a message if he just wanted to check in, or know what time Connor and I would be back later. Was Swede projectile vomiting something he'd eaten? Did Bryce accidentally refracture his wrist? Had Maisie choked on grapes at breakfast? She liked to goof off, tossing them in the air and catching them in her mouth…

Or, I didn't want to think, but did. *Or…*

Had something happened back home?

At Elkins?

That had to be it. That *had* to be it. Blood was pulsing in my ears by the time I turned onto the Farm's main road, beating so loudly that I barely heard my name called.

"Olivia!"

I glanced to my left to see Erica waving at me in her favorite oversized FAIRFIELD UNIVERSITY sweatshirt. How had she gotten here? Our car was nowhere to be seen.

By Boston Whaler?

"Hi," I said slowly, as she picked up her pace. Something in my bones told me to stop in my tracks, to wait for her. "Is everything okay?"

What a stupid question.

Something was clearly wrong.

Instead of answering, my stepmother wrapped her arms around me and squeezed me tight. The hug felt more like a straitjacket than a warm embrace, like she thought I might run away, or maybe she had really paid attention to how Annie delivered bad news to me over the years. When she'd told me about Pops passing, I could barely feel my blood circulating.

But I'd never felt safer.

Now, a hard lump rose in my throat. "Is Annie..." I started, but I didn't want to say the rest aloud, for fear that it might be true.

"No," Erica whispered, "but Elkins called this morning." She paused. "She's had a really bad fall, Liv."

Big, hot tears threatened to escape—*crocodile tears*, Annie called them—and everything in my body told me to pull away from Erica, but I didn't have the strength.

Or maybe I didn't want to.

"She's in the hospital," she continued, now stroking my hair. "It sounds like she might need surgery, so your dad is going to drive home today. He's packing right now, and we booked a ferry out of Vineyard Haven in a couple hours."

This time I did break away from Erica, suddenly desperate to move. Desperate to take action. "I need to get my stuff," I told her, wiping my eyes before wildly gesturing to the Annex. "We need to get back to the house. I need to talk to him."

"Okay." She nodded; her eyes were glassy. "Let's get your stuff."

~

According to Elkins, the last few days for Annie had been incredibly difficult. She'd been irritated with the nursing staff, refused to eat meals, and was endlessly restless. If she did manage to fall asleep at night, she woke up in the wee hours of the morning and insisted on taking a shower. A night nurse complied, and then she'd be dressed by 3:00 a.m.

Her fall had not been especially dramatic. She hadn't slipped in the shower or gotten up from bed and collapsed. "She stubbed her toe on the carpet," my dad told me when Erica and I got back to the house. Maisie and Bryce didn't know; they were making waffles with Nick. "She didn't lift her foot up enough when she took a step."

"Turf toe," Erica softly said. "That's what the lacrosse team called it in college whenever someone tripped on the turf."

My dad took her hand and tried to smile, but his lips were a thin line.

"When do we leave?" I asked, a rasp in my voice.

"Liv." He sighed. "You don't—"

"When do we leave?"

"A half hour."

That was all I needed to hear; I spun on my heel and hauled ass to my little room upstairs so I could start packing. *Only the essentials*, I told myself. I'd ask Maisie to grab my beach towel off the clothesline and bikini from the hook in the outdoor shower and bring them home next week.

Next week.

We had come up here for three, and I was ducking out after two. Topper and Peggy hadn't even had their anniversary dinner yet.

It's okay, I told myself. *This is an emergency.*

My heart hammered as I unzipped my huge suitcase and started throwing things inside, organization be damned. Pajamas, sneakers, bras, rain jacket…

I heard a knock on the door while I quickly balled up my socks. It was Erica, holding my two glittery cosmetic cases from the bathroom. "Light packer" would never be on my résumé. "I'm pretty sure I grabbed everything." She offered them to me. "If any nail polish is missing, Maisie probably has it."

"Well, at least it's safe," I said. "Thank you."

Erica folded her arms across her chest. I wanted to return to my turbo-packing, but she clearly had something to say.

And I didn't need to prompt her.

"You shouldn't feel obligated to go," she said gently. "Your dad can handle this."

I tried to keep my cool. "I don't feel obligated," I said. "I want—*need* to go. This is Annie."

"I know." Erica nodded. "I understand, but this trip has been so wonderful for you, Olivia. Do you really want to give up your last week of vacation to sit in the hospital?"

It felt like she'd slapped me in the face.

My cheeks certainly burned like she had.

"It's only her arm—"

"Are you serious?" I cut her off. "Are you *seriously* suggesting that I blow off Annie—who is hurt and sick and so alone—to continue running around this island?"

"No." Erica shook her head. "No, I'm sorry. That didn't come out right."

I didn't care.

"I get it," I said, gritting my teeth. "I've been paying attention these last couple weeks. You aren't close to your parents—you can't even decorate a scrapbook!—so it's impossible for you to grasp why I am the way I am with Annie." I laughed hollowly. "But just this once, I wish you would *try* to understand!"

Pulse pounding, I waited for Erica's rebuttal, but it came in the form of a step backward, like I'd shoved her. "Please say goodbye to your brother and sister before you go," was all she said, then she turned and disappeared into the hall.

"Don't worry, I'm hurrying," I said when I heard resolute footsteps a few seconds later. Definitely my dad, eager to get on the road.

But it was Connor who appeared in the doorway. My heart dropped like an elevator.

Were you even going to say goodbye? I expected him to say, because in the time it had taken me to return to the tent to track down my phone and then run into Erica, he'd woken up and volunteered to run to Morning Glory Farm with Wit for a desperately needed loaf of zucchini bread. I hadn't waited for him to come back, instead asking Meredith to give him a hug for me and tell him I'd call him.

Surprisingly, Connor mentioned nothing about my flimsy farewell. "Why are you so hard on her?" he asked.

My eyebrows knitted together. "Excuse me?"

"Erica," he said. "I heard you two from the stairs."

Perfect, I thought, stomach swishing. *I bet others did too.*

"Olivia, why are you so rough on her?"

"Because she's being ridiculous!" I sputtered.

He neither agreed nor disagreed. "You didn't need to yell at her. She's just looking out for you." He gave me a lopsided smile. "She loves you."

My heart twinged. I knew Erica loved me, she was sort of obligated to, but did she *like* me? I felt like she was critical of everything I did.

Because she wants what's best for you, a voice in my head said. *She might not be warm and cuddly, but neither are you. You never have been.*

For fuck's sake, I'd put glue in her shampoo!

Connor coughed. "And if you really think about it, she might be right," he gently ventured. "Your dad is Annie's emergency contact, and maybe it's better if you give him some space to handle—" He dropped off, likely because of the expression on my face. It wasn't an angry glare, but my eyes widened. He didn't support me?

Oh, I realized when his shoulders just barely slumped. He was disappointed.

Here I was leaving, and we had no plan for what came next.

Because he wanted something to come next; he wanted a *future*.

"Connor." I sighed. "I don't know what to say."

"Just say you'll call me tonight and have dinner with me next month," he said, taking a step toward me.

Okay, I thought, because that wasn't much. He wasn't asking for much. He wasn't asking me to marry him, let alone be his girlfriend. But I knew he saw that on the horizon.

"Why do you even like me?" I whispered, my insides twisting.

"I'm not her, Connor. I'm not the girl of your dreams, not the *Olivia Lupo* of your dreams." I swallowed hard. "Mads told me—"

"A joke," he cut in. "Mads—who I plan to murder, by the way—told you *a joke*. There is no Olivia of my dreams."

My eyebrows knitted together. *Huh?*

Connor sighed. "I've dated a lot and had a couple serious girlfriends. Like Mads says, I'm a serial monogamist. And I like being that way; I like having a girlfriend." He rubbed the back of his neck. "But all those relationships have ended, and most of them didn't tear me up too much. Mads and I would laugh and say it was because Kaylie or Brenna or Dani or Leah wasn't *Olivia*. It didn't last because she wasn't Olivia." His voice quieted. "I haven't ever fallen in fucking love because no one has been Olivia. Not even *Mads* is Olivia."

Oh, I thought.

My stomach sank, starting to get it. Connor hadn't spent the last several years pining after me specifically; no, he'd been yearning for...

"I had the biggest crush on you at Camp Skytop," he said. "I looked for you between every activity and at every meal and counted down the hours until phone time not only to beg my mom to come get me, but also for my promised face time with you." He shook his head. "I loved watching you talk on the phone; your face *lit up* as soon as someone in your family picked up."

Olivia! I could hear Annie's voice, even now. Music to my ears. *Dearest, tell me everything...*

"All you remember about me is my freckles and Red Sox jersey, because the thought of talking to you tongue-tied me. Literally. If you asked me my name, I guarantee I wouldn't have been able to tell you."

"Maybe not," I told him. "But your name tag would've been your wingman."

One side of Connor's mouth tugged up in a smile. We'd been required to wear pins for our entire Skytop session. "I've never again blanked like that with a girl," he said. "But god, I wish I would. I've always hoped someone would make me forget my name like Olivia Lupo." His blue eyes held mine. "Who I truly never imagined getting a second shot to introduce myself to, as melodramatic and daunting as that most definitely sounds to you."

I opened my mouth, but I couldn't speak; my heart had lodged itself in my throat.

"You think I don't know you." He shrugged. "Maybe I just don't know you at your best." He moved forward to take my hands. His calloused palms started to soothe my shaking fingers. "But I've absolutely gotten glimpses of the real Olivia, and all I know is that I love being with her. She's funny and caring; she's smart and so loving. She has the best laugh, and I feel like I can talk to her about anything while being totally tongue-tied." His eyes clouded. "Our timing must not be right, though."

Is it ever going to be? I wondered. Because even if I spoke or FaceTimed with Connor every day until he got home, who knew what next month would look like. I didn't know how intense Annie's recovery would be, but I knew every fall left her weaker.

And we would both be leaving for college in mid-August, which would be a big deal for both of us. The two Homebodies. A relationship just seemed like something we couldn't fit on our plates, no matter how much we might want to.

I could barely look at Connor when I told him that. Logic that sounded like lies. The corners of my eyes stung. "You know you can shift things around on your plate," he said. "You can move the mashed potatoes to make room for stuffing, especially when the stuffing is *this good*."

I laughed a little, letting the tears loose.

"Liv!" I heard my dad call as Connor wiped them away, thumbs brushing across my cheekbones. It made the backs of my knees go weak. "You just about ready?"

"Be right down!" My voice nearly cracked. I was nowhere near ready.

Connor exhaled a deep breath, sparking my pulse. "I hope Annie is okay," he said, hiding his hands in his pockets. "Please tell her I say hi."

"What did you talk about?" I asked, remembering the time he'd stolen my phone.

"Flowers," he said. "She told me about her hydrangeas. She'd cut them herself, from Erica's bushes. They were blue at first, then turned white overnight. I told her they sounded beautiful." He smiled sadly. "And then we talked about you."

TWENTY-FIVE

After disembarking the ferry, my dad and I only stopped once on the way home. Swede—seemingly fine with his vacation being cut short—was pretty vocal about his need for a bathroom break. We grabbed coffee after hitting the rest stop's bathroom ourselves, then we were back on the road. I put on my dad's favorite playlist, but he didn't drum along on the steering wheel like usual. We both stayed silent with our thoughts. Mine circled around Connor…

"*Fuck*," I whispered.

My dad switched lanes. "Mmm?"

"Fuck," I said again. "I was supposed to go out to lunch today." I winced. "With Christian Fox."

"Christian Fox as in Topper's friend?"

"Yes." I nodded, then I started to spill the story. "He knew Annie, Dad. He knew her back when she and Kathy Ryan came to the Vineyard."

"I knew Kathy would have some involvement," my dad mumbled.

"*Christopher.*" I poked his arm. "I'm serious. I found out he's the artist behind Annie's little watercolors. He was really important to her."

"Okay..."

"He's the *Chris* she's been complaining never visits, Dad. Not you."

My dad glanced over at me, now hooked. "What's the story?"

"I don't know," I said. "I was supposed to have lunch with him today to find out." I groaned. "He probably thinks I blew him off..."

"I'm sure that's not true," he said. "Olivia Lupo never blows anyone off."

I snorted, because she'd definitely done a fantastic job of blowing off Connor. He'd poured his heart out to me and what had I done?

Left.

Like I always do, I started to reflect. I left relationships so no one had the chance to leave *me*.

"Why don't you text Erica?" he suggested, our car speeding up. "I bet she can get in touch with Christian."

I bit the inside of my cheek, knowing it was a good idea but worried too. She'd only given me a shoulder-squeeze goodbye.

This was more important, though.

Hi, I wrote. I was supposed to meet Christian Fox today for lunch. Could you or your dad tell him I had to leave?

Of course, she texted back. I will call him.

I stared at her message for a few seconds, then typed, I'm sorry, Erica. I'm the worst.

She typed for a while after I hit send, but her response ended up being brief: Please give Annie a kiss for me.

My chest tightened.

"How are Erica and the twins getting home?" I asked later, when we finally crossed the Connecticut border into New York. Connecticut was such a small state, yet it took forever to get through because of its traffic. It suddenly hit me that we'd taken the car.

"They'll fly," my dad said as I scratched Swede's ears. He'd fallen asleep with his head on the center console. "Martha's Vineyard to Boston to Philly."

"Expensive?" I asked.

"Outrageously," he answered, and then he smiled the closest thing to a smile I'd seen this whole drive. Pilots and their families flew for free.

Onward we drove.

~

After finally dropping Swede and our suitcases at home, we drove to Capital Health, the closest hospital to Elkins Village. Annie was in surgery, so we sat in the waiting room until the doctor found us. Her surgery had gone well but sounded grotesque. She'd needed a few screws, along with a serious plate.

"You don't have to see her," my dad said when we were waiting for Annie to leave the recovery room and get settled elsewhere. He dug out his keys from his pocket. "Head back to the house, figure out what you want to order for dinner, and later I'll Uber—"

"Dad, no." I shook my head. Haddonfield was fifty minutes away, and I wanted to see Annie. "I'm staying by your side."

He pulled me close, wrapping an arm around my shoulders.

"Lupo?" A nurse eventually called. "Annette Lupo?"

"Yes, that's us." My dad and I sprung up from our seats. "Annette is my mother."

My heart grew heavier after the nurse escorted us to Annie's room; I hardly recognized my grandmother. Her still unfamiliar gray hair was flat but unkempt at the same time. And her skin was so eerily pale, which only emphasized her bruises. I sucked in my breath at the one on her face. Black and blue had blossomed on her left cheek, the color cradling her eye.

Oh, Annie, I thought, tears welling up. I took her hand and squeezed it, blue veins looking like lace on her skin. If Bryce were here, he'd call it a spiderweb.

He'd also want to sign her white cast, but if things were different, I knew she'd be horrified at the thought.

But things weren't different; we didn't have all of Annie, so I didn't think she'd mind some Sharpie action. Or even notice.

Her eyes blinked open once or twice during the two hours we spent there—and I swear we got the ghost of a smile—but she didn't speak. "See you tomorrow," I whispered before kissing her forehead goodbye. "The twins and Erica love you so much." A few tears drip-dropped into her matted hair. "They'll be here soon."

Would a week feel like "soon" to her? No one knew how time worked in Annie's head, not even Annie herself.

She only spent one night at the hospital, then she was discharged and brought back to Elkins. My dad handled that part, and I pulled into the parking lot a few hours later. The drive from Haddonfield had felt unusually long, and even though we'd only been gone two weeks, Finlay House didn't feel as familiar. There was the atrium, which tried so hard to be cheery with its bright skylight and colorful photographs decorating the taupe walls.

Unfortunately, I wasn't buying it today.

Residents had congregated at the rally point, like it was Groundhog Day. Women worked on a jigsaw puzzle while blind Bob Coleman wore his big headphones, off in audiobook land.

Other people dozed in their wheelchairs and strollers, keeping warm under their fleece blankets. A lump rose in my throat. How long until Annie became one of them?

She looked so small in her bed; my grandmother had *never* seemed small to me. She'd always been a statuesque five foot eight.

So much has changed, I thought. *So much has changed in two weeks…*

I told myself over and over that it had nothing to do with the fact that none of us had visited. That a lack of visitors had nothing to do with Annie's setback.

Setback, not decline.

"Hi, Annie," I softly smiled when she was finally *awake*-awake during my visit, three days after surgery. I kept my relieved enthusiasm in check, not wanting to frighten her. "How are you?"

She blinked, and I held my breath, preparing myself to be no one special to her. "Mmm…livia," she mumbled, and that was it.

But when she squeezed my hand, I squeezed hers back.

It was like this the next day too. Even if Annie's eyes were open, she didn't really engage with me or my dad. He stuck to asking questions about her bachelorette life in New York or telling stories from his childhood, like he had for a while now. Her long-term memory had hung on the longest.

But her responses were more or less the same: a combination of her dreamy voice and distant smiles. "Oh, yes," she whispered after we asked about living at the Barbizon Hotel. "My roommate would always…" She trailed off. "…and then stole…Daddy bought me…"

I willed my Martha's Vineyard memory book to come faster. I'd finished compiling it the night my dad and I'd gotten home and paid for express shipping. *Golden Hour Girls* was the title.

Seeing Connor throughout my camera roll had been harder than I'd thought, because there were more pictures of him than I realized I took. One I lingered on, perhaps my favorite, had been taken at sunset on the Farm. Meredith had secretly snapped it, she then sent it to Connor, who sent it to me. It was our last photo together.

Everyone had gotten off the Oystercatcher to find the best view, but Connor and I'd stayed put, legs dangling off the flatbed. He had his arm around my shoulders, and I had both of mine looped around his waist, hugging him close. We weren't grinning at the camera, but instead smiling slyly at each other in the pink-orange glow.

My heart heaved. I hadn't heard from him since I'd left the island, but why would I? Not only had he resumed minding Teddy and Finn, but I hadn't exactly signaled that I wanted him to call me. All I'd given him was a litany of reasons why we wouldn't work.

Shutterfly finally fulfilled their promise on Friday, and I didn't bother opening the box before driving to Elkins. Needing a breather, my dad had gone out to lunch with friends. It was only me today.

"I'm so sorry, Olivia," Tara said as I signed in at the nurses' station, excitement written all over my face. "I must sound like a broken record, but she's asleep. We had her in a chair for a couple hours this morning"—she gestured to the rally point—"and I think walking tired her out."

"Oh." My stomach sunk. It was good that they'd gotten Annie up and walking, but… "That's okay," I said. "I'll just sit with her."

I cracked the front cover of *Golden Hour Girls* once I'd

plopped down in my grandmother's cushy bedside "throne," but I kept checking on Annie. Her breathing was pretty steady, although the pained expression on her face made me shift in my seat. She still hadn't gotten used to her sling. My dad had to stop her from tearing it off the other day.

Two minutes later, my phone buzzed with a text. From Erica, a photo of Bryce and Teddy on the beach. Someone had buried them waist-down in the sand before giving them mermaid tails. *Connor and Finn sculpted the tails,* Erica had written. *Maisie collected "the scales."*

The scales were pebbles, shells, and bits of purple and white wampum.

Siri, play "Under the Sea", I wrote, hearting her messages. I wouldn't say things were good between us, but we had been updating each other throughout this week.

If my dad had any idea what I'd said to Erica before we'd left, he didn't let on.

And I didn't need Erica to remind me that today was Topper and Peggy's anniversary. The Carmichaels had been talking about it for the last couple weeks. I knew Nick and Sage had taken them on a boat ride around the island this morning (coffee and pastries included), and their children had a lunch reservation at Edgartown Yacht Club. Tonight was the big dinner at the Outermost Inn.

I thought about asking Erica to pass along my congratulations, but I realized there was nothing stopping me from reaching out myself. Topper and Peggy Carmichael had been nothing but welcoming to me this month…

And, I thought, stomach churning, *I didn't even say goodbye to them.*

I'd seen them through the kitchen window while I hugged Maisie and Bryce, reading together on the back deck, but I hadn't been able to take five seconds to slip outside to thank them for their hospitality.

I wanted to kick myself.

That wasn't me. That wasn't the person my dad and Annie had raised.

May I have your mom's number? I texted Erica.

Leaving the memory book behind, I left Annie's room and walked farther down the hall, to a door that opened out to a small courtyard. It was only open during visitor hours. Greenery outlined the flagstone patio, and bright zinnias burst from terracotta pots. I tapped on the contact Erica had shared, and I sat down in a wicker chair as the phone started to ring. On the third ring, I started to mentally compose my voicemail.

But Peggy picked up on the fourth.

"Hello?" she answered. "Who is this?"

Right, she didn't have my number.

"Hi, Peggy," I said, summoning a smile even though she couldn't see. "It's Olivia."

"Oh, Olivia, hello," she replied. "How are you?"

"Celebrating!" I joked. "I wanted to wish you and Topper a

happy anniversary. I hope you have some champagne on ice for tonight."

"Thank you, sweetie." She laughed. "We do have a bottle we've been saving for a very long time. Topper and Beth are just dying to pop it."

"I hope someone takes a video."

"Charlie has already been informed. I'm told he has the newest iPhone."

"Perfect," I said, then swallowed hard. "I also wanted to say thank you, Peggy. Thank you to both you and Topper. It was so kind of you to welcome me into your home this month, and I had a wonderful time." I started babbling. "And I'm sorry I didn't say goodbye before I left; I'm really embarrassed. I just didn't expect to leave so suddenly, and I was so worried about my grandmother..." I trailed off, to right myself. "I loved spending so much time with your family, and I hope you all have a fantastic dinner tonight."

"That means a lot to me, Olivia." Peggy sounded like she was smiling. "And I will pass the message along to Topper." She paused. "Frankly, I have no idea why Erica was so nervous about you making the trip."

My eyebrows knitted together. "Erica was nervous about me coming?"

"Oh, yes," her mother said. "She was so worried, so wrapped up in ensuring that you had a great time..."

Something bittersweet twinged in my chest.

"...I understand the last year has been a lot for you."

"Yes," I said. "It's been a lot for my whole family."

And with that, I thought of my family, who meant so much to me. My dad, Bryce, Maisie, and…

"Peggy, do you have Instagram?" I asked.

"Oh no, I don't." She laughed lightly. "Sage keeps offering to download it for me, but it sounds like there is a learning curve."

"Well, I think you should take Sage up on her offer, so you can follow Erica," I said. "Her feed is gorgeous. Annie always loved looking at it with me, and I know you'll love it too."

Peggy was quiet, contemplative. "How is she doing, if you don't mind me asking?" she asked after a beat. "Your grandmother?"

I bit the inside of my cheek. "I don't want to dampen the mood of your big day."

"Please." I imagined her waving a hand. "I got seasick on the boat this morning, and Jay spilled his beer on me at lunch. And the kiddies asked to give Posey a bath this afternoon and ended up dyeing her green. The day can only go up from here."

I couldn't help it; I tilted my head back and laughed.

My eyes were puffy from tears as I headed back to Annie's room, but talking to Peggy about her had been cathartic. She was a good listener.

She also said she'd speak to Sage about creating an Instagram profile.

It was a step in the right direction.

I nearly ran into Tara; she was exiting another resident's room and brightened when we made eye contact. "There you are!"

"Here I am…"

"I've been looking for you," she said, unable to contain her excitement. "Annette has a visitor!"

"Oh, my dad?"

The nurse shook her head, and my pulse sped up. Had one of Annie's old friends woken up and finally realized they owed her a visit? That, after being the world's greatest friend for forever, she *deserved* a visit?

I couldn't wait to see who it was and give them a piece of my mind.

But when I marched into Annie's room, I ended up swallowing my words. Because it wasn't one of Annie's golf buddies, or old neighbors, or a longtime rival from her bridge club.

It was Christian Fox.

TWENTY-SIX

He wore a green visitor's badge and sat at the edge of Annie's throne, paging through her *Golden Hour Girls* book, but he looked up at the sound of my steps. The book snapped shut. "Olivia," he said, rising from the chair and clearing his throat. "Hello."

"Hi." I tried to keep the mood light. "You forgive me then?"

Christian tilted his head, not quite following.

"For standing you up for lunch?"

He chuckled. "It's been years since I've been stood up, so my ego was a little bruised, but of course I do. Erica called and explained what happened..." He drifted off to glance at Annie, who stirred but stayed sleeping. "Which is how I ended up here."

Why didn't Erica warn me? I wondered.

"She didn't know I was coming," he clarified. "She only gave me the details." He rubbed his forehead. "I can't believe I didn't know."

"Why would you?" I asked, and I gestured for him to sit back down. I perched at the foot of Annie's bed, careful not to crush her toes. "How long as it been since you've spoken?"

"A *very* long time," Christian answered. "We ran into each

other at JFK airport once; it had to be ten or twelve years ago. I was flying out to Amsterdam, and she had just deplaned from…"

"Australia," I finished for him. "She took a six-week cruise to Sydney then flew home."

"Yes." He nodded, a bittersweet expression on his face. "And that's *all* she told me. I noticed her wedding ring, but she didn't mention if she'd had any children or where exactly she lived. It was only a quick hello." He chuckled. "I suppose she didn't want to devastate me further."

I raised an eyebrow. "You never knew she was Annette Lupo?"

"Never," Christian said. "I only knew her by her maiden name; before the airport, the last time we'd spoken was when she broke off our—"

"Your what?" I asked after he cut himself off. "When she broke off your what?"

Although the answer was suddenly obvious. I thought of Annie's favorite ring, safely stowed in my jewelry box. She'd worn it almost every day, as much as or more often than her engagement ring. My dad had brought back the two sapphires from Thailand, but the diamond's origin was a mystery. I'd surmised it was a family stone.

I tried to keep my voice from leaping an octave. "You two were engaged."

"We were." Christian nodded. "For a time."

My pulse pounded. I needed more information; I needed to know what happened.

"We spent four summers together," he continued. "Four incredibly *meaningful* summers on the Vineyard. They always went by too quickly, and it took a lot of strength to say goodbye to each other before returning to school. I was at Georgetown, and she was, of course, at Vassar."

"For two years," I whispered. Annie had only gone to college for two years before deciding that it wasn't for her. After that, she'd enrolled in secretarial school and started her life in New York.

"Mm-hmm," he hummed, and I sensed some type of subtext there. "Before that, we did everything together. Swim, sail, read, paint, dance, fish, and we played so much golf and tennis. Explore too." He half-smiled. "We truly were inseparable. I proposed toward the end of our fourth summer. I snuck back to Boston one day to buy the ring."

"What happened?" I asked quietly. The Foxes struck me as the type of family who'd pass down heirloom jewelry.

"My parents," Christian said.

"They didn't like her?"

"Oh, no." He shook his head. "They *loved* her; my father called her *enchanting*."

"Then what was wrong?" I folded my arms across my chest. Annie *was* enchanting.

"I did not grow up with her," he told me matter-of-factly. "We did not attend cotillions together, and she did not have a debutante ball in Boston."

I couldn't help it; I rolled my eyes. *Thwarted by the Junior League?*

What bullshit. Annie was classier than every one of those girls.

"I thought my parents would accept us after I proposed," Christian said, "but they did not; in fact, things grew worse. They were no longer kind toward Annette, when she had been such a part of the family for the last few years... She ended things in December...god, over fifty years ago now. I was supposed to stop in New York on my way home for Christmas, but she wrote me a letter earlier that month and told me not to come. She thought it was in both our best interests if we called off the wedding whose date hadn't even been set."

"And you listened?"

Before Christian could answer, Annie groaned in bed. I smiled when she blinked open her eyes. They were so blue. "Hi, Annie," I said softly. "Someone's here to see you..."

"Clearly, dearest." She was blunt. "You."

I shook my head, then gestured to her visitor.

My grandmother's eyes didn't widen, but I caught something spark in them. She recognized him, right? "Oh, Chris," she whispered, and when her summer love reached out to take her hand, she added, "Must you still bite your nails?"

I slipped out of the room to give them some alone time after Annie told me that Christian was a man she had "once corresponded with."

Some things she was always going to keep private, I guess. Even if the secret was standing and smiling a little cheekily right in front of us.

I hung out nearby, in one of the hallway's small alcoves. Phones weren't exactly encouraged in Finlay House, but they also weren't prohibited. "Hey, Liv," my dad said. "I'm just grabbing some dinner stuff at Acme. Everything okay?"

"Better than okay." I beamed at no one. "Annie has a visitor."

The line was silent for a beat, until he asked if said visitor was the ghost of Kathy Ryan. Like me, my dad wasn't impressed with the foot traffic of Annie's friends.

Or lack thereof.

"Two words," I told him. "Christian Fox."

"Huh," he said. "He drove all the way down here? At his age?"

I admit, he had a point. We knew plenty of octogenarians who drove…but six hours? Across multiple states?

"Dad!" I whisper-yelled. "He and Annie were once *engaged*!"

My dad, again: "Huh."

"She broke it off because the Fox elders were Knickerbocker snobs back then," I hurried. "But her sapphire ring's diamond? That was from *him*."

"And our names are suspiciously similar," he said wryly. "Did she love my father at all?"

I gasped. "Dad!"

"I'm *just kidding*, Liv." He chuckled. "Although I've always wondered where she got that diamond…"

"He has so many stories about Annie." I bit the inside of my cheek. "I'd really like to hear them."

There was another pause on his end, but I didn't think he was hesitating. Just thinking. "I would too," he said after several seconds. "If he likes chicken piccata, he's welcome to come for dinner."

I smiled and speed-walked back to Annie's room once we hung up. "And I have the sweetest daughter-in-law," I heard my grandmother saying, which made me stop short. Her voice was soft and a bit strained, but this was the chattiest and most coherent she'd been since her surgery.

And Erica? The sweetest? What happened to calling her *that woman*?

"She is such a good mother to my grandchildren and tries so hard with…" She lost her train of thought. "And she's just so wildly creative. I used to love decorating the house for the holidays with her"—her voice soured—"but my family no longer lets me leave this place. Did you know Olivia stole my car?"

The corners of my eyes prickled. I hadn't *stolen* her Mercedes, but guilt still coated my skin. Because I'd lied. "Please, Annie?" I remembered asking a couple years ago, playing it so cool. "The Jeep's going to be in the shop for a few days, and I need a car to get around…"

I'd convinced my grandmother to let me borrow her car, with no plans to return it. Annie couldn't be trusted on the road anymore, so my dad had sold it back to the Mercedes dealership. She'd asked about the car a few times, then she stopped one day. I still didn't know if it was because she'd forgotten about it or realized it was never coming back to Elkins' parking lot.

"Oh, Annette..." Christian laughed as I edged toward the doorway, not sure I wanted to interrupt. "Believe me, my daughter wants to steal my car too. Especially after today's road trip."

"Daughter?" Annie asked.

"Yes, Elise. I have two sons too."

"Oh, that's nice..." She didn't ask any follow-up questions, which meant she was no longer comprehending. My heart twisted. "You took a road trip?"

"Yes," he said. "A road trip to visit you."

"Why?" she asked. "We saw each other just last month." She laughed. "You almost drove the tractor into Job's Neck!"

Christian was quiet. "Right," I just barely heard him say. "Right, I'm so happy to hear that you haven't forgotten."

"Oh, I could never," she said as two tears slipped down my cheeks. "*Never*."

~

Christian didn't say anything once we'd said goodbye to Annie; instead, he wrapped me in a firm hug. *I'm so sorry*, it seemed to say.

"Would you like to come over for dinner?" I asked.

Swede barked up a storm when we got to Haddonfield, my dad immediately offering Christian a drink. If either of them thought this dinner date was weird, you'd never be able to tell. He smiled fondly at the photo albums I showed him while my dad cooked, and he beamed at Annie's old Polaroids and watercolors. "She nicknamed the Farm 'Summer Camp' as soon as she set foot on it," he confirmed, then he pointed out his inked but hidden initials. My favorite was a tiny CDF twisted into a tree trunk.

My dad and I loved hearing about Annie's adventures on the Vineyard—she ran around barefoot, she grilled the best tuna, she had the worst luck with skunks, and she won every late-night poker game—and I could tell Christian was enraptured by my dad's stories about growing up with Annie as his mother. "*Really*?" he asked when my dad started telling him about the time he and his best friend canoed as fast as they could down the Delaware River. "She *refused* to pick you up afterward?"

"Well, the guide told her that the route was supposed to take four hours, but if you don't stay with the group..." My dad shrugged. "Edwin and I did it in *two* hours, and afterward, we called her from the pay phone. She briskly told us her bridge guests just arrived, so we had to hang around the general store until the full *four* had passed..."

Christian was also heartwarmingly interested in my grandfather, but when my dad started telling him how Pops and Annie met, my phone started to chime from the kitchen counter. "My bad," I said, hurrying to silence it.

But once I saw the name on my screen, my heart slipped into my stomach, and it wasn't so easy to send the caller to voicemail.

Because the caller was Connor.

"Hello?" I said after I'd sequestered myself in our house's screened-in porch. "Connor?"

"Hi," he said evenly. "How are you?"

"I'm fine. We're in the middle of dinner."

"Oh, of course." He coughed. "I can call—"

"No, no, it's fine." I guess that was my word of the day. Fine. "How are you? Isn't Topper and Peggy's anniversary dinner right now?" (Erica had texted my dad some photos of the oasis that was the Outermost Inn.)

"It is," Connor confirmed. "And they invited me, but I stayed back and made some pasta. I'm not really part of the family."

"I get it," I said, even though I had thought about the Carmichael dinner more than once after calling Peggy today. I knew their grandchildren had an original song to sing, and Erica and her siblings had each prepared a toast. Plus, the scrapbook. Had Erica finished her pages?

"You have FOMO?" Connor joked when I didn't add anything else.

"A little, actually," I admitted, feeling my lips twitch in amusement. "It sounded like a really nice night." My heart twisted. "But I'm meant to be here."

Connor didn't say anything, then sighed. "I'm so sorry, Olivia. I can't believe I said or suggested that you should stay here. *Of course* you should've gone home to see Annie." He went quiet again. "It was nothing but selfish of me, and I'm sorry. I feel like such an asshole."

"Don't," I said. "Please. I was the asshole, Connor."

I am *the asshole.*

He shifted the subject. "How is Annie? Erica told me her surgery went well, but she hasn't said much since. Just that you and your dad are visiting a lot."

"Every day." I nodded. "And she's okay but still pretty weak. She sleeps most of the time, and when she's not sleeping, she's irritated by her sling." I bit my pinkie nail. "Although she did have a non-blood-related visitor today."

"Oh, really?" Connor sounded intrigued. "A white-haired man with a baseball cap, perhaps?"

"Wait, he told you?"

"He mentioned it to me on the beach the other day, that he *might* go." Long pause. "He also offered to give me a ride, in case I wanted to visit too."

A hard lump formed in my throat.

"And I thought about it," Connor went on, voice a little strained. "I know the Carmichaels would've understood and covered Teddy and Finn, but..." I could see him running a hand through his hair. "I really wasn't sure if you'd want to see me."

"Connor." I gripped my phone tighter. "It would've meant

so much to see you. Really, it would've. You turn everything to sunshine and magic."

So incredibly corny but also so incredibly true.

"I'm glad," was all he said.

We sat on the phone in silence. "I should go," I said after a minute of hearing nothing but blood pump through my ears. "Christian is telling us about *Annette* in exchange for stories about Annie, and I don't want to miss any good ones."

"Of course," he said. "I bet all of them are good ones. Please tell him I'm happy to hear he made it down okay."

"I will," I said, and even though his young charges had FaceTimed me with Bryce yesterday, I added, "Please tell Teddy and Finn hi from me."

His words were the equivalent of a salute. "You got it."

I squeezed my eyes shut, aware I initiated a goodbye but not wanting to be the first to say it. "And let me know if they share any funny sound bites from dinner, okay?"

"Sure," Connor said, then took a breath. "Have a good rest of your night, Olivia."

He hung up before I could whisper it back.

TWENTY-SEVEN

Christian went back to Elkins the next day to see Annie again before he drove back to Massachusetts. I took the elevator down to Finlay and got there right after he'd been buzzed through the maximum-security doors. His eyes were red, like he'd been repeatedly wiping away tears. I didn't need to ask to surmise that Annie probably hadn't recognized him.

"Please keep in touch, Miss Lupo." He gave me a hug. "If you ever want to talk, or if anything..." He trailed off, and I was grateful. I could imagine, but didn't want to *hear*, the rest of the sentence. "Let me give you my phone number, okay?"

After airdropping me his contact information—Christian was skilled with a smartphone—he asked about my "young man."

"Oh, Connor's not my young man," I said, flushing a little. Had Connor not mentioned I'd taken his heart and stomped on it? "I'm not sure he was ever my young man."

But he wanted to be, and it felt like he could've been.

If I'd only let him in.

"I'm going to pretend I didn't hear that last part," Christian said smoothly. "As I don't believe it to be true."

I folded my arms over my squirming lungs. "Our timing was off," I told him. "It couldn't have been worse."

Christian considered. "One thing about timing," he finally said, "is that it is fairly malleable. You can play with it, reshape it to your advantage. That doesn't mean it's always easy, of course. Your grandmother and I had perfect timing, but it ended the way it did because of an obstacle. We could not surpass my parents' disapproval." He paused. "But from what your dad told me about Annette and your grandfather... He told the timing to screw itself."

My heart twisted. Annie and Pops had met in Grand Central Station's oyster bar a few days after her twenty-third birthday. She was having lunch with her uncle while Pops was waiting for his train...because he had gotten an exciting new job and apartment in Washington, DC. He was leaving for his new life.

He never left.

I knew what Christian was insinuating. Everything was pushing my grandfather into his next chapter, but after he met Annie, he flipped back pages to stay in New York.

But how could I do that with Connor? It's not like I could go back to the beginning of vacation, that was impossible.

God, I'd made *such* a mess.

I reached into my purse and handed Christian an envelope; his eyes widened when he pulled out a picture: the Polaroid of Annie standing barefoot by the tractor. "No." He started shaking his head, but I caught his grip on the photo tighten. "Olivia, you must keep this."

"Don't worry," I told him. "I made copies, and I have a feeling this was your photo first."

His smile was nostalgic. "It was tacked above my desk at Georgetown, and she and Andrew helped me pack up my room after junior year. I guess she stole it." He slipped the photo back in the bag. "Thank you—thank you very much."

The corners of my eyes prickled as I gave him one last hug goodbye.

On Sunday afternoon, my dad went to pick up Erica and the twins at the airport, and when they got home, it looked like the last thing my stepmother wanted to do was unpack.

Luckily, I gave her an excuse not to.

"Do you want to walk?" I asked her, Swede already leashed and ready to roll. "Get some fresh air and feel the breeze in your hair?"

Erica loved a stroll to stretch her legs and unwind after a day of travel. "Sure," she said, releasing a deep sigh. "That sounds perfect."

I was too nervous for nuance, so once we were two houses down, I apologized. "I'm so sorry, Erica," I said. "I'm sorry for putting glue in your shampoo."

My stepmother gave me a quizzical look, as if to say, *Wasn't that almost a decade ago?*

"I know I was a total beast to you back then," I kept going. "And I'm embarrassed to say that I'm not much better now. The things I've said to you over the past couple months..." A lump formed in my throat as I searched for the right word. "Well, I'm surprised you still haven't stuck a bar of soap in my mouth."

We both fought a laugh. Annie used to have one threat when babysitting Maisie and Bryce; whenever they misbehaved, she'd say, "If you do that again, I'm going to wash your mouth out with soap!" (It was apparently a line she'd picked up from my great-grandmother.)

Erica neither thanked me for my apology nor told me it was okay. Instead, she said, "I understand I will never be your mom, Olivia, but I've never tried to be."

"I know," I said quietly, because I did.

"Then what am I doing so wrong?" she asked. We slowed at a break in the sidewalk, waiting for a couple cars to pass before we crossed. "You obviously find something about me terrible, but even after racking my brains, it's still not clear to me."

My pulse pitched, not wanting to touch that with a ten-foot pole. No matter how nicely I phrased my problems, I couldn't tear into Erica like that. My dad would never forgive me.

"*Really*," she pressed. "Tell me, Olivia."

She sounded desperate, like this had kept and still kept her up at night, but we passed three more mailboxes before I mustered up the courage to speak. "The Christmas card," I said as Swede barked and wagged his tail at the corgi watching us from his fenced-in yard. "Every year, the Christmas card is signed 'The Lupo family and Olivia.'"

Erica furrowed her eyebrows. "I think I did all our names last year," she said. "Christian, Erica, Maisie, Bryce, and Olivia."

I didn't point out that I was last, despite being the oldest. That wasn't really the point. "No." I shook my head. "I mean, I *feel* like that's how it is. I feel like you four are a family, and I'm just there." I swallowed and continued, not giving her a chance to speak. "And that you *can't wait* for me to leave. I didn't even ask for the biggest bedroom when we moved to Haddonfield, but you told me I couldn't have it. You said Bryce and Maisie were going to live here the longest, so they deserved the biggest rooms. And you gave me a full-on freaking luggage set for graduation last year."

"I did, didn't I?" Erica grimaced. "Yikes, I didn't realize how any of that came off. You know Maisie has way too much stuff, and I thought Bryce needed the biggest room because he's the only boy and needs his own space."

I sighed. "Why didn't you say that?"

"Because it's a cliché, and I worried that you would roll your eyes at me. You were already so bitter about the move."

"Hey, I didn't put up a fight!"

"No, you didn't, but it was all in your body language."

I bit the inside of my cheek. I guess I'd been so focused on keeping my sarcasm and facial expressions in check that I'd forgotten about everything else. I really didn't mind moving; it was the *reason* we were moving. Away from Annie.

"And the luggage..." Erica laughed. "Olivia, you were *always* drooling over Annie's European luggage. Your dad and I were *giddy* when we ordered your set. We thought we'd knocked it out of the park!"

"I didn't say I didn't love it," I murmured.

"I don't have some diabolical plan to push you out the front door and lock it behind me," she went on. "I'm just..." She sighed and took Swede's leash from me, wanting to walk him. "I'm just trying to help launch you the best I can—or guide you, or just *support* you. Your dad is away so much, and as heartbreaking as it is, Annie is no longer the most capable North Star."

"Is it?" I asked, voice brittle. "Heartbreaking?"

Erica stopped in her tracks; Swede strained against his leash. "Are you *really* insinuating what I think you're insinuating?"

My heart hammered. "No," I told her. "I know you care, Erica. I know you love Annie so much." A lump formed in my throat. "But you're keeping it all bottled up, and maybe you think that's best..." My voice hitched. "I want to know that I'm not the only one so completely gutted by this."

Erica didn't say anything, but I blinked to see her bottom lip quiver. I'd *never* seen that happen before, and I suddenly felt badly that we were in public, standing on the sidewalk just outside of town. "Someone needs to stay strong," she said. "I need to be there for your dad and the twins...and you, if you'll let me." She wavered. "But of course I'm a mess, Olivia. Annie was—*is*—more than my mother-in-law. She gets me and has always been there for me. I'm sure it took you approximately thirty seconds to notice that my parents don't understand, or try hard to understand, what I do for a living. Beth and Jay too. While Annie..." She shook her head. "We spoke every day about my work. What I'm most passionate about, how to appeal to multiple age demographics, which business opportunities are worth taking and which I should pass on. She taught me everything I know about flower arrangements, and she is a wonder at seasonal tablescapes and light hors d'oeuvres. I wouldn't be where I am without her, and to lose that special collaboration feels a little like losing a limb." Two tears escaped, trailing down her cheeks; she didn't wipe them away. "Not to mention, she welcomed me with *such* open arms when your dad first introduced me to her. I worried so much about pleasing her, worried about proving that I was good enough for her widowed son." She sighed. "That fear disappeared the moment I met her."

I didn't have any words, and I had an inkling that she didn't want me to make things more dramatic, so I just took her hand and squeezed it. "Should we turn around?"

"No." She squeezed my fingers back. "Let's go a little farther."

We shared a smile then resumed walking.

I asked about her scrapbook pages on the way home. "What did you end up doing?"

"I was going to do a collage of my parents and their dogs over the years," she said, pulling her hair into a ponytail. "But before I could, we opened up the scrapbook to the rest of the family and Finn and Teddy pre-empted that stroke of genius, with some help from Connor."

I sighed. "More evidence to support the claim that Connor McCallister is perfect…"

"Connor McCallister is not perfect," Erica replied, then affectionately poked me. "But I think he might be perfect for you."

I was powerless against the extreme heat flooding my face. Not even the sudden breeze could cool me off.

She gave me a look. "*I* know that *you* know that I haven't cared for any of the boys you've spent time with," she said. "Probably because *you* think *I* think they're dorks."

Dork, Maisie's code for *douche*.

Ha, who was my sister kidding?

"A few of them were, to be clear," she added. "But that's not it."

I raised an eyebrow. "What is, pray tell?"

"It's that they're people you knew you wouldn't let in, or at least let in enough to *matter* to you. People you can happily leave before they leave you, before they can break your heart."

My eyes instantly welled up.

"I am so deeply sorry about your mother and Pops…" she said slowly. "And Annie, in her way, but losing them doesn't prophesize that everyone in your life is going to leave you." She laughed. "You have been unfair to me, Olivia, and at times, properly *vicious*, but dammit, I will not be deterred!" She wrapped an arm around me as a couple crocodile tears escaped. "I love you so much, and I'm not going anywhere."

All I could do was nod.

"And neither is Connor McCallister," she whispered, squeezing me tight. "Believe me, and trust him."

I wanted to. I desperately wanted to.

"Anyway," she said, "one of my scrapbook pages was an ode to my siblings' hideous childhood haircuts."

I found it in myself to laugh. "Was a photo of you among them?"

"Of course not." Erica shook her head. "Because Peggy learned a thing or two by the time I came along. Instead of a pageboy cut, I had a Posh Spice–style bob."

"Hey, that's one plus of being the way-youngest," I pointed out.

"You know, I never thought of it like that." She giggled. "But I guess it is…"

TWENTY-EIGHT

A few weeks later, I had gotten back into the groove that was my normal life. I ran my morning loop around Haddonfield with Swede, went back to work at Inkwood Books, and goofed off with Maisie and Bryce after visiting Annie. I even took the train into New York to see my friends. "Have you heard from Connor?" Gwen asked the first weekend in August. The city was stifling so our plan was to do a "museum crawl" to cool off. Stop #1 was the Neue Galerie, the home of Gustav Klimt's famous *Portrait of Adele Bloch-Bauer I*, otherwise known as "The Woman in Gold."

It was one of Annie's all-time favorite paintings.

"Nope," I said, and thankfully Gwen and Quincy left it at that. They hadn't been the biggest fans of my decision to snip whatever we'd started, but they understood.

Or at least they'd said they did.

Connor hadn't called or texted me since that one night, and I knew it wasn't fair to him if I reached out. *What do you want from me, Olivia?* I could hear him asking.

To start over, I imagined answering. *And for you to promise to stay.*

But Erica said I had to trust him, and I still hadn't fully wrapped my head around Christian Fox's theory that, if we wanted it enough, we could manipulate timing.

So I thought a lot about Connor, and how much I missed him, and what a mistake I'd made, but I didn't do anything. Instead, I stewed.

Several days after our museum crawl, I presented Annie with the Gustav Klimt pictorial book I'd bought at the Galerie's gift shop. It was Wednesday, and I'd brought it to Elkins on Monday, too, but it had been an easy visit...so I'd kept it to myself, saving it for a not-so-good visit.

I didn't usually visit during the dinnertime, but Erica, Maisie, and I'd spent the afternoon lounging at the pool and just couldn't bring ourselves to roll up our towels. Annie had refused to eat in the dining room, so Kai brought a tray to her. Everything had gone to shit when my grandmother accidentally spilled chocolate milk on her sling. "I don't know why this is here in the first place," she insisted. "If you check my menu"—she brandished her light pink sheet of paper with her good arm—"I ordered *iced tea*, not chocolate milk!"

I grimaced as Kai left the room to get her a new drink, folding up her menu and slipping it in my pocket. A shaky circle had indeed been drawn around chocolate milk.

She calmed down a little once her tray had been cleared, but she kept asking when we could leave. "I do not like this hotel, dearest," she said as I felt pang after pang in my chest. "I've stayed in worse, but *really*. They mess up my dinner and forget yours entirely. The décor is tired, furniture uncomfortable, and the *smell*." She turned up her nose. "Doesn't it smell like…like… oh, shoot…" She squeezed her eyes shut, grappling for the right word. "It smells just like…"

"Here, Annie!" I said, hoping to redirect her. Forcing a smile, I gave her the coffee table book. "I went into New York to see Gwen and Quincy the other day and thought you would like this."

I saw my grandmother's eyes glaze over the words and she flipped approximately five pages before closing the book. "I'm very tired," Annie said softly, and when she shifted in her chair, the book fell from her lap. I tried not to wince when it bonked on the floor. "Can we leave now?"

No, I thought. *No, Annie, we can't.*

I felt like a failure, but unless Elkins Village wanted me to melt into a puddle of tears, I had no choice but to do what I did next. My voice was thick, my chest tight. "Of course," I said as I scooped up her discarded book and set it on her window seat. "Let me talk to Tara quickly. I need to…" I searched for an excuse, in reality wanting the nurse to supervise our goodbye. "*Check out* with her."

Annie nodded slowly, her eyes already closed.

She looked so peaceful, but also so tired…and so old. Even older than my visit seventy-two hours ago. How was that possible?

Battling back tears, I swiftly and silently gathered my stuff and slung my tote bag over my shoulder. “Good night, Annie,” I murmured before giving her the lightest kiss on the forehead. Something in the pit of my stomach told me not to wake her. “I love you, and I’ll see you soon.”

A thick haze engulfed me once I left Annie’s room. I vaguely heard people say my name and say goodbye as I crossed the atrium, and when I signed out at the nurses’ station, I could barely wrap my fingers around the pen. I didn’t return my visitor’s badge, and the nurse on duty didn’t ask for it. And I couldn’t remember pressing the security doors’ button, but someone buzzed me through anyway.

I was the only soul in the elevator, its hum almost lulling me into a deeper trance. The sunlight was bright through the windows when I stepped out onto the main floor. It was only a quarter after seven; the sun had yet to set. “Take care, Olivia!” I heard the front desk attendant call, and I managed a half wave before exiting the building.

The parking lot was crowded tonight; I wasn’t surprised. The weather was beautiful, most visitors probably taking an evening walk along Elkins’ trails with their friends or family members. Annie wasn’t allowed to do that anymore, not even with me or my dad. After she had tried to escape Elkins last spring, it was too risky.

Muscle memory took my feet where I needed to go while I wiped my watery eyes. I usually parked near the big magnolia tree, but I second-guessed myself when I spotted a familiar blue-gray Jeep under the dusk-to-dawn light.

Like mine, it had no top, but I squinted to see an *HH* bumper sticker and license plate for the Keystone State.

It hit me like a truck that today was Wednesday.

Connor brought his grandfather sushi every Wednesday.

Connor is here, I thought, my heart unsure whether to swoop or soar. *Connor is here, Connor is here...*

And just like that, I knew what to do.

I knew how to wrangle time.

Hands balling into fists, I speed-walked over to his car and whispered a wish before reaching for the driver door's handle.

Please be unlocked.

With no roof, it would've been easy to climb in through the trunk, but if the door opened, it was a sign. "There's no parking lot safer than Elkins Village," Connor had once said.

My breath caught when the door unlatched, and in one inelegant motion, I swung myself up into the suspended Jeep and slammed the door shut behind me.

Then I waited.

I waited and waited for Connor.

A strain of pure anxiety and excitement raced through my veins, and I tried to rehearse what I was going to say while gripping the Jeep's steering wheel. I willed it to ground me.

Eventually, the dusk-to-dawn light flickered on above me. The sun was now noticeably slipping in the sky, and I checked my phone to see that it was now 8:15. I'd been waiting an hour. Finlay House would've asked me to leave long ago, but since Connor's grandfather still lived independently, the rules were different.

I texted Erica that I wouldn't be home for a while.

Okay, just keep me posted, she wrote back. Anything interesting?

A grand gesture, I typed and saw her heart my message. Her extremely accurate Bitmoji—created by Bryce, polished by Maisie—also wished me good luck.

I couldn't help but smile, but before I felt a boost of confidence, I heard footsteps and someone say, "Miss, I think you have the wrong car."

At the sound of Connor's voice, I whipped around to see him framed in the passenger door's nonexistent window. He ran a hand through his hair, his summer tan making it seem more blond than red, and no one looked better in a white T-shirt than him. I'd never seen the silver watch on his wrist, but I instantly loved it.

A lump rose in my throat. "No," I told him. "I definitely have the right car."

"Alright." He nodded once, his blue eyes stirring the butterflies in my stomach. "As long as you're sure."

And with that, he opened the door and hopped into the passenger seat. I laced my fingers together when he didn't say anything else, both of us knowing the floor was mine.

Here goes nothing.

Or everything.

"If I wasn't so attuned to my suspension and seat orientation," I started, "I might not have realized I'd climbed into the wrong Jeep that night. Instead, I might've checked my texts and scrolled through Instagram for a while before cuing up a playlist and trying to start the car with the wrong keys. I might've spent so long dawdling that you might've discovered me." I swallowed hard. "Which means we would've met then."

Connor's neutral expression betrayed nothing, but I swear something glinted in his eyes. It was enough to keep going.

"I wish we'd met just like that, but right here and now," I told him. "It kills me to admit this, but we met at such a terrible time, Connor. We were pushed together right away, and you were right. I wasn't my best self. There was so much going on; I didn't know how to be." I took a deep breath. "I thought Annie's encouragement would make everything better. I thought I would be able to let go and push my problems aside for a summer fling, but I should've been as honest with you as you were with me."

"Yes," Connor murmured. "Although maybe not *that* honest."

I felt a twinge in my ribs, hoping he didn't regret laying his feelings about me on the line.

"Things are different now," I added, pulse pounding. "*I'm* different now."

"How?" He raised a slow, exaggerated eyebrow. I wondered

if he knew it made the backs of my knees weak. "Do you have less on your plate?"

I started to laugh. "No, I still have a heap."

"Then…"

"My full plate is my shield," I told him. "I *can* shift the mashed potatoes to make room for stuffing. I would move them in a heartbeat, Connor, but I've been so afraid."

"Of what?" he asked gently, though I suspected he knew.

"Loss," I answered, because it had finally clicked into place. "First my mom, most recently my grandfather, and in between, my dad when he married Erica."

I was ashamed to admit it, but in the deepest depths of my subconscious, I knew it was true. Ever since my walk with Erica, I'd been trying to see that so-called loss as a gain.

Because new family members *were* a gift.

"And I know I am going to lose Annie relatively soon," I told him. "She is going to stop knowing me, and then one day she is going to leave us for a place with pearly white gates and a glass of perfectly chilled pinot grigio." I blinked away tears. "The prospect of losing someone I love so much and so hard… I dread the idea of letting you in and losing you too, even if it's in a different way."

"Try a *drastically* different way," Connor said. "And I hope that wouldn't be the case, if we gave things another—a *real*—go." He reached for my hand. "I understand how you feel, Olivia. I really do." He sighed. "And everything on the Vineyard was too much too fast. I said I wasn't an arm-twister, but I'm sorry if I twisted your arm."

I shook my head. "You didn't. You offered me your heart."

We sat there in silence for a few seconds.

"I think about it all the time," he murmured, in this voice that made the hair on the back of my neck stand up. "I know we had fun together, but I would do most of it over if I could."

I exhaled. "Christian Fox has this theory about time," I said. "Timing good or bad, he thinks that if you want a happy ending enough, you can sweet-talk time to be on your side."

"Mmm," Connor hummed, then shifted in his seat. "You really wish we were meeting right here, right now?"

"Yeah." I smiled bittersweetly. "I do."

My pulse sparked when I heard his door unlatch, and I swallowed as he slid back onto the pavement. My throat was dry. He walked back toward Elkins with no goodbye.

I didn't call after him. I didn't ask if he'd be back.

Instead, I watched him in the rearview mirror until he'd disappeared into the building. And then I unlocked my phone to check my texts before tapping over to Instagram. Maisie loved watching Reels, so my algorithm was truly unhinged. In what world did AI singing cat videos and deep clean bathroom footage mix with stand-up comedy clips and spring style in the South of France?

I went to my Spotify after a couple one-pot-meal tutorials. Slowly, I scrolled through some of my recent playlists. Nothing seemed quite right, but as soon as I lost myself in starting something from scratch, I felt a tap on my shoulder.

His touch electrocuted every inch of my body.

"Hi there," Connor said, only inches away from me. The driver door was the only barrier between us. "I don't mean to scare you, but you're in my car."

"Wait, what?" I knitted my eyebrows together. "I could've sworn this was mine…"

"Unless you live in Pennsylvania and visit your floral wallpaper–obsessed aunt in Hilton Head when you're not playing in lacrosse tournaments, I don't think so."

"Oh, jeez, I'm sorry." I winced, and even felt myself blush. "How embarrassing."

"No, no, don't worry about it." The corners of his mouth quirked up in amusement. "I've seen another blue Wrangler in this lot."

I gave him a look. "You come here often?"

"At least twice a week. You?"

"Double that."

"Yeah, I was wondering," he said. "You look really familiar." He took a breath that made my pulse skip *one, two, three*. "I'm Connor McCallister."

"Olivia Lupo," I heard myself say, and while my mind flashed ahead to him leaning into the car to kiss me, his voice brought me back to the moment.

"Ice cream?" he asked, seemingly for a second time. "Are you in the mood for ice cream?"

"Yes!" I grinned as my heart ignited. "I'm always in the mood for ice cream."

"Great, so am I." He grinned back, then tossed me his keys and winked. "Let's go."

ACKNOWLEDGMENTS

Right now, I'm sitting at my kitchen table with a box of tissues. We're about seven months out from release day, and I have tried writing these acknowledgments a couple times without crying, but to no avail...so I'm just going to blubber my way through them.

Alright?

Alright.

The Summer of Second Chances is a romance, but it is also a love story between a grandmother and granddaughter. I wouldn't have been able dig into Annie and Olivia's deep bond without my paternal grandmother, Jo Ann (or "Nana," as my siblings and I call her). I am both her eldest grandchild and granddaughter, titles I treasure. Jo Ann is where I get my champagne taste and love for all things girly. She was an avid golfer, bridge player, needle-pointer, and she loved art, travel, tulips, chocolate, and a chilled glass of pinot grigio. In the winters, she kept her coat on when she came over for dinner (my dad kept our house at a brisk sixty-eight degrees) while evenings at her townhouse felt like a trip to the tropics (seventy-nine degrees, at least).

Gut-wrenchingly, Jo Ann passed away in March 2024 after a yearslong battle with Pick's Disease, a rare form of dementia. While many of her episodes inspired Annie's, my family and I are so fortunate that she never forgot our names or grew unkind toward us. I can still feel how hard she squeezed my hand when I showed her my engagement ring for the first time, and I'm still holding out hope that I'll someday solve the "Case of the Missing Cartier Watch."

I also struck gold with my maternal grandmother, Mary Lou, who was recently described by a friend as the "most gracious and lovely person I have ever known." She left us this summer at ninety-one (despite promising me ninety-seven!). Like Jo Ann, she was a shrewd bridge competitor, world traveler, and lifelong friend. No outfit of hers was complete without lipstick and pearls, and I've lost count of how many beautiful quilts she lovingly crafted over the years. "Grandmom" (or "Grammy," depending on the grandchild) also had a true talent for sniffing out family gossip; no secret was safe on our Stone Harbor beach days. I am one of her whopping eighteen grandchildren, but I will forever and always feel so uniquely adored and supported by her. *The Summer of Broken Rules*'s Honey would not exist without you, Grandmom.

And Pam, when I think about the grandmother I hope to be someday, I think of excitement for annual spring visits, delicious lunch dates, receiving the most delightful birthday cards in the mail, and watching *Downton Abbey* late into the night. I love sipping coffee with you, Rilla, while listening to stories about my grandfather (although shopping is never not fun, too). Thank you for keeping his memory so very much alive; what an honor it is to be one of your "grands."

Ross ("Poppy" to some grandchildren, "Granddad" to others, and "Wink" to readers), I won't ever have the best words to describe how much you mean to me. I am constantly inspired by your intellect, resilience, and capacity to love so many of us so much. Three cheers to your fourteen-year-old self for having such good taste in girls!

Now, on to the usual list of suspects.

(Unclear if the tears will lessen.)

Eva Scalzo, superstar agent and all-around girl boss: Thank you for always being only a text away and for traveling the world with me. I will never forget that moment in Rio (Hello to all my wonderful Brazilian readers!) when we were swooning over Marco but couldn't get Connor out of our hearts. There wouldn't be nearly as much sunshine and magic in this story if you hadn't said, "You know what? I think Connor deserves his own book!"

I once again want to raise a glass of champagne to Annie Berger, my editor. You are as much a part of the KLW Universe as its characters. Thank you for letting me draft the books of my heart (even if they aren't always what I originally pitch!) and thank you even more helping turn them into the books of my dreams during revisions. I am always so in love with and proud of what ends up shining on the bookshelf.

Team Sourcebooks, featuring: Dominique Raccah, Gabbi Calabrese, Karen Masnica, Lia Ferrone, Delaney Heisterkamp, and Thea Voutiritsas. I so appreciate everything you do and all the unwavering enthusiasm in my inbox. But let's all cross our fingers and toes that the Instagram collab invite goes through next time! More shout-outs to Jennifer Gonzalez, Kirsten Clawson, Corina Lupp, Stephanie Rocha, Erin LaPointe, Laura Boren, Diane Cunningham, Paula Amendolara, Jess Elliott, Trent Harmon, and Jenne Abramowitz.

Thank you, Monique Aimee, for another cover I want to take straight to the framers. I am in awe of your talent.

To Trip and Cindy Stowell, and the entire Flynn family: Summer is not summer without the Farm. Thank you for inviting me back again and again so I can delight in its wonder over and over. Hopefully our future morning walks involve more Remi and Ruger and less lone star larvae...

Josh Walther, you are one of my favorite people to ever exist. Probably one of Jo Ann's, too, from the way she never-stopped-talking about you!

Michael, wedding officiant and dear friend, thank you for your kind words of encouragement: "The cover is so incredible that the book doesn't even have to be good!" (Or something to that effect).

Thank you, Anthony, for still handling all things Squarespace and for remaining one of my fellow goofballs. Someone somewhere has the security camera footage to prove it. All they need to do is splice it together.

Jessica L. Cozzi, you are the author friend I always hoped I'd make someday. I am so grateful for your advice, sense of humor, pep talks, and insight into the publishing industry. I can't wait to hype up your books for years to come!

Tommy Tibble, thank you for ensuring the group chat's daily stream of dog content remains at a standard high enough to spark smiles. Timmy, the addition of Dolly has been nothing short of special.

Endless love and appreciation to the Palm Beach squad—Emily, Madison, Meredith, Nell, Scout, and Jackie. I needed that vacation so very badly, and after a canceled flight, two airports, and "frozen" luggage, you all made sure it was one to remember.

Thank you to my husband, Christopher, for a hundred reasons I will attempt to list when you get home from work in thirty-four minutes. You are brilliant and beloved, and I can't wait until you walk through the door.

My parents. Mom, this is the tenth manuscript of mine you've read chapter by chapter by chapter... Thank you for still hearting my "I sent you pages!" texts. Writing is one of the world's most solitary sports; I'm so lucky to have your wonderful feedback to prevent it from becoming a lonely one. And Dad, no book is complete without you, even if it's just me repurposing a witty one-liner from an overheard conversation with Trip. Keep the red corvettes coming, okay?

Finally, thank you to my devoted readers: I feel a wild urge to hug every single one of you, but instead, I'll play it cool and keep writing you books.

ABOUT THE AUTHOR

Photo © Suzanne Schenker

K. L. Walther is the #1 *New York Times* and *USA Today* best-selling author of *The Summer of Broken Rules*, *While We're Young*, and *A First Time for Everything*. Born and raised in the rolling hills of Bucks County, Pennsylvania, she is happiest when reading a romance on the beach or bantering with her better half while waiting in line for ice cream. She currently lives in Philadelphia with her husband and hopefully, soon, a golden retriever.

Visit her online at klwalther.com or find @klwalther9 on Instagram.